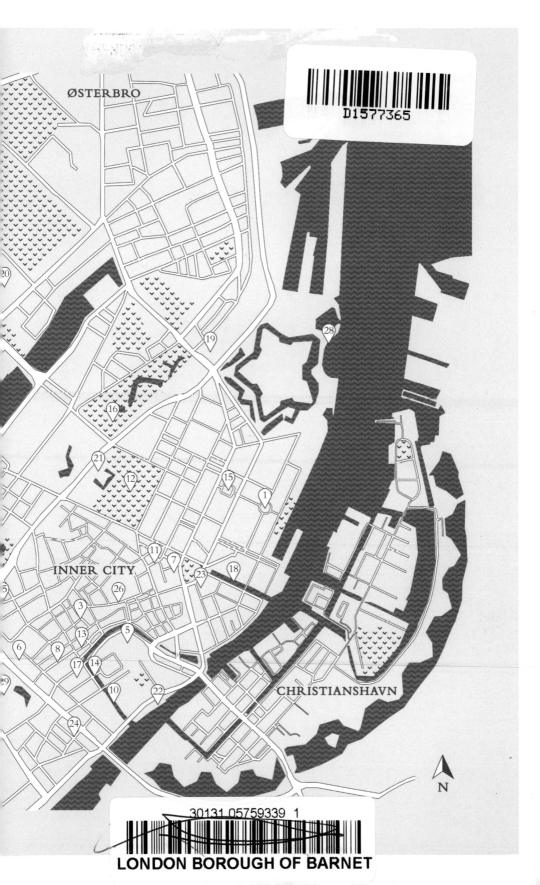

ØSTERBRO

INNER CITY

CHRISTIANSHAVN

N

MY NAME IS
JENSEN

MY NAME IS JENSEN

JENSEN

Heidi Amsinck

MUSWELL
PRESS

First published by Muswell Press in 2021
Copyright © Heidi Amsinck 2021

Typeset in Bembo by M Rules
Printed and bound by CPI Group (UK) Ltd, Croydon CR0 4YY

Heidi Amsinck has asserted her right to be identified as
the author of this work in accordance with under the
Copyright, Designs and Patents Act, 1988

A CIP catalogue record for this book
is available from the British Library

ISBN: 9781838110185
eISBN: 9781838110192

Muswell Press
London N6 5HQ
www.muswell-press.co.uk

1 3 5 7 9 10 8 6 4 2

To Frederik and Jules

Week One

1

Tuesday 07:13

Jensen sucked the cold air deep into her lungs and let the last few meandering snowflakes melt on her upturned face. Only a few windows were lit in the apartment buildings surrounding her. People on their way to work, their bodies still warm from sleep, were treading gingerly on the pillowy pavements, looking about them as if not recognising their own city. They had forgotten the snow could fall, how it dulled the sounds of their footsteps as though the sky were a lid fitted over Copenhagen. Even the mouthy drunks had vanished from their perch by the supermarket on Christianshavn's Square, chased indoors by the worst blizzard for many years. In time, the snowploughs would clear the streets, and normality claim the day, but for now the city was holding its frozen breath.

Jensen took her usual route across Knippelsbro to Holmen, past Borgen, the parliament building with its giant verdigris crown, forging a winding track in the snow with her bicycle. She watched the rear of a yellow bus slide out sideways in a wide arc. The windows were steamed up, obscuring the passengers inside, who might be little more than ghosts. Jensen decided she liked the city this silent and deserted, its majestic old buildings taking centre stage. Bar the bus, the scene would have been instantly recognisable to any nineteenth-century Copenhagener.

When she reached Snaregade, it became impossible to cycle any further on the slippery cobbles. She got off and pushed her bike in between the tall, leaning houses of the old town. Just like her to have picked this, of all mornings, to be heading into the newspaper early. Less than twenty minutes ago she had lifted the curtain by her bed to discover the strange bluish-white world outside. It had felt virtuous to get up and head out. Now she wondered if she ought to have stayed put.

Was it possible that she had simply forgotten how to be a journalist? Lost the curiosity and bloody-mindedness that had paid her rent for as long as she could remember?

Since returning to Copenhagen, she had felt enthusiasm seep from her like a slow puncture. To the point where she was no longer able to string a sentence together, let alone a whole article worth reading. Nothing worked, nothing mattered.

She was meant to be *Dagbladet*'s special reporter, going behind the news with features skewering Danish society. But what did she know about Danish society after fifteen years away?

For weeks she had been promising a feature on cutbacks in mental healthcare, citing delays in gaining document access as an excuse for not turning in copy, but in truth she hadn't even started researching the story. She supposed it was a crisis of confidence.

Her editor, Margrethe Skov, a woman for whom confidence had never been in short supply, wouldn't understand. ('Journalism is a craft, not bloody art; we don't sit around waiting till we feel inspired.')

Margrethe was right, of course. Jensen just needed to keep working at it. With a bit of luck, she could have made a solid start on her feature by this morning's editorial meeting, and how good would that feel, how satisfying to rub the faces of her (by now multiple) detractors in it? Plenty of unemployed journalists would kill to write for *Dagbladet*, Jensen reminded herself, as she pointed her bike forward, her boots squeaking resolutely in the snow.

She saw it when she was just a few yards into Magstræde.

Against the red building with the green door.

A waist-high mound of snow.

Lumpy.

She looked left and right down the curved street, wishing someone else would turn up, knowing what the lump was, but not wanting to know. For a moment, she considered continuing past it, but how could she?

Her heart was pummelling her rib cage, the sweat beginning to run inside her gloves. Resting her bike against a street lamp, she leaned closer to the lumpy mound, gently brushing away the snow.

She recoiled, stumbling backwards.

It was a man, his face turned towards the sky, his eye sockets filled with snow.

She recognised him. He had been sitting in exactly the same place last night, cross-legged, covered in the same red sleeping bag, though she was pretty sure he had been alive then. She remembered thinking it was an odd place to be asking for money, in the shadows between two street lights with a blizzard underway.

The man's palms were turned upwards as if he had been professing his innocence or praying when he died, neither of which appeared to have done him much good. He looked a good few years younger than her, perhaps in his early twenties. Hardly more than a boy.

'Not again,' she said out loud, only then realising the significance of the words.

Was this really happening?

She brushed away more snow, then stopped abruptly when it gave way to raspberry slush. The boy's puffer jacket was ripped; he had been stabbed in the stomach.

The other victim had been stabbed too, hadn't he?

On the ground next to the boy was a paper cup full of coffee and a pizza in a cardboard box. There was salami on the pizza; it had curled up and frozen, matching the colour of the dead boy's skin.

For a moment, Jensen was forced to lean forward with her hands on her knees, as saliva ran out of her mouth and melted a hole in the snow. She retched, her back convulsed, but nothing came.

Her hands were trembling; she shivered, all of a sudden feeling the cold deep inside her bones. How long had the boy been dead for? Hours at most, or someone else would have found him, wouldn't they? Despite the snow, or even more so because of it, Magstræde was the sort of quaint old street that tourists went mad for. Picture-postcard Copenhagen.

The sky above the tall Lego-coloured town houses was fringed with turquoise now, a fingernail moon fading into the dawn. The snow on the street was pristine except for the tracks she had made.

She looked at her phone, feeling a familiar loosening in her abdomen. She had put off calling Henrik since she had moved back home, ignoring his messages, but he would know what to do about this.

Death was his thing.

He would want to be the first to know.

Besides, calling Henrik would work in her favour. *Dagbladet* had milked the last murder for all it was worth. In London, homeless deaths might not make the front page, but on the streets of Copenhagen, capital of the happiest nation in the world, it was big news.

Why was the boy there? Who was he?

Henrik would be more likely to share information when the time came than a random patrol unit responding to a 112 call.

Henrik owed her.

He owed her so much that no matter what he did for her now, they would never be even.

She caught him in the car going to work, shouting on the hands-free over the din of the radio news. The timbre of his voice darkened when he realised it wasn't a social call. She heard the siren come on, his car accelerating.

'Stay where you are,' he said, in the rough voice he reserved for work. 'And don't touch anything.'

Too late for that.

She took a few pictures of the body, though she doubted the paper would be able to use something so graphic. The boy's open mouth made him look vulnerable, the fluffy hair on his chin not quite enough for a beard. Snowflakes had caught in his eyelashes, turning them white. He was so thin, there were shadowy hollows below his cheekbones.

With her foot, she brushed aside a little of the snow on the ground and saw that he had made a seat for himself out of a flattened cardboard box. His puffer jacket was of a good make, so too his woollen beanie. He had dressed for the weather. She had to keep moving up and down the pavement to stay warm, breathing on her hands. Her exhalations came fast, in little clouds of white steam.

A man walked past. Weirdly, he didn't give her and the boy a second glance. He had his headphones on and that unseeing gaze of busy city people on their way somewhere important.

That's how it happens, she thought. That's how a person dies in the street without anyone noticing.

Magstræde was never exactly busy, though, which made it an odd choice for someone hoping for the charity of passers-by on a night of heavy snow. Perhaps the ban on begging and homeless camps had driven him here? In the dark, half obscured by parked bicycles, he would have been less likely to attract the attention of the police.

She crouched down to look more closely at the dead boy, trying to find the reason for the voice telling her something was wrong, something about his empty hands. Had there not been a sign when she had passed him last night, a piece of cardboard with something scribbled on it? If not, why had she assumed he was a beggar? Of course, she hadn't actually read it, averting her eyes just like this morning's commuters. What had it said? Something about being hungry? Whatever it had been, the sign was gone. There was nothing else to see, no personal belongings of any kind, just the pizza and coffee.

She checked her watch.

Her resolve to get to the office early to work on her feature now seemed as much of a lost cause as the dead beggar's attempts to make a living.

Her eyes were caught by something in the boy's lap, the corner of a piece of paper protruding from the snow. She put her gloves back on and tugged gently at one corner.

It was a handwritten note:

Fuglereden (the Bird's Nest), Rysensteensgade

She took a picture of the note before replacing it, then looked up the address on her phone. It was a local hostel. The boy could have had a bed there, hot food, shelter. Yet here he was in front of her, staring up into the sky at something no one else could see.

'Why didn't you go there?' she said out loud, her voice sounding flat in the icy stillness.

As the first sirens approached, she stroked the remaining snow from the boy's face with her gloved hand and closed his eyes.

2

'What are you going to do now?' Jensen asked Henrik as the paramedics emerged from behind the screen set up by forensics.

Quickly, they put the stretcher with the body into the back of the ambulance, bringing to a halt the entertainment of the people who were craning their necks behind the police tape at the end of the street. Funny that not one of them had been around to help the boy when he was still alive.

Henrik's unmarked car smelled of his leather jacket; he had turned the engine on to warm them up, and Jensen was slowly regaining the feeling in her fingers. They were both looking at the scene in front of them, but his hand was stroking the inside of her thigh, leaving a trail of electricity in its wake.

She let him.

He had that effect on her.

'What would you *like* me to do?' he said hoarsely.

She knew it would be a disaster to turn and look at him. The brief glimpse she had caught when he had first arrived on the scene, taking charge with his football-player swagger, had been enough. He hadn't changed in three years. Same black jeans, same white shirt. It must be all there was in his wardrobe, a row of identical shirts and jeans, sleeves rolled up in the summer, down in winter.

Instead of turning her head, she forced herself to stare at a yellow toy tractor by her feet. Henrik bent over, picked up the tractor and tossed it into the back seat. His face was bright red.

'I meant what are you going to do about the boy?'

They sat in silence for a moment as the ambulance glided away, and the crowd began to disperse.

'I missed you,' he said, finally, when everyone but a couple of uniformed officers had left.

He reached further up her thigh. 'Why didn't you respond to my messages?'

'Henrik, you left me in a hotel room.'

'I had to get back home for my son. Come on, Jensen, you know the score.'

'You said you'd be five minutes. You said you were going to get a coffee. That was three years ago.'

'I did try calling.'

'Six months later. And you wonder why I didn't pick up?'

She brushed away his hand. Being angry made it a lot easier to look at him.

'For fuck's sake, Henrik, two beggars have been murdered on the streets in as many weeks. What are you going to do about it?'

He rubbed his bald head. 'The two may not be related. Could just be a coincidence.'

'And if not?'

He withdrew his hand from her thigh, sighing deeply. 'You heard what forensics said. We have to wait for the post-mortem; it's too early to tell.'

'So this is just another day in the office to you?'

'No, but I have learned never to jump to conclusions, and you would do well to stick to the same advice.'

'He didn't look like he was homeless or a typical beggar.'

'Oh, tell me, what does one of those look like?'

'His clothes were too clean, too good, for someone who lives on the street.'

'Why don't you just come and do my job for me,' he said, laughing, but she could hear the edge in it.

'He wasn't a drunk or some addict,' she insisted. 'He had clean clothes, good teeth, good skin. No smell on him, no bottles lying around.'

'Doesn't change the fact that we have to wait for the post-mortem in order to know what happened to him. Could have been some argument that went wrong.'

'You don't know anything about this boy. Young white male, no ID, no phone, no belongings, could be anyone.'

'Probably Romanian, or some other Eastern European. We still get the odd one sleeping rough here, though the begging ban has made a difference.'

'He had the address of a homeless shelter. Why didn't he go there?'

'Maybe he did.'

'What?'

'Last night would have been busy; they might not have had room. Or maybe they wouldn't let him in for some reason or another.'

'Why not?'

He held up his hands in mock surrender. 'Don't ask me.'

'All right, so as I was saying, you have no idea who he was or what happened.'

Henrik had no reply to that, and she wasn't going to wait around for another banal guess.

'Call me when you know something, anything at all,' she said and climbed out of the car, slamming the door.

He rolled the window down, imploring her to return, but she ignored him. She wanted to get out of there as fast as she could.

He had that effect on her, too.

11

As she headed for her bicycle, a delivery van drove up behind Henrik's car, unable to pass in the narrow one-way street. The driver made the mistake of tooting his horn. Henrik responded by tearing open his door and marching up to the van, shoving his police badge into the driver's face with such aggression that the man began reversing all the way back where he had come from.

Jensen couldn't help smiling.

Henrik really hadn't changed one bit.

3

From the corner office of *Dagbladet*'s editor-in-chief, Copenhagen's City Hall Square looked like an abstract painting, a damp mess of white pavements, yellow buses, red tail lights and people rushing to get out of the sleety weather. Jensen watched a group of pedestrians waiting patiently at the kerb for the lights to go green, though they could easily have crossed the road between the cars. In London, you never saw this respect for the rules, this reluctance to stand out from the crowd.

'Sorry, I'm late,' said Margrethe, barging into the room carrying a leather shoulder bag and a takeaway coffee.

She settled her tall, broad-shouldered form into the swivel chair behind her desk with a grunt. 'Had to go and see the prime minister,' she said.

'Oh?'

'Bloody waste of time, before you ask,' she said, taking off her steamed-up glasses and wiping them on her jumper.

Jensen was about to open her mouth, grateful for the opportunity to delay the conversation she knew was coming, but

Margrethe held up a hand to stop her. 'Save it,' she said, putting her glasses back on and reaching for her coffee.

Jensen shrank in her chair. Margrethe was one of the few people whose opinion she respected. It was Margrethe who had plucked her from the local paper as an eighteen-year-old without as much as a school leaver's certificate and given her a job at *Dagbladet*. Two years later she had sent Jensen to London as the newspaper's correspondent. There had been plenty of dissenting voices, but Margrethe had ignored them all.

She was taking her time, adding three sachets of sugar to her coffee. The wall behind her was lined with photographs of her all-male predecessors, going back to *Dagbladet*'s nineteenth-century origins. Compared to Margrethe, with her long grey hair, fleshy face and penetrating gaze behind thick lenses, they looked like a bunch of friendly uncles.

'I can't work you out, Jensen,' said Margrethe, stirring her coffee with a pencil. 'I fought to keep you when we closed London. They told me not to do it, that you were a pain in the arse, but I ignored them because I always thought you were a great reporter. I sacked someone, an old colleague with five years to retirement, so you could get a job back here. I protected you, took you off the daily beat to give you time for your so-called research, and this is how you repay me?'

She paused, sipping from her cup without taking her eyes off Jensen, who knew better than to interrupt her boss mid-flow.

'You've been back, what, three months? And tell me, how many articles have you written?'

Jensen wriggled her hands under her thighs and looked out of the window at the square below. As she watched, a man standing too close to the kerb got sprayed with dirty slush by a passing taxi.

'I don't know exactly. Ten?' she offered.

'Four.'

Margrethe rifled through a pile of papers on her desk and

pulled out a slim file. 'Let's see, ah yes, your reportage on Denmark's marginal communities.'

'Took me ages to write.'

'It's horseshit. No heart,' said Margrethe, tossing it to one side.

'Next, your feature on that dramatic plane crash in Sweden before Christmas.'

'I received a lot of nice emails afterwards.'

'Bollocks. I've read more engaging articles by sixteen-year-olds on work experience. Want to look at the other two?'

'No,' said Jensen.

'Right, so talk to me. What's going on?'

'I need time to settle in.'

Margrethe pretended to consult a printout on her desk. 'You've had three months, and while you've got yourself nice and cosy, we've lost . . . let me see . . . two thousand, eight hundred and seventy subscribers. Any more staff cutbacks, and we may as well switch off the lights.'

Jensen nodded. She had seen the figures. Despite ever-more desperate forays into digital, the 120-year-old newspaper was dying on its feet. Bar a couple of overworked proofreaders, the subs had all gone, and the section editors had to lay out their own pages. The few tired journalists who remained barely had time for more than holding up a microphone to a succession of so-called experts, let alone going digging for stories. You could no longer read *Dagbladet* confident of finding out what had happened in the world in the previous twenty-four hours, in order of importance. The newspaper was now a personalised 'experience' with stories churned out online at regular intervals through the day, clickbait first. Plenty of online readers, but you needed a handful of those to earn as much as you did from one paper subscriber. The traditional business model was irreparably broken, and *Dagbladet* was yet to find a new one that worked.

'Give me a chance to—'

'I have,' Margrethe snapped. 'Trust me, if you'd been anyone else, I'd have kicked you out months ago.'

Jensen hung her head.

'So, whatever is going on with you, fix it.'

'Yes.'

'Now leave,' said Margrethe. 'I am busy. There's been another murder. It's all over Twitter.'

The bells in the tower of City Hall struck twelve noon in the familiar sing-song chime that reminded Jensen of the midday news on the radio in her late grandmother's kitchen. That was the problem. The bells, Magstræde, City Hall Square, *Dagbladet*: on the surface they were the same as always, but Copenhagen had changed while she had been away. She felt like a stranger in her own city. Not that she would ever be able to explain that to Margrethe. Her boss had no patience with feeble emotions.

Only one thing impressed Margrethe: a good story.

'Still here?' she said, looking irritably at Jensen.

'Wait. I have something,' Jensen said, making a swift decision.

'It better be good.'

'It was me who found the guy. This morning, in Magstræde.'

'You did what?'

She told Margrethe everything, leaving only Henrik out of it. Margrethe's body language softened gradually until she was leaning forward on her elbows, the coffee growing cold by her side.

'It's a great story,' she said when Jensen had finished. '"Second homeless man found dead on Copenhagen street. *Dagbladet*'s reporter discovers the body."'

'It might be. I just—'

Margrethe's voice hardened. 'I said it's a great story. This joke of a government has finally gone too far. Now beggars are being killed in the street. Its cruel, heartless, bankrupt policies are bringing shame on the country. Denmark is better than this.'

She waved Jensen off. 'Write a feature. Eyewitness account,

all the trimmings. I'll get the guys at Borgen to chase down the government for comments. There's a social campaign in this. The opposition will go mental.'

'We can't be sure—'

'Do it, Jensen!'

Margrethe had already turned towards her desktop and picked up her phone, squeezing it under her chin as she typed. The conversation was over. Jensen headed for the door, already regretting owning up to finding the beggar. But what else did she have?

'Wait,' Margrethe shouted after her. 'Tell me you had the presence of mind to take some pictures before the police arrived?'

Jensen kept her back turned, closing her fist round her mobile phone, cradling the photos she had taken of the dead boy.

'Sorry,' she said, squeezing her eyes tightly shut. 'Must have been the shock. I completely forgot.'

4

'Marvellous, just bloody marvellous.'

Chief superintendent Mogens Hansen, known affectionately as 'Monsen' (to his intense dislike) was taking his massive corpus for a turn around his desk. From the way he was panting, Henrik guessed it was his first exercise in some considerable time.

It never ceased to amaze him how little work of any kind the head of the investigation unit managed to do. His desk, between two windows that left him backlit and imposing to visitors, was always swept clean of paperwork, and Henrik didn't remember ever seeing the computer on.

On the wall between the two windows was a portrait of Queen Margrethe II. Henrik remembered it from Monsen's office at the police yard before they had all been shipped out to the modern building at Teglholmen. Much like its owner, the photo had looked more at home in its previous surroundings.

Henrik resisted the temptation to quip how inconsiderate the Magstræde killer had been to strike just as the government was paying uncomfortably close attention to their department.

It was Monsen's hobbyhorse, and if Henrik got him started on it, they would be here for hours.

Monsen kept walking. 'Two stabbings in ten days, homeless men, a short distance from one another? Hardly a coincidence.'

'Might be. We don't know yet.'

'ID on the first victim?'

'Not yet.'

'And this new one?'

'Same. But our lead theory is that they were Eastern European, possibly Romanian.'

Abruptly, Monsen stopped his round-the desk jaunt, flopped into his chair and made a face like Munch's *The Scream*.

'Find out who did it, Jungersen, and make this stop. At the very least, we must be able to tell if these murders were committed by the same person?'

'Actually, no. Impossible to say before we have the results of the post-mortem.'

'So you are telling me we have nothing at all?'

Henrik held up his hands. 'We're working as fast as we can.' He made a move to get up. 'Talking of which, I'd better ...'

Henrik could smell Monsen's aftershave, the sweat that was just beginning to darken his armpits. The utter misery on the chief super's face stopped him in his tracks.

'Fast isn't fast enough. I just had the commissioner on the phone. Apparently the prime minister wants progress in the next twenty-four hours, she said, or she is going to come over personally and tear me a new arsehole.'

Henrik suppressed a laugh at the thought of the diminutive prime minister administering a spanking to his corpulent boss, though Monsen's fear was well founded. The police chief represented the old guard of establishment figures whose time had come and gone, in the view of the prime minister. This was the knockout stage. One false move, and Monsen would find himself drawing his pension.

Henrik, for one, would regret it if that happened. Monsen's face might not fit the prime minister's idea of inclusive leadership, but he was a solid policeman, old school, with no time for the touchy-feely nonsense that had become the bane of Henrik's life. Besides, deep down, though he would never admit it, Monsen had a soft spot for Henrik, preferring him to Henrik's immediate boss, Superintendent Jens Wiese, whom both agreed was a boring pen-pusher.

Monsen was almost a whole generation older than him, but Henrik knew that they came from the same mould: working-class lads who could so easily have come down on the wrong side of the law. They had never discussed it (Monsen wasn't the sort of man you reminisced with at the best of times), but he felt certain that for both of them, joining the force had been about the lure of boy's-own adventure, cops and robbers, more than any desire to save the world. No one could do that, not even the prime minister, for all her sanctimonious bluster. The world was beyond redemption, full of nasty people motivated by lust and greed, as the likes of Henrik and Monsen knew better than anyone. All you could hope for was containment, and these days perhaps not even that. When it came to the score, the criminals were winning.

Henrik saw all of a sudden how the chief super had aged. Cracks of weakness were beginning to show, and he didn't like it. It reminded him of his father, his energy all but sucked out of him by life's million disappointments. Monsen's most important (if not *only*) attribute had always been his unwavering self-confidence. Besides, if he was an anachronism, what did that make Henrik?

'I get it,' he said. 'Don't worry. We've got our best team on it. When have I ever let you down?'

Monsen stared at him, incredulous for a moment, as if counting in his mind the thousands of times Henrik had stepped over the line, but they both knew that Henrik was right. In the big scheme of things, which was all that really mattered, he had always come through.

Monsen made a show of looking at his watch. 'I want you to call me inside midnight with some good news. Is that understood?'

'Yes, Monsen, of course, Monsen.'

'Now get back to work.'

Henrik headed for the door, grimacing at the wall in relief.

'And Jungersen?'

'Yes?'

'Call me Monsen one more time and you will be the one with the new arsehole.'

5

'Shut up and listen,' Henrik said, looking around at his team of investigators. Lisbeth Quist and Mark Søndergreen, both decent, plodding detectives more than ten years his junior, had been out all morning and were now perched on the table in the meeting room, still wearing their coats and clutching reusable coffee mugs. He could tell from their downcast faces that they hadn't had much luck.

Six uniformed officers had crowded in around the door, as though they were expecting some kind of show. They would be sorely disappointed.

'This morning a member of the public (ha!) discovered the body of an unidentified male in Magstræde,' he said, pointing to the crime-scene photos fixed to the whiteboard.

'Preliminary findings suggest that he had been dead four to six hours. Cause of death almost certainly stabbing. No witnesses have come forward.'

He pointed to the second set of crime-scene photos, considerably grislier than the first.

'We can't rule out a connection to the murder ten days ago

22

of another, as yet unidentified, male found in Farvergade. Both men appear to have been homeless, both were found without belongings or ID, having sustained multiple stab wounds by a knife not yet recovered. On the other hand, we cannot say for sure that the two murders are linked. The first was a lot more violent than the second.'

He paused, thinking about this. Was it significant? A stabbing was a stabbing, and the two crimes had more circumstances in common than not.

'Mark, any progress on the first victim?'

'No. Still no sign of any belongings, and the murder weapon hasn't been found. We're looking for witnesses, but so far nothing of use. No CCTV, unfortunately.'

'Same story in Magstræde,' said Lisbeth. 'A few people saw the victim sitting in the street during the day yesterday, but no one witnessed the murder. It would have happened around the time that the blizzard was at its worst.'

'Excellent,' said Henrik. 'So, we've no ID, no personal effects, no confirmed cause of death for the second murder, no murder weapon for either, no witnesses and no CCTV. Any questions?'

Mark put his hand up tentatively.

Henrik sighed. 'What?'

'Could this be a serial killer? Some far-right nationalist going around taking out foreigners sleeping rough?'

Henrik felt the eyes of the police officers widening.

'Let's not start speculating until we have more evidence.'

Meanwhile, the press would be doing all the speculating for them. The headlines he had seen so far would be enough to whip up a frenzy.

'We do have one lead: a scrap of paper found on the second murder victim with the name and address of the Bird's Nest, a homeless shelter in Rysensteensgade. I'll take that one and, Lisbeth and Mark, I want you to go around to the other shelters in the city: find anyone who might have known our two victims or spent time with them in the past few weeks. Take interpreters, if you have to. Then head back to Magstræde and press some more doorbells. One of the residents must have seen or heard something.'

He turned to the police officers.

'Find the murder weapon or weapons. And look out for wallets or rucksacks or any other personal effects that might have been recovered and handed in to police in the past twenty-four hours. Turn every stone, I don't want to see you back here with nothing.'

Henrik looked out the window at two female officers striding across the road from the car park and envied their air of purpose. One of them, Henriette, had fancied him once. They had fooled around for a while, until she had got serious, and he had made his excuses. Now she treated him like a leper, something his wife already excelled in. And Jensen, too.

The absence of any personal possessions near the victims was bothering him. Even if you accepted the premise that either victim had possessed anything worth stealing (highly unlikely), you would have expected their empty rucksacks or wallets to have been found nearby. The only other reason he could think of why someone would have taken the stuff would be to delay detection. Unless someone had wanted to hide the identity of the victims, but what would be the point of that? Before long, the police would have all the information they needed.

He looked up to find his colleagues drifting out of the room, chatting among themselves and checking their phones.

'One more thing,' he shouted. 'No one is to discuss this case outside of these four walls, and that includes partners and spouses.'

He knew this was merely a case of delaying the inevitable. Two killings of homeless men in ten days would be irresistible. Little titbits from their investigation would start to find their way into the newspaper columns. *Dagbladet* would go to town with their coverage, spearheaded by the formidable Margrethe Skov, who would relish giving the government a shoeing for letting people die in the street. He could already see the head-line: *Shock discovery by* Dagbladet *reporter.*

It would get him into all sorts of trouble at home when his wife found out. She had been on high alert since she had discovered that Jensen had moved back to Denmark; it would not go down well that she was also now involved in a murder investigation that Henrik was in charge of.

'Not my thing, crime,' Jensen had always said. These days he had no idea what her thing was. Not him, it seemed.

Annoying all the same that he couldn't stop thinking about her. He got out his phone and checked for messages.

Nothing.

6

Tuesday 16:04

With her legs folded at forty-five degrees, there was just enough space for Jensen to perch on the dormer windowsill in her office. She stayed there as dusk fell over the red-tiled roofs of the city and crept into every corner of the room. The sky was the colour of tin, pregnant with more snow.

Most of her colleagues worked on the open-plan floor downstairs, without fixed seats, keeping their laptops and belongings in tiny lockers. She was one of a lucky handful who had their own offices on the unmodernised top floor of the building; yet another reason for her colleagues to hold her in contempt, as if taking someone else's job and gadding about under Margrethe's protection (as long as it lasted) wasn't enough. Though whoever had made the decision to let her have her private space had probably done everyone a favour. Fifteen years of working in London by herself had not exactly honed her skills at rubbing along.

Easy to see now that moving home had been a huge mistake. Margrethe had talked her into it over dinner and copious quantities of wine at an expensive Mayfair restaurant, a rare gesture

26

of generosity intended to soften the blow of her job as *Dagbladet*'s London correspondent being axed.

'What good would you be to anyone here – an uneducated Danish hack?' she had said, half cut and slurring at the end of the evening.

The people at the neighbouring tables had stared, perhaps taking the two of them to be mother and daughter. You would have to be blind to think they had emerged from the same gene pool, but then Margrethe had been acting with unusual familiarity and protectiveness that evening. With the candlelight reflecting in the restaurant's mirror surfaces, she had painted a picture of opportunity and rediscovery, but in reality, Copenhagen had only made Jensen fonder of London. Back here she felt like a stranger. In London, everyone was. The city was big enough to hide in, to reinvent herself over and over.

After being dismissed from Margrethe's office, she had spent an unproductive afternoon googling homelessness in Denmark. Rough sleepers were estimated to be in the hundreds in the past year, and a good proportion of the homeless were foreigners. Henrik had been right: the man might not have been able to get a bed for the night anywhere, as hostel facilities had been cut back.

She checked her phone. Henrik hadn't been in touch. Maybe he had no information yet, maybe he was still smarting from their exchange in Magstræde, but it was not that which had stopped her from writing as much as a single sentence of her article.

Nothing felt right.

She found the photos she had taken on the dead boy. No sign of a struggle or agony in his features. The peaceful look on his face was at odds with the violent injury to his body. And if he had been turned away from the hostel, why had he chosen to stay in Magstræde with his back against a door when there were nooks and crannies nearby offering more shelter and privacy? If he was begging and sleeping rough, how come he was so well

27

dressed? Had he written the address of the shelter on the scrap of paper himself, or had someone given it to him? And how was it even possible to be stabbed in the streets of a big city without anyone discovering it till hours later?

Margrethe was wrong: it wasn't a great story.

Not yet.

Not that she would tell her boss that to her face. Margrethe had called five times in the past hour alone, chasing for her eyewitness feature, without Jensen having had the nerve to pick up the phone.

She looked up at the familiar sound of shuffling footsteps approaching her office. Henning Würtzen was one of the former editors-in-chief immortalised on the wall in Margrethe's office, though you would scarcely recognise him from his photograph. Some of the older reporters remembered him retiring in the early 2000s, but no one recalled when he had come back. One day he was just there, shrunken and tortoise-like in his brown suit, with an unlit cigar in his mouth, haunting the corridors of the newspaper like the spectre of journalism past. By default, he had become *Dagbladet*'s obituary writer. No one of note died without Henning writing about it. He had a vast number of ready obituaries on file, including, rumour had it, his own.

Jensen liked Henning. With no interest in trivial conversations, he was oblivious to the backlash against her return from London as a staff reporter. He walked into her office without knocking, hit the light switch and headed straight for the paper coffee cup on her desk, shaking it to check for remains.

'Margrethe was asking after you,' he said, raising the paper cup to his mouth with trembling hands.

'That's from yesterday.'

Jensen made a face as Henning drained the cup without any outward sign of disgust.

'She told me to tell you that Frank is going to write the feature now, and that you should go home and think about how

28

you intend to make a living when you no longer work here,' he said, looking past her with his rheumy eyes, as if reciting a poem off by heart.

Frank Buhl. Crime writer in clogs. He must have loved being handed such a juicy story, even better seeing as she had shown herself unable to handle it. Well, Frank was welcome to it as far as she was concerned.

'Was that all?' she said in a mock-posh voice.

Henning refilled his paper cup and shuffled out of her office, holding up one trembling hand in the affirmative.

No sooner had he left than Jensen heard the sound of clogs approaching.

'What do you want, Frank?' she said, staring at the building opposite where an energetic box-fit class was in progress on the floor below.

'I want you to tell me what you saw. If you can't be arsed to write it yourself, at least give me something to go on.'

She looked at him. He had a notepad and pen at the ready.

'I saw a dead man,' she said.

'Thanks, that's brilliant, anything else?'

She made a show of thinking about it.

'Snow.'

'Blood?'

'Yes.'

'Signs of violence or a struggle?'

'Not really, except for the blood,' she said, reminding herself once more of how odd that was.

'Any belongings or ID lying around?'

She shook her head. 'No, nothing.'

'And the doctor attending the scene, what did he conclude?'

'I am not at liberty to say, I'm afraid.'

That much, at least, was true. Henrik had sworn her to silence, though she wasn't sure why, seeing as the doctor had only told them what was already obvious to them both.

Frank snapped his notebook shut. 'Well, that's terrific. You've been a great help. Thank you so much. If I can ever return the favour, just let me know. Perhaps ...'

'Perhaps?'

'Perhaps I can suggest that next time you're a little less of an arse about it. What the fuck's wrong with you?'

What *was* wrong with her? She didn't know.

When Frank finally left, shaking his head, she climbed down from the windowsill, grabbed her coat and switched off the lights, standing still for a few minutes in the dark office with her eyes closed.

Half a century ago the whole building would have trembled as the presses rolled on the ground floor. The corridor would have been buzzing with the tap-tap of typewriters and reporters rushing in and out of smoke-filled rooms, knowing that what they did mattered, that people all over the country were waiting for the thud of the newspaper landing on their doorstep in the morning. Now the place was dead, a mausoleum to the fourth estate.

She ought not to be surprised. The print media's decline had begun years before she had even considered becoming a journalist, but somehow working out of her London flat had cushioned her from the worst of it. Here, in the shell of what was once an important institution, there was no escaping the facts.

Her phone pinged. She fished it out of her bag and stood in the dark with her coat on, reading Henrik's message, her face bathed in the blue light from the screen.

I must see you.

7

The smell of the flat depressed her: the sweat and exhalations of strangers absorbed by the walls through the years, the meals cooked on the gas rings in the galley kitchen, the odour of mildew from the drains plunging deep below the building. It hit her as soon as she opened the front door, along with the sight of her cardboard boxes piled around the floor. In three months she had failed to unpack, let alone leave any personal mark on the place.

Markus had gone for the Icelandic homestead look, with wooden furniture, candles and sheepskins. It was hopelessly impractical. The sheepskins kept sliding off the chairs, and the table – a slab of wood on trestles – wobbled dangerously under any kind of weight. In one corner, under a red lamp, were the bearded dragons Markus called his 'girls'. His condition for renting his flat to Jensen while he travelled around the world with his boyfriend was that she fed and watered the girls.

Most of her books, furniture and clothes from London were still in a container in the south Copenhagen harbour, contents for a home of her own as soon as she found one. Hard to do when you weren't looking.

She opened the fridge. There was half a tub of vanilla skyr and two bottles of Carlsberg. She took the skyr and closed the fridge door, then opened it again, put the skyr back and grabbed one of the beers. She drank it sitting on the bed in the dark, listening to the neighbour's television, a child's footsteps on the floor upstairs, someone sneezing repeatedly. Across the street there was another apartment building, just like hers, with televisions blaring in dark rooms. When she sat still and held her breath, it was as though she wasn't there at all.

She opened her laptop. Frank's piece was online already: *Second homeless man found dead in Copenhagen street.*

'Oh, very creative, Frank,' she said, toasting the screen with her beer.

It was a solid piece, textbook. He had spoken to a handful of 'experts' about the shrinking number of hostel beds in Copenhagen and pointed to the obvious question mark now hanging over the controversial begging ban. Her own picture was there, the old mugshot from when she had first started to report from London. It had been during her short-hair phase. She looked like an obstinate boy. Her quote, a declaration of horror at the discovery of the body, was entirely made up (fair enough, she might have done the same in Frank's place). A spokesperson for the prime minister expressed the government's concern and promised a full investigation into the case and any failings on the part of social services. This close to a general election, they were willing to promise anything. There were photographs of Magstræde, where people had left flowers and messages, out of guilt, perhaps, for not helping the boy when he had been alive.

She lay back on the faux-fur bedspread and stared at the ceiling, where a leak in the flat upstairs had left a water mark on the plaster. Like the truth, water always found its way through eventually.

What was wrong with her? Why couldn't she just have

written the article and be done with it? What had made her think she was better than Frank or Margrethe, she who had cycled past a beggar in the street and left him to die in the night?

Margrethe would already have written the editorial for tomorrow's print edition, one of her hallmark takedowns of the prime minister and her assaults on the welfare state. The general of an ever-diminishing army, Margrethe wasn't backing down or languishing in some bedsit lamenting the death of newsprint.

Jensen's phone lit up. A row of hearts. The blue-and-white Messenger icon with the name Henrik Jungersen triggered the familiar pull from the centre of her being.

If I knew where you lived, I'd do something stupid.

He would have deleted the message as soon as he had sent it. She had left no more of a visible trace on his life than she had on Markus's flat. She told herself this was why she had saved and printed their entire correspondence, as a record for posterity that their relationship had existed, that it had been real. Held over many years, with pauses of months, it had been the world's slowest conversation.

'I trust you completely,' Henrik had once told her. For a long time she had thought it meant that he trusted she was his. Now she knew it meant that he trusted her with their secret.

She wasn't ready to play their old game of tag again.

Not yet, perhaps not ever.

8

Wednesday 09:31

'First of all,' said Margrethe, silencing the room with her reptilian stare. 'A shout-out to Frank for his work on the Magstræde case. Solid journalism, old school. We're leading from the front again with the best coverage by far of any of today's papers.'

To murmurs of assent around the room, she launched into a detailed appraisal of today's edition of *Dagbladet*, both the front-page article with the century's most predictable headline and the inside feature on the shrinking provision for society's most vulnerable.

Jensen looked at the people gathered round the elliptical white boardroom table. They were the cream of the crop, the lucky ones who had survived the latest round of job cuts, still decently paid with good pensions, thanks to the Danish journalists' union, though not even the trade body had been able to hold back the digital tidal wave wrecking the country's most esteemed newspapers.

It was someone's birthday, so there were warm rolls from a posh bakery on the table, along with thermoses of coffee.

Henning was helping himself, eating and drinking with a single-minded devotion and showing no signs of listening to a word Margrethe was saying, though Jensen knew he rarely missed a beat. She wondered what he did for meals at home, or where home was. She had no idea if there was a Mrs Würtzen. Henning at home, out of his beige suit, doing something normal like brushing his teeth or frying an egg, was harder to imagine than him sleeping on the chaise longue in his office upstairs. She had never caught him actually staying the night, but nor had she ever seen him leaving the building.

Frank was beaming, soaking up Margrethe's compliments. Even Jensen had to admit that he had done a decent job with what he had been given, which was virtually nothing.

Lise Dissing, the culture editor, a woman with strawberry-blonde hair scraped into a tight bun and a face covered in tiny copper freckles, reached out and patted Frank on the shoulder to his visible pleasure. Jensen was pretty sure she wouldn't have done that had Margrethe not been sitting at the head of the table. Everyone wanted to be friends with Margrethe.

She thought back fondly to her time in London, when she used to dial in to these meetings, lying in bed while reading the day's news and deciding which stories to pitch. Sitting in the full glare of the others made her uncomfortable, even more so as she was painfully conscious that (again) she had nothing in today's paper. Suspecting that her free ride was about to come to a crashing halt, she grabbed a bread roll and began to spread it thickly with butter. Not that she was hungry, but she needed to fade into the background, to make herself inconspicuous by doing what the others did. The coffee tasted bitter, but the older journalists were guzzling it like water.

Thankfully, Margrethe was steering the meeting on to discussing the content lined up for the day ahead. She rubbed her hands together as the politics team on videoconference from Christiansborg reeled off the interviews they had lined up.

Frank announced a Sunday feature on vulnerable young immigrants from Eastern Europe.

'Still no news on the identity of the two victims?' asked Margrethe.

Frank shook his head. 'No one has any idea who they are. Nothing through Interpol, not matching anyone reported missing.'

'Incredible,' said Lise. 'They must be someone's son or brother or friend. Imagine no one noticing you've gone.'

Margrethe shot her an impatient look. She had never been one for mawkishness.

'Unusual, but not unheard of,' said Frank. 'There was that woman last year in Hvidovre, Jeanette Thomsen. Took a week. And this chap was obviously a foreigner, so it could take a lot longer than that.'

'What do you base that on, Frank?' Jensen heard herself say.

Even Henning turned to look at her, his lips forming a large O, frozen mid-bite round a bread roll.

So much for staying inconspicuous.

'The police, actually,' said Frank, his face a deep puce. 'They said they know most of the Danes sleeping rough around the place, and no one has heard of these guys, if that's all right with you?'

'All I am saying is that we have no facts yet. We don't know who the boy was or what he was doing in Magstræde or what he died of. He might not even be a beggar.'

'Which is exactly what my article says, as you would have known if you had bothered to read it.'

'So, all we are doing is guessing, speculating, and we may be right, but we could also be very wrong.'

'Thank you, Jensen, for your value-add,' said Margrethe. 'I am sure no one here would have reached that conclusion without you. When is the post-mortem, Frank?'

'Soon. Tomorrow maybe.'

He was sulking now, avoiding Jensen's eyes and leaving the cup of coffee that he had just poured for himself untouched by his side. She thought of the scrap of paper with the name of the homeless shelter. Henrik must have decided to keep that detail to himself, or Frank would have mentioned it in his article. He had used every single piece of information in his possession. She wondered if he had thought of checking out the inner-city shelters himself and decided unkindly that he didn't have the imagination to do so.

Towards the end of the meeting, when people were picking up their laptops and coffee cups and heading for their desks, Margrethe looked straight at her. 'Oh, Jensen. I had a tip-off, some kind of accountancy scam doing the rounds. It's in your inbox, check it out.'

Jensen didn't have any particular beat at *Dagbladet*, as the newspaper's special reporter, but financial fraud was as far from her expertise as it was possible to get. It was obviously some kind of punishment.

'Seriously?' she said, but Margrethe was already striding away with her mobile phone to her ear.

'Use your instinct, if you still have one,' she shouted.

A few of the other journalists sniggered. Yasmine, Margrethe's long-suffering personal assistant, followed after her boss, balancing her phone on a stack of papers. She looked back over her shoulder at Jensen and shook her head with a look that said: 'Not now.'

'And when you get back, come and see me. I need to talk to you,' added Margrethe, without turning round.

9

Wednesday 12:36

Pigeons rose from the slushy road surface at the mouth of
Strøget, where Jensen had to wait on her bicycle for pedestrians to cross, conscious that she was in full view of Margrethe's
corner office and praying that her boss was elsewhere engaged.

She had decided that the fraud story could wait. Margrethe's
tip-off had turned out to be from a man with an anonymous
email account who described himself as 'the owner of a popular
Copenhagen restaurant'. It was directed at Karen Nordmann,
an accountant whom he claimed had defrauded his business of
almost a million kroner. The email was full of bizarre accusations: *You won't find Karen Nordmann anywhere. It is not her real
name. Besides, she is in Thailand now, spending my money.*

Jensen had received many emails of this kind over the years
from desperate, deluded people with personal scores to settle.
All had gone straight in the bin. She wondered if this was
Margrethe's idea of a joke.

Unlikely.

Margrethe never joked.

The restaurant at the top of Magstræde was open, the black

sandwich board outside inviting people in. A vent emitted a smell of pizza that made Jensen's stomach rumble.

Inside it was warm and cosy, with a nautical feel reminding her of West Jutland fishing boats. The sloping floor was crammed with wooden tables and chairs. A selection of colourful bottles was lined up on the windowsills, and candles flickered inside storm glasses on the counter.

She had the pick of the seats; snow was obviously bad for business. Almost immediately after she settled for a table in the corner of the room, a waitress with long hair in a loose bun came over and handed her the menu.

'Always this quiet in here?' Jensen asked.

The waitress laughed. 'You wouldn't have said that yesterday. Place was a circus with all those reporters hanging around.'

'Because of the stabbing?'

The waitress nodded, uncomfortable all of a sudden.

'What's good here?' Jensen asked, pointing to the menu.

'The Gitte Stallone is my favourite.'

'The what?'

The waitress laughed again. She had pretty teeth, a tattoo of some kind of insect behind one ear.

'Pizza with cured salmon and smoked cheese, wrapped around salad.'

'I'll have that. And a large pot of coffee. And water.'

'Help yourself,' said the girl, pointing to a jug on the counter.

While Jensen waited for her food, trying to work out the link between pizza and the pneumatic Danish-born 1980s Hollywood starlet, she checked the news on her phone. Nothing yet on the boy's identity. Most of the media outlets were still speculating that the man was Eastern European.

She wolfed down the pizza, watching the restaurant slowly filling with tourists. She still had half a pot of coffee left when she signalled to the waitress for the bill, her stomach full of warm starch.

'Actually, I was the one who found the boy yesterday morning and called the police. In hindsight, I should have stopped on Monday night when I first noticed him sitting there.'

The waitress looked as though she was about to cry. 'Me too,' she said. 'I did try, but I should have done more.'

Jensen wiped tomato sauce from her lips, feeling her mood lift by several degrees. It seemed not everyone was indifferent to the boy's death.

'When was that?'

'About eleven o'clock when I arrived for work. It hadn't begun to snow yet, but you could tell it was just about to. I saw the boy sitting there, so I went up and talked to him.'

'And what did he say?'

'Nothing. I tried in English, and German, but he just shook his head.'

'They think he might have been Eastern European, maybe Romanian.'

The waitress nodded miserably.

'It was you, wasn't it? The pizza and coffee?'

'It was the least I could do, but he didn't want it. He kept shaking his head, so I just left it there and walked away.'

'And the note?'

'Which note?'

Jensen stared at the waitress. So, it wasn't her who had left the scrap of paper in the boy's lap.

'Nothing, my mistake, I must have misheard you. Did you see anything else?'

'Nothing apart from his rucksack.'

'Rucksack?'

'Yes, it was right next to him. Why, did you not see it?'

'No. Someone must have taken it. What colour was it?'

'Blue, I think. Bright blue.'

'Big? Small?'

'Sort of medium-sized.'

'You know it's strange,' said Jensen. 'Stuff appears to have gone missing overnight. When I saw the boy on Monday, I could have sworn I saw him holding a piece of cardboard with something written on it.'

'Oh, but he was,' said the waitress, more confident now. 'I saw it, too. I told the detective about it when the police came round yesterday.'

'Bald guy, tough looking, black leather jacket, not young, not old, kind eyes?'

'Yes, that's the one.'

Thanks a lot for sharing, Henrik.

'And do you remember what the sign said? I am kicking myself that I didn't take a closer look and help the poor guy.'

The waitress nodded again. 'That's what was so weird. I mean, if he was really Eastern European, because there was just one word, and it was in Danish.'

'And that word was?'

'*Skyldig.*'

Guilty.

10

Wednesday 13:42

Jensen left her bicycle chained to a lamp post outside the restaurant and walked towards Snaregade.

If the boy had had a sign, then where was it now? Had it blown away in the blizzard, or been removed by the killer along with the boy's rucksack? She couldn't see why anyone would have bothered to do that.

The town houses, all different colours and sizes, were holding their secrets close. She walked past the junction with Knabrostræde, as far as Gammel Strand, glancing across Holmen's Canal to the ochre-coloured walls of the Thorvaldsen Museum. The only people she met were a few tourists hugging themselves miserably against the cold.

She turned and walked back to where the boy had been sitting when she found him. The flowers left by the mourning public had darkened with frost and were fewer in number than they had looked in the picture in *Dagbladet*. Someone had left a teddy bear dressed in the Danish flag. A card wrapped in a plastic freezer bag left by a bunch of roses, so dark red they were almost black, read: *Rest in peace.*

'Hypocrites,' said Jensen out loud.

Had his 'Guilty' sign been an indictment of society? A finger pointed at the people passing by for allowing a fellow human being to sleep in the street?

She stepped back and looked up at the building. The basement windows were covered in security grilles. Five doorbells, five name tags. She rang the bells, one by one; no answer. The tenants were out at work, or scared, or fed up talking to journalists, possibly all of the above. No one could blame them.

She sat down on her haunches facing the street, quickly feeling the cold rise from the wet cobbles. The thin sheets of cardboard the boy had been sitting on would not have offered much insulation.

Magstræde was narrow and bending, leaving only a section of it visible. The building opposite the boy's perch was four storeys, and small compared to its neighbours, with cleaner windows. The ground floor was raised above street level and the windows were half covered in white shutters, but you could just about make out two oversized brass pendants suspended from the ceiling. It looked like some kind of office.

Jensen noticed movement behind one of the shutters, someone looking out and locking eyes with her for a split second. She decided to take it as an invitation.

The sign on the door said CG Dentistry. Two doorbells with blank name tags, a camera. She pressed the lower bell and looked straight into the lens, holding up her press pass. There was another camera, CCTV, mounted above the door.

'Yes?'

A female voice, tentative.

'Jensen, *Dagbladet*. Can I come in and talk to you?'

The briefest hesitation. 'Do you have an appointment?'

'Do I need one?'

Silence.

Jensen raised her voice: 'All I want to know is what it feels

43

like to sit inside in your nice warm office across the street from where a young man was stabbed to death.'

The woman hung up. Jensen was about to press the doorbell again when the buzzer sounded, unlocking the street door and admitting her into a narrow hallway with a door on her left. It was opened almost at once by a busty, smartly dressed blonde woman in her thirties. She smiled apologetically.

'Forgive me if I wasn't very hospitable. We've had a steady stream of you lot calling in the last twenty-four hours.'

The reception desk was impressive. Curved round one corner of the room, it looked as though it had been crafted out of a single sheet of copper by elves with tiny hammers. There was an oversized bouquet of lilies and branches, comfortable chairs and posters on the wall of smiling men and women, alongside framed collages of newspaper and magazine cuttings about the clinic. On the counter, and in a tall shelving unit on the far side, were stacks of black boxes with *CG* marked in bold white letters.

A man came through from the office beyond the waiting room, smiling. In his mid-fifties, with thinning salt-and-pepper hair combed back from his forehead and horn-rimmed glasses. Striking rather than handsome, he had a tall, lithe figure and the kind of natural authority that comes with a white coat.

'Christian Grønfeldt.'

His hand was warm and dry. A smart room with a big desk was just visible through the open door behind him.

'Jensen, *Dagbladet*.'

'We already spoke to one of your colleagues. What was his name, Malene?'

'That would be Frank,' said Jensen. 'Frank Buhl.'

'That's it.'

'I am not here as a reporter. Actually, it was me who found the body yesterday morning, on my way to work.'

'I see. We heard what happened, of course. Horrifying, but, as we said to the others, we'd rather you didn't quote us. This

44

is a place of business, as you may appreciate. We wouldn't want to scare off our clients.'

'You're a dentist?' said Jensen.

Grønfeldt beamed. 'Cosmetic orthodontist, actually. I sell beauty, youth, hope. What everyone wants, a perfect smile.'

It had the sound of an oft-repeated mantra.

'Teeth whitening?'

'That too. And certain beauty treatments and our own range of products.'

He gestured proudly at the boxes with his initials.

'Botox?'

'We like to refer to it as injectables.'

'Did you notice the victim sitting there during the day on Monday?'

'*I* did,' said Malene.

'What time?'

'Maybe about five o'clock. It had started to snow heavily by then.'

'Did you notice him arriving?'

She shook her head. 'Neither of us did. I don't think he was there when I popped out briefly on Monday morning, but I was rushing, so I can't be sure.'

That was how it happened, thought Jensen again. You saw what you wanted to, and no one wanted to see a beggar in the street.

'Your camera,' she said. 'The one on the wall above your door. Could it have picked up anything?'

Grønfeldt smiled sheepishly.

'The police asked us that. I shouldn't tell you this, but you look so nice. The camera is not recording. It's a legacy from the company that owned the building before us.'

'How long since you bought it?'

'About four years, but we reckon the camera is a deterrent, so we've kept it.'

He glanced at his expensive-looking watch, the size of a saucer. 'I'm afraid we're expecting our next client any minute. Do come back another time. Call us first, we'll have coffee, and you can have a tour of the place.'

'I will,' Jensen said, grabbing a business card from a dish on the counter and seeing herself out.

It was obvious Grønfeldt and Malene were an item. He had that possessive look about him. Not bad going for a man who had to be twenty years her senior.

A man with a caveman beard walked past as she stepped into the street. The biting wind felt like an assault after the warm clinic.

'*Hej*,' she shouted, waving her arms. 'Excuse me.'

The man continued on his way. She ran after him, grabbing his arm. He stared at her, terrified, killing the sound on his headphones, but not bothering to remove them.

'A young man was stabbed here yesterday,' she said, pointing to the makeshift memorial. 'He had been here since Monday. I saw him, he was holding a sign. Do you live locally?'

He shook his head, wide-eyed. 'No.'

'But you come through here regularly?'

He shook his head again. 'I can't help you,' he said, more aggressively this time, and walked away, picking up the pace.

She felt a spike of anger at the city, its callousness and indifference. Whatever the boy had hoped for, it was unlikely he had found it in here.

A man with a ponytail and black cagoule came up behind her and began photographing the flowers with a professional camera. She vaguely recognised him from one of the tabloids, though obviously it wasn't mutual. He was doing what she was doing, grabbing anyone she could find to interview.

'Excuse me', he said. 'Can I ask if you . . .?'

'Get lost,' she said, and headed for her bicycle and what was shaping up to be an exceptionally tedious afternoon in the office, investigating a case of accountancy fraud.

11

Jensen was soaked when she arrived home from work after riding through the sleet all the way to Christianshavn. Her face and hands were numb with cold, her jeans clinging to her thighs and cutting off her circulation. She needed a long soak in the bath, but Markus's shower would have to do, if there was any hot water, which was by no means certain.

She tried to remember whether she still had a tin of soup left. Should she nip down to the Vietnamese for a phở instead? It would mean getting wet and cold again. The front-door key slipped out of her useless hands and landed on the doormat. The sound was drowned out by the evening news on her next-door neighbour's TV.

Inside, she didn't bother with the lights before throwing down her bag and wrenching herself out of her wet clothes, dropping them in a heap on the floor and heading for the bath-room naked.

She froze halfway.

It was a small sound, no more than the faintest sigh coming from the flat's only proper room, but definitely there.

Her heart began to thump. The lock hadn't been forced. Had Henrik found her and used his police training to gain access somehow?

Not funny.

Not funny at all.

She had no weapon but the element of surprise. With a probing hand, she found the light switch and counted silently to three before hitting it and pushing the door open with as loud a roar as she could muster.

A shape rose from the bed with a blood-curdling scream. She caught a glimpse of nut-brown skin, tattoos, wild black hair and a pillow held aloft.

'Markus, what the fuck?'

'Jesus, you scared me. Haven't you heard of knocking?'

'Why would I knock? I live here,' she said.

Markus looked at her naked body and his scream segued into roaring laughter. There was a popcorn smell about him, of sweat and unwashed clothes. She covered herself with one arm as best she could.

'Jesus, you stink,' she said. 'When did you last have a bath?'

He flopped back onto the bed and began to roll around, convulsing with laughter. She made a mental note to change the bedclothes. Then she joined in. Her neighbour, a man who kept his TV volume on max yet was hypersensitive to any noise coming from her apartment, began to bang on the wall. She knelt down, pulled the duvet over her head and abandoned herself to laughter, feeling the tension leave her body, until she realised that Markus had begun to sob loudly.

She noticed his rucksack on the floor still carrying the airline tag, alongside a hideous woven shoulder bag.

'What's the matter, Markus?' she said. 'Where's Luuk? I thought you two were meant to be in Australia.'

Markus's shoulders shook violently. She didn't know whether to touch him or not, having only ever seen him in his work

48

clothes behind the newspaper's reception desk. Their sudden intimacy felt awkward.

'Tell you what,' she said, standing up and pulling the duvet with her. 'Give me five minutes to throw on some clothes and I'll run down and fetch us a phở and some beers. You can dry your eyes and have a shower, and then I want to know exactly what happened. All of it.'

12

Wednesday 20:14

They used one of her cardboard boxes as a table. Markus sniffed loudly, with his face bent over the hot soup. His heart might be broken but there was nothing wrong with his appetite.

'Such a prick. Didn't even leave a note when he took off in Sydney. I just woke up one morning and he'd gone without me.'

'You'd no inkling?' she said, twisting lime into her soup, her mouth watering at the sour smell rising from it.

'A bit, maybe,' said Markus, slurping noodles. 'He'd started finding everything about me wrong. Said my legs were too short, that my feet were like trotters.'

She glanced quickly at his scab-covered feet, which looked welded into his flip-flops. Luuk had had a point.

Markus wiped his nose with the back of his hand and pointed to the bed. 'Sorry about earlier ... I'm so fucking jet-lagged. Only dropped in to pick up the keys to my mum's place but saw the bed and got overwhelmed. Don't even know what time it was, but it was still daylight, so must have been hours ago.'

He looked around the flat and she felt embarrassed about the

50

boxes, the dirty clothes on the floor and the empty beer bottles by the bed.

'What are you going to do now?' she asked him, feeling her nose begin to run from the chilli.

'Yeah, about that,' said Markus, avoiding her glance. 'Mum's in Spain, so I can stay at her place till she gets home, but then I am going to have to ask for my keys back.'

He drained his soup container and fished with his chopsticks for the noodles left at the bottom. Jensen wondered if his ex had also been disgusted by the way he smacked his lips when he ate.

'When?' she asked, calculating that a month should be enough for her to find another place.

Markus looked straight at her, a new edge of hardness in his eyes.

'Tuesday,' he said.

'What?'

'You've got five days,' he said, finishing his beer with a loud belch.

'But I don't have anywhere to go. What am I supposed to do with all my stuff?'

'Not my problem,' he said, staring straight at her with his beautiful, cold brown eyes, then softening a little and gesturing at the flat.

'Come on, it's not like you have to pack or anything. And you knew this was an informal arrangement. I'll pay you back to take us to the end of the month, promise.'

She looked at the soup and the beers that she'd bought, the T-shirt of hers that he was wearing, and felt that she was owed something better. Was she expecting gratitude? She berated herself for her stupidity.

After checking on the lizards, he left with his rucksack and ugly shoulder bag, heading for the metro and his mum's Hellerup apartment.

'I'll be here ten a.m. Tuesday. Great if you could be gone by then,' he said, before letting himself out and slamming the door.

Copenhagen wasn't going to work. Not in a million years. And now she was homeless to boot. She reached for her laptop and began to look up flights to London.

In the terrarium, under the red lamp, one of the bearded dragons leaned close to the glass and stared at her sideways with its unblinking eye.

13

'We've got something, boss!'

Mark came running up to him like a playful Labrador. Henrik, carrying his leather jacket and about to leave the office, felt a surge of affection for him. Most of his colleagues were cynical, jaded, playing it cool, but, if nothing else, Mark could always be relied upon for his enthusiasm.

'What, you found a witness?'

'No, not that. Me and Lisbeth drew a blank, I was going to tell you that before this new thing happened.'

Fuck. All they had to go on was the statement from the pizza waitress who claimed that the Magstræde victim had been holding some sort of sign. (If you believed her, which Henrik was inclined not to. Too often, people saw things that weren't there, and the sign hadn't turned up.) No one at the Bird's Nest shelter had offered any information of value. A whole day's work and, depressingly, they had got precisely nowhere. At this rate, he would have no update for Monsen.

'Well, spit it out then.'

'We had a phone call from Skovhøj, a youth home in

Roskilde, reporting one of their residents missing, a twenty-one-year-old man by the name of Casper Madsen. Not been seen since Sunday, and stuff's gone from his room, apparently.'

'Description?'

'Matches that of our second victim.'

'Have his parents been contacted?'

'Mother dead, father unknown. The manager of the youth home, Karina Jørgensen, said she'll be able to do the ID.'

'Well, what are you waiting for? Get her down here!'

'Already arranged for tomorrow first thing.'

'Good.'

Henrik shrugged on his jacked and headed for the lift but stopped on sensing Mark staying put behind him.

'For God's sake, what is it?'

'Just thinking, boss, that if it really *is* Casper Madsen, then this isn't about foreigners. So, what would the motive be for someone to kill him and the first victim?'

'Might not have been the same killer.'

'Still, why?'

'Theft.'

'But we know that our first victim was extremely drunk when he was stabbed. Would have been like taking sweets from a baby, no need to actually kill him.'

'God knows. People are sick,' said Henrik.

'And another thing,' said Mark. 'What makes someone leave a nice warm bedroom to sleep rough in Copenhagen during the worst snowstorm in years?'

That was a more interesting question. Henrik didn't have the answer to it, but with a positive ID, they would be a lot closer to finding out. Even better, now he would actually have something to say for himself when he phoned Monsen from his car on the way home.

14

The room at the Forensic Institute had been designed without any attempt at softening the blow of death. No flowers or tissues, just four tiled walls, strip lighting and a trolley with the ominous shape of a corpse under a sheet. The lab technician, a young woman with jet-black hair cut in a short bob with a blunt fringe, stood to one side, ready to lift the sheet from the body on Henrik's signal. Her name was Clara, and she would have been pretty (if a bit too young for him) had it not been for the thin silver ring in her lower lip. Henrik hoped the fad for mutilating one's body with piercings would have long passed by the time his own daughter got old enough to consider it. This thought made him feel like a dinosaur, his wife's favourite word for him but, strangely, not one he minded. The last couple of decades had brought little good in the way of human development, as far as he was concerned. Quite the opposite. If he had thought he could get away with it, he would gladly have locked up his daughter, and his sons too, to keep them from harm. Spotting danger at every turn was a daily burden, but what he had seen in his career could not be unseen. His wife, for all that she was better educated than him (according to his friends, he had 'over-scored' in the marital stakes), would never understand it, and so he kept these thoughts to himself. They barely talked anyway, so it made little difference.

He looked at his watch, exchanging a quick glance with Clara, whose eyes were welling up from a supressed yawn. They had been there for ten minutes already, waiting for the youth-home manager from Roskilde to stop sobbing and collect herself sufficiently for the task at hand. She kept eyeing the door as if expecting to be rescued by her colleague, who was waiting outside.

Henrik had taken an instant dislike to Karina Jørgensen, and sensed the feeling was mutual. She was the type who made no effort with her appearance. Big belly, copper-coloured hair growing out grey, ugly red spectacles. ('You're no oil painting yourself,' he heard his wife say.) As a means of navigating the female minefield, he had relied for years on flirting, but with a woman as ugly as this, he was unable to find it in himself, and they tended to be immune to the cheeky-chappie patter he would use to some effect on the elderly. Besides, he thought Karina Jørgensen was rather overdoing it. It was not as if she had known Casper Madsen personally. Since arriving she had been busy making excuses, conscious presumably of how bad it looked that no one at Skovhøj had noticed the boy's absence until last night, when another resident had raised the alarm. Mark had been to Roskilde already, collecting the CCTV recording showing Casper leaving at 5.43 a.m. Monday morning, with a bright blue rucksack slung over one shoulder. He had been wearing the woollen beanie that was now stowed away in a specimen bag at the technical investigations centre in Glostrup, while his rucksack had vanished off the face of the earth.

'You can only cut back social services so much before something has to give,' Karina had insisted.

Henrik wondered what cutbacks had to do with it. His

56

instinct told him the manager was feeling guilty about something and that not realising that one of her charges had run away was only the start of it. He handed her a box of tissues with a 'Take your time,' meaning the exact opposite. She blew her nose noisily, her shoulders heaving in dry spasms. After another five minutes of sniffling, she said, 'OK, let me try now,' and approached the trolley.

Henrik held his breath and kept his eyes on Karina's face as Clara pulled back the sheet. The woman did what everyone did in this situation: covered her mouth with her hands. She let out a strangled scream, then wobbled dangerously, before Henrik caught her under one arm.

'That's him,' she managed to stammer. 'That's Casper.'

He nodded to Clara who re-covered the body, triggering another gush of tears from Karina. He managed to get her to drink a glass of water. She shook so hard that most of it ended up on her jumper.

'Any idea what might have led him to leave Skovhøj and travel to Copenhagen on Monday morning?'

'None whatsoever. He was a disturbed young person with multiple issues. All our residents are.'

'You say that,' said Henrik, 'so I find it odd that no one missed him for three days.'

Karina Jørgensen promptly stopped sniffling.

'Skovhøj's not a prison. Our residents are free to come and go as they please. Besides, even if we had wanted to, we're so severely understaffed that we can't possibly keep an eye on everyone.'

'Really? Not even a daily census? A quick knock on the door to ensure everyone is where they should be? Surely that can't take more than a few minutes.'

'You make it sound as if Skovhøj were some sort of borstal,' said Karina Jørgensen. 'Actually, we believe strongly in the individual freedom of the young people in our care.'

57

Really? Were we now supposed to be defending the freedom of vulnerable youngsters to get themselves stabbed to death in the street? Henrik decided to let it go.

For now.

'You'll need to give a formal statement. I'll take you and your colleague down to the station, get it over and done with.'

'Wait – there is more I need to tell you. In confidence,' said Karina Jørgensen, nodding at Clara, who looked only too grateful to be dismissed, wheeling away the remains of Casper Madsen with indecent haste.

As she turned to Henrik and began to speak, there was a new expression of grim determination in Karina's eyes that brought him sharply to attention for the first time since this sorry investigation had started.

15

Before heading into work, Jensen cycled to Magstræde and walked from there to the Bird's Nest in Rysensteensgade on the other side of H. C. Andersens Boulevard. The slush on the pavements had frozen overnight and she had to walk slowly not to slip, but still it only took her nine minutes. So the boy had been no more than nine minutes from safety when he died.

Had he gone there, and been turned away, as Henrik had suggested? She didn't want him to be right.

The shelter was on the corner of a red-brick apartment building, down a flight of stairs in a glass-fronted basement. She could just about make out the word 'butcher' on the wall, the outline of an old shop sign. A note taped to the door said *No drugs*, in Danish and English.

Maybe that was why the boy had been turned away, if he had ever got this far. Jensen was about to ring the bell when a woman of indefinable age came out, with long hair, puffer jacket, pom-pom hat, jeans and trainers, carrying two plastic bags. She didn't look up, but propped the door open for Jensen as she left. Impossible to tell whether she worked there or had stayed the night.

Inside was a narrow hallway with a tall counter and a door leading to the back of the basement. The door was locked with a key code. Another notice, pinned to the counter said, *Wait your turn* and *Respect our rules*. Jensen could smell coffee and hear the clattering of crockery being stacked somewhere towards the back of the building.

A woman in her fifties sat behind the counter, typing furiously on a laptop. She had short-cropped curly hair and round, black-rimmed spectacles, and looked utterly worn out.

'We're open again at six this evening. Come back tonight, as early as you can,' she said, without looking up from her work.

When Jensen didn't move, she repeated the same sentences in English, then pushed a laminated sheet across the desk, with what Jensen assumed to be the same message in a dozen languages.

'My name is Jensen. *Dagbladet.*'

The woman finally looked up. 'Oh,' she said. 'That policeman did say you'd turn up sooner or later.'

Damn Henrik.

'I am not here as a journalist, actually. I just need to know what happened to that homeless boy who was stabbed. It was me who found him in Magstræde on Tuesday morning.'

'Yes, he said that too.'

She waited for the woman to say something else. They stared at each other for a few long seconds, until the woman caved.

'What do you want?'

'To find out if he turned up here on Monday night.'

'I will give you the same answer I gave to the policeman: he might have done, I have no idea. We have thirty-three beds here. It was snowing hard. Fifty-five people turned up. We took an extra four, though we don't have the licence for it, which means we had to turn away eighteen people.'

60

'First come, first served?'

'No. We draw lots.'

'That's nice.'

'It's inhumane. We try to send the ones who lose to other shelters, but there is a lack of beds everywhere in the city. Especially in bad weather.'

'So, you don't remember him? Medium height, thin, dark hair, fluffy beard, puffer jacket, bright blue rucksack?'

'That would fit the description of a lot of the people we see here. It's possible he did come, and that I turned him away. There. Is that what you want?'

She looked close to tears.

Jensen spoke more gently. 'Can you think why he would have had on him a scrap of paper with the name and address of this place?'

The woman shrugged. 'Could be a thousand different reasons.'

'None of your colleagues would have gone around the city handing out the address to the homeless?'

'Look, we're four people on duty here. All volunteers. Much as we'd like to, we don't have the time to advertise.'

She tried to stare Jensen down, but years of hard practice had made Jensen good at saying nothing. In the end the woman relented.

'Sorry,' she said. 'I am just so angry. This sort of thing was bound to happen one day. We've reached a new low in society; it's shameful. No one should be sleeping rough. We can well afford to give everyone a roof over their heads.'

She would get on well with Margrethe.

'Yes, we can,' said Jensen. 'But there is always the possibility that the victim didn't want one. Maybe he didn't come here after all.'

'Who doesn't want shelter? Something hot to eat, a bed to sleep in, a shower and breakfast in the morning?'

'That's what I am trying to find out.'

A man came out, in army fatigues and a red padded jacket, wearing a blue rucksack. He didn't look at them before heading for the street.

'Tell you what,' said Jensen, nodding at the door to the back. 'I promise to get out of your hair, but do you think I could just have a quick look? I won't talk to anyone.'

'Can't see why not, most people have left for the day, anyway. Everyone has to be out by nine, but no photos, and don't quote me for any of the things I have just said.'

Seemed the woman wasn't keen to stick her neck out for the dead boy either. Aside from herself and the pizza waitress, the poor lad had few people in his corner.

'I don't know what sort of image you have in your mind of this place,' said the woman as she flashed her staff pass to unlock the door, 'But it's not the Ritz. I want you out in ten minutes.'

There were three rooms. Metal bunk beds with blue plastic mattresses, a bank of lockers against one wall. Water pipes ran along the ceiling. A woman had to keep her neck bent as she sat on a top bunk, packing her belongings. She didn't look up when Jensen passed her. No novelty in a stranger coming and going in this place, obviously. Better to keep one's head down.

Jensen walked past two bathrooms and came to a dining room and kitchen at the back. Two people were finishing off their coffees, and a man was cleaning the tables.

The woman in the reception had been right: the shelter was basic, but it was warm and dry. Better than a square of cardboard, in a blizzard, on the pavement of a dark street. Any day.

16

From the Bird's Nest, Jensen cycled in under a minute to the tiny green coffee van parked in Sankt Peders Stræde by an old-fashioned street lamp next to black-painted fence plastered with posters. The morning rush of workers from the nearby offices and shops was over, and the narrow street, with its tall, pastel town houses and gable ends covered in graffiti, was quiet, with just a few pedestrians shuffling along on the slushy pavements.

No sooner had Liron spotted her than he began stuffing freshly ground beans into an espresso scoop and compressing them with his thumb. Five minutes later, she was warming her hands on a large paper cup of double-shot latte. She never ordered anything from Liron, and he never asked what she wanted, just brewed her whatever he thought she needed. In return, his was the only coffee in town Jensen was willing to pay for.

'Uh-oh, someone's in a bloody bad mood,' said Liron with his toothy grin, more at home in the Danish vernacular than the natives after twenty years in the country.

The Danish girl he had followed from Israel and married had

long since vanished, but Liron had stayed put and made it his mission in life to educate the Danes about coffee.

'Leave it, Liron,' she said.

She closed her eyes and sipped the foamy, nutty-tasting drink. It was excellent, thick like chocolate and, slowly, she felt herself calm down. There was no two ways about it: it wasn't worth falling out with Margrethe over what had happened in Magstræde. She was going to have to check out the accountancy fraud. As soon as she had finished her coffee.

The weather had changed. It was blustery with a harsh, low sun that cut into her eyes. Her hair was whipping around her face and getting into her mouth. Liron, dressed in a long coat, bobble hat, fingerless gloves and a leather apron, stamped his feet and blew on his hands. With his pale hazel eyes, set into deep, grey sockets, he would have been handsome were it not for his goatee, plaited and tied with a single red bead.

'Sorry, I was grumpy,' Jensen said, draining her cup and handing it back to Liron. 'Bet you wish you were back in Jerusalem now.'

'Fuck, no,' Liron said, holding out his arms, his face cracking into a wide smile. 'I fucking love it here. Bloody wonderful Copenhagen.'

Before she could stop him, he bent down, poked his head through her legs and lifted her onto his shoulders, ignoring her screams as he staggered around in the snow roaring with pleasure. He smelled of tobacco and Christmas spices: cinnamon, nutmeg, cardamom. She held onto his head, closed her eyes and turned her face towards the sun. Surprisingly, there was some warmth in it.

17

Friday 10:29

Jensen was still chuckling to herself when she cycled away past City Hall Square. There was someone she needed to see before she headed back to the newspaper. Liron had reminded her that she still had friends in her home country.

The wind numbed her face as she rode down Vester Voldgade, past the posters for a new Viking exhibition at the National Museum, and down Ny Vestergade, towards the ornate Marble Bridge, where Copenhagen briefly turned into Venice. Mirrored in the glazed-over waters of Frederikholms Kanal, the pale arches of the bridge formed three perfect circles. She turned onto the cobbles and cycled between the two crowned arches that led onto the old riding grounds in front of Christiansborg Palace, squinting in the sunlight. A few lacklustre tourists were drifting around taking photos, oblivious to the dramas going on inside the building.

She had always given Borgen a wide berth, hating the incestuous environment of political journalism, the slippery nature of facts once they had been through the machinations of spin doctors and parliament members, but she needed to see Esben.

He was the only politician she trusted. They had launched each other's careers. Without Esben, no scoop for her and her local newspaper, no discovery by Margrethe, no *Dagbladet* and no London. And, though he would never admit it, without her, Esben would still be selling duvets in Aalborg.

She asked the woman in the porter's cubicle to call his office, looking in vain for his tall figure in the crowds of school pupils and staff milling about under the high lobby ceiling.

'Are you . . . err, Jensen?'

A panting man in jeans with a staff badge dangling over his soft belly shook her hand. His skin was damp, his forehead running with sweat.

'I am Ask, Esben's . . . err, assistant. He's really busy, so just five minutes, OK?'

No, thought Jensen, that couldn't be right. Esben was the laziest man north of the Alps. A great talker, efficient, a consummate politician, but never ever *busy*.

She followed Ask up the marble staircase. He reached back with one hand to pull up his waistband and tuck in his shirt, but didn't quite manage it, leaving the hem tucked into his burgundy underpants. There was a large sweat patch on his back. All in all, he was about as far from the usual profile of Esben's assistants as it was possible to get.

Ask made her wait while he knocked and entered Esben's office, closing the door behind him. Then she heard a chair being pushed back and Esben's booming North Jutland voice: 'Yes, you clown, let her in this instant!'

Esben waved Ask off with a look of distaste and kissed Jensen on both cheeks. Though he had to be some way north of fifty by now, he was still almost shockingly handsome: a runner's body, winter tan, recently whitened teeth. She wondered if he might have been to see Grønfeldt. A newspaper lay open next to his phone on his otherwise empty desk. He had been reading the sports section.

Busy, my arse, thought Jensen.

'Heard you'd moved back,' Esben said with a flirtatious smile. 'Why didn't you call me?'

'New assistant?' she said, ignoring his question. 'Your tastes have changed, Esben.'

He rolled his eyes. 'My wife's choice. MeToo and all that shit. She's worried I'll be next.'

'Smart woman.'

Esben made Ask go and get coffee, to the man's evident displeasure, though he held his tongue, obviously having learned by now that Esben always got his own way.

Well, almost always.

'So, Jensen. You've been back home for three months with not as much as a word, and now this. What's up? You finally decided to come to San Sebastian with me? I know this great little place – five stars, food out of this world, bedrooms upstairs.'

'You know the guy who was stabbed over in Magstræde?'

'Read about the same in your paper.'

'Well, it was me who found him.'

'So I gather. Tell me, why did you let that clown Frank Buhl steal your gig? Are you losing your touch, Jensen?'

'I'll tell you another time. But what do you make of the murder, and the one before it? Do you think someone is out to make a point about homelessness in Copenhagen?'

'I see. You *are* still working on the story. Does Buhl know?'

'I'm *not* working it, just wondering.'

'Sure. Whatever you say. Well, personally I think nothing, but a few people here at the circus are getting quite het up about those murders.'

'Why?'

'It's budget time. Government's cutting back, making the hard choices no one else has the guts for. And here come our homeless poster boys and get themselves killed. And now it's the government's fault.'

'Isn't it?'

'Of course not. It's a total red herring.'

Esben leaned across the desk and grasped her hands, serious all of a sudden. 'Steer clear of this madhouse, Jensen. The boy was killed. Find out why and then write the story as only you can. This,' he said, gesturing dramatically at the room, 'is nothing but smoke and mirrors.'

'You're a great advert for parliamentary democracy, Esben, did anyone ever tell you that?'

She bit her lip. 'Thing is, I may not have a newspaper to write for much longer. Margrethe is pissed off with me and on top of that I am about to lose my flat. I should have stayed in London.'

'Yes, you should, but you are here now. You can borrow our summer house in Hornbæk until you sort yourself out with new digs. Here.'

He pulled out a key ring and wrenched off a key, throwing it on the table. Then he narrowed his eyes.

'You're not still seeing that policeman, are you?'

'No! And anyway, if I were, it would be none of your business. Shall we just remind ourselves that you, of all people, are in no position to lecture anyone about adultery?'

He held up his hands. 'OK, guilty as charged, but the man's a bastard. You deserve better.'

He rose from his desk. 'Come on, I'm buying you a drink.'

'It's eleven in the morning!'

'Tsk,' he said. 'I told you years ago, Champagne has its own rules.'

18

'Who are you?'

There was a boy making himself at home in her chair with his dirty trainers on the desk. He was wearing huge over-ear headphones and filling her office with vape stinking of cherries.

The room was dark but for her anglepoise desk lamp. Night had fallen without her noticing. Drinks with Esben had dragged out (when did they ever not) and she was now feeling the after-effects, along with a growing sense of guilt at having done nothing yet to investigate Margrethe's tip-off.

The boy at her desk didn't react. Jensen crept up behind him, lifted one headphone and shouted in his ear.

'WHAT THE HELL ARE YOU DOING?'

The boy collapsed and slid onto the floor with his hands on his head, screaming as though she had struck him.

Eventually he stopped. She stared at him as slowly he collected his wits and got up.

'No need to shout,' he mumbled.

His face lit up, a bright red spreading from his neck across his pimpled face. 'My aunt told me to wait here.'

'Oh well, if your aunt told you.'

The colour in the boy's face darkened as he stuck out his chin.

'Margrethe, your boss.'

'You what?'

The boy shrugged like it could have been Queen Margrethe for all he cared. Jensen grabbed him by the arm and marched him out of her office.

'Let's go and see Aunty Maggie, shall we?'

Yasmine waved her arms in front of her when she saw the two of them approaching. 'Don't go in, she's got visitors.'

Too late, Jensen had already opened the door. Margrethe looked up, inscrutable behind her thick glasses. Jensen took in the scene. Two men in dark suits seated by Margrethe's desk, coffee in the blue-and-white Royal Copenhagen china reserved for special occasions, vanilla biscuits. This had to have something to do with money.

'Ah,' said Margrethe to her visitors, not missing a beat. 'Here is my next meeting. Gentlemen, I believe we were finished?'

While Yasmine saw the visitors out, the boy helped himself to biscuits, a stack of three, which he shoved into his mouth before slumping into a chair.

'This,' said Margrethe, pointing to the boy, 'is what I needed to talk to you about. Meet your new trainee.'

'My what?'

'Gustav is finding himself . . . at a loose end, shall we say.'

'In the middle of January? Why isn't he at school?'

'Let's just say school and Gustav don't mix, but I reckon he might make a good reporter.'

'With no journalism degree? And what is he, sixteen?'

'Seventeen. And you're hardly one to talk about degrees. Wasn't it you who once told me you can't learn journalism from a book?'

'It's nepotism!'

70

Margrethe made a show of looking around her. 'Who is going to complain? It's not as if we'll be giving him a salary.'

Gustav looked up. 'What?'

'I am busy,' said Jensen. 'I don't have time to babysit some teenage delinquent.'

'That's precisely my point: you're not busy. You haven't written anything since you arrived home last year that I'd as much as wipe my arse with. How did you get on with the tip-off I sent you?'

'Still working on it, not sure there is much there.'

'Look again. I have had stories from this person before, all turning out to be spot on. Bit of a mover and shaker, obviously.'

'You know who it is?'

'Absolutely no idea, but should be child's play for you to find out. God knows why, but I am willing to give you one last chance. On the condition that you help me out with Gustav here. He knows some stuff; the two of you will get along.'

'But . . .'

'We're not going to discuss it any further. You're taking him on and that's that.'

Yasmine came back in. She avoided Jensen's gaze, but the corners of her mouth were turned up in the tiniest of smiles as she looked at Margrethe and pointed to her watch.

Damn it, she had been in on it from the start.

'Yes, yes,' said Margrethe. 'It's late, I know. Everyone get lost. I have half an hour to write my leader, and then I'm taking Gustav out for pizza.'

19

Friday 16:58

'Don't say a word,' Jensen said to Gustav when they got back to her office.

She pointed to the sagging armchair opposite her desk. 'Sit there! Wait for pizza time with auntie.'

'I don't want to be here either,' Gustav spat, his voice almost breaking. 'She's got me by the balls.'

That sounded like Margrethe all right.

'You don't understand. This is my last chance, or she'll send me back to dad's.'

'And what's so bad about that?'

'You've obviously never met my dad. My life won't be worth living.'

'Shush,' said Jensen. 'I've got work to do.'

Gustav opened his mouth to add to his sob story, then thought better of it and reached for his vaper. One death stare from Jensen and he dropped it back in his pocket with an irritated sigh.

She turned on her laptop, reminding herself that things could be worse. She still had a job and an understanding boss, as long as it lasted.

What had Margrethe meant about recognising the tipster from other emails? Who was it who was so keen on them investigating their accountant? She read the message again.

'So how do I find out?' she said out loud.

'Find out what?' said Gustav.

She had forgotten he was there.

When she showed him the email, he feigned disinterest at first, but as he read it and began to concentrate, his face was transformed into something almost charming.

'This is the tip-off Margrethe wants us to work on.'

'Why don't you just ask them who they are?'

'All right, smartarse.'

Jensen looked at the cursor on her laptop screen. It flashed as if goading her to start. Margrethe had been right; she hadn't written anything for a very long time. She didn't know any more if she could.

She quickly typed a message: *Margrethe passed me your message. I want to help you. Can we meet? P.S. Who are you?*

'Not as stupid as you look, maybe,' she said to Gustav, packing up and putting on her coat.

'Come back Monday morning, nine o'clock sharp. Editorial meeting at ten. Keep your feet off my desk, and if I catch you vaping in here one more time, you're out, no mercy. Got it?'

She had reached the door when her phone dinged in her pocket.

Henrik.

Positive ID on Magstræde man: Casper Madsen, reported missing from Skovhøj in Roskilde. You didn't hear it from me. Please let me see you, I am going mad here.

That explained why the beggar's sign had been in Danish.

But not what it meant.

Or where the sign had got to.

Skyldig.

Jensen ignored Gustav's curious stare and returned to her desk

73

to look up Skovhøj on her mobile phone. Run by the council, the centre offered assisted living for vulnerable young adults with psycho-social issues: 'Your own flat, company when you want it, and carers at hand around the clock.'

It sounded depressing, but it would take more than that, surely, for someone to travel to Copenhagen to sleep rough on the night of the worst blizzard for many years. Unless they were insane. But would someone insane have enough presence of mind to dress warmly and pack a rucksack?

She found the name and email address of the centre manager and asked for a meeting in the morning. It was not as if she had anything else to do with her time now that Margrethe had passed the story to Frank. And you would be pretty heartless to decline a chat with the 'traumatised' passer-by who had found the corpse of one of your so-called charges, wouldn't you?

20

Skovhøj was nothing like the woodland idyll its name suggested.
A huddle of low buildings set around a courtyard in a suburban
area of Roskilde, it couldn't have looked more like an institution if
the word had been mounted in neon above the door. Not even the
golden light spilling from the windows into the monochrome mist
of the winter morning was enough to make the place look inviting.
No wonder the boy had done a runner. Jensen rang the doorbell.

She needn't have worried about the centre manager being
willing to see her. Karina Jørgensen had replied inside ten minutes, urging her to come as soon as possible.

Now, as she welcomed Jensen inside, Karina's puffy face and
raw eyes told of a long night of crying and no sleep. Jensen was
ushered through a common area smelling of coffee and new
carpet. Aside from a very large young woman in a beanbag
playing a shoot-out game on the Xbox, the room was deserted.
There were still fairy lights up from Christmas, and gold paper
stars in some of the windows. A poster on the wall reminded
tenants that Skovhøj tolerated no bullying, violence, aggression
or behaviour that put others at risk.

75

'We're all deeply affected by what has happened,' Karina said.

Jensen assumed that excluded the girl, who seemed engrossed in her game.

There was a thermos of coffee on the table in the staffroom. Three mugs.

'I asked my colleague Tobias to join us,' said Karina, indicating for Jensen to take a seat. 'He spends a lot of time with Casper,' she said, immediately realising her mistake.

'Spent, I mean.'

She began to weep. Overegging it, thought Jensen.

A man in his thirties with a topknot and a heavy, rust-coloured beard entered the room.

'Tobias,' he said, shaking hands with Jensen.

The two of them sipped their coffees in silence, waiting for Karina to pull herself together, which she did finally, blowing her nose noisily into a tissue.

'I am sorry,' she said. 'Only, it's come as a terrible shock. We had all got so fond of Casper. I was the one who had to identify him. It was . . . well, you found him, so I guess you know.'

Jensen thought of the pictures on her phone but decided they would only upset Karina further. She didn't exactly relish the thought of looking at them herself.

She told the two of them as much as she could about how she had found Casper, exactly where he had been sitting, and how peaceful his face had looked, as if it knew nothing of the trauma that had befallen his body. 'He was well wrapped up against the cold. Nice warm puffer jacket, woollen hat, both new looking,' she said.

Tobias nodded miserably. 'We went and bought those together. If only I'd known what he was planning.'

Karina laid a hand on his shoulder, and Jensen noticed him pulling away a fraction.

'None of us had any idea,' said Karina. 'Not till Wednesday

evening, when one of the other tenants raised the alarm and we realised that no one had seen Casper for a couple of days. We broke into his flat, found it empty and reported him missing straight away.'

She began to cry again, big wet tears rolling down her cheeks and falling onto the table. 'I'd seen the news about the body in Magstræde, and when we realised that Casper had taken off, I got such a horrible feeling.'

Jensen waited for Karina to gather herself. She seemed in no hurry to do so.

'I saw him on Monday evening when I cycled home from work,' Jensen said. 'Forgive me for asking, but how come it took you two days to discover he had gone?'

Karina looked at her sharply. 'We're not to blame.'

Tobias smiled sadly, defusing the tension. 'Casper always kept himself to himself. He was very quiet. We didn't have any reason to suspect that anything was wrong.'

'Since when had he been living here?'

'Arrived last November.'

'From?'

'I'm afraid we're not in a position to tell you that,' said Tobias.

'Can't or won't?'

'Look,' Karina said, setting her cup down hard. 'All the young people here are vulnerable, challenged, damaged. They're here because they need to be. Casper was no different.'

She got up, taking Jensen's mug and dumping it noisily in the sink. 'Thank you for coming all the way up here and for . . . what you did. It was good of you, but I don't want you to turn this into a story for your newspaper. Casper never got much from life — at least let's give him some privacy in death.'

'Who says I am not going to?'

'The police detective told me yesterday when I went into Copenhagen to identify Casper — Henrik something — to be wary of the press.'

Bloody Henrik again. Jensen wondered who else he had given a heads-up.

'If you want to write something, write about the council's senseless plan to close this place down. We've got twenty-two residents here. Where do they expect them all to go? They have cut back so far already we can't do our jobs properly, as Casper's death has now proved. It should never have happened. Never.'

'I'm sorry,' said Tobias later, when he and Jensen had left Karina behind in the staffroom. 'Karina has dealt with calls all morning. She is under a lot of pressure from the council. What's happened is very bad – for Skovhøj, for all of us.'

'I get it,' said Jensen. 'I am just trying to make sense of it all. Did you know that when he first sat down in Magstræde, Casper had a sign with him, a piece of cardboard with the word "guilty" on it?'

By the way he looked straight at her, she could tell this was news to Tobias.

'No.'

'Can you think why he would have done that?'

'I wouldn't know . . .'

He looked away, and Jensen reckoned that he *did* know, or had at least made a fairly good guess in his own mind.

'How well did you know Casper?' she said.

'We would hang out now and again. I'd take him shopping, stuff like that. But he spent most of his time by himself in his room.'

'He didn't have a mobile on him. Do you know if he owned one?'

'The police asked me that, too. I am fairly certain he did.'

'Laptop?'

He shook his head.

'Was there anyone else he spent time with, besides you?'

'Not really. Look, I don't want you writing any of this.'

Tobias gestured at the notebook Jensen had finally succeeded in digging out of her bag.

She put it away again. 'Force of habit,' she said.

This was true. The notebook was a prop more than anything these days. She would only jot down the odd word, and never referred to it when she actually sat down to write. By that time, she had already formed the story in her head.

'Don't worry about me,' she said. 'But you do realise that as soon as this gets out, there will be other journalists knocking on your door, as nosy as I am, but a lot less amenable. Casper's death is a story.'

'We won't let them in,' said Tobias.

'Right.'

'Karina is drafting a statement. That will be all we'll have to say.'

Jensen strongly doubted that the woman would leave it at that but decided that Karina would have to take her own chances with the press. She would be more than a match for the likes of Frank Buhl.

'Before I go,' she said. 'Would it be all right to have a quick look around Casper's flat?'

Tobias stroked his beard and glanced at the door to the staffroom, as if considering whether to go back in and ask Karina for permission. Jensen reckoned she had a pretty good idea what the woman's answer would be.

'I won't touch anything,' she pleaded. 'Just five minutes?'

Casper's flat was at the end of a long corridor throbbing with clashing beats coming from behind closed doors. His rooms were clean and dark, the kitchen and lounge area empty, no sign of dirty clothes or any personal items lying around.

Jensen's heart sank. 'I see you tidied already.'

'No,' said Tobias. 'Casper always kept it like this.'

'In that case, can I ask how you could be so sure he had left?'

'His rucksack was missing, and his sleeping bag. He had those when he first arrived here.'

'Did the police tell you that there was no sign of the rucksack when I found him? Someone must have taken it.'

79

'Yes, they mentioned that. They wanted me to try and work out what had been in it, but I have no idea. I don't think any of his clothes were missing, apart from what he was wearing, of course.'

Casper's flat looked like the home of a soldier. The bed was made, the duvet tightly tucked under, as flat as a sheet of ice. The only object in the room that wasn't nailed down was a piece of paper on the bedside table with the words *NO, THANKS* written on it in block capitals.

She looked questioningly at Tobias.

'Ah,' he said. 'No one told you? Casper didn't speak.'

21

Jensen was still thinking about this later as she stood by the bike rack, putting on her helmet and gloves for the twenty-minute ride back to Roskilde station. Tobias had told her Casper had had no problem with his hearing, but when he wanted to say something, he used pen and paper. Seemed sad that 'No, thanks' was a phrase he had used often enough to keep it by his bedside.

And why had he left for Copenhagen without most of his belongings? She had seen clothes and trainers in his cupboard. Everything suggested that he had planned on coming back.

She felt the tap on her shoulder a split second before she sensed the shadowy presence behind her. For her size, the Xbox girl was surprisingly light on her feet.

'He came from Søvang,' she said.

'Excuse me?'

'Casper. You asked where he came from. That's why they wouldn't tell you. It's a young offenders' institution.'

Guilty.

'You were eavesdropping?'

81

The girl shrugged, her gaze unflinching. Jensen wondered why she was at Skovhøj – what her story was.

'How do you know he was at Søvang?'

'I am good at finding stuff out.'

'What was he there for?'

'I don't know yet.'

Jensen cocked her head to one side. 'Not *that* good then.' She smiled. 'You knew Casper?'

The girl looked away at the bike rack and down the driveway disappearing into the icy fog. She was welling up. 'He was my friend. It was me who raised the alarm.'

'What made you do that?'

'We were supposed to be gaming on Wednesday, but he didn't turn up. He had never not turned up before.'

'I am sorry.'

'Who killed him?'

'I don't know.'

'Are you going to find out?'

'The police are on the case.'

'And you?'

It was a good question. Jensen evaded it. 'Tell me about Casper. What was he like?'

'Kind.'

'I understand that he didn't speak. Do you know why?'

The girl shook her head. She was crying properly now, tears rolling down her cheeks.

Jensen wrote her number on a piece of paper and handed it to the girl. 'Tell you what, why don't you call me when ... *if* you find out more?'

The girl looked at the note, her red eyes squinting. 'Jensen? What more than Jensen?'

'Just Jensen. And your name is?'

'Fie.'

'Fie what?'

'Just Fie,' the girl said.

They shook hands. Fie's was as hot and puffy as a yeast bun, wet with the tears she had wiped off her cheeks. As Jensen cycled into the mist, she felt the girl's eyes on her.

22

Saturday 11:43

The dull winter landscape of east Zealand passed by the train in a misty-brown blur. Two days ago, Casper had made the same journey, passing through the calcified suburbs to the pulsating heart of the capital. Had he written his sign at home in his room, or had he picked up a piece of cardboard on impulse once he had reached Copenhagen?

Skyldig.

What had he been guilty of? Or had he meant that society itself was guilty, that it had let him down somehow and was to blame for his predicament, whatever that was?

Jensen leaned against her bicycle and checked her phone, rocking with the motion of the train. The floor was muddy, the carriage smelling of steaming winter clothes.

Henrik's increasingly desperate messages contained no new information, and Margrethe had gone quiet, satisfied, presumably, with her new childcare arrangements for Gustav.

The train was already approaching Copenhagen, past block after block of red-brick apartment buildings and railway cuttings covered in graffiti.

At the Central Station, Jensen took the lift to the concourse and lost herself in the crowd. The old terminus building with its tarnished iron chandeliers suspended from a blood-red ceiling reminded her of trips to Tivoli when she was a child. On hot summer days you could hear the screams from the fairground rides and smell the ice cream and frying fat long before the turnstiles came into view on the other side of Bernstorffsgade.

Today, however, it felt damp and draughty, full of grim-faced people rushing to catch their trains. Had Casper locked eyes with anyone when he passed through, or had he kept his head down, like most people travelling through this morning, seeing nothing?

23

Saturday 12:33

She left her bicycle in the newspaper's basement and climbed the back staircase, creaky and smelling of century-old dust. She had almost made it to her office without meeting anyone when she heard the telltale sound of clogs approaching along the corridor. Unusually for Frank Buhl, they were moving at speed.

'Come to grovel?' he said as he passed, shrugging on his red puffer jacket and zipping it over his sizeable belly.

He was going to have to invest in a new jacket soon or give up on the fried hotdogs and chocolate milk from the sausage stand across the street that he favoured at lunchtime.

'You seem to be in a hurry?'

'They just released the identity of your dead beggar. Turns out he was some youngster from a mental home in Roskilde. I'm on my way there now. Some of us have to keep this news-paper running.'

'Frank, I am sorry,' she shouted after him. 'About the way I questioned you at the meeting the other day. I don't know what came over me – must have been the shock of finding the body.'

Frank looked unconvinced.

'Between you and me,' she said. 'I think you're much better at covering this sort of story than I am, and Margrethe knows that, too.'

He stopped. 'You do?'

'Absolutely.'

He reached into his mouth with one finger, probing for something stuck between his teeth.

'And you're sure you didn't notice anything at all when you first saw the body, anything out of the ordinary?' he said.

Jensen shook her head. 'Honestly, there is nothing aside from what I told the police. He was just sitting there dead, on his own, in the snow with a sleeping bag over his legs.'

Frank shrugged. 'Unlucky. Wrong place at the wrong time,' he said, disappearing down the stairs.

She ought to have told him about Casper's sign or the missing rucksack or the note with the address of the Bird's Nest. But the words wouldn't come. Like the pictures she had taken of Casper in the snow, it felt wrong to share. Besides, the police would release the information soon enough, when they felt it would serve a purpose.

She went into her office and sat down at her desk without turning on the light or removing her coat. She had already been to Skovhøj and talked to the staff and knew more about the case than anyone, aside from Henrik. What was she doing leaving the story to someone else to write?

She rang Henrik's number. The profile picture that came up on her screen was one she had taken once in a bar. It was her only photo of him and, even then, he had almost succeeded in covering his face with one hand.

'*Hej*,' he said, answering on the first ring, and just like that she was thrown back to the first time he had called her, years ago, after they had met in London and he had returned home to Copenhagen. His next words back then had been almost whispered: 'This is crazy.'

87

'Good to hear your voice,' he said now, breathing out slowly.

It sounded as though he was settling into a comfortable armchair. She imagined him sitting in his office – somewhere she had never been – but there was none of the usual background noise on the line. Could he be at home? She wanted to break through the intimacy he was trying to create.

'Why didn't you tell me about Casper's sign?'

'What sign?'

'The pizza waitress told me. You spoke to her yourself on Tuesday, so don't pretend you don't know about it.'

Henrik swore. 'That's police business. Besides, I thought you'd handed the story over to Buhl. He's been on at me constantly since.'

'I know what the sign said, and now I think I know what it means. Casper was inside for something, until last November, wasn't he? I am guessing that holding a sign was some sort of public show of *mea culpa*. Or else, an accusation aimed at the world for failing him.'

'Mea what, professor?'

'A confession.'

'I knew that,' he said.

'I *had* wondered why someone would choose to beg in such an inauspicious location as Magstræde.'

'And?'

'Now we know he wasn't.'

Silence. She knew Henrik was mulling over how best to manoeuvre the conversation back onto personal territory, but she was not in the mood to let him succeed.

'Still doesn't explain why he chose to sit in Magstræde, though,' she said. 'Higher footfall elsewhere if the idea was to broadcast his message to the world.'

'Listen to me, Jensen – let it go,' said Henrik. 'We're dealing with it. You found a body, you called it in, end of story. What time do you finish work?'

She ignored him. 'What was he inside for?'

'That's confidential.'

'You don't have anything at all, do you?'

'Come out for a drive with me. I need to see you. Jesus, Jensen, what do I have to do?'

She hung up. He had nothing to offer her but drives around Copenhagen where no one would recognise them. Just like three years ago. Sometimes they had gone as far as Helsingør and risked a walk in the dark along the beach, but that was as far as their public outings went. If he wanted to see her this time, he would have to take her out for a meal in a restaurant, like a normal person.

Jensen's online search for Casper Madsen returned a huge number of articles, as expected. His surname was almost as common in Denmark as her own. She spent the rest of the afternoon trawling through cases, but unearthed nothing that appeared to match. When she felt herself nodding with sleep, she decided to call it a day.

On the way out, she found Henning in his office, dressed in his customary beige suit. She could tell from the smell of cigar that he had been smoking out of his Velux window not too long ago. He was seated at his desk with a pair of ornate silver scissors, cutting articles from copies of the leading Danish newspapers, more than a month's worth, judging by the height of the stack. The radio was on – some kind of jazz. It was obviously a slow news day as far as Danish celebrity death was concerned. Each time Henning finished a cutting, he carefully dated it with a fountain pen and set it aside for stowing away in one of the five man-sized filing cabinets lined up along the wall.

Henning was firmly analogue. He didn't own a mobile phone and only reluctantly agreed to use a laptop to type out his obituaries. His old typewriter still had pride of place on his desk, next to a stack of empty paper cups scavenged from other people's offices, like so many trophies.

'You know all that stuff's on the internet, don't you?' she said.
He didn't look up from his work.

'You still in the doghouse with Margrethe?' he said, cutting deftly around a jagged column edge. His fingers were trembling, and grey with newsprint.

'Not since I agreed to babysit her nephew. Listen, Henning, ever heard of a Casper Madsen? Locked up in a youth prison until last November?'

He kept cutting. 'No.'

She nodded in the direction of the filing cabinets. 'Want to have a look under Madsen to be sure?'

He shook his head without taking his eyes off the scissors. 'No need. Never heard of him. Who is he?'

'He is the young man who was stabbed down in Magstræde, the one I found on my way into work last Tuesday. You know, the second victim?'

'Casper Madsen doesn't sound very Romanian,' Henning grunted.

'Because he is not. People jumped to conclusions, same as ever. Say, Henning?'

'Yes.'

'How do you decide who gets to go in the filing cabinet?'

'Anyone who has done something worth reading about.'

'According to you.'

'Yes,' he said and looked up at her with his with watery eyes. They were astonishingly blue.

'Do you have any coffee?'

'You finished it yesterday,' she said. 'So, am I in the filing cabinet?'

'No,' said Henning, without hesitation.

24

Saturday 21:16

Outside now.

You know where I live?

I have ways.

You can't come in.

Who says I want to? We're going to the Forensic Institute.

On a Saturday night?

Got anything better to do?

Jensen threw on jogging pants and a sweatshirt, splashed cold water on her face and tied back her hair. Henrik shot her a lingering glance as she got in the car. The icy cobbled street was shining like black metal as they drove along the canal, past the basement restaurant with candles in the windows, and people hunched outside in the cold, smoking.

'You were asleep, weren't you?'

'None of your business.'

He laughed. 'That means you were.'

He had tidied his car (no toys this time). There were two cans of Coke in the cup holders, one of them opened. This was another of his unchanging habits: he always kept multipacks

91

of Coke in the boot of his car. She declined his offer of the unopened can.

The Coke, his leather jacket and man-spread across the car seat: everything was always the same, including the feelings he managed to produce in her.

She forced herself to look out of the window as he navigated northwards. The Saturday shoppers had been replaced by the pleasure crowd, seeking the easy oblivion of the inner-city bars. This was Henrik's world; its ebbs and flows were in his blood. The few times they had met in London over the years, he had looked smaller somehow, almost awkward without the vague air of threat he exuded in his natural habitat.

They passed the lit-up façade of the National Art Gallery and crossed the Lakes, black mirrors ringed with lights reflecting from the windows of the stately apartment buildings.

'What about Casper's relatives? Did you speak to them?' she said.

'There is an aunt, that's all. Took a while to track her down. Lives in Jutland, in a commune near Silkeborg, total loon. Told us to go to hell.'

The concrete towers of Rigshospitalet, the national hospital, also known as Riget (the Kingdom), loomed into view. Henrik drove round it and went down a side street lined with trees to one side. He parked by a low-rise concrete building and turned off the engine.

It was quiet in the car. A man was walking a small white dog on a strip of grass, scooping its poo into a bag.

Henrik touched her hair. 'You've been avoiding me.'

'I am here now.'

'Because I bribed you into coming.'

He looked straight at her, with the grey-blue eyes that had pinned her to the spot when they had first met, that slightly sideways glance, with a warmth that told you he wasn't the thug he appeared to be.

'If you want to see me properly, you'll have to take me out for dinner.'

'Maybe I will,' he said, glaring at her.

No sooner had they slammed the car doors than he was back in work mode. She preferred him like this. In his element, no-nonsense to the point of being brusque.

'Keep your mouth shut in there. If it gets out that I brought you, it's a disciplinary at best for me.'

'So why bring me?'

'Call it an olive branch. This way,' said Henrik, heading for the entrance.

As they waited to sign in, he stood behind her, too close. She felt the heat radiate from his body onto her back, his chin somewhere above her head.

Don't turn around, she commanded herself.

Don't.

They came to an office with low lighting and a stuffy, over-heated atmosphere. A man with hooded eyes, a Tom Selleck moustache and greying chest hair protruding from the neckline of his white T-shirt turned from his computer screen and smiled at them. He was wearing white trousers, white clogs and an unbuttoned white tunic.

'Ah, there you are,' he said to Henrik, removing his rimless glasses. 'I was just about to give up on you. And who is your friend?'

'No one,' said Henrik. 'Forget her, she is not here. I'll explain later.'

'Well hello, *No One*. I'm David. Delighted to meet you.'

They shook hands. She smiled and left it at that, lest she made an inappropriate remark. David gave them paper gowns and overshoes and disposable caps. His hands were large and strong, his forearms hairy. Jensen imagined them wrenching apart a rib cage.

'Let's go,' he said.

He led them through a series of doors to a high-ceilinged hall with a row of separate, stable-like booths. The floor tiles were wet from a recent hose-down. Jensen dared not think what had been there before. A row of white wellies of varying sizes were lined up along the far wall, with heavy-duty plastic gloves, like gauntlets, suspended from hooks above. Each of the booths had its own stainless-steel autopsy table, but just one was occupied, with a slight body covered in a blue sheet.

'You stay on this side,' David said to Jensen, pointing to a line between the tiles and a darker grey linoleum floor.

'If you feel faint, sit down on one of those chairs and put your head between your knees.'

He handed out face masks to herself and Henrik and fitted one over his own mouth and nose.

Henrik's eyes said: *Do as you're told.*

He swaggered over and stood with David next to the table as the pathologist lifted the sheet. The stab wounds were like gaping mouths on Casper's body. Jensen looked at the ceiling for a while.

'So, as you know already,' said David, 'Casper was stabbed. I counted fourteen stab wounds in his abdomen, one in his groin.'

Henrik nodded, staring intensely at Casper, as if expecting him to sit up and tell him who did it.

'And this one here was fatal,' said David, pointing. 'But . . .'

'But?'

'Casper would likely have died anyway. Certainly, he would have been unconscious when he was killed.'

'Why do you say that?'

'There was enough benzodiazepine in his system to knock him out. He wouldn't have felt the cold till it was too late. A sober person would have found shelter before their body temperature dropped below the level of danger. On a night like last Tuesday, ingesting benzodiazepine would have been suicide.'

'What's benzodiazepine?' said Jensen.

Henrik shot her an irritated look, but David's eyes were smiling over the top of his mask. 'It's a kind of sedative sometimes given to patients before operations or prescribed for anxiety disorders,' he said.

'Or taken as a recreational drug. Always plenty of benzos knocking around,' said Henrik, addressing himself to David.

'And you're sure there's no sign that he fought his attacker?'

'Yep, none. In contrast to the victim from Farvergade. Nothing under the fingernails, no scratches or marks consistent with self-defence.'

'Who would have stabbed someone who was already as good as dead?' said Jensen.

'That's up to Jungersen here to figure out. Speculation is not my department. Talking of which . . .'

He turned on the light above the table. Someone had shaved Casper's body hair. He was so thin his ribs were clearly visible.

'He has an older scar on his right thigh. There, can you see it?'

Henrik nodded. 'He was injured in a knife fight in a young offenders' institution about four years ago. He was sixteen at the time.'

'It would certainly be consistent with a stab wound,' said David. 'There is also evidence of significant self-harm, on his lower arms and legs. Some of it very recent.'

Henrik shook his head slowly at Casper's silvery skin. It had a textured look, as though it has been woven on a loom.

'And then there's this.'

David pointed to Casper's upper arms. 'See these marks?'

'They look like bruises,' said Henrik. 'Could he have been moved by someone after he died?'

David shook his head. 'No, he would have got these while he was still alive. He would have been handled roughly by someone.'

'Man or woman?'

'Could be either, judging by the size of the marks, but I

95

would say that whoever did it was either very strong or very angry.'

'Doesn't help us much.'

'No, I can see that.'

'Last meal?'

'At least eight hours before he died, though the contents of his stomach suggest that he had a milky chocolate drink not long before.'

'Chocolate milk?'

'Could have been hot when he drank it.'

Henrik nodded. 'Maybe he had brought it with him, in a flask. Probably in his rucksack, wherever that's got to.'

David shrugged.

'And time of death?'

'The medical examiner who was first on the scene estimated that he had been dead for four to six hours when he was found, so sometime between one-thirty a.m. and three-thirty a.m. I saw no reason to contradict that when I performed the post-mortem.'

The two men stood close together, looking down at the corpse. They had begun to wobble in and out of Jensen's vision.

Perhaps it was the sight of Casper's boyish, undernourished body, perhaps the animal stench, which was at odds with the tiled, bathroom-like surroundings, like an abattoir.

Henrik caught her before her legs buckled, pushing her into a chair and forcing her head down between her legs. The last thought she had before she was overcome by darkness was how utterly useless she was.

Week Two

25

Monday 08:57

By now Jensen was almost getting used to finding strangers in her office. 'What's going on here?'

The sagging armchair she had grown rather fond of had gone. In its place was a desk, scavenged, presumably, from the office of yet another unfortunate colleague whose job had been canned. The desk was facing hers. A man wearing overalls emerged from under it and smiled proudly at his work.

'I understand there's going to be two of you in here now?' he said. 'Tell you the truth, I am more used to taking stuff down than putting it up these days. Makes a nice change.'

Jensen knew protesting would be futile. Margrethe obviously meant business. As long as she played along, she was unlikely to get fired and, at least for now, she desperately needed to buy herself some time.

'Yes, it would appear I have an apprentice. Can we just . . .?'

She pulled the two desks apart an inch and looked at them for a moment with her head cocked to the side.

'No, still not right . . . I know, could you get one of those

99

partitions from the meeting room downstairs, the kind that doubles up as a noticeboard? Stick it between us?'

'OK, but you won't be able to see—'

'Please,' said Jensen, folding her hands in front of her face. 'Trust me, we need a partition here.'

At that moment Gustav walked into the room with his headphones on, plunked himself in the desk chair and began to swivel. To his credit, the man in the overalls said nothing, just nodded his understanding at Jensen and left.

'This laptop is ancient,' said Gustav.

'Oh, I am sorry – you thought this was Google?'

'It was just a statement of fact,' said Gustav.

Jensen searched her bag for paracetamol, longing for one of Liron's coffees. The weekend had been a washout. By the time she had come round on Saturday night and Henrik had persuaded her that he needed to drive her home, it had been after midnight.

'Remember, I know where you live now,' he had said when she left the car.

She had gone straight to bed and stayed there with her laptop most of Sunday, doing nothing about finding a new place to live, and tomorrow Markus would be claiming back his flat. She felt in her pocket for the keys to Esben's summer house. It would have to do.

Ignoring Gustav, she checked her email, surprised to find a reply from Margrethe's tipster.

Tomorrow evening at six. Assistens Cemetery.

There was a map with a pin. Somewhat elaborate for a story about an errant accountant, she thought.

'What are we doing today?' said Gustav, booting up his laptop.

'*We* are not doing anything. *You* might be, but first I want to know who I am dealing with.'

He looked at her, frowning, lifting his headphones. 'Dealing with?'

100

'You. Ever read the papers?'

'Not really.'

'Follow the news on TV or radio?'

'Sometimes.'

'Do you write? Were you good at Danish at school?'

'Top of my class, until I got expelled.'

'Expelled for what?'

He glared at her in silence. Fine, she would find out sooner or later.

'Right, so you want to be a newspaper journalist?'

'Maybe. I don't know.'

'Gustav, look around you. Does this place look attractive to you? Half the people who used to work here are gone, there are no subeditors left, hardly any photographers. Three years from now, five, tops, and these offices will be a museum. Take my advice, pick a different career, anything but this.'

'That's not what my aunt said. She said there will always be a need for reporters. She said you will teach me how to be a good one.'

Oh God. Had she been this stupid at his age? Almost certainly yes. She hadn't read the papers then or had anything like a remote interest in the news, or writing, for that matter. It was something else that had made her apply for a job at the local free paper, aside from needing the money. A vague sense that journalism was cool, that it would legitimise the lazy belligerence that had got her into trouble with her teachers. Both had turned out to be wide of the mark, of course. Her first editor had been entirely deaf to her charming excuses, and she had been given her final warning when, out of the blue, Esben had phoned her one evening in the office, sowing the seeds for what had later become a scoop big enough to hit the national papers, including *Dagbladet*.

'Why me?' she had once asked him.

'I saw your photo in the paper, and there was this cheeky look in your eyes that I couldn't resist. I thought, *She will be fun.*'

101

'Nothing whatsoever to do with my journalistic prowess, then?'

'That too, though I thought it was about time someone liberated you from the lost-pet column.'

It was Esben's story that had made her. Once hooked on discovering the truth, there had been no stopping her.

If Margrethe had seen the same idle irreverence in her nephew and reckoned journalism would make him too, then Jensen couldn't fault her.

On the other hand, her own road-to-Damascus moment had been years ago, before smartphones, Twitter and Instagram. When newspapers were just beginning to spot the edge of the cliff they were hurtling towards.

'Listen,' she said. 'Before you get all misty-eyed, we both know we're not here together out of choice. We've got to keep auntie happy, but in the meantime, you may as well make yourself useful. Google the Casper Madsen case, the guy found dead in Magstræde a week ago, and read the coverage, every last word of it. And when you're done, head down there, talk to anyone you can find and ask them whether they saw anything on Monday night or Tuesday morning. What time did the boy first pitch up in the street? Did they notice a blue rucksack? Did any of them leave him a note with the name and address of a homeless shelter in Rysensteensgade?'

'Margrethe said you found the body. She said you didn't want to write about it, and now someone else is working on the story.'

'So?'

'So, are you sure you want me to go to Magstræde?'

'It's for your education.'

'Margrethe won't be happy.'

'Except she isn't going to find out, is she, Gustav?'

He folded his arms across his chest, looking unconvinced.

'It's just a bit of research. I am curious, that's all. Probably won't lead anywhere. Anyway, we'll look into that tip

Margrethe gave me, don't worry. I've got a meeting with Deep Throat tomorrow evening.'

'Who?'

'You know – guys in trench coats, secret meetings in underground car parks?'

Gustav stared at her blankly.

'Are you seriously telling me you never heard of *All the President's Men*?'

'Nope.'

'Look it up,' she said.

She had a similar conversation with her first editor when she had been not much older than Gustav. Her turn to be overbearing.

'Can I come?' said Gustav.

'Depends.'

'On what?'

'On whether you behave yourself.'

She got up, grabbed her coat and bag.

'Where are *you* going?' Gustav shouted after her as she walked out into the dark corridor where the slow tap-tap of Henning's keyboard was the only sound to be heard.

'To get the strongest coffee I can lay my hands on.'

26

Henrik had chosen the dingiest corner of Café Victor and was sitting with his back against the wall. He had told her once that he could never be ambushed, that he could spot danger a mile off, an occupational hazard that ruined most holidays and social occasions in public spaces for his family. He was scanning the room now, fixing his eyes on Jensen as she walked towards their table.

His eyes.

Dear God.

She took in the lit candle, the tiny vase with the white roses matching the giant bouquet on the stainless-steel bar: props for the kind of romantic dinner the two of them could never have, at least not here, nor anywhere else in Copenhagen.

The shiny surfaces reflected their awkward glances. For a Monday in winter, the place was positively heaving. Too many people, far too close.

Henrik was wearing his usual white shirt and black jeans, though he had exchanged his ancient paint-splattered engineer's boots with the black brogues he referred to as his 'dancing shoes'. She supposed she should be honoured at this gesture of effort. On the other hand, he had kept his leather jacket on.

All the faster to run.

'Fuck, I missed you,' he whispered, checking the room behind her. He was touching her under the table.

They ordered burgers and beer.

'See?' said Jensen when the food arrived. 'You and me, in a restaurant, like proper grown-ups. A journalist interviewing a police detective about a case.'

He attacked his food as if he was late for an appointment. 'But *she* knows you're more than that.' (*She, her*, never *Louise.*)

'You told her I am back?'

'No, but it's not that hard to work out. Your byline is in the paper.'

'Not much lately.'

'Still, she knows there's something about you and me.'

'And if she saw us together?'

'There'd be an earthquake. She'd kick me out, no mercy. And I'd be OK with that, if it wasn't for Oliver. He is only seven, and him and me . . .'

He touched a fist to his heart. 'And to think I didn't even want a third child.'

'What happened?'

'She told me she'd divorce me if I didn't agree to it,' he laughed.

Not for the first time, Jensen thought that for all his machismo, Henrik was a weak man, and she was disappointed in herself. What was the definition of insanity again? Doing the same thing over and over and expecting a different result.

Café Victor was his favourite, but she could tell by the look in his eyes that it had been a mistake to meet here. This was his domain, where he had been free to imagine a different identity for himself, free of baggage, the tough-looking man in the glitzy bar. She was trespassing.

'It was you who pursued *me*,' she said. 'I never wanted anything from you, but you couldn't leave it alone.'

'Really? That's not how I remember it,' he said, throwing his napkin on his plate and smiling at her provocatively, while his hands slid up her thigh.

She looked away, alarmed at the sensations he was provoking.

He had left his onions and lettuce in two neat piles on the side of his plate, scraped the cheese off the burger. Still fussy about his food, especially where cheese was concerned.

She had barely made any inroads into her own meal. The two of them didn't function as a couple. She had often suspected that whatever was going on between them, however strong the draw of it, was largely in their heads and didn't bear exposure to daylight.

'I've been thinking,' she said, changing the subject, 'about why Casper stayed put that night instead of going to the shelter.'

'What of it?' said Henrik.

'I think he was making a point. He didn't care any more what happened to him. I thought at first that he had left most of his belongings at Skovhøj because he intended to come back, but he probably didn't expect to be needing them again.'

'Or he was just off his head. Remember the benzos. Drugs were endemic at Skovhøj. We're looking for a dealer who is supposed to be supplying most of the kids.'

'Strange.'

'Why do you say that?'

'His room was so tidy. He seemed to have been a self-contained person, organised, in control of himself.'

Henrik leaned back, folded his arms across his chest. 'If I overlook the fact that you just admitted to having been in his room, there is no stereotypical profile of a recreational drug taker. The stuff is everywhere. Besides, bound to be a few bad boys hanging round Casper from his time inside. He wouldn't have had to look far for someone willing to sell to him.'

Henrik ducked, suddenly, violently, like someone suffering from grenade shock.

'Fuck.'

'What's happening?'

'That's one of her girlfriends over there.'

'Where?'

'Don't look, for fuck's sake!'

He grabbed his keys and got up, kept his head down and his back to the room.

'Have to run. I'll wait for you outside in the car, around the corner in Grønnegade. Give it five minutes, and sorry but you're going to have to pick up the tab. I've no cash and I can't use my card. She'd kill me if she saw this on the bank statement. There'd be an explosion.'

He headed for the toilet and came out again after a few minutes, his eyes darting round the room, avoiding hers. Then he left the restaurant, his swagger reduced to an anxious shuffle.

Jensen sat for five minutes looking into the empty space he had left behind. Then she pushed back her plate and went to the counter to pay the bill. On the pavement outside, she stood for a while looking in the direction of Grønnegade where Henrik would be waiting in his warm car with the engine running, then turned resolutely in the opposite direction.

As dates went, it had been a resounding fiasco. She wished for the one-thousandth time that Henrik was prepared to let her go from his life, entirely and for good. It was a choice she felt unable to make herself. Until one of them did, she feared they were condemned to repeating the same mistake over and over.

Her phone vibrated in her pocket: Fie, the Xbox girl from Skovhøj.

Casper Madsen is not his real name. I can find out, but it won't be quick or legal.

Jensen hesitated before responding, but only for a second.

Do it.

27

Monday 21:42

Henrik Jungersen sat by the desk in his office staring outside, where the snow had begun to fall again. He was still wearing his leather jacket: far too much effort to remove it.

'That went well,' he said out loud. 'Bravo, Jungersen, bravo.'

There was paperwork on his desk (he could cover the walls in his office with the amount of paperwork he was behind on), but he couldn't concentrate on it; his reading glasses, which, embarrassingly, he was now unable to do without, remained tucked into the pocket of his white shirt.

For half an hour he had waited in Grønnegade, ducking his head every time someone passed his car. All that time before he had realised that Jensen wasn't going to show.

Of course not.

And could he blame her?

He picked up his phone. There had been no new messages in the past minute – a good sign, but it was too early to believe himself safe. If his wife's friend had seen him with Jensen and spilled the beans, he would have to protest that it was work (technically correct). It was why he was here now, seated at his desk.

Deniability.

Fucking Jensen.

If he had never met her, his life would have been simpler.

Less fun, but definitely simpler.

Come to think of it, the fun times were some distance behind them now. Jensen had changed. If possible, she had become even more annoying over the years.

He had never been able to explain to himself why he was so attracted to her. She wasn't even his type – slight and dark and flat-chested with gappy teeth and an air of stubbornness about her. But her dark blue eyes always got him, the intensity of her gaze and expressions. There was a fire in her that he yearned for, that always kept him coming back.

He looked at the sofa opposite his desk and thought of lying down and going to sleep, which would be preferable to going home at this stage. His wife was no fool. ('Is there someone else?') If he were to walk through their front door in this state, she would know for sure.

He felt sick, as though he had a bug that was unable to shake off. His stomach ached, he had palpitations and was unable to rest. He knew the symptoms for what they were.

It was happening again.

There was a triple knock on the door, Mark's gratingly chipper call sign.

'Working late, boss?'

'If you didn't think I was, why did you knock?'

'I don't know. It was a rhetorical question, I guess.'

'What do you want?'

'Remember how we said it was odd that there were no CCTV cameras anywhere near the spot in Magstræde where the second victim was murdered?'

'I could hardly forget,' Henrik snapped.

It was virtually impossible to move an inch in Copenhagen these days without being caught on camera, but somehow every single CCTV in the vicinity of the murder scene in Magstræde was either broken or pointed in wrong direction.

'Well, I found one.'

'What did you say?'

'It was a little tricky. The occupier in number nine, some sort of advertising agency, I think, had gone bust, and the premises were empty, but it turned out the camera—'

'For the love of God, Søndergreen, spit it out.'

Mark edged his way into the office, pointing at Henrik's laptop. 'May I?'

Henrik held up his hands and leaned back. 'Please.'

An image flicked onto the screen, a collage of white and grey.

'The camera is mounted over the door of number nine, pointing down the street in the direction of Gammel Strand. That means it's not capturing the stretch of wall where our man was sitting, but ...'

He pointed to the middle of the screen. 'This white bit here is the light from the street lamp three metres east of the victim, and the darker grey is the opposite pavement.'

'The picture is poor – it was snowing pretty heavily at the time – but now see this ...'

Mark fast-forwarded. The time in the top right-hand corner moved to 02:12.

They sat side by side and looked at the grainy image.

Nothing.

Henrik sighed irritably.

'Wait,' said Mark.

And there it was, at 02:14: a figure with their back turned, running towards Gammel Strand, out of the picture.

'Go back,' Henrik said, alert now.

They watched it again, and again, and then a fourth time.

Henrik pointed at the screen. 'Man or woman, would you say?'

'Hard to tell with the hood they're wearing,' said Mark.

'I think it's a woman. Women run differently.'

'I don't know. Would you bet on it?'

No. Henrik had to admit it was no more than a hunch.

'Check all the CCTV you can find in the vicinity, see if this person turns up anywhere else around this time.'

'Already did that,' said Mark.

Mark was irritating, but Henrik had to hand it to him: he was a very thorough policeman.

'And?' he said, suddenly hopeful.

Had they turned a corner, finally?

'Absolutely nothing.'

28

Tuesday 10:04

The partition Jensen had asked for had appeared overnight, and her office now resembled a 1980s telesales firm. Not that she was complaining. She would far rather stare into a felt wall than the spotty face of Gustav, whom she could hear on the other side, humming to whatever garbage was coming through his headphones.

Her arms were aching. She had persuaded Markus to let her put her cardboard boxes in his basement lock-up until she could decide what to do with them. It had taken her two hours to carry everything down the four flights of stairs, and during all that time Markus had been on the phone. She had left his flat without saying goodbye, carrying only a rucksack of clothes.

Gustav was doing something that was making the partition wobble. She dug a one-hundred kroner note out of her pocket.

'GUSTAV!'

She got a grunt in return.

'Nip down to the coffee van in Sankt Peders Stræde and get us a couple of coffees, will you? Guy's name is Liron, goatee,

112

swears a lot. Tell him I sent you, and that I need something strong.'

Silence.

'What, right now?' Gustav piped up, emerging from the other side of the partition.

'Yes, now!'

He snatched the banknote out of her hand and left, dragging his feet, his underpants almost fully in view above the dropped waistline of his black jeans. Jensen stretched and rubbed her face vigorously, desperate for energy. She had hardly slept. By the time Henrik had finally stopped messaging his apologies (none of which she had replied to), it was 2 a.m., and her mind was churning with Casper's case and her disastrous move back to Denmark. Should she stay? Was there any point?

She had been flat hunting for a lacklustre few minutes after yesterday's editorial meeting, knowing that Margrethe had gone to a conference and wouldn't be checking up on her. It had turned out rental flats in Copenhagen were rarer than sunshine in January. She would be stuck with Esben's summer house for a while, but perhaps that wasn't so bad: a bit of peace and some decent sleep until she got her head sorted, no strings attached.

Gustav had left his phone behind. It was ringing on the other side of the partition, the theme music from Star Wars. It stopped, then began to ring again. She pushed back her chair and headed across to his side of the office. She picked up the phone and turned it off. It was sticky; she wiped her fingers on her trousers, grimacing. Everything Gustav touched was grubby.

She stopped in her tracks and gawped at the noticeboard.

Gustav had pinned up an enlarged map of Magstræde. By each building number he had listed the different floors and apartments, leaving ticks against some of them and question marks against others. He had obviously been working on it all weekend.

The pizza restaurant at the top of the street had been ticked and marked with a smiley and a phone number. The friendly waitress, perhaps?

Fast work, Gustav.

Jensen noticed that CG Dentistry occupied the floors above the clinic too. Presumably Grønfeldt was living above the shop. She began to jot down a list of questions and was still going when Gustav returned.

'I got mocha, and yours is muddy coffee or whatever.'

'Mud coffee.'

Gustav consulted the paper cups in his hands. He wore the cold on his jacket, the smoky, wet smell of the outside.

'Liron said the coffees were on the house. Congratulated me on having landed a job with you. He is clearly a big fan.'

Liron and his silver tongue.

'It's not a job, Gustav,' she said, smiling.

She held out her palm. He stared at it for a moment, before fishing the crumpled banknote out of his back pocket and handing it over with an irritated sigh.

Jensen removed the lid from her cup and sipped slowly from the thick, black drink, careful to leave the ground coffee undisturbed on the bottom.

Liron never got it wrong.

'Nice work,' she said, pointing to the noticeboard.

He blushed.

'I haven't finished. So far, no one has any information. A couple of people reckoned they might have seen Casper much earlier on Monday, before lunchtime, but nobody is certain.'

'How did you get them to talk?'

'I said it was a project for school. Magstræde then and now. We chatted a bit first, and then I asked them about what happened, all casual-like. I can be cute when I want to.'

'I sincerely doubt it.'

'Well, it works. People see boys my age as either helpless kids, or semi-criminal troublemakers, if they notice us at all.'

Jensen nodded, thinking how this teenage cloak of invisibility could have its obvious advantages. She had to admit that Gustav had surprised her in his thoroughness.

'By the way, you had a missed call, pretty persistent.'

He consulted his phone, frowning. 'Weird, I already spoke to her, wonder what she wants.'

'Who?'

They both turned their heads at the sound of shuffling footsteps. Henning appeared in the doorway, a geriatric bloodhound, his body stooped and unsteady.

'Do you have any coffee?' he said, scanning the room, his eyes homing in on Liron's paper cups like a heat-seeking missile.

'Henning, meet Gustav, our new trainee. Gustav, meet Henning, the man who knows everything about anyone in Denmark worth knowing.'

'Cool.'

Henning ignored him.

'Are you finished with that?' he said, pointing to Jensen's coffee.

'No,' she said. 'But I am sure you can have the rest of Gustav's mocha.'

Gustav looked outraged but handed his cup over. Henning left, smacking his lips. A few weeks after she arrived in Denmark, Jensen had bought him an expensive coffee machine, bean grinder, milk frother, the lot. He hadn't used it once.

'Do you have a bicycle?' she said to Gustav.

'No, but I can get an e-scooter in, like, two minutes.'

29

Tuesday 10:54

'What is this?'

Gustav got off his scooter and looked searchingly at Jensen.

'It's a murder scene.'

He looked disappointed. God knows what he had been expecting. A chalk outline of a body on the tarmac? Jensen walked over to the doorway, where someone had placed a fake candle that had run out of battery. There were no flowers. She supposed they were long gone, to the extent that anyone had bothered in the first place.

'This is where the other man was killed.'

'The homeless guy?'

'Yes. They still don't know who he was, but they reckon the two murders might be connected somehow.'

'Why? Casper Madsen wasn't homeless.'

'Maybe not, but he was on the street under a sleeping bag when he was stabbed. And his stuff was stolen. The police will have to at least consider the possibility that the two crimes were linked.'

They fell silent, looking at the doorway. It belonged to a bric-a-brac shop with a tinted front window full of old crockery, brass lamps, figurines and beer mats. The deep and sheltered entrance made it immediately obvious why someone would have chosen it as a perch for the night.

Jensen leaned closer to the lower part of the door, ran her finger over it.

'What?' said Gustav.

'It was painted recently. Look, this part is slightly darker than the top of the doorframe.'

Gustav stared at her. 'So?'

'There must have been a lot of blood. Believe he was stabbed in the neck, probably nicked an artery.'

'Yuck,' said Gustav, but he couldn't tear his eyes from the paintwork.

Jensen looked down the street to where a group of red-faced, gruff-voiced men and women had congregated. They were sitting on the edge of a pebble-dashed concrete planter containing a sickly shrub. Nothing else stood out about the street. It was like any other around the neighbourhood. The homeless man would probably have felt lucky to find it, a quiet, dry doorway. The weather had been milder then, but wet. What a way to die, metres from warm, dry homes and restaurants, surrounded by indifferent strangers. No one had reported him missing; after nearly three weeks, he was yet to be identified. The papers were calling him Victim A, just as, for a while, Casper had been Victim B. She hoped it wouldn't be necessary to go through the entire alphabet.

A coarse laugh rose from the gaggle of drunks around the planter. She walked resolutely up to them, leaving Gustav standing where he was. A stale, unwashed smell hung over the group.

No point in pretending to be friendly. They didn't look like they were easily fooled. She went straight in.

'*Hej.* Did any of you know the man who was killed over there?'

They followed the direction of her pointing finger and looked at Gustav as though he was the murdered man. He looked back at them, shrugging.

'It's about two weeks ago now, before the snow came.'

'Who is asking?' said a tiny man with an impressive amount of aggressiveness for his size.

The others laughed. 'Piss off,' said a woman. 'We don't know anything.'

The aggressive man shushed her. The others fell quiet.

'Jensen, *Dagbladet*.'

They booed her.

The little man folded his arms across his chest. 'Like she said, we don't know anything. And even if we did, we wouldn't speak to you lot. Now scoot.'

More laughter.

Jensen looked at their faces. Even the woman who had just been reprimanded was howling with mirth, but there was one who wasn't laughing: a large man with an unruly beard and military fatigues, sitting at the back of the planter slightly away from the others.

Jensen thought she recognised the look on his face.

'Suit yourselves, but there might be some cash in it, should your memories magically return.'

She turned and walked away, winking at Gustav.

'Let's go,' she said.

They were two streets away when the big man in the army fatigues caught up with them. A plastic bag full of bottles and cans was rattling from the handlebars of his bicycle. The recycling deposit from the empties, collected from rubbish bins, would be enough for a beer or two.

Jensen took a 200-kroner note from her wallet. The man immediately made a grab for it, but she snatched it away.

'Talk first,' she said.

He looked around him and gestured at an alley leading to the bike sheds behind a block of flats. He and Jensen left Gustav to keep an eye on the street.

'I saw something,' said the man. 'That night.'

118

'Tell me,' said Jensen, looking into his bloodshot eyes. It was impossible to tell how old he was.

'I was passing, trying to get out of the rain. I heard them shouting.'

'Them?'

'There were two of them, two men.'

'What were they saying?'

The man shrugged. 'I couldn't hear very well, but I don't think it was Danish.'

'Were they arguing?'

'I think so. When I returned later on that morning, there were police everywhere.'

'Anything else? Can you say what the men looked like? Black, white, young, old?'

The man chewed his lip. 'White, not old. Sorry, I don't remember anything else about them. I didn't stop to look.'

'Did you tell the police? They've been appealing for witnesses; it's been all over the news.'

He shook his head. 'I don't want any trouble.'

'At least tell me your name?' Jensen said. 'Do you live round here?'

'Can I have the money now?' he said by way of reply.

He left immediately, with the banknote tucked into his trouser pocket, flashing her with a wodge of his white belly. She got a picture of him cycling away.

'Shit, I didn't get his face.'

'I did,' said Gustav.

She felt a buzz in her pocket as he airdropped the images to her phone.

'Well?' he asked.

'Interesting. If they were arguing in another language, it would be fair to assume they knew each other.'

'So?'

'So that's not someone randomly going around killing the

119

homeless. *If* Victim A was stabbed by the man he was seen arguing with, that is. Might have be someone different, later on that night.'

In any case, it was something she could offer to Henrik in return for new information. If he had any, which was by no means certain at this stage.

Gustav sniffed loudly. 'You could have had that for a hundred.'

30

Assistens Cemetery was not the sort of place anyone would rush to spend a January evening. Jensen had checked the map a hundred times, but this was definitely the right section of graves. The deserted avenue, flanked by tall, naked trees, disappeared into the mist at either end. Difficult not to think of the generations of dead Copenhageners beneath her feet.

She had been up and down a few times, done the tour, pointing her mobile torch at the gravestones and calculating the ages of the dead. Most had been over seventy. Casper Madsen, or whatever his name was, had been twenty-one. His funeral had not even been held yet.

She checked her watch; Deep Throat was twelve minutes late. At fifteen minutes past six she turned towards her bicycle, reckoning that she had waited long enough, and could now tell Margrethe she had tried.

'Wait.'

The man startled her, stepping out of the shadows into the cone of street light in which she was standing. Short of stature, with heavy horn-rimmed glasses and a neatly trimmed beard.

He was wearing sensible shoes and an expensive-looking camel coat with leather gloves and a burgundy scarf wound twice round his neck. Inconspicuously affluent; the sort who would blend into the background in a posh neighbourhood like Charlottenlund.

'Jensen?' he said.

His voice was as posh as his attire; she put him at near seventy, though he moved like someone far younger.

'You're late.'

'I wanted to make sure you were alone.'

'Have you been watching me?'

'Sorry.'

'Who are you?'

'I am a great admirer of your boss. Best journalist of her generation.'

'Hard to argue with, but I meant what is your name?'

'It doesn't matter. Nobody knows me, and I like it that way.'

'You're in the restaurant business?'

'Among other things.'

'You could still tell me your name.'

'I don't know yours. Tens of thousands of people in Denmark are called Jensen.'

'Almost a quarter of a million, actually.'

'There you go, so what's your first name?'

'I don't use my first name. Not since first grade.'

'Why?'

'Let's just say my mother had a moment of madness when she named me.'

'Then we have something in common.'

'What?'

'Embarrassment.'

'How so?'

'Your name embarrasses you, and I am embarrassed about the matter that brings me here. I was caught out. One of my businesses, a restaurant, employed an accountant who turned out not to be who she said she was.'

'She ran off with your money.'

'She siphoned off nine hundred and fifty thousand kroner from the restaurant's account. Then she left for Thailand.'

'You should be telling the police.'

He smiled. 'Did you know that the police don't investigate financial crimes involving less than one million kroner, unless the money has been stolen from the public purse?'

'No.'

'Me neither, but Karen Nordmann did. She thought she had hidden her crime well, but she reckoned without me. Still, she is not worried; she knows the police won't do anything about it, and she is smart enough not to use her real name.'

'Maybe you should let it go? Put it down to experience?'

Jensen could no longer feel her toes. She thought fondly of a nice warm bar she knew, under five minutes' bike ride away.

'No. People don't cross me and get away with it.'

'But what can I do?'

'I looked you up. You're a good reporter. There is a lot more to this story, more accountants like this so-called Karen Nordmann. All of them work the same scam, and they are very good. Most people never find out where the money has gone. They circulate around the businesses in Copenhagen. Karen Nordmann will surface again when her money is used up. There is a chap I suggest you speak to; they have virtually bankrupted his business, and I believe he has been threatened. I will email you his details; you should go and see him.'

'I don't know — it sounds like a weak case to me. If you're so certain, why don't you just do something about it yourself?'

The man smiled again. 'I am talking to you.'

He dug deeper into the pockets of his coat, looked around him. His steamed-up glasses concealed his eyes.

'My father is buried in this cemetery. He always kept

Dagbladet at home, and his father before him. It's why I suggested we meet here.'

'Right.'

'I am fond of journalists.'

'That makes one of you.'

He laughed softly. She noticed that his breath was hardly visible in the frozen air, unlike her own. He was making her nervous.

'So, you'll look into it?'

It was cold, she wanted to get away from cemetery, and a tiny part of her was intrigued.

'OK, but I am not making any promises.'

He nodded and walked down the avenue away from the light. A few seconds later a car drove up noiselessly, he got in and disappeared, and the cemetery fell quiet again.

A fox barked in the distance.

'You can come out now,' she said.

Gustav crashed out of the bushes with maximum noise. 'Jesus, five more minutes in there and I would have died of hypothermia,' he shouted.

'It was you who wanted to come.'

'I didn't know that I'd be spending the evening in a frozen hedge.'

'Did you get a photo?'

'No, and before you say anything, the bastard kept his back turned the entire time. It was like he knew I was there.'

Maybe he did, thought Jensen. He had said that he had been watching her. Perhaps he had decided Gustav didn't constitute a threat.

An email from him flashed up on her screen with the name of the source he had recommended (Carsten Vangede) and a mobile phone number. Why had he gone through the trouble of meeting her, only to direct her to someone else? This seemed to her an oddly cowardly move.

124

'So, are we going to see the guy he talked about?'

She put her phone away. 'Another time.'

She got back on her bicycle, her thoughts turning to the warm, candle-lit bar. There was just about time for a quick one before she had to begin the long train journey up the coast to Esben's summer house.

'See you tomorrow in the office.'

He shouted something after her. To her delight, it was a Danish expletive for the female of the species that she hadn't heard since her earliest youth. He was likely to have picked up the term around Margrethe, who had always worn that particular insult like a badge of honour.

'*Møgkælling.*'

Bitch.

31

Henrik stopped breathing in through his nose. The rucksack on the plastic sheet in front of him stank of things he was trying not to think about. They were hovering around the boot of a patrol car next to Frederiksholms Kanal. One of the uniformed officers had called Mark, knowing Henrik would want to have a look before the rucksack was sent on to forensics.

'Who found this?'

'Resident checking on his boat,' said the officer who was shining his torch into the boot.

'And?'

Mark piped up: 'The ice has been melting in the last few days. Guy noticed it bobbing in the water, thought it was a rubbish bag. Apparently, there's an issue with people dumping rubbish in the canal, and it's really—'

Henrik held up a hand.

'Spare me the detail. What else?'

'He used an oar to get it. When he saw what it was, he rang the police.'

'And no one has opened it?'

126

Mark and the officer both shook their heads, probably remembering previous occasions when they had jumped the gun and got an epic bollocking.

'Good.'

He donned latex gloves and began to open the rucksack. It was black, so he knew that it couldn't have belonged to the youngster in Magstræde, but Farvergade, where the first victim had been stabbed, was not far away. The perpetrator would have run off, ripping anything of value out of the bag and tossing it in the water. Unlikely to be useful to them, but they would have to go through the motions of finding out.

Going through the motions. If his life had a tagline, that would be it.

The first five items in the rucksack were clothes: a large hooded jumper, Nike T-shirt, two odd socks, a scarf and a pair of men's underpants. He held them at a distance, grimacing. There was a plastic bag with some sodden biscuits, a pouch of tobacco and a set of keys. No wallet, no phone, no documents of any kind.

'Do you think it's his?' said Mark. 'Victim A?'

Henrik rested his knuckles on the edge of the boot and looked at the rucksack. He would be willing to bet that it was.

'Probably,' he said, pushing the rucksack to one side.

'Can I just . . .' Mark cautiously pulled the rucksack towards him, all the while keeping his eyes on Henrik. ('Stop making people so jumpy,' his wife would have said.)

He nodded his assent and watched as Mark checked the front and side pockets, and the zipped-up compartment in the lid. He found nothing but some remnants of sweet wrappers.

Henrik began to walk away.

'Wait,' said Mark, his hand deep in the interior of the rucksack.

He pulled out a photo. Some of the picture came away when he unfolded it, but you could tell that it was a baby, weeks old at most.

127

'There is some writing on the back and what looks like a phone number,' he said.

Henrik snatched the photo from Mark's hand. Reluctantly, he reached into his shirt pocket for the reading glasses that made him look like his father, but he could not make sense of the letters.

Nu uita de noi.

'What does it mean?'

'It's Romanian,' said Mark, consulting his phone. 'Means "Don't forget about us".'

Henrik smiled to himself.

'Check that phone number, quick as you can.'

For the first time in days, he felt a spring in his step as he walked to his car.

32

Tuesday 21:23

Jensen turned into the drive to Esben's summer house, the icy gravel crackling under her tyres. She hadn't considered how dark it would be to cycle there from Hornbæk station on a Tuesday evening in February. Her bike light picked out Neighbourhood Watch signs and padlocked gates, but a burglar could work undisturbed here. The police were half an hour down the road, at best, and who was going to call them?

She had already gone the wrong way twice in the warren of narrow lanes with pastel-coloured wooden houses all looking the same.

Esben's holiday home was far from what she had imagined, given its location in Hornbæk, home of the rich at play. Esben was the biggest show-off she knew, with his palatial villa in Klampenborg and eye-wateringly expensive taste in suits and cars. Of course, the money was all his wife's. That explained why he had chosen to stay married, though not why Ulla hadn't told him to get lost years ago. Yet the yellow wooden cabin with its white-painted window frames, standing on a modest plot close to its neighbours, was unashamedly traditional.

The inside smelled of summer and pine needles and raincoats. There was a pile of wellies in assorted sizes by the front door, a handful of fishing rods, two worn golf bags and shelves full of books, airport novels and biographies mostly. And pictures of Esben and Ulla and their four kids, only one of whom, an 'afterthought' as he liked to call her, was still living at home with them.

For all his clumsy attempts to come on to her over the years, and the countless of times he must have succeeded with other women, Esben also wanted to be the family man in his paint-splattered overalls, manoeuvring his ride-on lawn mower around his rectangle of grass and drinking beer in front of the football on TV.

She thought of Henrik and how much he and Esben were alike in this respect, if only this one. Happy at home with their wives and children, guarding them from the truth of who they really were, having their cake and eating it.

I trust you completely, she heard Henrik say.

'You're not marrying material,' Guy had told her a lifetime ago in London, when she had tumbled into his bed, bruised and weak, the first time Henrik had decided to go back to his wife. Guy had meant it as a compliment – having entertained her in a crowded bar with tales of the many vacuous women his wealthy Lord and Lady parents had tried their hardest to make him settle down with – but now it hurt her to remember.

Everyone in Denmark was at home with someone, but she was by herself in a wooden cabin in a deserted summer-house district on the tip of Zealand.

Shut up, Jensen, and stop pitying yourself.

I know where you live now.

No, you don't.

She smiled at the thought of Henrik turning up at the flat in Christianshavn to be met at the door by a wild-haired Markus in his underpants.

Can we go away somewhere and find out what this is? he had asked her. In the middle of a murder case that had the whole country exercised, was he seriously suggesting they go off on a dirty weekend?

He did have a point, though. You could count on two hands the times they had seen each other in all the years since they first met in London. There had never been enough time to put a relationship to the test, let alone have one in the first place.

They almost hadn't met. Henrik had been attending a European policing conference with his boss. On the last evening there had been a dinner at the Danish ambassador's residence in Sloane Street, to which a couple of the London correspondents had been invited. She had just returned from Edinburgh, and dinner with some dusty old men in uniforms was about the last thing she had wanted, but her colleague from *Jyllands-Posten* had pulled up outside her flat in a black cab and refused to leave unless she joined him. To this day, she remembered exactly where she had been sitting in the ambassador's dining room, with Henrik diagonally across the table from her. They had stared at each other all throughout the meal, as if trying to remember where they knew each other from. Later, in the lift down to the street —magically, he had managed for the two of them to ride alone – he had kissed her.

What he had forgotten to tell her, however, was that he was married. For which she had made him do penance ever since.

Jensen flicked on the lights in the open–plan kitchen and living room. There was a note on the counter: *Look in the fridge. Big hug, Esben xxx*

Six bottles of Louis Roederer all lined up in a row, a carton of smoked salmon from Letz delicatessen in Østerbro, a loaf of sourdough bread with caraway seeds. He would have got the summer house ready for her over the weekend.

She lit a fire in the wood–burning stove. Esben had left bunched-up newspapers, logs and kindling, so all she had to do was strike a match. She dragged an ice-cold mattress through from one of the bedrooms, got undressed in front of the fire, and poured herself a glass of champagne, staring into the flames as she warmed up under the duvet. Perhaps the summer house wasn't so bad. If she got hold of a car somehow, she could make it into the city in under an hour.

She got out her phone. Henrik would be in bed by now, but she knew his mobile was virtually taped to the palm of his hand. She sent him Gustav's photo of the witness and composed a message. The champagne had softened her.

This man saw the first victim arguing with someone on the night he died. Now give me the name of Casper's loony aunt and we're quits.

She thought of Casper, seated in Magstræde, with the sleeping bag over his lap, alone, under the influence, on the coldest night of the year, holding a sign proclaiming his guilt.

Skyldig.

Guilty of what?

What had he done to get himself locked up in a youth prison?

There had been no word from Fie since Monday's message; it was time for another visit to Roskilde.

33

'Cinnamon pastries from Ole & Steen, chocolate icing.'

Jensen held up the white cardboard box like an offering to a goddess. It was tiny in Fie's hands; she looked uncomfortable with the gift. Jensen quickly changed the subject.

'There is someone I'd like you to meet.'

Gustav stepped forward.

'This boy wants to be a journalist. God only knows why. They forced me to take him on as a trainee and now I can't go anywhere without him following me.'

Fie smiled.

'I'm deadly serious. He is a right pain in the neck.'

'Learning from the master,' said Gustav.

Fie took them to her flat, past the common area where she had been playing on the Xbox the first time Jensen had visited. Like then, the place was dead, the only sign of life a faint throbbing R&B bass coming from next door.

Again, Jensen wondered why Fie was there and not in a flat of her own, holding down a job.

She was wearing the same clothes as last time: black

133

leggings and a greyish, floaty tunic, her feet stuck into uni-corn slippers.

Her flat was diagonally opposite Casper's. Warm to the point of stifling, cloying with scented candles, a cave full of things. There were fairy lights dangling from the walls and dozens of stuffed toys on the bed. In the middle of the living room stood a faux-leather gaming chair pointed at a giant screen, with an armchair pulled up beside it. Against a wall to the right of the chairs was a desk with three blank monitors and a serious-looking laptop open on a coding page. Jensen wondered if she had been searching for clues about Casper when they arrived.

'Take a seat,' said Fie, seating herself on the swivel chair by the desk, and leaving Jensen and Gustav side by side, awkwardly facing the screen. Gustav immediately began to play with the settings on the gaming chair.

'Casper and I brought the extra chair in here, so we could play together,' said Fie. 'He wasn't bad.'

Jensen heard the grief in her voice. Casper had been a friend where few friends were to be had, and now he had gone. 'Do you have any pictures of him?'

'Just one,' said Fie, scrolling through her phone, a pastry in one hand. She had taken a large bite out of it, leaving the shape of her crooked teeth in the icing.

She showed them a photo of Casper glancing up at the camera, his face half-obscured by a hood. He looked surprised, a reluctant subject. His expression reminded Jensen of Henrik. In the few public photos that existed of him, he was wearing sunglasses, hiding from view.

'Tell me,' said Jensen, wondering how best to broach the subject before settling for head-on, 'did Casper ever take drugs?'

Fie stared at her. 'Why do you say that?'

'No reason. I was just wondering, since he sat outside in the cold like that, how he could stand it, unless he was on something.'

'There are drugs, if you want them. Most people here are into them.'

'And Casper?'

'Took them a few times in the beginning, maybe to blend in, but they made him crazy, he'd do all sorts of stupid stuff, so he stopped. He was totally clean.'

Not strictly speaking true, but how could Jensen tell Fie without revealing how she knew?

'And the people here,' she said. 'What sort of stuff do they take?'

Fie shrugged. 'Amphetamines or ecstasy, sometimes coke.'

'What if you get found out?' asked Gustav, clearly impressed.

'They turn a blind eye if you keep it discrete,' said Fie.

She looked forlornly at the remains of the last cinnamon pastry for a few moments, then popped it in her mouth and chewed with grim determination.

'Where do people get the drugs from?' asked Jensen.

'There's this guy near the Central Station.'

'In Copenhagen?'

She nodded. 'I don't know his name. There's no number or anything. You just go where he hangs out. It's like a sweet shop – you can have anything you want, if you've got the money.'

'Could you show me the place? Describe the guy to me?'

Fie brushed pastry flakes off her thighs, pulled the sleeves of her tunic over her wrists when she noticed Jensen looking at her scars.

'Maybe. But there is something you need to know about Casper. I found out that—'

There was a knock on the door. Fie looked from Jensen to Gustav and held a finger to her lips. She went to the door and Jensen recognised the gentle, peace-making voice of Tobias. There was a pause, a brief mumbled exchange, then Fie called out to Jensen.

No point in trying to fight it.

'Maybe I'll see you another time,' she said to Fie, nodding vaguely at the room, where Gustav remained seated.

Thankfully, he had enough presence of mind to keep his mouth shut. No point in them both getting thrown out before they had got what they came for.

'How did you know I was here?' Jensen asked Tobias outside in the corridor.

He pointed to the flat belonging to Fie's neighbour, the one with the poor taste in music.

'Guy in there heard Fie talking to someone and called us. Fie never talks to anyone. Well, not any more.'

Jensen was taken to the staffroom again, but this time there was no coffee on offer. Karina was waiting for them; she looked even more drained than last time, as if she hadn't slept since. Her mouth was pinched.

'I am sorry,' Jensen said. 'I didn't know visiting was forbidden.'

'You're taking advantage,' said Karina. 'Fie is vulnerable. Trying to get information out of her about Casper by pretending to be her friend is disgusting.'

That word again.

Vulnerable.

Used liberally whenever Skovhøj needed to defend itself against accusations from the outside.

'Fie wants to help find out what happened to her friend. What's wrong with that? She shouldn't be cooped up in here anyway.'

Karina smiled thinly. 'You people have no idea what Fie or any of our other residents have gone through' she said. 'We don't want you hanging around here. We've already told you everything we know. The only good thing that's come out of this mess is that people now understand that you can't simply keep chipping away at funding for youth homes without it causing tragedies like this.'

Tobias checked his phone, handed it to Jensen to see for herself.

'Look, we've already got 87,678 signatures to keep Skovhøj open.'

'So we don't need you stirring up trouble,' said Karina.

Jensen held up her hands. 'I only want to find out the truth. Why don't you want that, Karina? What's wrong with the truth?'

'Get out.'

'Before I do, did you know that drug-taking is endemic here, and that Casper took drugs the night he died?'

'Right now,' said Karina.

Tobias was looking down at his feet as Jensen gathered her coat and bag and headed for the door. 'Does the council know and the government and all those people you got to sign your petition? And if they did, do you think they might change their minds?'

34

Wednesday 12:44

At long last Gustav appeared from the back of the buildings, traipsing through bushes covered in hoar frost. He was looking at his mobile, his headphones round his neck. Jensen was sitting on a boulder by the side of the road, far enough away not to be seen from the entrance.

'What took you so long?'

Gustav blushed. 'I couldn't get away. She begged me to stay, just one game of GTA, she said. Then she totally destroyed me.'

They began to walk back towards Roskilde station, through residential streets lined with yellow-brick bungalows with red-tiled roofs, each with their own rectangle of lawn surrounded by a brown beech hedge. The houses were abandoned, the carports empty. Everyone was out at work or at school.

'So, did she tell you who Casper was?'

Gustav was pensive.

'Beaten by a girl,' she said, nudging him with an elbow.

He recoiled from her touch and she left him to his thoughts.

After a few minutes, he said: 'What's wrong with Fie? Why is she in there?'

'I don't know.'

'If I don't pull myself together, my aunt says she'll report me to the police, and they'll put me in an institution.'

Jensen didn't doubt it, not in the slightest. It was exactly the sort of thing Margrethe *would* say.

'Skovhøj is not that sort of institution. People like Fie are there out of choice. They have issues, psychological problems, social problems. They need therapy, someone to check in on them now and again.'

'Didn't work too well for the guy who got stabbed.'

'Gustav, no one is going to send you to Skovhøj.'

'You don't know what I did.'

'What *did* you do, Gustav?'

He didn't reply. They watched a postman pull up in a bright blue van and try to deliver a parcel to one of the yellow-brick houses. No one home. The neighbourhood was dead.

'Fie said Casper had done something bad before he came here. She told me to tell you that his real name was Thomas, Thomas Mørk. Changed his name in prison.'

Jensen stopped walking.

'For Christ's sake, Gustav, why didn't you tell me that at the start?'

'Is it important?'

'Um, yes? We're trying to find out what went on here, why Casper . . . why Thomas ended up at Skovhøj, what made him travel all the way down to Copenhagen and sit down in the street with a sign announcing his guilt to the world. Did Fie say what the bad thing was?'

Gustav shook his head. 'She said to read all about it in *Dagbladet*. I was just looking it up when you tore into me for being late.'

Jensen stopped on the pavement and logged into the newspaper's archive on her phone.

There it was.

The whole thing.

Right there all along.

She must have missed the story during her years in London, when Danish news, while bad enough, always, inevitably, seemed overshadowed by something bigger or worse.

Thomas had killed his mother, Sandra Mørk, stabbing her twenty-seven times with a bread knife in the family kitchen. Having just turned fifteen, he was old enough to be tried in court. Frank had covered the story for *Dagbladet*, which had dubbed it 'the Langelandsvej Murder'. At first his identity had not been disclosed. But someone had talked to the media, and Thomas's entire life's story had come out: his difficulties at school, issues with drugs, mother with a succession of boy-friends, police cautions for the minor offences of a desperate teenager.

Skyldig.

Thomas had left Skovhøj last Monday and caught the train into the capital to proclaim to everyone what he had done. But why then and not when he had left the young offenders' insti-tution in November? Why wait so long?

Jensen needed to get back to her office to think.

'Walking is too slow. We need to get you your own bike,' she said.

'I can always get a bike,' he said, smiling broadly and nodding at a shed in someone's garden.

'Gustav, did you got thrown out of school because you stole something?'

By way of a reply, he put his headphones back on.

'What is it with you and those headphones?' she shouted. 'Could you just for once not wear them?'

Gustav shook his head solemnly.

'It's better for everyone if I do. They help me stay calm. Or at least that's what the psychologist said.'

35

Still no messages from Jensen. Henrik put down his phone for the seventeenth time and looked out of the car window at the gap in the football-pitch fence, through which his eldest son was due to emerge any minute now. Only a year ago he would have been watching the training session from the touchline, but these days only the uncool kids still permitted their parents to watch. Henrik understood this. The same thing had happened when he was a boy, but much later, when he was fifteen or so. Mikkel seemed to have grown up without him noticing. It had all started with his mobile phone, a reluctant gift from his parents on his tenth birthday. He now had a private space unreachable by Henrik's benign but dedicated policing. Not two weeks ago he had caught the boy watching porn, and had had to have 'the conversation', received with much embarrassed squirming and rolling of the eyes. During his (admittedly lacklustre) mono-logue, he had felt like the world's biggest hypocrite: who was he, a failing husband – himself not averse to watching porn when he could get away with it – to teach morals to anyone, let alone his own child?

In truth, it wasn't the porn that had upset him, but the realisation that his three children, even Oliver, would one day soon grow away from him, removing the protective screen that kept him and his wife from having to face up to the disastrous state of their marriage.

The training session was coming to an end. He recognised one of the mothers from Mikkel's school, the hot single one (Mille or Mia – he could never remember her name), walking with her son along the pavement towards his car. She fancied him, he could tell. One nod from him, and she would be straight in there. For a bald, rough-looking man, he had had more than his fair share of success with the opposite sex. It would be easy to step out of the car, start chatting.

'Fuck's sake, Henrik, what are you doing?' he said out loud to himself.

('You pathetic loser,' he heard his wife say.)

He ducked and pretended to be texting as the woman passed the car. Still nothing from Jensen. Where the hell *was* she?

He had been back to her Christianshavn flat, of course he had. He couldn't control himself as far as she was concerned. Having that suntanned bloke opening the door had been a nasty shock. Henrik had pretended to be there on official police business, but the guy had told him Jensen had moved out and that he had no idea where she had gone.

'Leave a message for her at *Dagbladet*, if you're so keen to get hold of her.'

He seemed not to care two hoots about Jensen. If Henrik hadn't been so ashamed of himself, he would have taught the man a lesson there and then.

More kids were emerging from the sports ground and disappearing into waiting cars or getting on their bikes and cycling off. Mikkel was always one of the last. Henrik could hardly blame him, as he was often late for the pick-up, though he had never entirely missed it, not once. His colleagues knew that, whatever else was going on, he always collected his boy from football training. Tonight he would have to drop Mikkel home and take off again for the police station almost immediately.

Karina Jørgensen's revelation at the Forensic Institute that Casper Madsen was Thomas Mørk, the Langelandsvej killer, had thrown a spanner in the works, to say the least. Two murders of rough sleepers in such close succession could hardly be a coincidence, but that one of them should be Thomas was a bizarre turn-up. Henrik remembered the case well. Thomas had been fifteen at the time, only three years older than his own son was now. Mikkel had his moments, and so did his wife, but the idea that the boy would stab his mother with a kitchen knife was unthinkable and abhorrent.

Thomas had been found by his stepfather, covered in blood and still holding the knife, slumped over the body on the kitchen floor. The fact that his mother had been thirteen weeks' pregnant at the time had made it even more horrific. It was hard not to think that Thomas Mørk was better off out of this world. How could anyone have a normal life after doing something like that?

He wondered what Jensen would make of it all, and suddenly he longed to speak to her about it. He tried her phone number again, but she still wasn't picking up. She was giving him the cold shoulder, obviously, after the incident at Café Victor (luckily, there had been no other fallout). Jensen was the most stubborn woman he knew and, given who he was married to, that was saying something.

He had considered calling the newspaper and demanding to get her home address under the pretext of needing her urgently as a police witness (not a million miles from the truth) but had thought better of it. He was knee-deep in trouble as it was. No need to add further complications.

Mikkel emerged as the floodlights on the training ground were switched off, leaving the surroundings in darkness. Henrik felt a rush of guilt at the sight of his son's slumped shoulders as he walked towards the car.

'What took you so long?' he said, jest-punching the lad on the shoulder, but Mikkel shrank from him, putting his seatbelt on and turning his face to the passenger window.

'Good training session?' tried Henrik.

'No,' said Mikkel. 'I don't want to talk about it.'

Like father, like son. The Jungersen men never had been any good at talking. Henrik patted the boy on the thigh and pulled out of the parking bay.

36

They moved the noticeboard from the space between their desks to the wall behind Gustav's chair. In the centre, they pinned up the photograph of Thomas that Fie had shared with them, and round the sides, printouts of articles about the Langelandsvej murder case in chronological order. Gustav crossed out 'Casper Madsen' and wrote 'Thomas Mørk' in bold capitals.

There were thirteen stories. *Dagbladet* had lost interest quickly after the case had first been reported, with a second wind around the time of Thomas's name leaking. Psychologists had been interviewed, speculating about the root causes of matricide. Some had argued that Thomas may have been obsessing about incest and killed his mother as a means of putting an end to feelings he knew were wrong. Others said the stabbing could have been his response to excessive control or (more likely) the polar opposite, a total lack of interest on Sandra's part.

The same few photos had done the rounds. There was one of the house where the murder happened, a mirror image of the bungalows they had walked past in Roskilde. A large chunk of the Danish population lived in houses like that. The photo would have served as a chilling reminder to readers of the horrors that might be lurking behind seemingly mundane façades.

Another picture was a school photo of Thomas, taken three years before the murder: chubby, smiling, long-haired, with virtually no similarity to the skinny, bearded twenty-one-year-old who had gone to sit down in Magstræde, let alone the bluish corpse now residing in a stainless-steel drawer at the Forensic Institute.

Dagbladet's photo of Sandra had been cropped from a holiday snap in happier times, a beach bar at sunset. She had been a pretty blonde with skin that reddened easily.

There were interviews with teachers at Thomas's school, most of whom were 'shocked' or 'saddened', and the usual fillers from neighbours who couldn't believe that something so gruesome could have happened in their peaceful street, to a family that always seemed so nice, so quiet.

No one could ever believe it.

'Are you going to tell Frank who Thomas was?' said Gustav, as they stood back and admired their work.

Jensen told a half-truth. 'No. I don't want to get Fie into trouble. It will come out soon enough anyway, making a sad story even sadder. Doubt it will detain the media for very long.'

'Then why are we doing this?'

It was an excellent question.

'Because I found him, I suppose. I need to know what happened. So far, pieced together, the story raises a number of questions. What made Thomas choose last Monday, the day of the blizzard the media had been talking about for days? Why Magstræde? Where did he get his drugs from? What makes a fifteen-year-old kill his mother and then, seven years later, scribble his guilt on a cardboard sign and hold it up for everyone to see? If he was a psychopath juvenile killer, how come he was so kind to Fie, at least according to her? And what made him go mute?'

'OK, OK, I get it,' said Gustav holding up his hands. 'So, what do we do now?'

'We talk to some more people.'

'How long do we have to do that for?'

'Till we get somewhere.'

'Or nowhere.'

'Right. It's called journalism. If you want to sit at your scavenged desk and listen to chill-out music for the next three months until Margrethe finds you out and sends you back to your dad, then be my guest.'

Gustav looked at her defiantly. 'Or I could just tell her that you're still working on this story.'

'Still working on what story?'

Margrethe was darkening the door, dwarfing the two of them.

Jensen had never seen Margrethe in her office before, nor anywhere on the top floor of the building. She glanced pleadingly at Gustav, vaguely shaking her head.

'Your tip-off,' he said to Margrethe.

'Why would I mind that?'

'I meant still working on it, as in no significant progress made.'

'None?'

'Some,' said Jensen. 'We met your secret source. Or, should I say, your number-one fan.'

'And?'

'He has given us the name of someone who will talk.'

'Good. Pleased the two of you are getting along. Keep me posted.'

Jensen took a step towards Margrethe, blocking her path to the noticeboard with their pinned-up investigation.

'I think there might be something in the story,' she said.

Margrethe smiled.

She never smiled.

Jensen decided she disliked it profoundly.

'Shut your mouth,' she said to Gustav's grinning face when, finally, Margrethe had left.

She was yet to make up her mind about him. What had he done that was bad enough to get him thrown out of school? And more to the point: how had he subsequently managed to sweet-talk the most cynical woman in Copenhagen into believing that he was not beyond redemption, to the point of making her climb two flights of stairs in order to smile like a giddy schoolgirl?

She looked at the noticeboard again. Gustav had crossed out the names of people in Magstræde he had already spoken to. One or two still had a question mark against them.

'By the way,' she said. 'That woman you had a missed call from the other day, the one you said you'd already spoken to – who was it?'

'Oh, just Malene from the dentist's in Magstræde.'

'What did she want?'

'No idea. I called her back a few times. Not picking up.'

37

Henrik belched loudly and set down his can of Coke on his desk, looking at what was left of his chicken shawarma with a mixture of disgust and self-loathing. He had taken off again almost immediately after bringing his son home after football practice, preferring a dirty takeaway to the meal his wife had left for him in the kitchen. She knew full well that he wouldn't eat lasagne because of the cheese sauce. He detested cheese in all his forms, always had done, always would. He reckoned that these days she was doing it on purpose, serving him food that disgusted him as a means of making him leave.

He was about to call Mark for news when Lisbeth showed up, wearing a coat and looking worn out. Still young, still trying to prove herself. He remembered well what that was like. It had been ages since he had asked her how she was or taken her out for a few beers. He knew that she and Mark looked up to him, and they had notched up some notable victories together, but Henrik was first to admit that he was not much better at being a boss than he was at being a husband.

149

'Come in,' he said, sweeping the remains of his supper, such as it was, into the wastepaper bin. 'Where's Mark?'

'Went home to his kids.'

'Why are you still here? You should go too.'

'I am,' she said. 'Just wanted to tell you that I think we now know the identity of Victim A. If the rucksack recovered from Frederiksholm's Canal belonged to him, that is.'

'Oh?'

'We rang the number, and a woman answered the call, but she didn't speak English, so we tried again with an interpreter.'

'And?'

'She confirmed that she had written the message and given the photo to her child's father before he left their town but said that she hadn't heard from him for eighteen months.'

'Name?'

'Andrei Ciobanu. From Sibiu in southern Transylvania. Originally from Bucharest. She wasn't very complimentary about him.'

'Get his medical records.'

'Already on it. Should be with us tomorrow. With a bit of luck, they should confirm what we already know.'

'Good work, Lisbeth.'

Monsen would be thrilled. Finally, some progress in this moribund case. Though if the first victim really was Andrei Ciobanu, then it raised a whole lot of questions about what his murder had to do with the stabbing of Thomas Mørk. Unless the victims were picked at random, which didn't bear thinking of.

If Mark was a Labrador, Lisbeth was a greyhound. Quiet, intelligent, fast. He didn't know anything about her home life, was pretty sure she had never mentioned a boyfriend or a partner. Not that he would go there. ('As if *she* would!' he heard his wife say.) Lisbeth was blonde, sporty and big-boned, the type who was good at handball, and one of the boys. For all Henrik

150

knew, she might not even be into men. ('You think everyone who doesn't fancy you is a lesbian.')

What he did know was that between her and Mark, she was the one with the most potential to replace him when the time came. Which would be sooner rather than later, unless he got his skates on and solved the case.

38

Gustav slept most of the way to the ferry port at Odden with his head lolling against the backrest. His mouth was open, like Thomas's when she had found him in Magstræde, but Gustav had pink cheeks and saliva glistening at the corners of his lips and his eyelids were fluttering with dreams. His hands were soft like a young boy's, nails bitten to the quick.

Jensen had almost lost faith in Henrik when, finally, the name and address of Thomas's aunt in Jutland had pinged through from him on Messenger.

The sun had emerged for the last bit of their journey along the narrow spit of land with the sandy beach on one side and, on the other, a row of wooden summer houses, empty until their owners escaped Copenhagen on Friday evening, though not many did at this time of year. The water in the bay was dark turquoise and dotted with white horses, the lime grass whipping in the wind. It was as beautiful as a summer's day.

As long as you stayed inside your nice warm car.

Jensen's life had become a lot easier since she had persuaded Margrethe that she and Gustav needed their own set of wheels to pursue her story. Either Margrethe had ordered Yasmine to lend them her car, or Yasmine, who was a smart woman, had volunteered, seeing which way the wind was blowing. In the red Beetle, a large sunflower dangling from the rear-view mirror, the journey back and forth from Esben's summer house was barely forty-five minutes. It had made the commute bearable.

Jensen had decided against calling ahead to ask Thomas's aunt about paying her a visit. Few people with any information of value welcomed talking to journalists. Better to just appear on the doorstep. It was always more effort to turn someone away physically than hanging up on them.

Ditte Mørk had told the police to go to hell when they informed her Thomas has been killed. Either because she wanted her nephew to rest in peace, or because she didn't care what had happened to him. Whichever, she was unlikely to want to have a nice chat about it over a cup of tea.

39

On the ferry Jensen bought hotdogs and Cokes, reflecting on how her diet had deteriorated since Gustav had been foisted upon her. He seemed to exist on meat and white starch, preferably processed and fried to within an inch of its life.

The sun was shining through the greasy windows, leaving the passenger lounge stifling. They had taken off their coats and were leaning back in the soporific atmosphere, staring out to sea.

'I hate Jutland,' said Gustav.

'Why?'

'Flat. Boring. And Dad lives there.'

'Where?'

'Aalborg.'

'Aalborg is lovely.'

'Not with Dad in it. Loves bossing people around. Used to fly fighter planes, now he trains pilots in the air force.'

'What happened, Gustav?'

'Mum died. Got breast cancer when I was nine. They said she was cured, then last year it came back and killed her inside four weeks.'

He said it as though he was imparting the football results, a honed routine, designed to rebuff any attempts at sympathy.

'Your mum was Margrethe's sister?

'Fuck no. My mum was nice. Margrethe is Dad's sister. Fascists, the two of them.'

Jensen chuckled inwardly. Margrethe would be outraged to be called a fascist. But if Gustav was referring to his aunt's authoritarian leadership style and take-no-prisoners attitude to those she loathed, then he was pretty much spot on.

'Tell me about your mother.'

'Not much to tell. She was a piano teacher, a good one. I used to ask her to play for me. I could listen to her for hours. She was a kind person, happy. I feel terrible now, though.'

'Why?'

'I was a nightmare to her, made her cry. Sometimes I can't even remember her face, and it makes me kind of desperate, and then I have to get all the old photos out.'

'I am sorry.'

'Yeah, well, whatever.'

He shook his head and wiped his eyes with the back of his hand.

'So, between your aunt and your dad, you reckon Margrethe is the lesser evil?'

'Something like that. We never saw her much when I was living with mum, so I don't know her very well yet, but so far, she is all right. Besides, I already tried staying at Dad's in Aalborg. Didn't go so well.'

Jensen had known Margrethe for more than fifteen years. She had never spoken of her family, least of all her brother and nephew. She lived in a large apartment in the Østerbro district, but Jensen had only been to it once, and besides that they had never socialised outside of the office, except that one time in the Mayfair restaurant.

'When you say it didn't go well, you mean that you did

155

something so bad it got you thrown out of school and your father and your aunt threatened to put you into an institution?'

Gustav shrugged.

'And the bad thing was?'

At that moment, the announcement came over the tannoy telling people to return to their cars. Aarhus Harbour had slid into view, the sunlight catching in the windows of the cars lined up for the return leg to Zealand.

Gustav grinned at her, picked up his coat, and joined the crowd heading for the stairs.

40

Thursday 14:06

It wasn't hard to spot Ditte Mørk's house, not after they asked one of her neighbours for directions and were told to follow the mess.

The commune was in the Danish Lake District, in patchy woodland out in the sticks between Skanderborg and Silkeborg. Hobbit houses with curved, thatched roofs and porthole windows next to log cabins. A few chickens were pecking at the naked earth on the tracks where the snow had melted. Outside each house there were neatly kept kitchen gardens with onions and cabbages, stacks of firewood and rows of wellies.

Outside every house but one.

A tethered goat stared as Jensen and Gustav approached Ditte Mørk's cottage, passing a clapped-out orange VW camper van. The weatherboarded house, once painted yellow, had seen better days. A recent delivery of firewood had been dumped in a pile out front and left to the elements. Tossed in the garden, half-obscured by snow, like debris from an explosion, were old bicycle tyres, a red washing-up bowl, a tin bucket,

157

wet newspaper and a shopping trolley. You had to admire the woman for getting the trolley here, given the nearest shop had to be at least five miles away.

Wood smoke was rising from the back of the house. Someone was chopping logs, grunting with exertion. Jensen told Gustav to take a walk and leave Thomas's aunt to her. Ditte Mørk might not appreciate coming across a teenage boy on her property. Seeing as the woman was wielding an axe, it wasn't worth taking any chances.

'And take your hood off!'

Gustav made a face and walked away, hands firmly in his pockets. Thirty seconds later she watched him remove his hood with an angry swipe of his hand.

Cautiously she walked round the side of the house. The wood smoke grew stronger and made her eyes sting. Bits of burnt paper and ash drifted past her face.

'Hello? Ditte? Ditte Mørk?'

The back garden was overgrown and bordered by pine trees. She couldn't see for the smoke. Then she felt a hard poke in her back and prayed to God it wasn't the blade of the axe.

She turned and stared into a pair of watery blue eyes set deep into a rough red face framed by hair that was grey at the roots but had at one point in the not-too-distant past been dyed with henna. If there had ever been a likeness between Sandra Mørk and her sister, it had all but gone now; there was nothing of the pretty, suntanned blonde about Ditte. She was wielding a spade, holding it aloft like a club. 'You've got ten seconds to get off my land, or I'll deck you.'

'My name is Jensen.'

'Eight, seven . . .'

There was a sour smell coming off her. She had had a drink not long ago. Perhaps several. Her hands were red raw.

'I drove here from Copenhagen.'

'Four, three . . .'

158

'I am the one who found your nephew. I found Thomas. In Magstræde.'

'Ha!' shouted Ditte Mørk, showing stained, crooked teeth.

She was still holding on to the spade but seemed to have forgotten about the countdown momentarily.

'You thought I'd be grateful, did you? You thought I'd like to hear all the details, that I'd care? Well, I don't. I'm glad that evil runt is dead. Glad. I hope he suffered.'

'Did they tell you he had been sitting in the street holding a sign that said *skyldig*?'

'My sister should never have had him; she should have got an abortion. Child of the devil, never left her alone, always mithering, the needy little fuck.'

'Did he talk back then, when your sister was still alive?'

'Never fucking stopped.'

'Well, he wasn't talking recently. Not in the last four months or so of his life, perhaps longer than that.'

'Conniving little shit, trying to get sympathy. Always someone else's fault, but Sandra paid the price, didn't she? Twenty-seven times he stuck that bread knife into her. They found him covered in her blood. Well, there was no getting out of that one.'

'But now that he has been murdered, aren't you curious what happened to him?'

It was the wrong question. Ditte remembered her threat again and held the spade aloft. Jensen didn't fancy calling her bluff.

'Couldn't give a fuck. Hope he burns in hell. Now scarper, or I'll knock out those pretty little teeth of yours.'

Jensen walked to the car, seeing Gustav emerge from one of the hobbit houses carrying a silver-foil parcel. An old man with a grey beard was waving him goodbye. Then the man spotted Jensen looking at him and shut his door hastily.

'What's that?'

'Home-made vanilla cookies. Told you I can be cute.'

'What did you find out?'

Gustav opened the foil parcel and began to stuff his face. Jensen's mouth watered at the Christmassy smell of the cookies.

'Kurt said no one likes her. Moved in about five years ago. She was all right in the beginning, but now they just want to get rid of her. She's an alcoholic, he said, shouts at everyone, always lighting fires, leaves rubbish all over the place. The kids are frightened of her.'

'How did she find the money to buy a house here? Can't be cheap.'

'That's just it,' said Gustav, in between mouthfuls of vanilla cookie. 'Kurt says he's never seen her do any real work. Yet she's always got money for booze.'

'Anything else?'

Jensen snatched a cookie and popped it in her mouth before Gustav could protest. It was delicious, still warm from the oven.

'Only a lot of other stuff about the council and taxes that I wasn't really paying attention to. Can we go now? Please, please can we go back to Copenhagen?'

41

By the time they drove off the ferry at Odden and joined a car-
avan of cars heading for the capital, it was dark and sleety. She
rang Henrik on the hands-free. Gustav was looking out of the
window at the passing summer houses, nodding to his music
and drawing faces on the steamed-up glass.

'What do you want?' Henrik said.

'Nice.'

'I'm on my way to the gym. You've got three minutes.'

Every day without fail Henrik trained for an hour. Work,
training, football. Those were the interests in his life, and he
had had years to perfect them.

'Charming lady, Ditte Mørk.'

'Told you she was a loon; didn't think you'd be stupid enough
to actually go and see her.'

Jensen overtook a car whose driver appeared to be accelerating in a bid to out-race her. Did people do that in England,
or was this a peculiarly Danish thing? A spin-off from the

Scandinavian Law of Jante, condemning anyone who tried to stand out from the crowd? *Don't think your car is faster than ours.*

'So that's it then – a dead end,' said Jensen.

'Not quite.'

'What?'

'We tracked Ditte Mørk's movements. Turns out she was in Copenhagen the night Casper died.'

'Or shall we call just him Thomas?'

Henrik fell silent for a moment. When he spoke again, it was in his policeman's voice.

'How do you know that?'

'I have my sources.'

'It's illegal to access confidential police records.'

'Don't worry, I won't tell anyone. I've been taken off the story, remember? So you think Ditte had something to do with it?'

'Don't know.'

Jensen remembered the marks on Thomas's arm, a sign that he was handled roughly by someone before he died. Ditte Mørk was certainly angry enough to have done it.

'Could she have been prescribed tranquillisers at any point, like the benzos Thomas had taken? Or got hold of them somehow?'

'It's possible. We're checking it out.'

'But why would Ditte have looked up Thomas in Copenhagen, and how would she even have known where to find him?'

'If we had his mobile phone, or his laptop, we might have been able to tell you. As it is, we've got no idea who he was in contact with before he died.'

'What about the dealer, the one all the kids up at Skovhøj were buying from?'

'What of him?'

'What's his name?'

162

'I'm not going to tell you that, because then you'll go and see him.'

'Never mind, I'll find out myself. If he supplied the drug Thomas took before he died, he might know something, or maybe he's involved somehow.'

'You're incredibly annoying, you know that, Jensen? Anyway, time's up – you are de-prioritised.'

'Suit yourself.'

'But if I find you have been interfering with our enquiries, I will have no choice but to arrest you.'

'I'll look forward to it. Don't forget the handcuffs.'

When the call was over, she felt Gustav's eyes on her. He had taken his headphones off and was smirking.

'What?' she said.

'Was that your boyfriend?'

'No.'

'Sounded like it.'

'Well he isn't.' She hit the accelerator. Now she too was anxious to get back to Copenhagen. 'You couldn't be further from the truth, Gustav.'

42

Thursday 19:11

Starving and miserably cold, they headed straight for the newspaper's canteen to regroup and forage from the vending machine. To Gustav's joy, they ended up with Mars bars, crisps and Cokes. If they didn't improve their diet soon, they would both end up with scurvy.

As they went to sit down, they spotted Frank, on his own with a whole booth to himself, tucking into a large slice of Othello layer cake and leafing through *Dagbladet*. It was deadline time, and everyone was busy producing tomorrow's edition.

Everyone but Frank.

'What's this, Frank, haven't you got work to do?'

'Nah,' he said, turning a page. 'The circus has moved on.'

'What do you mean?'

He looked at Jensen over the rim of his reading glasses. 'Haven't you heard? They just called a general election. It will be well-nigh impossible to get anything in the paper for the foreseeable. And anyway, there's been no development in the investigation, since it turned out that the second victim was just a troubled Danish kid who ran off from an institution.'

'So, it's less of a story, because there is no serial killer after all, going around and finishing off Eastern European beggars?'

'I didn't say that, and there might still be a serial killer. The kid could easily have passed for a migrant if the murderer was out to make some sort of point, but the police now have to broaden their investigation.'

Frank was right. Jensen reminded herself that Thomas had been an elective mute and thus unlikely to stop any would-be racist killer.

'Fact is, people are sleeping rough in our streets, and two have died. It's like Margrethe puts it: this has become a nasty little country,' she said.

'Well, now the nasty little country is having an election, so people can decide for themselves what they want to make of it.'

Everyone had known that the election was coming, but it had been expected much later, May at the earliest. As far as Jensen was concerned, it was good news. Margrethe would be preoccupied for weeks. No one would be chasing her for copy for a good while.

Frank saw the relief on her face and mistook it for glee.

'What are you looking so smug about?' he said, frowning. 'What are you two up to?'

Gustav opened his mouth to speak, but Jensen grabbed his arm hard.

'We've been looking into the story Margrethe got tipped off about.'

Frank laughed, his mouth full of cream cake. 'Well, good luck getting that crock of shit into the paper before Easter.'

He looked up, taking in the two of them. There were flecks of marzipan and droplets of whipped cream in his beard.

'How about you come and learn from a real journalist who has actually been to school?' he said to Gustav, pointing at Jensen with his fork. 'This one's past her best.'

'Really?' said Gustav, innocently. 'That's not what my aunt told me.'

'No?'

'No, my aunt said she may be the best reporter this newspaper has ever had.'

Jensen looked at Gustav, astonished.

'She said that?'

Frank clasped his hands to his heart. 'Aw, isn't that nice.'

Jensen dragged Gustav away with her, before one of them said something they were going to regret. Frank's laughter followed them all the way up the stairwell to her office.

43

Thursday 21:31

Jensen felt self-conscious in her ripped black jeans and biker boots, perched on the slippery leather bar stool. She kept looking at the entrance, trying to ignore the group of inebriated Swedish businessmen doing their best to attract her attention.

It was Esben who had insisted on them meeting at the hotel d'Angleterre. Decked in velvet, glass and gold, the champagne bar was practically his second living room. He rarely bothered going anywhere else.

The Swedes fell quiet as Esben made his way through the room, his teeth brilliant white against his suntanned skin. She thought again of how devastatingly handsome he was in his well-cut blue suit and white shirt – Savile Row, no less. His trips to London to refresh his wardrobe were an annual pilgrimage; many times they had celebrated his purchases at Claridge's afterwards. And on all those occasions Esben had tried to talk her back to his room.

'Sorry I am late,' he said, kissing her on both cheeks, his aftershave enveloping her in the scents of a Mediterranean spring.

Real life, including something as trivial as winter, never

appeared to leave any mark on Esben, who always looked and smelled as though he had just risen from a warm, fragrant bath. Nor did he ever remark on how scruffy she looked by comparison. It was one of the many reasons why she loved him. For a man so apparently vain and shallow, he was surprisingly blind to how others dressed.

'Over here,' he said to the bartender. 'Louis Roederer. Two glasses.'

'What's this for?' she said, as the bartender sprang into action.

'For the election, of course. I am heading back home to Aalborg on Saturday to begin campaigning.'

'You don't actually think you lot are going to win again, do you?'

'Win? We're going to walk it.'

The bartender popped the cork and began filling their glasses with a ridiculously elaborate manoeuvre. Esben winked at her.

'Skål,' he said, touching his glass to hers.

'I admire your confidence. Margrethe thinks you and the rest of the government parties are finished. She says she'll personally be clapping you out on the steps of Christiansborg the day after the election.'

Esben laughed. People turned to look, a few of the women letting their eyes linger on him, then flicking onto Jensen, obviously trying and failing to make sense of the two of them together.

'Good old Margrethe. Never gives up on her ideals, does she? But she is backing the wrong horse. The Social Democrats are done for.'

'She said the pendulum is swinging against you. The Magstræde case was the last straw. People have had enough of austerity.'

'Nah,' Esben said, draining his glass and reaching out for a refill. 'That won't fly. Just wait and see. So, how are you enjoying Hornbæk?'

He didn't like talking politics outside of work, got bored with it quickly. Fine by her.

'Hornbæk is great, if you're into summer-house neighbour-hoods off season. No seriously, thank you Esben. Very kind of you.'

'I'd let you have our place in Klampenborg, now that I am going to be away for a while, except Ulla won't be going back to Aalborg with me. She hates it up there.'

'I'm all right as I am.'

'I know you are. How's the story coming along? The one you're not working on?'

'Turns out the boy was high on drugs, but no one knows it yet.'

'What was he doing in Magstræde that night?'

'No idea.'

'Well, make sure you find out.'

'Do you know they collected thousands of signatures to keep Skovhøj open? The manager is convinced the boy wouldn't have taken off if it hadn't been for the staff cutbacks they've endured in the past few years.'

'Bollocks – he was a free agent. If they'd had him under observation twenty-four seven, they still couldn't have prevented him from going.'

'Maybe not. But he might not have wanted to leave.'

'Let me tell you, Jensen, if that home had been clad in marble and the bathroom taps made of gold, with ten staff per resident, the lad would still have left. This has nothing to do with money.'

'Maybe not.'

'All in all, his was quite a convenient death, wouldn't you say?'

'What do you mean?'

'It couldn't have been more helpful to those wanting the place to stay open, or to get more budget for social services.'

'What, you think someone at the home might have some-thing to do with what happened to Thomas?'

'I don't think anything,' said Esben, holding up his hands in a gesture of innocence. 'I am just saying that it's quite the coincidence, if you believe in that kind of thing.'

Jensen was feeling the effects of the champagne and told herself, *No more*. Esben, by contrast, looked like he was just getting started.

'I should get going,' she said, finishing her drink. 'Long way to Hornbæk.'

'Must you?' said Esben, refilling her glass. 'I promised to take Ulla out for dinner tonight. I was hoping I'd have an important last-minute meeting to attend. I have a room here; you could be at work in five minutes in the morning.'

He looked at her meaningfully, and she thought how easy it would be. Her and Esben, no ties, no promises, but she also knew he would tire of her, as he did of everyone eventually.

'I won't touch you,' he said, brushing a strand of hair from her face. 'Unless you want me to?'

'Sorry, I've got work in the morning. I am heading back over to Magstræde to talk some more to the residents. One of them is bound to have seen something,' she said, getting down from the bar stool and pecking Esben on the cheek, whispering in his ear:

'Call your wife and say you'll meet her in ten minutes. I reckon she deserves it.'

44

Magstræde was sunny but freezing, a tunnel of sharp wind whipping through the centre of town. A few tourists huddled near the southern entrance to the street, taking photos. She spoiled their shots, walking directly in front of their outstretched mobiles.

Gustav had taken the train back out to Roskilde. He reckoned a few more games of GTA with Fie and she would tell him where the dealer who supplied the Skovhøj kids was hanging out. Jensen had let him to go on his own, conscious that Karina and Tobias wouldn't be letting her anywhere near Fie now, not after the last time. And she and Gustav needed the dealer's name, or they wouldn't get much further.

'But that's all you're doing,' she had told him. 'As soon as you have the details, I want you straight back here, so we can work out what to do next.'

Gustav had agreed, reluctantly. She had made him swear on it.

The lights were on at CG Dentistry. She rang the bell and waved at the camera, leaning against the door with one shoulder

171

as Malene buzzed her in. There was no awkward preamble this time. She had called ahead and was expected.

The clinic was warm and fragrant, like a bathroom in a luxury hotel. There was a tape on, birdsong and raindrops. The copper reception desk was shining with polish, reflecting the winter sunlight across the sanded oak floors. Malene greeted her from behind the desk and pointed to one of the waiting-room chairs.

'Do take a seat.'

Jensen remained standing,

Malene blinked at her. She had perfect teeth, perfect skin and perfect hair scraped back into a ponytail as straight as a whip. She was wearing a white uniform this time.

'You and Grønfeldt,' said Jensen. 'Are you . . .?'

Malene pointed to the ceiling, smiling. 'Married. We live upstairs.'

'I see,' said Jensen, looking at a framed article from an in-flight magazine, in which Grønfeldt was pictured seated with Malene standing behind him, one hand on his shoulder.

'Tell me,' said Malene. 'There was a boy here on Monday, said he was working on a school project about Magstræde that *Dagbladet* is going to print. Know anything about that?'

Gustav. He must have been trying hard to impress.

'Gustav Skov?'

'Do you know him?'

Jensen decided not to try and explain how she had ended up with a teenager in tow.

'You could say that. He is my editor-in-chief's nephew.'

'Nice boy. Very curious, kept asking about the murder. Anyway, I thought of something he might be interested in. Tried to call him a few times, but so far no luck.'

'Oh?'

'Ah, Jensen, good to see you again,' said Grønfeldt loudly, emerging from his office. 'Coffee?'

They left Malene to man the phones. Jensen wondered what she had been about to say.

In his office, Grønfeldt closed the door and turned towards an expensive-looking coffee maker. He began by grinding the beans, then tamped the ground coffee into silver scoops. He placed two cups under silver taps, working with tight, precise movements.

There was a desk at one end of the room, sideways on to the window, no family pictures, no objects or artefacts of any kind on the black lacquered surface. The shelves behind the desk were stacked with pyramids of black boxes with the white CG logo. To one side was a dental chair in black leather, overlaid with white paper.

'Have a seat,' said Grønfeldt, with his back to her.

Jensen knew he meant the armchair in front of the desk. He wanted to sit on opposite her, the big man in his office. She chose the dental chair. Her boots made a dirty mark across the tissue paper.

If Grønfeldt was surprised to see her there, lying back, her hands folded across her belt buckle, the man had a remarkably good poker face. He sat down on his dentist's stool and passed her a tiny gold cup of bitter espresso with a foamy layer of milk. Then he set down his own cup, held up a mirror to her face, leaning in to add his reflection to hers. This was obviously his sales routine. Force clients into confronting their dislikes from the off.

'You have great teeth,' he says. 'That's down to luck. We could close the gap between your front incisors,' he said, touching Jensen's lips and turning her face towards the light.

'Good, full lips.'

She stared into his eyes. They were deep brown, inscrutable, steady, ignoring her, absorbed by professional interest.

'You look tired,' he said. 'Botox would do wonders for you, and with that skin you only need very little. It would take ten years off you.'

173

'You promised me a tour of the place,' she said.

He made a sweeping motion with his hands. 'This is it,' he said. 'You've seen it now. The inner sanctum. There's a storage room at the back, a toilet and a kitchen. Would you like to see those as well?'

She smiled. 'So, this is where you treat your patients?'

'Clients. No one here is ill, though I do make them feel better.'

He paused for Jensen's reaction.

She said nothing.

'You'd be prettier if I sorted out that gap between your teeth.'

'But a lot less like me.'

'Even more like you, and I would give you a discount.'

'Tell me again,' she said. 'About the boy. When you saw him. What you saw.'

Grønfeldt reached for his coffee cup, drained it, swallowed, all the while keeping his eyes on her.

'I already told you everything, the same as I told the police. Malene saw him sitting there in the evening. I didn't see anything. It snowed heavily all night. I only found out what had happened when the ambulance arrived the next morning.'

'He had a sign, with the word *skyldig* on it.'

Jensen watched Grønfeldt's face closely, but there was no inkling of surprise.

'You knew?'

He didn't blink.

'I must have been asked about it before.'

'Any idea what the sign could have meant?'

He shook his head. 'None whatsoever.'

There was a knock; Malene stuck her head round the door. Her eyes widened as she clocked the two of them, Jensen lying in the dental chair, Grønfeldt by her side, wide-legged on his stool. Then she collected herself and smiled.

'Your eleven o'clock is here, Christian.'

Jensen got up. 'Do you mind if I just . . .?'

Not waiting for an answer, she walked over to Grønfeldt's desk, sat down in his swivel chair and looked out of the window at Magstræde. On the other side of the street, directly below, she saw the blackened roses and the teddy bear wrapped in the Danish flag. Someone had put a storm lamp beside them with a candle that had burned itself out. It looked like one of the lamps from the pizza restaurant. The waitress, perhaps?

Whatever his motive, Thomas had travelled to Copenhagen and sat down directly opposite Grønfeldt's place. Why there? Why not twenty metres further down the street?

Grønfeldt cleared his throat.

'Are we done here, Miss Jensen?'

45

Friday 11:32

The top floor of the newspaper was deserted when she got back, clutching a cup of strong, sweetened coffee handed to her by Liron without comment. Grønfeldt had been right, then: she was definitely looking exhausted if Liron reckoned she needed this amount of caffeine to keep her going. She went straight to Henning's office. His radio was on, a sombre jazz trumpet, and his anglepoise lamp was lit, but the man himself was out for the count, snoring gently with his chin resting on his chest. A half-smoked cigar sat on the edge of his ashtray. She leaned over the desk, tried to read upside down what was written in his old-fashioned joined-up handwriting on the cardboard folder in front of him. It was the name of a famous actress she remembered from TV in her childhood and whom she thought had died years ago. On the screen, Henning had written the first few lines of her obituary. Perhaps he had got nostalgic thinking about his long-lost youth. The room smelled of newsprint and old man.

'What do you want?' he said suddenly, startling her.

She decided to hand him the paper cup from Liron.

'I brought you coffee.'

He began to drink immediately, grunting with pleasure.

'Why are you still here?' he said, when he had finished, one eye open.

'Nothing,' she said.

'You want something. What is it?'

'All right, does the name "Grønfeldt" ring a bell?'

'What more than Grønfeldt?'

'Christian Grønfeldt. He is a dentist.'

'Why do you want to know?'

'He owns the building across the street from where I found the murdered boy last week.'

Henning slurped his coffee.

'You're clutching at straws, young lady,' he mumbled.

The radio played a jingle. A newsreader announced the results of a poll predicting a landslide election victory for the opposition. She thought of Esben and his cockiness, which now felt foolish and misplaced.

After a while, she realised Henning had dozed off again. She prised the almost empty cup from his hand and placed it on the desk, so it wouldn't dribble down his shirt. Then she walked along the corridor to her own office, which was shadowy and silent and cold.

She was kicking herself for not having asked Malene what she wanted to tell Gustav, but Malene had ushered her out quickly, past the smart-looking middle-aged man waiting to be seen by Grønfeldt, and the moment had never arisen.

She checked her phone and found a message from Gustav.

Got the info on the dealer.

She quickly typed her reply.

Don't do anything. Come back to the office and we'll discuss.

Gustav's side of the partition was messy, with empty Coke bottles and sweet wrappers littering the desk. She stared for a long time at the pinned-up drawing of Magstræde with all the

177

names of the people who lived or worked there. There were only a couple left now that he hadn't crossed out. Going door to door was unlikely to yield much more information. In the half-light their display looked pathetic, almost childish. They had nothing.

After half an hour, there was a shuffling sound in the corridor: Henning stood in her doorway with the paper cup crumbled in his veined hand.

'Grønfeldt, you said?'

'Yes.'

He looked at the ceiling. 'Anton Grønfeldt, heart surgeon at Riget. Died about ten years ago. But Christian Grønfeldt, his son, is still alive. Something of a ladies' man. Dentist, with a private practice in Magstræde.'

'That's the one.'

'It was a dreadful business.'

The palms of Jensen's hands tingled.

'What was?'

He handed her a thick folder with 'Christian Grønfeldt' written on it in snarly blue ink.

'His girlfriend was killed, in their kitchen, by her fifteen-year-old son. They called it the Langelandsvej Murder.'

46

'Jungersen. What is it?'

Henrik fumbled with his watch in the darkness of his bed-room. Beside him, his wife pulled the duvet over her head and slept on. Years of being married to a policeman had desensitised her. To most things, regrettably.

Mark's voice: 'We have another one, boss.'

'Another what?'

'Body.'

Pause.

Henrik sat up, put his feet on the floor and grimaced at the icy floorboards. 'Mark, for the love of God, speak!'

'OK. White female. No ID, no belongings. Between twenty-five and thirty years of age. Addict. Stabbed. Sometime between midnight and two a.m. Found in Badstuestræde by passers-by.'

'Fuck.'

He dressed quickly without his wife stirring once. He needed a coffee badly, but there wasn't time to make one and the Baresso on Vesterbrogade, where they knew him by his first name and made his coffee without him having to open

179

his mouth (single-shot tall latte, not too hot), wouldn't be open yet.

'Fuck, fuck, fuck,' he said, as he drove through the slushy streets towards the centre of town.

Two murders might be explained away, but a third would make it into a definite serial killing, at least in the eyes of the press. Someone was going after rough sleepers.

He had been through it with Mark and Lisbeth over and over again. There was no connection whatsoever between the first victim and Thomas Mørk, which suggested they had been picked at random.

By whom? Why?

Was it, as Mark suggested, some right-wing moron out to make a point? In Henrik's experience, fundamentalist crack-pots were into grander gestures and rarely worried about detection. Yet whoever their perpetrator was had gone to the trouble of removing the victims' belongings and avoiding being caught by cameras or seen by witnesses. This in itself required a certain amount of planning beyond the wits of the average lunatic.

He spotted the blue lights a few streets away. Someone with half a brain had blocked off the street at both ends and kept the ever-curious public from entering. Where did they spring from, these nocturnal voyeurs, who were nowhere to be seen when the crimes themselves were committed?

Mark approached him at a trot, a worried expression in his eyes.

'Who found the body?' said Henrik.

Mark pointed to a couple of hooded lads huddled by a police car. Henrik sidled over, poking out his chest, conscious that, no matter how hard he trained, these days it required a greater effort for him to be intimidating.

'Right, who's first?' he said.

One of the boys spoke with the exaggerated soberness of the

extremely drunk. 'We saw the dog. It was kind of wandering about, so we followed it.'

The other boy was by far the worse for wear of the two. He looked very close to vomiting. Years of late-night street service had taught Henrik the signs. He took a step back.

'And?'

'That's when we saw her. She was kind of slumped over. We thought she was asleep but, when we touched her, she fell onto her side and her eyes were fucking open.'

At that moment, his mate heaved and brought up his last meal, laced with lager and bile. Despite his precaution, Henrik felt a splash hit his engineer's boots.

The talking boy began to laugh hysterically. Henrik looked slowly down at his boots and back up at the boy with his best death stare.

The boy stopped laughing.

Henrik turned to Mark. 'Have these two imbeciles taken down to the station and interviewed. Thoroughly.'

There was never anything glamorous about a murder scene, but this one was about as miserable as they came. The woman was lying as she had been found, on her back, staring blankly into the sky. It was impossible to tell her age. She had the emaciated, rough and desperate features of an addict, but could well be young. Her perch, a huddle of blankets and plastic bags, stank of piss and the blood that had spilled from her chest.

'Where's the dog?' said Henrik.

'Here. Why, do you want to interview it?' said one of the scene-of-crime officers, a woman named Lotte, whom he had had a fling with some time ago. Clearly, in her mind this gave her licence to be sarcastic at every opportunity.

'What will happen to it?'

She shrugged. 'It'll be put down, I suppose.'

The dog, some sort of bulldog cross, with a dirty red scarf round its neck was in a sorry state, wheezing loudly on its little bowed legs. It was gazing up at him with its big brown eyes. He swore under his breath.

'Give it to me.'

Lotte looked bemused but she was only too glad to hand him the lead.

'Found anything?' he asked her, changing the subject.

'Not yet,' she said.

'Any CCTV?' he asked Mark.

'Nothing obvious, but we're checking, boss.'

'Witnesses?'

Mark shook his head. 'We'll issue the usual appeal, of course.'

Like that was going to help. Henrik looked up and down the street. As with the other two, it was easy to see why the woman had chosen her spot, with the wide shop doorway providing shelter from the elements, if no warmth whatsoever. The thin layer of newspapers she had spread on the concrete step would have done her little good.

'Isn't the Bird's Nest near here somewhere?'

'The homeless shelter? Yes, not far.'

'Find out if she went there. They might know her. Then try all the other shelters, like last time.'

'Yes, boss.'

'This will all go mental in the morning. Monsen will want a press conference. With the election coming, this will be front-page news, and our backsides will be on fire till we find out who did it. Let's see how far we can get before all that happens.'

He walked across to his car with the dog waddling along by his side.

Mark ran after him.

'Where are you going, boss?'

'Back to the station to think. On my own.'

47

Saturday 02:51

Jensen was staring at her phone, listening to the waves breaking on Hornbæk beach. There had been no word from Gustav since Friday morning, and he hadn't turned up at the office. Four times she had rung him, but he wasn't picking up, nor replying to her increasingly anxious text messages.

She pictured Margrethe's Østerbro flat: high-ceilinged rooms lined with bookshelves and abstract paintings, golden light spilling from table lamps between comfortable chairs. Gustav was probably slumped in one of them now, with his headphones on, vaping.

She told herself that he was a teenager, that his phone was out of battery, that he had simply forgotten about her and found something better to do. She would be seeing him on Monday in the office, with his size tens on the desk.

Gustav was only two years older than Thomas had been when he stabbed his mother.

Skyldig.

Now it made sense. The Magstræde sit-in had been Thomas's *mea culpa*. Grønfeldt must have known all along. Why hadn't he said anything?

She messaged Henrik: *Why didn't you tell me about Grønfeldt?*

She thought of Grønfeldt running out into the street, covered in his girlfriend's blood and screaming for help. In her imagination, he was wearing his dentist's whites and the blood was dripping cherry-red onto the snow.

Thomas must have been consumed by guilt and wanting to send a message to Grønfeldt. Had he tried to get in touch and been turned away? Had the two of them had an argument, and this was Thomas's way of saying he was sorry? Or was it a wider protest, pointed at Grønfeldt but aimed at the wider public, who would never allow him to be free of his crime, no matter how earnest his penance?

It was hard enough to think of the answers without also getting her head around how Thomas had found himself the victim of a stabbing on the first night he had ventured away from the safety of Skovhøj. Whichever way she turned it, it seemed implausible that the two were not connected.

Somewhere between these questions without end, sleep crept up on her, ushered in by the sound of the waves crashing relentlessly against the beach.

48

When she woke up it was still dark outside, and she knew that there was someone else in the summer house. She sat up in bed, listening with her blood rushing in her ears.

Silence.

Had she dreamed it?

No.

She heard footsteps, a stumble, just outside the door to her room. Her fist closed round the bedside lamp, the only weapon she could think of. She unplugged it and held it aloft like a club.

Esben's house was surrounded by other summer houses, all of them empty, a smorgasbord of flat-screen TVs. Whoever had broken in could not have failed to see Yasmine's red Beetle parked outside; they would know there was someone in the house, but it wasn't stopping them. Either they didn't care, or it was her they were after.

Could it be Gustav? She had told him where she was staying. That he could sleep at hers, if things got tricky with Margrethe. Maybe he had been travelling and lost signal on his phone?

'Gustav?'

No answer.

'Anyone there?'

She got out of bed and stood in the pitch black, holding the lamp above her head. The door opened and she struck, shattering the lamp on contact. She had to move out of the way to avoid the intruder falling on top of her.

When, finally, she managed to find the light switch, she was staring at a scene she could not at first make sense of. A man was slumped on the floor, blood on his face and down the front of his pink shirt. The room stank of alcohol and expensive aftershave.

'Esben? Oh my God, are you all right?'

She managed to hoist him up into a seated position.

'Jesus, Jensen, that's some punch you've got,' he moaned, touching his forehead.

Then he laughed, blood on his perfect white teeth.

'What the hell are you doing here? Please tell me you didn't drive.'

He held up a finger, tried and failed to look serious. 'Never drink and drive. Aziz took me.'

'Aziz?'

'Guy who drives for me. She threw me out, Jensen. Read a message on my phone from some woman I have nothing to do with.'

'Nothing?'

'Nothing except this one time, ages ago. Won't stop texting me. Can't remember much about her, except she had these huge—'

'Stop. Too much information. Let's get you to A & E.'

'No hospital,' he shouted, grabbing her by the wrist with surprising strength. 'No publicity.'

So he sat on her bed while she knelt in front of him and washed off the blood, which turned out to come from a small cut on his forehead. She found a plaster in the cabin's ancient first-aid kit, gave him paracetamol and took off his bloodied shirt, all the while trying to avoid his piercing eyes. When she was done, he used her moment's hesitation to reach behind her and pull her towards him.

'Jensen,' he whispered. 'That is the sexiest nightgown I have ever seen. Let me just . . .'

And then his mouth was on hers and he tasted of cigarettes and blood. He was pulling down her shoulder straps. It was a while before she could speak again.

'This is a really bad idea.'

'No, it's an excellent idea,' he mumbled, kissing her breasts and reaching down between her legs.

She pushed him back on the bed and stood upright, though in that moment she wanted to do the opposite. Just once, to know what he felt like.

'Get some sleep, Esben. You're going to need it if you are to stand any chance in the election.'

She ignored his pleading. Eventually, he lay back on the bed and nodded off, snoring noisily. Even when drunk, he was handsome.

The rest of the night she didn't sleep at all for worry about Gustav.

Just after 6 a.m. there was a reply from Henrik: *Grønfeldt is not the story. Just ask that boy assistant of yours.*

49

Saturday 11:04

When Jensen turned up at the newspaper that morning, having waited for Aziz to arrive to sort out Esben, she knew something was very wrong. It was the way Markus, back on his perch behind the reception desk, stared at her as if she had come to work naked. She looked at him questioningly, but he just pointed to his earpiece, miming that he was on the phone. She was pretty sure it was a lie.

Yasmine intercepted her on the stairs. Unusually for her, she looked flustered.

'Margrethe wants to see you right now.'

'Can I take my coat off first, dump my stuff upstairs?'

Yasmine shook her head. 'Not if you value your life.'

Jensen had witnessed Margrethe's anger on many occasions. She had watched her rip people apart, leaving the carcase out as a warning to others, but she had never seen her frightened.

'What the hell have you done?' said Margrethe.

Yasmine made herself scarce, closing the door behind her. The newspaper was always quieter on Saturdays, but now no sound whatsoever could be heard, which meant everyone on the floor was straining to hear what was going on in Margrethe's office.

'What is it?' Jensen said, but she already knew. 'Don't tell me something has happened to Gustav.'

Margrethe was shaking.

'Where is he? Is he upstairs? Let me go and see him.'

She turned towards the door, but Margrethe raised her voice, stopping her.

'He is at Riget. Concussion, three fractured ribs, lost a front tooth. Found unconscious in the street by a member of the public last night.'

Jensen stared at her, trying to take in what she was saying. 'What?'

'You heard me.'

'I tried to call him, several times. I was worried.'

'Not worried enough to call me, or the police.'

'I knew you wouldn't approve.'

'Of what? You and Gustav working on the Magstræde murder behind my back, behind Frank's, and coming up with some cock-and-bull story about investigating the tip-off I gave you? Or you sending a seventeen-year-old to do your dirty work?'

'Did he say that?'

'Gustav hasn't said anything; he has been under heavy sedation since they took him to hospital. But they found a piece of paper on him with the details of a known drug dealer. The police are out looking for the scumbag as we speak.'

'He was meant to come straight back here, not go off investigating on his own. I told him that.'

'And I thought you were smarter than the rest, smart enough to have worked out by now that Gustav never listens to anybody.'

'I'm sorry.'

'You abused my trust. And I was dumb enough to let you. Though everyone kept telling me that you were a freeloader.

189

You practically had that Magstræde story served to you on a silver plate, but you couldn't do it. I hand-fed you another story, but you did fuck all about it, and instead you messed around and put people's lives in danger.'

'I'm sorry.'

'Go upstairs, now, and clear your desk. Do what you want, head back to London, as long as I never see your face again.'

50

Saturday 11:16

Jensen found Frank in her office, staring open-mouthed at the display she and Gustav had put together on the noticeboard. He was taking pictures with his phone.

'What are you doing here, Frank?'

He didn't even attempt to make a funny remark.

'You said you were glad Margrethe had put me on the story, and then you continued to work on it behind my back?'

'I just wanted to get at the truth, not turn Thomas into some sort of political campaigning fodder. He was an individual, with a story that deserved to be told.'

'And you thought only you could do that?'

Jensen looked at her feet.

'I covered the Langelandsvej Murder back in the day. You didn't tell me Casper was Thomas.'

'I was going to.'

'I know you and I aren't exactly on each other's Christmas-card list, but I thought that at least we were colleagues.'

'Not any more, if it makes you feel better. Margrethe sacked me. I am here to pack my things.'

'You know what's really tragic about all of this?'

'What?'

'None of it has anything to do with the Thomas Mørk case. Another homeless person was stabbed last night, a woman. There is some sort of crazy serial killer out there. Thomas was just unlucky enough to get caught up in it. You're way out of your depth, and now Margrethe's nephew has paid the price.'

When he had left her office, Jensen sat for a long time and gazed into mid-air and wondered how everything had gone so wrong so fast. If she hadn't cycled through Magstræde that Tuesday morning, she might still have been flying under Margrethe's radar, and Gustav would have been in one piece.

Why hadn't Henrik told her about the latest murder? What had happened to the two of them?

She took her unused notepad, unpinned the items on the noticeboard and folded them carefully before putting them into her bag. Then she looked at the thick folder that Henning had given her, and added that too, along with her work laptop, which she told herself she was borrowing until she could get herself a new one.

The last thing she did before leaving was to look out at the rooftops of Copenhagen, red and gold in the wintery murk. Her head felt heavy and empty.

51

When he saw her, Liron did something he had never done before. He reached into the front seat of his mini-van and pulled out a tiny folding chair. He pushed her into the seat and covered her legs with a woollen blanket. Then he made her a chai latte, heady with cinnamon, ginger and cardamom, and left her to breathe in the fragrant steam while he took care of his other customers, none of whom looked brainless enough to have got themselves sacked from their jobs.

She checked the news on her phone. Impossible to miss the story under the bright yellow 'BREAKING' banner. The election campaign had been momentarily forgotten in favour of grainy photos of police tape and emergency vehicles, which did little to hide the absence of any actual information on the third stabbing. In the vacuum, the usual 'experts' had rushed in, pointing fingers at the government for allowing the vulnerable to be picked off in the street one by one. The government had responded with new emergency shelters and round-the-clock street patrols across the capital.

'These killings are going to stop right now,' said the prime minister on the steps of Christiansborg, child-sized, flanked by the chests of her minders.

'I messed up,' said Jensen when Liron had finished the lunchtime rush. 'No job, no place to live, and a teenager is in hospital because of me.'

'Not the boy I met, your apprentice? He was so fucking nice. I gave him drinks on the house. Liron fucking never gives away coffee for free. Never ever.'

He made her tell him everything, from when she first discovered the body in Magstræde to her conversation with Margrethe. He was surprisingly gentle.

'Tell Uncle Liron. What do you want to do now?'

'I want to go to Riget to see Gustav, make sure he is OK, but I don't even know where he is.'

'Wait,' Liron said, getting his phone out. 'What's his full name? '

'Gustav Skov.'

'One of my customers works there. I am asking her.'

'Do you keep phone numbers for all your regulars?'

She couldn't recall ever giving him hers. Somehow that had never felt like the right thing to do.

He smiled, showing a mouthful of crooked teeth and gold fillings. 'This one's special.'

Ten minutes later, by the time she had finished her tea, his phone pinged.

'Gustav Skov? Admitted last night?'

Jensen nodded.

A forwarded message with Gustav's ward and room number lit up her phone.

'Told you, just ask your Uncle Liron.'

52

Saturday 13:04

Riget. The kingdom within the kingdom, a world unto its own. Parking her bike by the hospital, she saw a patient in a white hospital gown with a blanket over his legs being wheeled through the sliding doors by a younger man who could be his son. The patient got out a cigarette and lit up. She supposed you could get to a point in life when smoking could no longer be the thing that killed you.

No one stopped her as she walked through the sliding doors to the main high-rise block. She passed doctors in green surgical scrubs, riding on scooters, their white coats fanning out behind them. Bored-looking cleaners pushed their trolleys down the corridors, while patients in slippers and bathrobes took a break from their beds and the interminable waiting for one of two options: discharge or death. The hospital, a brutalist castle of a thousand rooms, surrounded them indifferently. Life went on.

In the rattling stainless-steel lift, she wished Henrik was standing behind her again, like he had done in the reception at the Forensic Institute, radiating his warmth onto her back. This

195

time she would have turned. It would have been like being back in the ambassador's lift in London all those years ago.

She quickly berated herself for these thoughts. How could she love a man who was so flawed, so set in his ways, so unreconstructed? How could the two of them, about as alike as fire and water, have connected so deeply that she was missing him now, of all days?

The corridor smelled of rye bread and linoleum, like school. A man in a hospital gown with a drip by his side was sitting on a sofa watching a British detective series with subtitles. He didn't look up as Jensen headed for Gustav's ward. She spotted his room immediately, but waited for a couple of nurses to pass before going in. Visiting hours weren't until later and she didn't want to be turned away after getting this far.

For once, she was in luck. Gustav was alone, sleeping. Under the light blue hospital duvet, he looked tiny. There were scratches on his boyish hands. She felt a surge of affection for him on realising that he must have fought back. There was plastic tubing connecting a cannula in his hand to a drip. His face was a purple, swollen mess. Someone had swept back his long fringe and fixed it with a slide. Gustav would have hated it.

'I am so sorry,' she said to his vacant face. 'I should never have let you go on your own.'

She sat on the wipe-clean plastic chair by his side and rested her forehead on his duvet.

Sometime later the door opened. If it was Margrethe, Jensen wouldn't be leaving the room alive.

'You must be Gustav's mother.'

An older nurse, bald with a face that showed he had been around the block a few times, touched her gently on the shoulder. He took her silence as an affirmation, and she didn't bother to correct him. It might as well be her. After all, Gustav's own mother was dead, and Margrethe was hardly the mothering type.

196

'I am Martin,' he said. 'I am looking after your son today.'

His handshake was warm and firm. He was wearing white clogs, white trousers and a blue, short-sleeved tunic. There was a tattoo of a snake on his wrist.

'He was lucky,' he said, checking the drip and fitting the blood pressure collar round Gustav's arm.

'Lucky?' Jensen looked at Gustav's face; it was the colour of raw steak.

'Whoever did it used some kind of bat, but it's the kicking that usually does it. Once you've hit the floor, you don't stand much of a chance if someone goes for your head. I am guessing he must have managed to stay standing for most of it. Tough kid.'

Jensen wiped a tear from her face, while Martin noted Gustav's blood pressure on a clipboard at the foot of the bed. He pointed to Gustav's headphones on the nightstand, smiling. 'He was found still clinging on to those. I guess they must be important to him?'

She nodded. How to begin explaining Gustav to strangers.

'He'll be OK,' said Martin, touching her shoulder.

After he had left the room, she sat immobile for a long time, with the familiar sensation of not really being there. She was the chair, an inanimate object and, outside, Copenhagen went about its business as though nothing had happened.

The room was stifling, and after a while she dozed off again, her sleepless night catching up with her.

When she woke up, she was looking into Henrik's angry red face. He gestured at her to follow him outside into the corridor, which she did once she had checked on Gustav.

'What are you doing here?' he said, broad and tall in his leather jacket with his hands on his hips. 'Haven't you done enough damage?'

He looked like he hadn't slept in days.

'You said I should ask my assistant.'

197

'I didn't mean literally!'

'Henrik, I told him to go to the office immediately after returning from Roskilde. You've got to believe me. If you'd told me the name of the dealer when I asked you, it wouldn't have happened.'

'You should have known better, Jensen. I told you we were handling it.'

'Well, you weren't, were you? If you'd arrested the guy before, Gustav wouldn't be lying in there.'

'We were about to. Then boy scout here wades in, and our man panics and disappears.'

'Did he kill Thomas? And the other two?'

'We don't know. We're doing some DNA tests. Plenty of tissue under the nails of your apprentice in there. He will have done some damage. David's team are comparing it to samples found on Thomas and the other two victims.'

'There were samples found on Thomas?'

'Don't get too excited. Most of us walk around with foreign fibres and dead skin cells on our persons. It might not mean anything. What we do know is that Thomas owed the dealer money, or so people claim. And, like I said, we have witnesses saying the dealer was in Copenhagen the night he was killed.'

'Is he Danish?'

'Yep.'

The man I spoke to, who saw the first victim argue with someone on the night he was stabbed, said they were speaking in a foreign language.'

'Might have been English; doesn't mean it wasn't the dealer.'

'Any connection between Thomas and the other two?'

'We don't know who the first victim was yet, so I can't answer that.'

'And the third?'

Henrik shook his head.

'But at least we now know what Thomas was doing sitting in Magstræde with that sign pointed at Grønfeldt's clinic.'

'I've known since his body was identified.'

Grønfeldt. The sly bastard.

'Thanks a lot for telling me.'

'Confidential police business.'

'I went to see him on Friday. He could have said.'

'I guess he was embarrassed. He had had no contact with Thomas since the court case years ago and, all of a sudden, the boy rocks up in front of his windows. Anyway, I thought his mad aunt would have mentioned the connection.'

'I got no sense out of her.'

'Hard to do.'

'So, let me get this right. You think Thomas took off from Skovhøj with his sign, or picked it up on the way, or whatever, then went to sit with it in Grønfeldt's line of sight, and on the same night he is stabbed by his drug dealer? Who has already killed someone else, and has now struck again? So this is all about drugs?'

'Could be.'

'But if Thomas owed the dealer money, how did he lay his hands on the drugs he took?'

'Maybe they were given to him deliberately. Less resistance.'

'Bit of a coincidence that it should happen on the night of his grand gesture of contrition, isn't it?'

'Not really. He hardly ever left Skovhøj, and even when he did go out, he was always in the company of others. There was someone, one of the carers, who used to take him shopping from time to time.'

'Tobias.'

'Yep.'

The two of them sat down, side by side on the red plastic chairs in the corridor, looking at the nurses rushing between the rooms. A porter pushed a trolley past them. The patient was in a neck brace, his face covered in bandages, his heavily tattooed arm hanging down to one side. Jensen read the name 'Anja' in the motif and wondered who she was, and if she was still in the injured man's life or a legacy of happier times.

'You don't really know anything yet, do you?' she said.

'No, we're totally fucked.'

He turned to her. 'For the last time, Jensen, find another story'.

She thought about mentioning Deep Throat but decided against it. Henrik would ask for details, which she would be unable to give him.

'I would, if I still had a job.'

'What?'

'Margrethe chucked me out. I am done at *Dagbladet*.'

'Why?'

'Let's just say that she wasn't overjoyed with what happened to her nephew.'

'What are you going to do?'

'Ask me in a couple of days.'

She closed her eyes, wobbly with exhaustion.

'Are you busy?' she said, after a while.

'You mean aside from solving three murders and a serious case of GBH?'

'I was talking about right now this moment.'

'I need to ask your friend in there some questions, but according to the nurse it might be hours yet before he wakes up. Why?'

'How about giving me a lift back to Hornbæk?'

Henrik smiled broadly.

53

Saturday 14:26

They drove through the city, the energy between them throbbing and pulsing. Henrik had shoved aside footballs, sports bags, children's jackets, empty paper cups and fast-food packaging to fit her bicycle in the back. The dog sat in the passenger footwell, breathing noisily. It was looking up at Jensen with its doleful eyes, and she was stroking its head, trying to ignore the stench of it. Its fur left a greasy feel in the palm of her hand.

'My wife blankly refused to have him in the house another night. He was howling the place down, waking the kids,' Henrik said.

He had tried to bundle the creature into the back of the car, but the dog was having none of it, until Jensen had taken it into the passenger seat. It had no tag, no name.

'How did it end up with you?' she asked.

'They were going to put the old boy down,' he said, avoiding her gaze.

She decided not to press him any further, knowing that

201

Henrik detested talking about his feelings. The second time they had met in London, years ago, they had watched a runaway dog being hit by a car in Kensington. Henrik had leapt into the road and cradled it till it died, stopping traffic and roaring at anyone trying to come near him. Later that night, trembling with shock and covered in the dog's blood, he had told her that once, as a teenager, he had punched a man unconscious for kicking his dog in the street.

'The only thing I remember is being at the police station afterwards. An officer gave me a Coke and told me I was lucky that the man had declined to press charges. Then he took me to see the police dogs.'

Heading northward, they passed the slate-grey lakes, dotted with swans and surrounded by stately apartment buildings. One summer afternoon years ago, they had walked there together in the shade of the chestnut trees; he had kept his gaze down and his hands in his pockets all the way around. She was wondering whether he, too, was remembering that day now.

This way out of the city, through Hellerup, Copenhagen grew more gentrified by the mile, and soon the apartment buildings were replaced by private villas with ocean views. Øresund lay to their right like a great silver dish. It was sunny and windy and bitterly cold. Jensen looked at the water, at a tiny boat far out towards the coast of Sweden.

When they got to Skodsborg, Henrik reached across the gearstick and took her hand. Jensen closed her eyes and felt the years peel away.

'I don't know what it is that you do to me,' he said. 'I can't work it out. You've got to be the most irritating woman north of the Equator, but here I am again.'

'We're best when it's just us, no other people, no everyday stuff,' she said, knowing the truth of the words as soon as she had said them.

He squeezed her hand. 'Will you return to London now?'

'Is that what you would like me to do?'

He glanced at her quickly, his expression obscured by his Mafia sunglasses. They both knew the answer: he always and never wanted her to leave.

'I have nothing to go back to. No job, no flat.'

'What about that British upper-class ex of yours, can't he help?'

Guy? The answer was yes, absolutely. One call and he would send her a ticket and have her brought back to his mansion and into his bed. She would have to share it with others, but he would look after her. Guy had never understood why she wanted to be slumming it as a reporter in a minor European language when she didn't have to, when he was ready to give her everything she wanted, for life.

Tempting.

'No,' she said to Henrik after a pause. 'I need to be working.'

'How?'

'I don't know yet,' she said, scratching the dog behind the ears. 'I suppose I will need to start again.'

54

When they got to Hornbæk, Henrik wouldn't let her leave the car. He lowered his forehead to hers, touched her hair.

She felt herself weaken.

'Nice place,' he said.

'It's Esben Nørregård's.'

'What does that old Lothario want with you?'

'Why should he want something?'

'Men always want something, especially with you.'

'So?'

'I'd rather you didn't see anyone else than me.'

It was a joke that wasn't a joke.

'I think I'd better come in,' he said.

She opened the car door and the dog jumped out into the snow, wobbling off for a pee. They left it to its business.

Aziz had thrown away Esben's bloodstained shirt and sheets and tidied the place before driving Esben back to Aalborg. There was no sign of habitation. The house was ice cold and smelling faintly of wood smoke, a summer cabin out of season.

Jensen lit a fire and made coffee while Henrik took a tour of the

place. She watched him traipsing around outside on the frozen lawn
with the dog around his feet, looking at the windows and checking
the door handles. He was cursing visibly and shaking his head.

'You can't stay here,' he said when he returned.

'Why not?'

'It's unsafe.'

He pointed to the French doors to the garden. 'Any half-wit
addict off his head could force that lock in about three seconds.
It's not as if you have to worry about the neighbours calling the
police round here.'

'No one is going to break in. Why would they?'

'If you had my job, you wouldn't ask.'

'I am fine,' she said, handing him his coffee.

'I've got to go back to town now,' he said, making no move
to go.

'OK.'

They stood opposite one another in the galley kitchen, leaning
against the counters. She felt his penetrating eyes on her, the solid,
warm, throbbing mass of his body as she stared into his chest.

She had no more small talk.

She was falling.

Again.

He put down his mug, grabbed her by her wrists and pulled
her into his embrace. There was a softness to his body now,
which moved her. He was still boyishly slender, but his muscles
had lost their steel.

It was like the first time all over again. He led her to the
wood-burning stove, and undressed her, right there on the floor.
He undressed himself. His eyes never left her body.

When she tried to cover herself with a cushion, he took it
firmly from her hand and laid her down and looked at her,
kneeling by her side.

'I want to see you,' he said.

She could have stopped him, but she didn't.

205

55

Saturday 17:41

When she woke up, he was gone, it was dark, and every inch of her body was tingling. By her side, the dog was snoring loudly. There was a note from Henrik on her pillow.

I think he likes you.

56

If she wanted to go to Copenhagen, it would have to be by bike and train. When she had left *Dagbladet,* Yasmine had been standing in the lobby holding out her hand for her car keys. Jensen could cope with Markus's blank stare from behind the reception desk, but she had always liked Yasmine, who had been Margrethe's PA for as long as she could remember. Though Yasmine and Margrethe were an odd couple, known to the newspaper's reporters as 'the Beauty and the Beast', the two of them were inseparable. Jensen doubted that her boss would last long on her own without the young lawyer who – for reasons only known to herself – had exchanged dazzling career prospects to become deck hand to the captain of a sinking ship.

She called the hospital to ask for news of Gustav, relieved when Martin came on the phone. He told her Gustav had been awake briefly in the morning, though he hadn't made much sense.

'Did he tell you what happened?'

'No, but then memory loss is quite common in these cases, and the sedative we gave him won't have helped.'

207

There was a new message from Henrik.

Fuck, I love you.

Dagbladet had taken a break from the election coverage and run a big piece on Thomas next to their frenzied speculation about the third murder: *Street Victim's Tragic Gesture of Apology*.

The old schoolboy picture of Thomas had made a reappearance, along with photos of the shrine in Magstræde and a snippet of copy from one of Frank's old articles about the case. Frank had spoken to a vicar from an inner-city outreach centre, who had waxed lyrical about the private misery of tormented souls and how everyone deserved forgiveness: 'Remember that Thomas was very young when he committed his terrible crime.'

Jensen could barely remember herself at fifteen and wondered what her teenage self would have made of the different woman she had become. Were you still culpable as an adult for sins you committed as your child self? She had read somewhere that the equivalent of all the cells in the human body were renewed every few years. Did that not mean that it was not culpability itself that stayed with us, but merely the memory of being culpable?

Grønfeldt had declined to comment on Thomas's murder, asking for privacy at 'this difficult time'.

A spokesperson for Copenhagen Police said: 'We will continue our enquiries in order to piece together what happened to Thomas during the twenty-four hours leading to his tragic death.'

Henrik would have put it less diplomatically. She knew that these days they kept him away from the press conferences. Safer that way.

At the bottom of the article, there was a mention of the petition to keep Skovhøj open, saying that the district council had launched a review.

She couldn't fault the coverage. It was sober, thorough, well written. Margrethe would be praising Frank again at this morning's meeting.

Jensen knew she ought to leave it, but she had to know what had happened. All of it.

She thought of Thomas seated in Magstræde, a frozen Buddha crowned with snow, eyes raised to the sky. She told herself she was doing it for him, but knew that it was more than that: an inability to let things rest once her interest was piqued.

She found her notepad and wrote:

Pills from whom?

Why Monday?

Sign, rucksack, phone, where?

Mute, why?

There was nothing but champagne left in the fridge. She scavenged in the cupboards and found a tinned ham for the dog and some dry biscuits for herself that she smeared with Nutella and ate in front of the fire.

When she had showered herself warm, she went outside and chopped more firewood and stacked it by the fireplace. There were no tracks in the snow, no sign of humans as far as she could see in any direction. All she could hear was the waves lapping the nearby shore.

She made a thermos of instant coffee (Liron would have poured it down the drain) and sat on the sofa with a blanket and Henning's folder. The dog jumped up, snuggling in close beside her. She wrinkled her nose, making a note to give bath it in the morning, but its warm body felt comforting.

There were hundreds of articles, and not just from *Daghladet*, diligently cut by Henning from each newspaper or magazine and marked with the date and name of the publication. It was going to take her hours to read them all.

She divided the articles into three piles: one on the Langelandsvej Murder, one on Grønfeldt's career, and one with pieces in which Grønfeldt was a mere tangential figure.

The first pile was by far the largest, and she spread the articles out on the coffee table and floor, ordered by publication.

The most extreme coverage was in the two tabloids, not surprisingly, with an even distribution between the three national broadsheets and a smattering of articles in the main left-wing-intellectual rag.

The first pieces were harrowing. Both the tabloids printed pictures of Sandra Mørk's yellow-brick bungalow in Farum, with police tape strung across the door and close-ups of blood in the snow.

They had interviewed several women who claimed to be colleagues or friends of Sandra, saying she had talked to them about her anguish over her son and his trouble with the police.

'She was afraid of what he might do,' someone called Charlotte Friis had said.

There was a photograph of a gaunt-looking Grønfeldt standing in the garden by a birdhouse, with a thousand-mile stare and the headline: *I Feel Sorry For Thomas.*

She read every single word of every single article. When she was hungry, she ate biscuits with Nutella and tinned peaches. When the fire began to die, she added more logs.

Towards the end of the coverage, when Thomas had been named and his life spilled across the pages, there was an article in the intellectual daily, a double-spread interview with Majbritt Johansen, the lawyer who had been assigned to Thomas during the case. The topic was the vulnerability of young offenders. Majbritt Johansen raged against those who had deliberately revealed Thomas's identity.

'He was a child,' she said. 'No one listened to his story. They took it and made it public for their own ends.'

By the time Jensen finished reading, she had made three additions to her notes:

House in Farum

Charlotte Friis

Majbritt Johansen

She wanted to speak to Majbritt, to hear Thomas out through

her. The lawyer had been right: his side of what happened was nowhere to be found in the articles. How would she find out where Majbritt lived?

Fie had found out about everything else. *Let's see how good she really is*, thought Jensen. She messaged Fie, telling her what had happened to Gustav, and that he would be OK.

Fie replied that Karina kept asking her questions about Thomas. 'It's almost as if she had something to hide.'

While she waited for Fie to send her Majbritt Johansen's address, Jensen opened a bottle of champagne and threw more logs onto the fire, plucking up the energy to start reading from the remaining two piles of cuttings.

Sometime after dark, headlights flashed across the living-room ceiling. The dog began to bark half-heartedly as a car pulled up outside. The possibilities darted through Jensen's mind. She thought it might be Esben again, or worse, his wife or one of their children who didn't know that she had borrowed the place.

She opened the front door, ready to explain herself, and saw a tall, broad figure emerging from Esben's black car.

'Aziz?'

There were plastic bags in his huge hands. His Danish was accented but almost flawless: 'I brought a takeaway, and some other stuff for the fridge. Esben reckoned you might be hungry?'

'Starving, but why are you here?'

'He told me to tell you he is very sorry about what happened yesterday.'

Aziz was making the cabin look small. His eyes were scanning the newspaper cut-outs and the half-drunk bottle of champagne, but whatever he thought of her was not showing on his face. She assumed that, working for Esben, he would have seen worse.

'Is that your dog?' he asked.

'Yes. No. It's a long story.'

She unpacked the food and put the takeaway in the micro-wave to heat. Aziz refused to share it with her, said he was going home to eat with his wife and children later. He watched her with his diplomatic, expressionless eyes as, greedily, she wolfed down the vegetable pakoras and chapatis dipped in spicy daal, with spoonful after spoonful of rice fragrant with cloves.

'Do you have everything you need?' he asked when she had finished and made him drink a cup of coffee with her. 'Esben told me to stay close. He doesn't need me for the next couple of weeks. Here is my number. Whatever you want, wherever you need to go, just call me and I'll drive you. OK?'

Her phone pinged. Fie was as reliable as clockwork.

'Actually,' she said, looking at the screen. 'There *is* something you can do for me. I need to see someone in Gentofte, and we're going to have to take the dog.'

57

Majbritt Johansen lived in a smart neighbourhood with white designer houses rising out of the snow like icebergs. Expensive cars lined the driveways, Audis and Volvo four-wheel drives. Sunday night and everyone was home.

She hadn't phoned ahead, for the same reason that she hadn't called Ditte Mørk. If Majbritt was at home, Jensen was unlikely to be a welcome guest. Throughout her career, she very rarely had been.

She waved at Aziz as she pressed the doorbell. Where she and Henrik had failed, the big man had succeeded: the dog was seated in the boot, looking at her reproachfully.

A man in his sixties wearing jeans and a woollen jumper came to the door. She held up her press card. 'Is Majbritt Johansen here? My name is Jensen.'

The man began to shut the door.

'Wait,' she shouted. 'I am not here to write anything.'

The door slammed in her face.

She rang the bell again, then bent down and spoke through

213

the letterbox. 'Please, I am the one who found Thomas. I just want to talk, to understand what happened to him.'

Nothing.

She turned to look at Aziz, shrugging. He rolled the car slowly towards her as she headed back down the front steps. She had almost reached him when she heard the front door open again. In the light from the hall, she saw an elegant woman with grey, almost white hair scraped back from her forehead. She was in jeans, a white shirt and a grey cashmere cardigan that she had wrapped tightly across herself. There were dark rings under her eyes.

The man from before was trying to persuade her to come back in, to close the door on Jensen, but, in the end, he gave up and walked away in a huff.

'Show me your press card again,' said the woman in a tired voice.

She nodded on seeing Jensen's name. 'I recognise your byline from the paper. It's unusual, or rather it's not . . . well, you know what I mean. Didn't you use to be in London?'

'Yes, but I am based in Copenhagen now. Or was. I no longer work for *Dagbladet*.'

'Why not?'

'Let's just say my editor and I had a disagreement.'

The woman nodded. 'I read the pieces on Thomas in your newspaper.'

'My colleague wrote those, Frank Buhl.'

'Utter garbage.'

'Would you let me come in so you can tell me why? I would like to know. It might be hard to believe, but I care about Thomas.'

Majbritt Johansen opened the door wide to let her in, averting her eyes. The house was warm and clean and tastefully decorated. Majbritt showed Jensen into her study, a cave lined with books. She leaned against the teak desk, folding her

214

arms across her chest. Obviously it wasn't going to be a long conversation.

'Working on a Sunday?' said Jensen, gesturing at piles of papers and an open laptop.

Majbritt shook her head. 'I retired three years ago. This is a labour of love. I am writing a book.'

'About what?'

'You wouldn't be interested. Look, you turning up here brings some unhappy memories. My husband is only trying to protect me. I used to get reporters showing up here all the time.'

'Because of Thomas?'

'Him too. Defending young offenders doesn't exactly make you the people's favourite. You were the one who found him, you say?'

'Total coincidence. I always cycle to work via Magstræde. I was early that morning. I'd seen him sitting in the same spot the day before, but assumed he was a beggar, so didn't think any more of it. Yes, I know, I should have stopped, offered my help. Maybe I could even have prevented what happened. When I saw him the next morning, I knew straight away that he was dead. We'd had all that snow overnight and it hadn't melted. It was all over his face.'

Majbritt looked at her hands. 'Why didn't you write about it?' she said after swallowing a few times.

'I couldn't do it. I felt like we didn't know enough.'

'Hasn't stopped most of your colleagues,' said Majbritt.

'Maybe in this case it felt different because I found him myself. He looked so ... vulnerable.'

Jensen hated using Karina Jørgensen's word for the residents at Skovhøj but somehow there was no better.

'Why are you here?' said Majbritt, glaring at her, and Jensen got a glimpse of how formidable an opponent the woman would have been in court.

'I read all the articles about the case today. You were never

215

quoted, but then suddenly there was this long interview with you, after the sentencing. The one with a picture of you outside the house in Farum?'

'I remember it.'

'Why did you speak after all that time staying silent?'

'I was angry. Thomas's identity had been blown, I still don't know by whom. He was only fifteen. He deserved our protection, but once the media circus started . . . well, the press didn't exactly allow him a fair hearing, and he wasn't able to give his side of the story.'

'Which was?'

She smiled miserably. 'Thomas always maintained that it wasn't him. He said that his mother's partner must have done it.'

'Christian Grønfeldt? But wasn't Thomas found with the breadknife still in his hands, covered in his mother's blood?'

'Yes, that's a factual statement.'

'Did he mean it metaphorically? As in Grønfeldt drove him to it?'

'He was in shock, not exactly coherent. He just kept saying over and over that it wasn't him.'

'When did you first meet Thomas?'

'That night, at the police station. Someone had made him take a shower; his hair was still wet. He was clean, but I remember . . .'

Majbritt broke off and made a steeple with her hands, touching them to her lips for a moment. She closed her eyes. 'He had blood under his nails.'

Jensen thought of Gustav, lying in the bed at Riget with the red half-moons on his fingertips.

'What did he say to you?'

'Nothing at all. He was in shock. They gave him something to sleep on. It was only the next day that he began to talk, and then it all came out in a rambling, disjointed narrative that I could make no sense of.'

'Tell me.'

Majbritt visibly pulled herself together. 'Why?' she said. 'What does it matter? It's done now, he is dead, and in a way, I am glad he was spared any more pain. He could not have lived a normal life after everything he went through.'

'Seems to matter a great deal to you.'

The courtroom lawyer was back. 'They all do. All the kids. Nothing comes out of nothing. Their stories would make you weep.'

Jensen wondered if Majbritt and her husband had been able to have children themselves. There was a wistful undertone to her words.

'When did he stop talking?'

'It was when we found out that he was getting seven years in the young offenders' institution. We were in court, he was sitting next to me, and afterwards when I turned around to look at him and ask him if he was OK, it was as if the light in his eyes had gone out. When I said goodbye to him, he didn't reply, and I had to just watch as they led him away. I went to visit him once, months later, but he refused to talk to me.'

'Was it normal for you to visit young offenders after they had been locked up?'

Majbritt shook her head. 'Actually, I had never done it before, nor since. But Thomas had no one. Expect for his mother's sister, who hated him, and he was so young. Anyway, he gave me this when he saw me.'

She opened a drawer in her desk and pulled out a piece of paper. It was soft to the touch, like it had been in and out of a hand or a pocket many times.

Leave me alone.

She got up, rubbing her temples. 'I am rather tired. I would like you to leave now.'

'Perhaps we can talk another time?'

'No,' said Majbritt. 'I really have nothing more to say.'

'I am staying in a summer house in Hornbæk. No one around for miles; we'd be quite safe talking there,' said Jensen, scribbling down her number and address.

Majbritt took the note and tossed it on her desk without looking at it.

Later, when Jensen was approaching the car, she noticed Majbritt's husband looking at her angrily from the living room. He was standing in the window with his hands by his side; she imagined they were bunched into fists. After a few seconds, he reached up and jerked the curtain across with one rapid movement, and Jensen was cut off, standing outside in the cold, and there was no human in sight, just the white blocks of the upmarket housing estate, icy and barren.

Skyldig.

Thomas hadn't meant himself. He had been pointing his finger at Grønfeldt.

58

If Aziz was annoyed at taking a detour to Magstræde, he was not letting on. Once more, Jensen reminded herself that whatever he was doing for her had to be as nothing compared to being Esben's fixer.

There was a soft light in the windows on the top floor above CG Dentistry.

'Wait for me here,' she told Aziz, leaving him in the car.

The windows were foggy with dog breath.

Grønfeldt answered the doorbell on the third buzz.

'Jensen, back so soon.'

She could hear music in the background.

'You knew all along that it was Thomas down here in the street, pointing a sign at your windows, and you knew full well what it meant.'

'Yes, you're right, I did.'

Jensen was taken aback. 'You're not denying it?'

'Why would I?'

'Because only the other day you told me that you had no idea who he was.'

Grønfeldt released the door lock. 'You'd better come in. Though I'm afraid you've got the wrong end of the stick.'

This time the door to the clinic on the left was locked. Jensen continued up the stairs to Grønfeldt's apartment.

Grønfeldt was in running gear, black leggings and a black zip-up top, bare feet. The Lycra clung to his body, showing off his flat stomach and muscular legs. There was mud on his shins, and he was drinking from a bottle of water.

'You're lucky to have caught me. I have been out running – twelve kilometres,' he said, leading her into the lounge which Jensen figured was directly above his waiting room.

Was he expecting applause for his endurance? She remained silent.

The apartment was a mirror image of the clinic downstairs, with its raw floorboards and designer furniture, but here there were modern paintings on the walls, by a Danish artist Jensen recognised: bald, naked, bluish-skinned, pot-bellied middle-aged men and women with their faces turned to the moon. An ironic antidote to the perfect-looking specimens Grønfeldt was creating downstairs in his clinic. He offered her water and fruit from a large bowl. She declined both but took a seat in a cowhide swivel chair, while he stretched out in the sofa.

'Look,' he said. 'See it from my perspective. What happened to Sandra ...' he stopped and looked as though he was about to cry.

She left him to gather himself.

'As you can imagine, it was an extremely traumatic episode of my life. I wanted to put it behind me.'

'You never spoke to Thomas after it happened?'

'Would you speak to the person who had killed someone you loved?'

'Did he contact you?'

Grønfeldt nodded. 'He wrote me tons of emails, text messages; it never stopped.'

'Show me?'

'I can't, I deleted them all. They were . . . well, they were rather upsetting.'

'Did you show them to the police?'

'No point, he was already locked up by the time they started to come, and a lot of them made no sense. They were all just threats – mad, rambling accusations.'

'Of what?'

'Things I never did. You don't understand: Thomas wasn't well. He was rebelling, falling in with the wrong people, getting into petty crime. He gave his mother hell. She tried to deal with it all, did her best.'

'What happened that day?'

'It was a nightmare. I went to the house straight from work, but Sandra didn't come to the door to greet me like she used to. The house was quiet, which was also unusual as Sandra nearly always had the TV on. I came into the kitchen. She was lying on the floor and Thomas was sitting next to her on his knees, leaning over in a sort of trance. There was blood everywhere. I slipped in it and fell. I shouted at him to help Sandra, to call an ambulance, but he just sat there, frozen to the spot. So I ran outside into the street, screaming. It had been snowing, like now. I had blood all over me. I didn't realise Sandra was already dead by then.'

He buried his face in his hands. For the first time, Jensen felt a stab of sympathy for the man. When she spoke, her voice was softer.

'Do you know what they might have been arguing about?'

He shrugged. 'Sandra had found some tablets in his trouser pocket that morning. It might have been that. You do know he was high when he did it?'

'I think I read that somewhere, yes.'

'Look, you're obviously a very good reporter, conscientious, thorough. I would hate to have found him like you did. It was

221

a sad death, a tragic end to a tragic life. Thomas was sick, misguided, tormented, but no one deserves to have their life snuffed out like that. I blame myself. I should have done something that night, but I honestly had no idea he'd be crazy enough to stay put in all that snow. I went to bed early to try and forget about it.'

She said nothing.

'Obviously, I was wrong not to have helped him, but I swear I didn't stab him. Why would I have done that? It wasn't the first time he accused me and wouldn't be the last. And you can't blame me for wanting to keep the truth about our relationship to myself.'

'Can't blame you for trying. You didn't exactly succeed, though,' said Jensen. 'It's all in the online edition of *Dagbladet* right now.'

'I am aware of that. That's why I am sitting here talking to you now. You can treat it as an exclusive, a scoop, if you like, the only candid interview I am prepared to give. If you're quick, you might still make tomorrow's front page. It's the least I can do for you after being less than honest, though I hope you can now understand my reasons.'

Jensen heard the sound of a door close somewhere on the floor above them: Malene, Jensen assumed, walking around in the couple's bedroom. She thought of her attempts to get hold of Gustav.

'Do you think I could have a quick word with your wife before I go? There's something I want to ask her,' she said.

'I am sure she would be glad to help you, but I'm afraid you're going to have to come back another time. Malene has a migraine. I am here, though, and willing to give you a story.'

'I am grateful, really I am,' Jensen said, all of a sudden feeling immensely tired. 'Except I am not here as a reporter. I am just a person wanting to know what happened.'

She grabbed a shiny red apple from the fruit bowl and sank her teeth into the flesh. It was bitter and dry.

Week Three

59

Skovhøj Kirke, once provocatively postmodern, had seen better days. Its white walls were streaked with mould, its church tower a brutal finger pointing at the sky. A ring of dirty snow marked its perimeter. Jensen guessed the architect would be mortified to see it in this state.

Jensen had failed to persuade the dog of the virtues of soap and water, so Aziz had refused to take it.

'It makes the car smell bad,' he said.

The dog had been barking and whimpering its head off when they left the summer house, but Aziz had refused to relent.

'It can look after the house while you're gone,' he had said.

Some guard dog. It couldn't walk five yards without needing a lie-down, never mind chase a burglar.

She asked Aziz to park at the end of the street. The funeral was meant to be a private affair, but just in case the time and date had leaked to the press, Jensen didn't want Frank Buhl to start asking questions or, worse, some of her colleagues from the other newspapers recognising Aziz as Esben's factotum.

She could have saved herself the worry. Only three other

people had turned up: Karina, Tobias and Fie. They were bunched up closely in the front pew. Karina glanced at her angrily over her shoulder. Jensen decided to take a seat further back on the opposite side of the aisle.

The church was even uglier on the inside, with varnished pine cladding making it look like a giant sauna. Which was ironic, seeing as it was possibly colder inside than out.

Jensen shuddered in her coat, glad that she had finally caved in last night and called Guy. Five more days, and she would be flying back to London. Her earthly possessions, stowed in the container out at Sydhavnen, would be dispatched after her as soon as she sorted out the shipping. She would be staying at Guy's town house in Belgravia until she decided what to do. He was in Cape Town and wouldn't be back for a fortnight. ('Keep the bed warm for me, dear.')

Thomas's coffin was white and plain-looking, the spray of red and white carnations embarrassingly small. Probably the best the council could afford, or maybe Karina and Tobias had clubbed together to buy the flowers with their own money.

The vicar, a woman with short red hair, was seated by the altar, beneath a huge wooden Cross. Discreetly, she checked her phone and pushed it back into the pocket of her black cassock. The abstract stained-glass window behind her cast a kaleidoscope of colours across the floor.

No one else arrived.

No Grønfeldt.

No relatives.

No friends aside from Fie.

The organist began to play, a hymn Jensen remembered from assembly in her school days. 'This Blessed Day'. The four of them sang it feebly. In the middle of the last verse, the door was flung open. They all turned to look.

It was Henrik in his black jeans and white shirt with his bald head lowered. He picked the pew behind her.

Right behind her.

She could smell his leather jacket, feel his eyes on the back of her head.

She turned and whispered, 'What are you doing here?

He held a finger to his lips. 'Shush.'

The rest of the service he was touching her hair and neck.

Again, she could have stopped him.

Again, she didn't.

The vicar did her best with Thomas, a young man she had never met. Jensen wondered if she had a go-to eulogy, a template for those about whom there is little to say, or little good. Unconvincingly, she preached understanding and forgiveness. 'Let he who is without sin cast the first stone.'

Fie sobbed, her body shuddering with the effort. Tobias put his arm round her.

'We commend to Almighty God our brother Thomas and we commit his body to the ground. Earth to earth, ashes to ashes, dust to dust.'

The vicar threw soil from a wooden box onto the coffin with a tiny shovel, and Fie released a loud cry that hung in the air, reverberating under the pine rafters.

No one heard the doors open again. It was only when Jensen saw a shadow rushing past her that she realised what was happening. The smell was familiar: smoke, alcohol, unwashed clothes.

Henrik was faster, but not fast enough. The woman with the wild henna and grey hair made it to Thomas's coffin before he could stop her. Her roar rose up, echoing chaotically as she knocked the coffin off its trestles, sending the carnations flying.

'Fucking brat, you have spoiled everything!' she shouted, spitting on the coffin, then looking about her wildly. 'Why are you here, you fucking do-gooders? You didn't even know him, the little shit.'

'And as for you,' she said, approaching the vicar. 'You know

227

he was a murderer, yes? Killed his pregnant mother, stuck a knife into her belly twenty-seven times?'

The vicar retreated, her back up against the altar, her ruff askew. The rest of them recoiled in horror.

Well, not quite all of them.

Soon Henrik had the intruder's arms locked behind her back and was sitting across her legs. She was screaming and kicking, but it was doing her no good.

'Ditte Mørk, I am arresting you for disturbing the peace,' he said, calmly, before getting out his phone and calling it in.

60

The four of them stood in the car park watching Ditte being driven away in a patrol car, followed by Henrik in his unmarked vehicle. Jensen never got a chance to tell him her news.

'I'll call you,' he had mouthed at her.

The undertakers were tidying up, having done their best to calm down the vicar before her husband had come to collect her.

'I thought she was going to kill me,' she had kept saying, over and over.

It was bright and cold and windy, and Jensen was squinting, shielding her eyes with a gloved hand. Someone was there, in the distance beyond the conifers that marked the far end of the cemetery and the common plot where Thomas's ashes would be interred when his body had been cremated. There would be no stone, nothing to mark his passing, or that he had ever lived.

'Who is that?' she said, pointing at the figure, but Tobias and Karina were preoccupied with Fie, who was crying inconsolably.

Karina led Fie towards the car park. 'I think we'd better get you home. This was all too upsetting,' she said, glancing back at Jensen as if she was responsible for what had happened.

229

'Coming, Tobias?'

'Yep,' he shouted, but Jensen could tell he was hanging back.

He came up to her quickly with his back to Karina and Fie and pressed a note into her hand. She waited till the Skovhøj minibus had disappeared down the drive and Thomas's coffin had been placed in the back of the hearse and driven off before reading it.

Tomorrow 7 p.m. Bruun's Coffee Shop. Christianshavn.

She knew the place. It was just by the canal, round the corner from Markus's flat.

There was no one to be seen now beyond the conifers. The cemetery and car park were empty and forlorn.

'Aziz,' she said, as they drove off, 'while you were waiting, did you see anyone?'

He caught her eyes in the rear-view mirror. He was frowning. 'No, except the policeman and that crazy woman. Why?'

'It doesn't matter. I thought I saw a person in the distance, but I must have imagined it.'

He frowned, but thankfully left it at that. For once, she was glad to be sitting in the back of the car. She leaned her head against the ice-cold windowpane, and folded herself into the corner of the seat, away from his questioning eyes.

The person in the cemetery must have been a random passer-by looking at the gravestones, just like she herself had done at Assistens Cemetery, or someone grieving for a loved one. She dismissed it from her mind.

The apartment buildings of the inner city flashed past her eyes. She thought of the people in their homes, together, gathered around in the light and warmth. Husbands and wives, lovers, children, dogs. Who in their right mind would choose to stay by themselves in a summer house out of season? In time, the lights petered out and the car became a sleek projectile shooting through the moonless dark. She drifted off.

61

Mark stuck his head round the door.

'I've got Ditte Mørk downstairs, interview room three.'

'Wait,' said Henrik, holding one hand up, trying to hang on to the brilliant thought he had just had.

Nope. Gone.

The day had long since begun but it had stayed dark and gloomy outside. In the winter months, most days the sun barely got a look-in.

Mark lingered in the doorway.

'What?'

'I just . . . aren't you coming?'

'In a minute! For Christ's sake.'

Mark scarpered and Henrik instantly felt guilty. He had been asking for Ditte Mørk to be fetched since the email had come through from her GP that morning: Ditte had been prescribed diazepam, a type of benzos, a couple of years ago for sleeplessness and agitation. This was enough for him to want to see her. She had told all and sundry about her hatred for Thomas, so there was no shortage of motive.

However, Henrik had to admit that drugging and then stabbing Thomas seemed like an extraordinary amount of planning for Ditte, a heavy drinker who could barely organise her own life. Henrik could imagine her stabbing the boy but doubted she would have had the presence of mind to sedate him first.

Despite himself, his thoughts kept leaping back to Jensen's theories on Christian Grønfeldt. Dentists had access to drugs, including benzos. Given their history, there was hardly any love lost between Grønfeldt and Thomas, but the motive was less obvious. Jensen might be right that Thomas had been pointing his 'guilty' sign at Grønfeldt, but the dentist had had a pretty watertight alibi for the time of Sandra Mørk's murder, meaning he could have had nothing to fear from Thomas's wild allegations.

Besides, Thomas had been out of youth prison since last November, so if Grønfeldt really *had* wanted to kill him, he could have done so a lot sooner. That left the elusive Skovhøj drug dealer, who had vanished from the surface of the earth after Gustav Skov's little show of initiative. The boy was lucky not to have got himself killed, but as long as he was suffering from amnesia, that particular lead would be going nowhere. Henrik had not had as much as one word of sense out of the boy.

He heaved himself up to standing, with an old man's grunt of effort. ('You sound like your dad,' his wife would have said.) That reminded him that it was weeks since he had last seen his father. There was a home match on at the weekend. He could take his father there with Oliver, the three of them wearing their football scarves in various stages of fading. At least then he and his father would have something to talk about. Over the years, the football chatter had become a means of avoiding the more serious issues going on in real life. His stepmother's Alzheimer's, for example, or the death rattle of Henrik's marriage. ('You do your family, and I'll do mine,' as his wife had once put it. Rather that way round, Henrik had always thought.)

The office was dead, the corridors murky and empty. Henrik shook off the feeling of not belonging there. Younger people were coming in; he didn't recognise a lot of his colleagues these days. Soon he would have to start thinking seriously about what to do after policing. The obvious choice was some sort of security job. Or he could set himself up as a private investigator, finder of lost dogs and photographer of the adulterous (ha!). These thoughts depressed him profoundly.

By the time he pushed open the door to the interview room, he was in no mood for Ditte Mørk's crazed rantings. She had spent the night sleeping it off in a cell, attended once for a cut on her hand by a doctor who had fled inside five minutes. There would be no more than a caution in it for her, despite the upset she had caused at yesterday's funeral, topped off with her being sick in the patrol car on the way back to the station. He didn't envy the poor sod who had had to clean up the mess.

Ditte sat with her arms crossed and her considerable arse on the edge of the seat, like a bored teenager. There was a glass of water and a cup of coffee in front of her. She looked rough, fixing Henrik with a bloodshot glare as he took up his seat next to Mark, who was taking notes on his laptop.

'Feeling better?' said Henrik.

'You can't hold me here.'

Her breath stank of alcohol and coffee and unbrushed teeth. Henrik sensed Mark wriggling in discomfort beside him.

'We can until such time as we judge that you no longer constitute a threat to the peace.'

'I never did.'

'Tell that to the vicar. She will be off for months with PTSD after your little stunt.'

'What do you want?'

'I want to know what you were doing the night between Monday and Tuesday a fortnight ago. Your car was spotted crossing the Storebælt Bridge earlier that morning.'

233

'So?'

'You went to Copenhagen.'

'Yes – is that illegal now?'

'And what were you up to that day?'

'Visiting friends.'

Ditte Mørk socialising seemed like an unlikely scenario. 'Can we have their names and addresses, please?'

'No. It's a free country, I can do what I want.'

'You went to visit Christian Grønfeldt in Magstræde, didn't you? Your late sister's former partner?'

She tried to stare him down, but he could see something flickering in her eyes.

'Why, Ditte?'

More staring.

'You saw Thomas sitting there, didn't you? And later that night, you came back and gave him drugs and then you stabbed him.'

She laughed, a witch-like cackle that segued into a prolonged coughing fit. 'If I was going to stab him, which I didn't, why would I have drugged him first?'

'Thomas was twenty-one years old, and in considerably better physical shape than you. He would have fought back.'

'If you say so,' she said.

'You were prescribed diazepam by your doctor.'

'And?'

'Do you still have the tablets?'

'I might do, but then again, I might have thrown them away.'

'So, what were you doing on that night?'

In the quiet of the interview room, he could hear Ditte Mørk parting her lips into a wide grin.

'I was sleeping in my camper van out in Hellerup.'

'Alone?'

'Yes, alone.'

'Did anyone see you?'

234

'No idea.'

'Where were you parked?'

'Dunno. Some side street. There was a blizzard. It wasn't as if I was able to run about town.'

'You need to show us the exact place. We will be looking for witnesses who are willing to corroborate your statement.'

He turned to Mark, who made a note on his pad in his careful joined-up writing.

'Am I a suspect now?'

'We need to rule stuff out.'

'Because I tell you what, if I had known the brat was there, I *would* have done it. Whoever stabbed him saved me the trouble.'

'We know from witnesses that Thomas had been sitting in Magstræde all day that Monday. And Christian Grønfeldt has told us that you made a visit there in the afternoon, trying to gain entry to his property. So are you telling me that you didn't see Thomas sitting directly opposite the clinic? Come off it, woman, you must think I was born yesterday.'

62

'And then she knocked the coffin to the floor and screamed at the vicar that Thomas was a murderer.'

'Ah, ah, don't make me laugh!'

Gustav was stretched out awkwardly on Margrethe's sofa, wearing a neck brace and his headphones. His missing front tooth gave him a mischievous look, like an urchin from a musical. He winced every time he moved.

Jensen had brought pizza from her favourite restaurant at Nørrebro: sourdough, peperoni, extra hot. They were eating it straight from the cardboard box. Or rather she was. Gustav had complained that chewing hurt too much.

Aziz had declined to join them. He was standing by the window, parting the blinds to keep an eye on the street, with a face on him saying they shouldn't be here.

It was Gustav who had called to let them know that the coast was clear, after he had managed with some difficulty to convince Margrethe that he could be left home alone.

The apartment was less elegant than Jensen had remembered from the one and only time she had visited: an awkward drinks

236

party for the newspaper's staff when Margrethe had turned fifty. In the grey light of winter, her furniture and belongings looked old and beaten up, the parquet floors fuzzy with dust. There was a grand piano covered in papers, and a stack of leather-bound books served as an occasional table next to an old armchair. Jensen remembered reading about Margrethe having lived with her mother till she died.

After a few attempts, she had finally persuaded Yasmine to give her a heads-up by text when Margrethe left the office, giving her and Aziz a chance to make themselves scarce. She had pleaded with Yasmine to be allowed to apologise to Gustav for her stupid mistake.

'But why did she do it? It doesn't make sense,' said Gustav, still puzzled about her story about Ditte's tantrum.

'Only she knows. Some sort of personal vendetta, I suppose.'

More to the point, how had Ditte found out about the funeral? Grønfeldt was one possibility. She would have to ask him about it.

'What happens to her now?' said Gustav.

'Nothing, I expect. Can't see the police bothering to charge her.'

'I still don't understand,' he said, peering up at her warily from under his long fringe. 'She must have said something.'

Jensen resisted an urge to sweep his hair away from his face so she could see his eyes again, like when he had been lying in the hospital bed at Riget.

'She shouted, "You have ruined everything," or something along those lines.'

'What does that mean?'

'No idea. That's what I am trying to work out. Also, I heard Ditte was in Copenhagen the night Thomas died.'

'Did you hear that from the policeman who is not your boy-friend?' said Gustav.

She slapped him on the wrist, and he howled in pain.

'Sorry, Gustav, so sorry I forgot. Are you all right? If you must know, the policeman is married and has three children.'

Aziz shot her a look. She returned it blankly. Given his boss's antics, what right did Aziz have to expect her to be a beacon of morality? Besides, what was happening between her and Henrik was not some sort of sordid affair. It was far worse than that.

'Gustav, what happened on Friday?'

'I don't remember.'

'You went and saw Fie, and then you came back to Copenhagen. Do you recall that much?'

'Sort of.'

'Do you remember what you were thinking about? Or whether you met or spoke to anyone?'

'I remember being at the Central Station.'

'Good, and then?'

'Just fragments.'

'Was there anything on your phone to give you a clue? A message from someone perhaps?'

'They must have taken it.'

'You shouldn't have gone off on your own.'

'Who says I did?

'CCTV. Apparently you were seen leaving the station in the direction of Vesterbrogade.'

'So?'

'If you had been heading back to the newspaper you would have gone the other way.'

'Not necessarily.'

'Wait a minute – your phone was taken?' said Aziz to Gustav.

'I was found without it, according to the police, and I don't think I could have lost it by accident.'

Jensen grabbed another slice of pizza; a shame for it to go to waste. 'So, either the person who did this to Gustav took it, or someone else who saw him lying there helpless. Never underestimate the callousness of scumbag passers-by,' she said with her mouth full.

'That's not why I asked,' said Aziz, addressing her pityingly, as one might a person of low intelligence. 'It will have your messages to Gustav in it.'

She bit her lip, dropping the pizza slice back in the box. True enough, she had texted Gustav the address of Esben's summer house; he had told her about locating the drug dealer. That meant she could be in danger too

'Fie thought Thomas must have bought the drugs,' said Gustav.

'He had no money.'

'You can always get money. Maybe he sold something to raise the cash?'

'It's possible.'

'But you don't believe it's what happened.'

'I don't know, and the dealer has disappeared, so we might never know the truth.'

She had lost her appetite.

'Get some rest now Gustav, just be grateful you lived to tell the tale.'

He looked sullenly at the floor.

'Gustav, I have nothing to teach you. I don't know what I am doing myself half the time. I haven't even been able to hold down my job, so if you want to be a journalist, you're going to have to find someone else to learn from. Frank Buhl offered his services. Maybe you should take him up on it?'

'I spoke to my aunt about you, tried to change her mind. I am still working on it. It's hard.'

'Pretty much impossible, in my experience. Anyway, by the time you get out of here, I'll have moved back to London.'

Gustav looked at her angrily. 'But you can't. What about me? What about the tip-off we were supposed to look into?'

'Ah yes, I didn't get a chance to tell you. I looked up the guy Deep Throat told us about. Carsten Vangede?'

239

Aziz turned to face them. 'Deep Throat?'

'The Watergate Scandal, not the porn,' said Jensen.

He shrugged and turned away.

Gustav looked searchingly at Jensen. 'And?'

'Owns a couple of restaurants and a bar that's seen better days. All in Nørrebro.'

'Which one?' said Aziz.

'Zoom Bar,' said Jensen.

'That's near me,' says Aziz. 'Always loads of drunks hanging out outside.'

'So are you going to go and see him?' said Gustav.

'Probably won't get the time before I leave,' said Jensen. 'Look, just forget about it. I am sure your aunt has by now.'

She walked down the hall to call Henrik, counting five bedroom doors. There were framed black-and-white photographs on the wall, people squinting into the sunlight of Copenhagen past, men with hats and pipes, and in between them nudes painted in oil. Margrethe's mother, Gustav's paternal grandmother, had been a well-known artist.

Henrik wasn't picking up, and she felt disappointed. Partly because she wanted to know if he had any news on the case, but really because she was dying to tell him that she would be moving back to London in under a week. She could message him, but she wanted to catch the emotion in his voice.

Not sadness.

Relief.

In Copenhagen, there would only be his car and stolen hours in hotel rooms and Esben's summer house. They would never be walking down the road together in the sunshine, holding hands. It was far easier when he stayed here and she stayed over there.

He knew it.

And she knew it.

But she wanted to hear him say it.

An email flashed up on her screen. The anonymous email account. Deep Throat.

Carsten Vangede is expecting you at Zoom Bar tomorrow evening at 7 p.m. Don't let him down. Or me.

63

Tuesday 17:56

M on her way. Leave now.

The heads–up from Yasmine had come sooner than expected. With an hour to kill before meeting Tobias, Jensen had asked Aziz to drive her around the town centre. The bars and restaurants were gearing up for the night, the windows of the old houses filling with golden light. It was slow going, with commuters and tourists straying into the narrow streets, but Jensen didn't mind. She wanted to think about Deep Throat and his struggle for justice by proxy. Why the cloak and dagger? And if he was as well informed as he had had her believe, then he must know that she was no longer with *Dagbladet*, or had the news not reached him yet? She disliked the hectoring tone of his email but resolved to go and see Carsten Vangede anyway. It wasn't as if she was going to be busy in the next couple of days and, in a crowded bar, what was the risk?

Aziz glanced at her in the rear-view mirror now and again but said nothing. Jensen wondered what he was making of her. They hadn't exchanged much besides logistics in the time she had known him.

'What are you called besides Aziz?' she asked.

He shifted in his seat. 'Almasi.'

'How did you meet Esben?'

'It's a long story,' he said.

'I have a long time.'

Aziz didn't respond.

'Tell you what, could you drive past Sankt Peders Stræde? There is someone I'd like you to meet.'

Liron's van was shut for the day. He was outside talking to a girl with red hair. He kissed her on the cheek and she walked off smiling to herself, carrying a large paper cup. Jensen wondered with a stab of inexplicable jealousy if the woman was the regular who had got the number of Gustav's ward at Riget, and smiled at her broadly, getting a puzzled look in return.

'Where have you been? I fucking missed you. I thought, shit, Liron, that cute journalist lady is never coming back again,' he shouted, holding out his arms for a hug.

He recoiled dramatically at the sight of Aziz coming up behind her.

'Liron, meet Aziz. Aziz meet Liron.'

'He is a bloody giant,' said Liron, pretending to be in great pain when Aziz shook his hand. 'Aaah . . .'

Aziz smiled for the first time since Jensen had known him. Liron reached up and put one hand on his bulky shoulder. 'Wait, my friend, just wait.'

They watched as Liron unlocked the van and brought out a tiny, battered, brass coffee pot that Jensen had never seen before. Liron spooned in finely ground coffee, so dark it was almost black. He poured in water and placed the pot on a gas camping stove, adding cardamom pods from a jar. When it was done, he poured the thick liquid into a paper espresso cup and handed it to Aziz, offering him brown sugar from a bowl. Aziz heaped in five spoonfuls and stirred before sipping his cup with surprising daintiness.

Liron watched his face with a wide, toothy grin. 'You like?'

'Syrian coffee,' says Aziz, smiling. 'Almost perfect.'

Liron made Jensen a cortado, and she and Aziz took their coffees back to the car. She decided to join him on the front seat, ignoring the uncomfortable look on his face.

'So, tell me how you met Esben,' she said. 'From the beginning.'

He rubbed his beard, looking out at the passing cyclists heading home from work in the slush, and at Liron packing up his van. It was a few long, awkward minutes before he spoke, but in the end her steady, silent gaze broke him.

'We had to leave Syria. My wife was six months' pregnant; we couldn't stay. So, we left, travelling up through Turkey and Greece, joining a group in Macedonia for the stretch through Serbia and Hungary. In Hungary, they held us for a week at a railway station, but they finally let us go. Then, in Austria and Germany, they put us on coaches, and we got the train from Hamburg to Puttgarden and then the ferry to Denmark. It had taken us a long time to get there and my wife was exhausted. The Danish police tried to persuade us to come with them, but I wanted to get to Sweden. I knew people who had gone there, so we kept walking north.'

Jensen remembered watching on the news the refugees walking on the Danish motorways, hundreds of them, mostly young men, carrying rucksacks and sports bags and dragging wheeled suitcases behind them.

'It was hard for my wife. Some people shouted at us to go home, but we just kept on walking. There were so many of us that no one could do anything about it.'

'What about Esben?'

'I guess he must have been watching it on TV and decided he had to do something. All of a sudden, he was just there, parked by the side of the road. He had an expensive car and wore a hood over his head. He kind of crept up on us through the crowd. I don't know why he chose us; maybe because of my wife's condition. She wasn't feeling well. He asked me to let him drive us to shelter and to give us food, just for the night, and then he would take us to Sweden himself. My wife begged me to agree. So Esben took us to his house in Klampenborg, and his wife was there, and two of his children, and they gave us a bedroom, and hot food, and clean clothes to wear. When the others had gone to bed, Esben and I stayed up and talked through my plan. He said it was a good plan, that Sweden was a good country, but that he believed Denmark would be a better home for us. He persuaded us to stay, and then he helped us apply for asylum. We stayed with him and his wife until we got a flat. He gave me work; I owe him everything.'

'Strange, Esben never told me, and I don't remember reading it in the papers.'

'He didn't want it to come out. No one knows about it.' A flinty look flashed across his eyes. 'You mustn't tell anyone.'

'I swear.'

Jensen was proud of Esben. It was typical of him. Aside from the story that had made his career, the same story that had made hers, he had kept a low profile through the years.

And beside that story, which had very nearly won her Denmark's Cavling Prize for exceptional journalism, what had she done with her life?

Aziz took her empty cup, placed it inside his, and crushed both in one hand. Then he walked over to Liron, and she watched the two of them shake hands as Aziz put one hand on Liron's shoulder and said something.

When Aziz returned to the car, Jensen was in the back seat.

'I think you prefer that no one sits in the front, am I right?'

'Only Esben,' he said, smiling.

'Just one last question, before we go.'

'Yes?'

'What did you use to do for work? Back in Syria?'

'You won't believe it.'

'Try me.'

'I was a rich man's driver.'

64

Tuesday 19:07

Tobias looked around him nervously as Jensen crossed the floor to his table at Bruun's Coffee Shop. Outside, across the black waters of the canal, she could see a yellow apartment building. A woman was standing by the window on the second floor, bouncing a child on her hip and talking on her mobile phone. Parked in the street below, Aziz sat in the black car, waiting to drive Jensen back to Esben's summer house or anywhere else she cared to go.

Tobias was drinking green tea from a reusable mug and asked if he could get her something. Jensen declined, still buzzing from Liron's cortado, but when she sat down, she knew it was a mistake to have turned down the offer. She was coming across as too impatient and businesslike. Tobias was losing his nerve.

'Before we go any further, I must tell you that I no longer work for *Dagbladet*. I'm flying back to London on Sunday,' she said, in an effort to appease him.

He looked puzzled, but after a little while his shoulders relaxed. He rubbed the corners of his mouth and caressed his caveman beard. Jensen thought about what he would look like without it and imagined soft, boyish features, a snail without its shell.

'Bit of a commute from here to Roskilde, isn't it?'

He shook his head. 'I have a room at Skovhøj, but my girl-friend has a flat five minutes from here, so I stay over now and again. It was her who persuaded me to talk to you.'

'I'm glad she did. I have some more questions for you.'

'I thought you said you no longer work for *Dagbladet*?'

'I don't. This is just me needing to know what happened to Thomas. Call it an occupational hazard.'

'You go first,' he said.

'You know the mad aunt who turned up at the funeral?'

Tobias nodded.

'Ever see her at Skovhøj?'

'No, never, but then Thomas had been given a new identity, hidden from anyone who knew him from before. His aunt would only have found out that he had died when Karina disclosed to the police who he really was, after she identified the body.'

He was right and, instead of pitying her lost-and-found nephew, Ditte had caused havoc at his funeral.

'What do you think she meant when she said it was all Thomas's fault?'

'The obvious, I suppose. He killed her sister.'

'But it's hard to imagine that the two of them were ever close. Ditte Mørk doesn't seem like the type who forms loving relationships with anyone, let alone members of her own family.'

'I don't know anything about that,' he said.

'Of course not, why would you. It just feels odd, all that anger after eight years.'

'Not really. Thomas and his aunt were estranged. His new identity wasn't revealed till a few days ago. She would have read about his murder in the newspaper, just like everybody else. I

247

guess she wanted to make a point that she hadn't forgotten what he did back then.'

'Make a point to whom, though? Only five of us there, no media. How did she even find out where the funeral was being held?'

'Not from me and I am pretty sure Karina wouldn't have told her either. Maybe the police? I wouldn't read too much into it, if I were you. The woman is clearly unhinged.'

'True enough. OK, final question: did Thomas ever tell you about what happened the day he stabbed his mother, or why he did it?'

Tobias shook his head. 'He and I never talked properly. Very occasionally, if there was something he needed to say, he would communicate with hand signs, or write it down. Like I said, I knew he'd been to a young offenders' institution, but I didn't know what for, and he never volunteered the information. I remember that the Langelandsvej Murder was on the news when I was at university, but I never thought . . . In fact, I would have said . . . No, it doesn't matter.'

'Go on?'

'It's just that we see a lot of different people at Skovhøj. People who've suffered or done stuff you wouldn't believe. But Thomas was different. Not because he didn't talk, but because of how tidy he was about himself and his flat. On the few occasions I took him out to go to the shops, he was always on time. I would find him waiting for me in his room, sitting on his bed with his coat on.'

'Did you enjoy his company?'

'In a way, but it was odd walking about with him in total silence. It was as if he had locked all the bad stuff away inside of him, but you could tell it was still there. It was rather intense.'

'But he was friendly enough to you.'

Tobias nodded.

'And to Fie, by all accounts.'

'Her too.'

'So, you don't understand how this could be the same person who stabbed his mother?'

'That's just it. I know full well he did it and, anyway, you can't tell from looking at a person what they are capable of. Working at Skovhøj has at least taught me that. It's just I think there was a lot more to Thomas than people wanted to see. There was a lot of depth there. He wasn't the monster he had been made out to be.'

'Apparently he always insisted that he didn't do it. That's probably what the trip to Copenhagen was all about, a kind of protest.'

'But the evidence was indisputable, I thought?'

'I believe so.'

'And I understand that he was in trouble at the time, with school and with drugs. I read somewhere that he had taken something that day.'

'Apparently, yes.'

Tobias had talked himself warm. He was as ready as he would be to tell her whatever it was that he had brought her there for.

'Your turn,' she said.

He spun his empty mug on the table, peered around nervously at the sprinkling of other people in the coffee shop, though not a single one of them was looking in their direction.

'I debated with myself whether to do this. I don't like going behind people's backs, but it's not right to just keep it to myself either. I haven't been able to sleep these past few days. That's why my girlfriend persuaded me to talk to someone. The only person I could think of was you.'

She smiled at him encouragingly.

'It's Karina,' he said. 'She lied to you.'

'What?'

'She told you she had no idea what possessed Thomas to take the train to Copenhagen that day, but that's not true, because I overheard her shouting at him the night before.'

Jensen remembered seeing Tobias recoil at Karina's touch when she had first visited Skovhøj. Now it made sense.

'Shouting what?'

'All sorts of horrible things. She accused him of being a free-loader, said there were plenty more deserving people waiting for a space at Skovhøj. She said that he was perfectly capable of speaking, and that he was a spoiled brat who was only after attention.'

'Any idea what had brought all that about?'

'We eat together all of us once a fortnight, take it in turns to cook and tidy afterwards. Thomas never once joined us.'

'Is it mandatory?'

'Not really, but we encourage people to come along. It's easy to become isolated if you stay in your own flat the whole time.'

'But Thomas refused.'

'Pretty much. He was never at table tennis either, or any of the group outings we arranged. As I have said before, Karina is under a lot of pressure, with the council threatening to with-draw their funding for Skovhøj. I supposed she had a really bad day and took it out on Thomas.'

'How?'

'She went to his room. It was Sunday evening, film night. Most of us were in the lounge watching, but as usual Thomas hadn't turned up. At one point I noticed Karina had left the room, so I went looking for her. When I passed Thomas's door, I heard her in there. She was yelling at him to leave Skovhøj if he was so independent and didn't need anyone else.'

'And then what happened?'

'Nothing. I went back to the film. Karina came into the lounge a few minutes later and sat down. But Thomas must have taken what she said literally. No one saw him alive again.'

'Did you confront Karina about it? That it might all have been her fault?'

'No, I knew she'd only deny it, and I don't want you to ask

250

her about it either. She will know where it's come from, and then she will find some way to get rid of me. She has done it before with people she doesn't like. A few weeks go by and, one day, they don't turn up for work. I just thought that maybe it would help you find out what happened to him.'

'You should have told the police.'

'I didn't want to attract attention to myself.'

'What do you mean?'

Her phone pinged. Gustav.

I just received this from Malene Grønfeldt. What do you think it means?

She read the message.

Sorry, we keep missing each other. I have some information for you. Can we talk? P.S. Don't share this with anyone, I don't feel safe any more.

Jensen forwarded Gustav's text to Henrik, ignoring the pings that immediately followed. He could go and speak to Gustav himself if he was interested.

When she looked up, Tobias was studying her face.

'What's happened?' he said.

'Nothing.'

She smiled in yet another attempt to reassure him. He wasn't buying it.

'You know you could tell someone else, anonymously, about Karina.'

She got a piece of paper from her bag and wrote down Frank Buhl's name and contact details.

Tobias studied the note closely

'I remember this guy,' he said. 'Karina refused to let him in when he came to Skovhøj. By then we had people with TV cameras outside and were under strict instructions not to speak to anyone.'

'She can't sack you if she doesn't know it's you speaking to *Dagbladet*.'

251

'Don't be so sure.'

'Why didn't you want to attract attention to yourself anyway? I mean with the police?'

'Because I also lied. I told them Thomas didn't have a laptop. In actual fact, he did . . .'

He paused, opened his rucksack and pulled out a laptop that had seen better days. It had a yellow-and-black nuclear-hazard sticker on it that said: *Keep Out.*

He placed the laptop on the table between them.

'The day the police came to search the place, I was upset and thought that Thomas should be allowed privacy and respect, so I took this from his room. I knew that he kept it hidden below his mattress. I haven't looked at anything on it, swear to God. I don't have his password, so I couldn't, even if I wanted to. I want to hand it to the police now that all the stories about him have come out, but I worry that it's going to look suspicious this late in the day, as if was trying to hide something before. What should I do?'

'That laptop is evidence. The police are still trying to piece together what happened the night Thomas was killed. There might be some clues in there as to what he was thinking.'

'I know, that's why I feel so awful about it all, but I can't afford to lose my job, not now. Me and my girlfriend are moving in together.'

She waited a moment before speaking, as if the idea had only then entered her mind. 'I could hand it in for you without saying where I got it from.'

'Would you?'

'Leave it with me.'

She wasn't lying.

She was going to give Henrik the laptop.

Absolutely.

Just as soon as she got the chance.

65

The sound of gravel crunching under tyres as Aziz turned into the Hornbæk drive reminded her of when she was a child and her mother used to carry her from the car into her bed. She would pretend to be asleep as she nestled into her mother's chest, inhaling her distinct smell of perfume, chewing gum and cigarettes. Until she had become too heavy to lift and their physical closeness, such as it was, had ended. Aziz would think nothing of carrying her into her bed now; he could probably do so in one arm. The thought made Jensen sit upright.

Aziz undid his seatbelt.

'No,' she said, touching his shoulder. 'I'm fine: go back to that lovely family of yours.'

'Just a quick look,' he said, 'To make sure everything is OK.'

What was it with the men in her life that they always needed to check on her safety?

'I can look after myself, you know, Aziz. Besides, I've got the dog now.'

'But Esben—'

'Oh, sod Esben. Take a look for yourself – there is no one out there.'

He made her promise to phone him if she needed anything, no matter how late. She waved him off, relieved when he turned the corner and disappeared from sight.

'Thought you'd never leave,' she mumbled, turning her face to the sky and exhaling mist into the blankness.

She stayed put until she could no longer hear the car. Then she realised the dog wasn't barking.

A faint whining noise that she couldn't identify was coming from the direction of the house.

She didn't see what it was till she was practically right in front of it.

A loud scream pierced the air. She fell, scrambling backwards in the snow on her hands and bottom, before realising that the scream was coming from herself. It evolved into a protracted, airless moan, like a scream in a nightmare.

The dog had been strung up on the front door, hanging from its front legs, its tongue lolling between its teeth and its bloodied white belly exposed.

The noise she had heard was the rope moving against the door.

The dog was twitching.

It was still alive.

Barely.

She got up, yelling, '*Nej, nej, nej.*'

Fumbling, she untied the dog from the door and held it in her arms, sitting on the front step. She thought of Henrik in the Old Brompton Road in Kensington, roaring at people to stay away as the stricken dog in his arms drew its last breath. But this dog wasn't dying. It was whimpering in pain.

Once, Jensen had watched her mother drown a sick baby rabbit they had found abandoned in their field. In tears, she had begged her mother not to do it, pledged to take care of it. But

254

her mother had carried on, holding the rabbit under the water of the horse-trough. ('It is a crime to let an animal suffer.')

There was a rounders bat in Esben's shed. Crying now, Jensen looked away as she struck, once, as hard as he could.

The twitching stopped.

She sat in the snow for what seemed like hours, sobbing, blood on her hands, rocking over the animal in her lap and stroking its body as it began to cool.

'I am sorry,' she said over and over. 'I am so sorry.'

Henrik answered on the fourth ring. He sounded muddled with sleep at first, but when she told him what had happened, he swore furiously.

'On my way, and whatever you do, don't enter the house. Do you hear me?'

While she waited, she tried to clean up the mess as best she could. It wasn't working too well. Whoever had killed the dog had been watching her coming and going. It could have happened any time in the past ten hours; she had been out all day.

She went around the garden, shouting 'Hallo' into the darkness, but the snow on the lawn was pristine, and there was no sound but her footsteps and the hush of the wind in the pine trees.

She was trembling with shock and cold when, at long last, Henrik came speeding up the lane. He ran out of the car, roaring with rage when he saw the dog.

He entered the house first, with a torch and his gun drawn. The living room had been ransacked, clippings, notes and printouts scattered everywhere, as though it had been snowing inside. In the mess, she couldn't tell whether anything was missing, but it hardly mattered. Whoever had been there now knew what she had been doing.

'Did Thomas's killer do this?' she asked Henrik, her teeth clattering.

'Fuck knows, but they won't be getting away with it,' he said, trembling with rage.

If the aim was to scare her, whoever had broken in and tortured the dog almost to death had succeeded. But scare her off what? To whom had she got too close?

She thought of Ditte Mørk. She was mad enough to have done it. Or the drug dealer could have got the address from Gustav. Or Karina Jørgensen could have managed to wangle the address out of Fie.

Henrik picked up some of the notes from the floor, a look of dismay on his face. 'I told you to stay out of it,' he said. 'I thought you might have stopped all this when Gustav got beaten up. That was the first warning. This is the second, and it might be your last.'

'It was exactly *because* Gustav got beaten up that I didn't stop.'

'You can't stay here now,' said Henrik, his eyes roaming wildly around the room.

'I don't have a choice – nowhere else to go.'

'I'll take you to a hotel.'

'It's after midnight, and there's none for miles.'

He insisted on staying the night. They climbed under the duvet with their clothes on. He put his gun on the bedside table and wrapped his arms round her, holding her close as she wept for the dog.

'The way it looked up at me with those big eyes, so trusting. I should have been nicer to it, loved it more while it lived, not left it here alone.'

He told her in a croaky voice that she had done the right thing, putting the dog out of its misery, that he would have done the same, that she had been brave. It felt like the opposite. Like something shameful and dark had been exposed that she didn't know she had in her. It made her want to throw up.

She slept badly, haunted by images of the dog dangling from

the door, the ghostly feel of its body in her arms, blood in the snow.

And, all night, she sensed Henrik awake behind her, rigid, eyes open in the pitch dark, like a sentinel.

66

'This feels wrong.'

Fie was sitting at the summer house dining table, the chair creaking under her. Aziz was at the end of the table, and Jensen directly opposite Fie. Between the two of them, she felt like Alice in Wonderland after swallowing the 'Drink Me' potion.

They all had a cup of coffee in front of them, made by Aziz. They had talked about the weather, the snow that was still thick on the ground outside, and the warnings issued by the Danish Met Office for another blizzard by the weekend.

Aziz had told them a story about driving his rich boss over the border to Lebanon in a snowstorm, and Fie had marvelled at the fact that snow falls in the Middle East.

Henrik had left at dawn, making Jensen swear to call him at the slightest sign of anything untoward. She had been trying to dig a dog-sized hole in the ground behind the summer house when Aziz had pulled into the drive. The ground was frozen solid, and she had been too shaken to make any headway. Aziz had come up beside her and looked at the dog, stiff as a board,

258

the bandana round its neck bright red against in the snow. There was nothing for it but to own up to him.

'I found it strung across the front door last night when I got back,' said Jensen, wiping her nose. 'A little message from someone telling me to mind my own business, and if I don't . . . that they know where to find me.'

'Who?'

'I can think of a few options.'

'You should have called me,' he said, gently taking the spade from her hand.

'The policeman came,' she said.

He nodded imperceptively, as if in approval.

Aziz had made quick work of the grave, placing the dog in the hole and filling it in with soil. Afterwards they stood for a while together in the bitter cold, him with one hand on her shoulder as hot tears rolled down her cheeks. Whoever had thought this would make her stop looking for Thomas's killer was mistaken.

Now she, Fie and Aziz were all staring at Thomas's laptop and the USB stick on the table next to it.

'How did you get it?' asked Fie.

'I could tell you, but that's not the question that matters most in this context.'

'What is?'

'Whether you think Thomas deserves a fair hearing. Whether you think his story is important enough.'

'I do.'

'Then help me find out what happened to him. Can you get into the laptop?'

'I think so.'

'Look, all you have to do is to copy the files to this USB stick, and afterwards I will personally hand the laptop to the police.'

'I am not sure we should be doing this.'

'You want to find out what happened to Thomas, don't you?

Because I have to tell you that I am not confident the police will get there. They've got three bodies so far, and not a clue what happened. There may be a lot of stuff on this laptop that they would just ignore, stuff that could mean something.'

Fie squirmed. 'I have a court order banning me from doing this sort of thing. I shouldn't have gone as far as I have for you.'

'What do you mean, a court order?'

'An injunction.'

'Oh?'

'You've no idea how I ended up at Skovhøj, do you?' Fie asked, after a pause.

'Will you tell me?' said Jensen.

'I was always fat, really, really fat. School was not good for someone like me, so I played truant a lot. I used to sit in my room and talk to people online, pretend I was someone else. I got into this whole new community of people who taught me all sorts of things. I learned fast, hacked into some sites. After a couple of attempts, I managed to book plane tickets to Florida for myself and my mum and little brother, but I got found out, and the police came to our flat. I only wanted us to go on holiday together.'

'You got arrested?'

'I was eleven years old.'

'Right.'

'They gave me a caution and I learned to be more careful. When I was thirteen, my mum went to prison, and me and my brother went to different foster parents. I didn't like the new people, so I tried to break into the system to alter my mother's criminal record and shorten her sentence. I got found out again, and my foster parents threw me out and I got sent to this residential school, which was really prison by another name. That's where I got the injunction taken out against me. I was still too young to be sentenced, but I am old enough for it now, so I need to be careful. I like it at Skovhøj; it's the best place I have ever lived.'

'Where's your mum now?'

'Dead. Overdose. I think that's why me and Thomas got on so well. We were both orphans.' She looked down at her hands. 'That and the self-harm. Thomas understood.'

'And your brother?'

'Last time I heard, he was on a container ship off the coast of Singapore. That was two years ago.'

Jensen looked at the USB and cleared her throat.

'I see why you wouldn't want to jeopardise things at Skovhøj, so tell me, will anyone be able to tell that you have copied the files?' Jensen asked.

'Not if I cover my tracks.'

'Then do that.'

'Always. But it's also . . .'

'Yes?'

'It's Thomas's private stuff on here.'

She looked Jensen in the eye and Jensen could tell that she was dying to have a look at her dead friend's stuff but wanted to be given permission.

'I will take full responsibility. You are not here today. You are at the cinema in Copenhagen with Tobias.'

'How did you persuade him to cover for us?'

'Let's just say he owes me a favour. Besides, he has a girl-friend in Christianshavn, so he wasn't particularly reluctant to be dropped off at Roskilde with a return ticket to Copenhagen. Come on, Fie. I am so close to finding out what happened to Thomas. Will you help me? Please?'

67

Wednesday 17:34

Night had fallen by the time Jensen and Aziz got to the city. Turned out Thomas had gone to great lengths to protect his information; Fie had spent ages getting round the password. In the end, Aziz had gone to wait in the car. Meanwhile Jensen had tried to read through the remaining articles about Grønfeldt, but she had been unable to concentrate, and had kept popping over to the dining table to check on progress until Fie had snapped the laptop closed and locked herself in the bathroom.

When she had emerged, much later, clutching the laptop to her chest, Jensen could tell she had been crying.

'Well?' she had asked. 'Can I have the USB?'

Fie had shaken her head, wiping her nose on the back of her hand. 'You won't be able to read any of it. It's all encrypted. I will need to take this back with me, run it through some different software.'

For most of the journey to Roskilde station and their rendezvous with Tobias, Fie had kept her face turned away, leaning against the window of the black car with the USB stick wrapped inside her fist. Jensen wondered what could be so important that Thomas would try so hard to conceal it.

Henrik was waiting for her at the entrance to the police building, looking even shiftier than usual. He marched her round the corner, through a gate into a shadowy courtyard full of bicycles. Then he opened her coat and reached up under her shirt, embracing her hard. His hands were warm and strong.

'Are you OK?' he mumbled into her hair.

She nodded.

'How did you get here? If you can wait, I'll finish up work and drive you to a hotel. I was going to do so anyway.'

Jensen freed herself. 'Thanks, but I have my own transport. Esben's driver has been at a loose end since he went back to Aalborg on Saturday, so I am borrowing him for the time being.'

'Esben has a driver? Why doesn't that surprise me? And you're sure the old goat isn't expecting anything in return?'

'None of your business.'

'Who is he anyway, this driver?'

'Aziz from Syria. He is lovely.'

Henrik frowned at her.

'He is married and has three kids,' she said.

'Somehow that doesn't make me feel better at all.'

He made a show of looking around for Aziz. Jensen ignored him.

'Henrik, I didn't get a chance to tell you. I am going home. I mean, back to London.'

He leaned his forehead towards hers, their noses touching. 'I am sorry,' he said, but she could tell that he wasn't.

Not really.

He had thought she was what he wanted, but he had made a mistake. Again.

'When?' he whispered, pressing his body against hers.

'Sunday.'

'I'll take you to the airport.'

'No, it's all right, Aziz will do it. Besides, it's probably best that you and I don't see each other again.'

She pulled away from him, took a step back, but he took a step forward, grabbed her shoulders.

'Listen, I love you. You can't end this. Well, you can try, but it won't work. You and I, we will always be bound together.'

They stood like that for a long time. Jensen could hear cars spraying slush in the road, a nearby siren, people walking close by talking. Copenhagen in winter.

'I came to give you something,' she said finally, feeling his body tensing as he came away from her. 'I am sorry, I should have done it last night.'

She reached into her bag and pulled out Thomas's laptop. The yellow sticker radiated its warning in the dark.

Keep out.

'What's this?'

'It's Thomas's. Before you say anything, I am just the messenger. Someone went into the flat and took it after Thomas died, before you arrived and searched the place.'

'I knew there was a laptop, I just knew it. Shit, Jensen, that's tampering with police evidence. Tell me who gave it to you.'

'Let me see. It could have been a lot of people. Twenty-two residents at Skovhøj, minus Thomas, that's twenty-one, plus nine members of staff, or eleven including the cleaners. That's thirty-two.'

'It's not what I asked. I asked who gave it to you.'

'And I am saying there are a lot of options.'

'You're withholding information from the police.'

'I am protecting my source.'

'I could arrest you.'

She held out her wrists. 'Go ahead.'

'Fuck, Jensen. Tell me you didn't look at it.'

'I didn't look at it.'

'You're lying – I can see it in your eyes. Just as well you're

264

going back to London, where you can't do any more damage. I'm starting to wish you hadn't called me that morning.'

'You don't mean that.'

'You're putting my job on the line.'

'Hardly. I no longer have a newspaper to write for, remember? Even if there were any new information on that laptop, which is by no means certain, exactly what would I be doing with it?'

'I can think of loads of things, and so can you.' Henrik looked beyond her to the street, his eyes narrowing.

Jensen turned to see the black car creeping up alongside the kerb. Aziz got out and stood silently by the passenger door, looking at the two of them impassively, hands the size of shovels by his side.

'Sorry, I've got to go now,' she said.

'Not back to Hornbæk. It's not safe. Jensen, for fuck's sake, what do I have to do?'

'Don't worry, Aziz won't let anything happen to me.'

She left him gaping as she walked towards the car, waving goodbye with her back turned.

68

Wednesday 18:51

Aziz must have got it wrong; there were no drunks outside Zoom Bar. Perhaps it was too cold, even for them, or the night hadn't got started yet. She was a few minutes early, but all the same, she would have expected the place to be buzzing already. The newsagent's next door was open and so was the kebab shop a little further along the street. The smell of the grilled meat made her mouth water, reminding her that it was a while since she had last eaten. Aziz had gone home to see his family. If Carsten Vangede stood her up, she would order a doner kebab with lettuce, tomatoes and onion and garlic sauce and eat it seated on one of the high stools by the window.

The faded green velvet curtains covering the lower half of Zoom Bar's windows were drawn, the door locked and guarded with a padlocked grille. She peered through the gaps and thought she saw a light, but it could have been the reflection of the street lamp behind her. She knocked on one of the windows, waited, and knocked again.

Just as she turned and began to walk towards the kebab shop, a ruddy-faced man pulled back one of the curtains. He looked her up and down for a while before gesturing at her to go through the gate to the back of the building. A security light came on as she approached, picking her way past beer kegs and crates of empty bottles, then the back door flew open and the man appeared. His burgundy shirt was untucked and he hadn't shaved for a few days, judging by his greying stubble. Gold sparkled on his neck and wrist.

'My name is Jensen,' she said, showing him her press card. 'Are you Carsten Vangede?'

'I thought you were a . . .'

'Man? I get that a lot,' she said.

He looked like he was debating whether or not to let her in, obviously not seeing a reporter of the calibre he had been expecting.

She got that a lot too.

'I was told to meet you here. It's freezing – is there somewhere warmer we can talk?'

'Be my guest,' he said, disappearing into the darkness of the bar and leaving her to see herself in behind him.

The smell that hit her sent her back to her earliest youth and the local bars she had frequented before she was old enough to drink legally. The Danes called them *bodegas*, these basic watering holes with pine-panelled walls papered with beer mats, postcards and old advertising signs. Far from the quaint country gastro pubs in England that attracted all generations, these places were for hardcore drinkers. Zoom Bar stank of beer and illicit cigarette smoke mixed with disinfectant from the toilets at the back. The bar was lined with black metal stools topped with faux leather. There were four other tables, all with upturned chairs. A billiards table was just visible through a gap in the door to a side room.

Carsten Vangede sat on a stool behind the bar, having made considerable inroads into a bottle of vodka. A cigarette was smoking itself in an overfilled ashtray. Soft American rock played from a speaker mounted on the wall next to a Route 66 sign.

'You're not opening tonight?'

'Nope,' he said. 'Nor tomorrow, or the next day, or ever again. Want to buy a bar?' he said, laughing humourlessly.

'What happened?'

'The bank called in my loan. I can't pay my creditors, can't pay my staff, can't pay my cleaners. I am bankrupt.'

'Because of Karen Nordmann?'

'Who?'

'The accountant. I thought—'

'It was the accountant all right. Bjarne Pedersen, or whatever his real name is.'

'Tell me, from the beginning.'

He looked up at her with his bloodshot eyes. 'What are *you* going to do about it?'

'I am here because our mutual friend thought I might help, by investigating, or maybe by publicising the scam and making some people pay attention.'

'They will eat you whole.'

'Who will?'

'The people behind this.'

He knocked an inch of ash off his cigarette and sucked deeply from the remains, pushing the smoke out through his nose. Jensen waited. With men like Carsten Vangede, you often had to wait a long time.

'I own three places,' he began after a long silence. 'This bar and a couple of restaurants, one of them a pizzeria. Everything was ticking along OK until this woman who has been doing the books for me retired last year. I advertised for a new account-ant, part-time, freelance, all that. Bjarne seemed great, used to spend way more hours than he charged for. Well, of course, the joke is now on me. For eight months he drained cash out of the operation, duplicating every third invoice in the system, and paying the proceeds into a bank account owned by himself.'

'How come you didn't discover it?'

He drained his glass and refilled it. 'I never paid any attention to the books before. Went like clockwork. Except one day, after Bjarne had gone off for Christmas, when a payment to one of my suppliers bounced. I tried myself to get to the bottom of what had happened, but nothing appeared to be wrong. Had I really been sailing so close to the wind without having the faintest clue? In the end I showed everything to my retired accountant, and it was her who discovered what Bjarne had done.'

'Then what did you do?'

'Went straight to the police, of course. Gave them all of Bjarne's details, the whole kaboodle. I thought they'd go and arrest him when he returned from holiday. But he didn't return, and they made no attempt to find him. You know what they told me?'

'They don't investigate private financial fraud of less than one million kroner.'

'Yeah, the arseholes,' he stubbed out his cigarette and lit a new one.

'Bjarne stole 900,078 kroner from me. I went to look for him myself, found his mobile phone number disconnected and someone else living at his address, who had no clue who he was. Then I met . . . our mutual friend, who told me the same thing had happened to him.'

'Do you have a picture of Bjarne?'

'Of course not. He was far too clever to fall for that.'

'Well can you describe him to me?'

'Blond, thinning hair, metal-framed glasses, medium tall. Not a Copenhagener; came from somewhere in Jutland.'

A poor description and lots of options for 'Bjarne' to have changed his appearance since. This story wouldn't be going anywhere.

'He did leave these behind. Not that they are of much use,' said Carsten Vangede, throwing a spectacle case onto the bar.

Jensen opened the case, which contained a pair of metal-framed glasses. The name and address of an optician in Randers was printed in gold letters in the lid. Seemed he had been right about 'Bjarne' hailing from Jutland.

'Already rang them, dead end. But sometimes I wonder . . .'

'If?

'If the people who ransacked my flat a couple of weeks ago were looking for these.'

'You had a break-in?'

'That's what they made it look like.'

'Was anything taken?'

'No, that's just it. They made one hell of a mess, but nothing was missing.'

They looked at each other for a while. Then she put the spectacle case in her shoulder bag. 'I'll take the glasses. If someone's looking for them, at least they are not going to find them here. Give me your number; I will think of something and call you back.'

He scribbled his number on the back of a beer mat and tossed it along the bar to her with as much disinterest as he could muster.

'By the way,' said Jensen. 'Before I go, do you know who our mutual friend is?'

'Never met the guy. We've only been in touch by email,' he said, refilling his glass.

'But you must know his name?'

'Not a clue,' he said. 'You?'

'No, but I intend to find out.'

'Yeah, well, whatever. One more business going down, who gives a shit,' he said, knocking back vodka once more and looking well on his way to paralytic.

Behind the bar a handwritten notice on a blackboard announced: *Every hour is happy hour at Zoom Bar.*

Not any more, thought Jensen as she jumped off the bar stool and let herself out into the dark back yard. She stopped for a moment, looking around her. Was it the conversation with Carsten Vangede that had managed to spook her, or was someone watching her somewhere in one of the dozens of windows stretching six floors above her to the tiny square of black sky? She ran for the gate and the safety of Aziz and the black car.

69

There was something on the doorstep to Esben's summer house, a murky outline against the snow. Footsteps led up the front door. Someone had been here while she was out.

Jensen felt fear prickling her palms. 'Oh God, not again.'

'Stay where you are,' said Aziz.

She watched in the light from the headlamps as he touched the dark shape with the nose of his boot, then bent down slowly to pick it up. It was a plastic bag from Magasin, the Copenhagen department store.

It couldn't be something to do with Carsten Vangede, could it? Not this soon after they had met?

'What's in it?' she shouted.

'Don't know. Looks like a folder with papers inside.'

She felt her shoulders relax a little. 'Maybe it's something for Esben?'

They took the bag into the house and put the folder on the dining-room table. The papers gave off a smell of mildew and were marked *Confidential*. There were notes, transcripts of interviews, copies of fingerprints and photographs.

Graphic photographs.

Sandra in her kitchen, the floor painted in her blood.

Aziz mumbled something in Arabic.

'Holy shit, it's a copy of Thomas Mørk's entire police file,' said Jensen.

'Same person who killed the dog?' said Aziz.

'No. The person who did this would never have laid a hand on an innocent creature. They wanted me to see this, to look for more clues.'

She thought of Majbritt Johansen's sad, worn face, the angry glare from her husband as he jerked their living-room curtain shut. Had the lawyer decided to drive to Hornbæk with the folder as an act of sheer defiance? Or had she too got curious about what happened to Thomas in Magstræde, and wanted Jensen to come up with the answer?

The last thing she needed was for Henrik to find out. Besides snatching the files from her pronto, he would kick up an almighty fuss about her having gone to see Majbritt in the first place.

'That's it – I am staying the night,' said Aziz.

'What?'

'More than one person knows where you are now, and with the dog and what happened to Gustav, it's not safe for you to be here on your own.'

'I'm perfectly fine.'

'I can sleep in the car; I am a very light sleeper. If anyone comes, I will wake up immediately.'

'Aziz, whoever killed the dog did what they came for, which was to frighten me. If they had wanted to do me harm, they would have done so by now.'

'Not necessarily. They tried to stop you, but you haven't stopped.'

'I don't tend to, once I get going.'

'Esben would never forgive me if something happened.'

'Nothing will,' she said with more confidence than she was feeling. 'I will sleep with a knife by my bed.'

She knew he was right to be concerned, but her weakness was making her embarrassed and stubborn.

Finally, Aziz relented, after she promised under pain of death to text him the second she woke up in the morning. She waved him off from the front door. Then she closed all the curtains one by one and checked that the doors were locked. She put music on, lit the candles, made a fire and opened another of Esben's bottles. But not even the champagne could distract her from the thought of a killer, cold-blooded enough to torment a defenceless dog, creeping towards the summer house in the snowy darkness.

She realised that she was afraid.

Her phone lit up with a message from Henrik.

No way I am letting that bearded giant take you to the airport. Besides I need to make sure that you definitely are leaving the country. See you Sunday!

She smiled despite the icy unease that had taken hold of her body. Then she opened the first of the folders with the documents from the Thomas Mørk case and began to read.

70

'Will someone please shut that woman up, I can't hear myself think,' said Henrik, closing his eyes and pinching the bridge of his nose.

The dog walker was sitting in the back of the open ambulance with a blanket wrapped round her shoulders, howling like a wounded animal, which had set off her yapping cocker spaniel.

One of the officers jogged over and had a word with the ambulance crew. The crew helped the woman inside with the dog, shut the doors and drove off, the barking and screaming mercifully fading from earshot.

Henrik breathed out slowly through his teeth, gesturing at the photographer from forensics to move away from the dilapidated orange camper van rust bucket. He shone his torch through the rear window. Whoever had taken issue with Ditte Mørk had left nothing to chance. She had been stabbed so violently that the front windscreen had been sprayed crimson.

Henrik spat on the ground, feeling his empty stomach turn. He reckoned the murder had happened not long before the dog walker had raised the alarm, perhaps due to the vague residual warmth that radiated from the inside of the van as he opened the door. The car park was obscured from the surrounding apartment blocks by a cluster of naked birch trees, but people going to work were bound to be heading for their cars soon and would stop to look and make a nuisance of themselves.

There was snow on the van, and no visible tyre tracks, so Ditte must have been parked up there overnight. Judging by the blood-soaked blankets, she had been sleeping in the vehicle when she was attacked. The rear window had been smashed with a brick. It was impossible to tell if she had fought back. David would be able to tell him, but Henrik would have to wait for answers. Unlikely they would know anything significant before tomorrow.

He peered inside the open driver's-side door, using his torch. The car was a pigsty, the footwells caked in mud and filled with empty bottles, food containers and a makeshift ashtray in a tub of yogurt. There was a beach bag on the passenger seat, ancient and threadbare. Henrik put on latex gloves, reached across the steering wheel and rifled through it.

The photographer stopped snapping away and looked up at Henrik expectantly.

'Benedikte Mørk,' he read from the driving licence, the photo on which, taken more than a decade earlier, bore no likeness whatsoever to its owner.

Ditte.

'She's known to us already,' he said.

A powerful spotlight came on, turning the blood on the windscreen a lurid purple. Perfect timing, thought Henrik, lighting the stage for the audience that was gathering slowly in the surrounding darkness. He stepped back to allow the scene-of-crime officers through in their white moon suits, then noticed a man on a bicycle holding up a mobile phone.

Fucking mobile phones.

Fucking people.

'Tape off the whole car park, now!' he shouted to a uniformed officer, who stared back at him gormlessly. 'And get rid of those rubberneckers. I don't want anyone sharing this online. Go!'

The officer sprinted towards the man on the bicycle while the white-suited investigators began crawling all over the car.

Bit too much of a coincidence, he thought, that Ditte Mørk had got herself killed a matter of days after Thomas. She hadn't stabbed her nephew; he was certain of that now. Her alibi had checked out. Henrik hated curtain-twitchers as much as the next person, but when it came to his job, he had learned to appreciate them immensely. A resident in the street in Hellerup where Ditte had parked her van on the night of the blizzard had noted down her licence number and reported her to the police for blocking his driveway. A couple of officers passing by in a squad car had received an earful from her around 3 a.m. According to them, she had been in no fit state to walk, let alone commit murder.

Henrik felt the beginning of a headache tighten its grip around his scalp. Maybe Jensen had had a point after all about Christian Grønfeldt being involved somehow. After all, he was the only person who had known both Thomas and Ditte.

He would have to haul the man back in. As soon as he could get away from this godforsaken dump. Whatever anyone had thought of Ditte – which in Henrik's case had been very little indeed – this was no place to die.

71

Thursday 09:16

Jensen woke to the sound of pounding on the front door. Only one person she knew was capable of striking a surface with such force.

'Aziz,' she said, conscious how she must look to him in her crumpled clothes and wild hair.

Come to think of it, he didn't look too good himself.

'Are you OK?' he shouted.

'Why are you asking? What's happened?'

'I couldn't leave. I wouldn't have been able to look Esben in the eye, so I parked down by the road, where I would see if anybody entered the lane. I must have fallen asleep around five, and when I woke up and saw there was no text from you, I thought . . .'

'Jesus, Aziz, you must have been freezing. If I'd known, you could have slept here.'

'No, I shouldn't have been sleeping. I should have been keeping a lookout.'

He looked half dead with tiredness.

'Well, nothing happened. As you see, I am fine. I was up half

278

the night reading the files that were left on the doorstep. Can't have slept more than a couple of hours myself. Come in and warm yourself.'

She made a fire and went to the kitchen to make coffee. While she waited for it to brew, she got out her phone, scrolling fast through the news. The latest poll was predicting that a far-right candidate campaigning on a platform of deporting all Muslims from Denmark might get enough of the public vote to make it into the Danish parliament.

'Nazi,' she mumbled under her breath, eliciting a sharp look from Aziz.

'Not you,' she said, waving her phone at him. 'It's just . . . something on the news.'

He took the cup she offered him, looked at it sceptically. 'I never understood how you Danes can drink this warm brown water.'

'Liron would be with you there,' she said.

He yawned, set down his untouched coffee on the dining table and rested his forehead on his arms. 'Wake me up when we're going.'

Jensen began to scroll through the news again, her eye caught by a *Dagbladet* story about the funding difficulties at Skovhøj. Frank reported that not all was as it seemed at the youth home, and that the manager had screamed at Thomas to leave on the eve of his departure for Copenhagen.

Yes! Finally, Tobias had given Karina some of her own medicine.

'Good luck getting that funding now,' Jensen said to the grainy picture of Karina, trying unsuccessfully to shield her face from the photographer's lens as she headed into work.

She took her coffee through to the living room and stopped mid-floor. A bright yellow notification on her phone told her that there had been another murder.

A woman had been found stabbed in her camper van in

279

Amager, near the airport. The circumstances weren't clear, but someone had posted a blurry scene-of-crime photo on Twitter, which had been reproduced by one of the tabloids.

The victim is thought to be forty-nine-year-old Benedikte Mørk from Mosebo near Silkeborg.

Jensen flopped onto the sofa.

What?

Ditte, stabbed?

It made no sense. She began to compose a message to Henrik but stopped halfway through. There was no point. He would be too busy to talk and had long stopped sharing information with her anyway.

Gobby and provocative, Ditte had not been the sort of person who picked up friends along her way. Few people would shed a tear at the news, but who had hated her enough to kill her? Could she be the fourth victim of the serial killer, though she didn't fit the pattern? Jensen checked the various news sites, but they were all just circulating the same scant facts.

There had been two new pieces of information in the section of the case file that she had managed to read so far. One was that, on the day of the murder at the approximate time when Sandra had been stabbed, Thomas had claimed that he had been visiting a friend from school who had also skived off that day. However, this had not been corroborated by the friend.

The second piece of information was that a neighbour opposite the Mørks' house had been identified, but later dismissed, as a potential witness, and their statement in Thomas's defence struck from the record. She had looked through the file, but not been able to locate the statement itself.

Both were worth checking out, but first she had to speak to Charlotte Friis, the friend who had been quoted for saying that Sandra had been afraid of Thomas, her own son.

Charlotte had owned a boutique in Ordrup, and the shop was still there, with the website listing her as the proprietor.

Jensen wanted to ask her about what the relationship between Grønfeldt and Sandra had been like. Had she ever seen the couple argue? Had she known about Sandra's pregnancy and what Grønfeldt thought of it?

He had had an alibi for the time of the murder, Jensen was sure that she had read that somewhere. If he hadn't had an alibi, then surely he would have been a prime suspect?

According to the post-mortem, Sandra had died sometime between noon and 2 p.m. Thomas had claimed to have come home no earlier than 2.30 p.m., directly from his friend's house, which was five minutes away by foot. Then, around 2.45 p.m., Christian Grønfeldt had arrived. It was a Wednesday, one of two days during the week when he shut his clinic early.

It took Jensen a while to find it. A typed statement dated the day after the murder. Christian Grønfeldt had seen his last patient at 2 p.m., and his assistant had waved goodbye to him at 2.30 p.m. precisely. The house was at least twenty-five minutes away by car, so that made it impossible for him to have killed his girlfriend.

She got to the bottom of the page.

And stopped, her heart skipping a beat.

The assistant's signature was a neat girlish snarl, the name printed in block capitals right next to it.

Malene Jansen.

She frowned.

Could it be?

The future Mrs Grønfeldt?

Was there not some sort of rule against that? Someone in an intimate relationship with a suspect providing an alibi?

She tried Henrik's phone, but he still wasn't answering, so she messaged him to call her back as soon as possible. Then she shrugged on her coat, grabbed her bag and went to find Aziz.

His muscular shoulder felt like marble under his jumper. She shook it gently. He sat up instantly, alert, if bleary-eyed. 'What?'

'I need to go to Ordrup. Please.'

A minute later, as they turned into the main road and headed for the motorway back to Copenhagen, her phone pinged. Not Henrik. Gustav.

Can you come over? I think I just remembered something.

72

Charlotte Friis was waging a one-woman war against ageing and, so far at least, she was winning. She had to be somewhere in her late forties by now, but she still looked striking. Jensen watched her as she finished serving a customer, bright of smile and bleached of hair, with a January suntan. She was wearing a long floaty dress, high-heeled boots, and a tight navy-blue leather jacket showing off her skinny frame. The skin was taut over her cheekbones, her eyes cat-like and observant beneath her dark, painted-on brows. The shop was warm and heavily perfumed with only a few garments on the rails. Riffling through them, Jensen dismissed them as ridiculous, one by one. She held up a silk blouse, as delicate and intensely patterned as a butterfly's wing, and did a double take on the price tag. Charlotte wouldn't need to sell many of those to keep her business afloat.

The customer left the shop laden with bags, and Charlotte's dazzling smile vanished off her face as she busied herself folding clothes and tidying, her bangles jingling energetically. Jensen thought she had been forgotten, when, without looking at her, Charlotte suddenly spoke.

'Can I help you?' she said vaguely in Jensen's direction.

When Jensen didn't answer, Charlotte looked up, frowning. 'Are you looking for something in particular?' she asked with a face that said she knew the answer to her own question.

She had taken up position behind the counter, her arms folded across her chest.

'My name is Jensen,' said Jensen, catching herself before she added that she was a journalist.

Was a journalist without readers still a journalist?

She cleared her throat. 'You may have read in the papers about the stabbing of Thomas Mørk. I was the one who found him.'

Charlotte wasn't softening one bit.

'I understand that you were a friend of Sandra Mørk, Thomas's mother, whom he is alleged to have stabbed seven years ago?'

'Alleged? He totally did it, no doubt about that.'

'It's true that there was a lot of evidence against him, but he said that he didn't do it, that his mother's boyfriend did it.'

Charlotte laughed cynically. 'Christian? Give me a break. Christian adored Sandra – he couldn't do enough for her. But Thomas, he was something else, drove her to the brink.'

'What about his biological father, was he not on the scene?'

'Sandra never spoke of him. Scarpered when Thomas was born, apparently, and, frankly, who can blame him?'

Unwanted and difficult, put away in a young offenders' institution and stabbed to death in the street at twenty-one. Thomas's life had been mostly shade and very little light.

'You said at the time that Sandra had told you she was scared of what Thomas might do. Did you mean she was afraid of him harming her?'

'What else would it mean?'

'That he might harm himself, or another person?'

Charlotte rolled her eyes. Time to change tack; the woman displayed no trace of warmth or empathy, something that was generally in short supply where Thomas was concerned.

'Did you know that Sandra was pregnant when she was stabbed?' said Jensen.

Finally, a crack in the woman's hostility, a flicker of surprise in her feline gaze.

'She was just thirteen weeks gone, so it wasn't really showing yet, and it was kept out of the media as a mark of respect of Grønfeldt's privacy.'

'I didn't know,' said Charlotte, and Jensen believed her.

Then the shutters came down once more.

'What do you want and why are you here?' Charlotte said, her stance hardening.

'I just want to understand how it all fits together. Did you ever see Grønfeldt and Sandra argue? Did she talk much to you about him?'

'Get out,' said Charlotte, marching up to the door and opening it to a blast of January chill.

There was a one-minute stand-off, but Jensen decided that Charlotte had probably said as much as she was going to. She held up her hands.

'I'm going. Didn't mean to offend.'

The door slammed after her, and Jensen walked away in the direction of Aziz and the black car. When she turned in the wintery grey street and looked over her shoulder, Charlotte was eyeing her from the window of her sparkling boutique, like an exotic bird in a cage.

73

Thursday 12:39

'Why did you bring me here?'

Henrik pressed the button on the Dictaphone, ignoring both Grønfeldt's hard stare and the message from Jensen on his mobile.

'Interview commences at twelve forty. Present are Christian Grønfeldt, his lawyer Pia Fløng, Detective Sergeant Lisbeth Rygaard and Detective Inspector Henrik Jungersen.'

'Can I just remind you,' said the lawyer to Christian Grønfeldt. 'You don't have to say anything at all. You have not been charged with any crime.'

'I know that,' said Grønfeldt, shaking off the calming hand she had placed on his arm.

Henrik cleared his throat. 'We would simply be grateful at this stage if you would help us with our enquiries,' he said.

'For God's sake, would someone tell me what this is about?'

'Formal identification is yet to take place, but we believe that Benedikte or "Ditte" Mørk, your late girlfriend's sister, was murdered sometime between two a.m. and four a.m. this morning.'

Henrik watched for Grønfeldt's reaction. The man's eyes widened.

'Where? Why?'

He was looking straight at Henrik. Only those telling the truth did that, in his experience, or psychopaths, because they had no compunction about lying to your face. Sometimes it was hard to tell which of the two you had sitting in front of you.

'You've told us that you were home alone last night.'

'That doesn't make me a murderer.'

'It makes you someone without an alibi.'

Grønfeldt stared at Henrik. Henrik stared back. He could sit there all day and stare if it came to it. Eventually the dentist looked away.

'Isn't it true that you hated your former girlfriend's sister?'

'There was no love lost between us, if that's what you mean.'

'Worse than that. Wasn't it you she had come to Copenhagen to see yesterday?'

'Might be, but I didn't meet her, if that's what you're implying.'

'What did she want?'

Grønfeldt sighed deeply. Henrik noticed with an undignified sense of satisfaction that the man had missed a bit of stubble on his neck when he had shaved that morning. Not perfect then.

'When my girlfriend was killed, when Sandra ...'

'Yes?'

'Sandra was always protective of her older sister. We argued about it, but when Sandra died, I took pity on Ditte and began to send her money now and again. I helped her buy her house on that commune over in Jutland.'

'But something happened.'

'Yeah, Ditte happened. She was always her own worst enemy. Drank like a fish. The money was never enough.'

'So you decided to call an end to your charitable giving.'

Grønfeldt looked up sharply. 'I did more than most would have done for that woman.'

'Was your decision prompted by Thomas's murder, by any chance? Ditte turned up at Thomas's funeral, screaming that he had ruined everything. What would she have meant by that?'

'No idea.'

'She came to plead with you.'

'I don't know what she wanted. Like I said, we didn't speak.'

'She'd been blackmailing you for years, hadn't she?'

'No.'

'Because she knew something, and when Thomas was killed, she lost her hold on you, but she still needed the money, so she begged you to pay her one more time. She was making a real nuisance of herself at your clinic, so you agreed to meet her somewhere else, only you couldn't control your temper, so you stabbed her.'

'That's not how it was,' shouted Grønfeldt.

'Where is your wife?'

Grønfeldt glanced sideways at his lawyer. She shook her head, but that didn't stop him.

'She took off.'

'When?'

'Yesterday.'

'Where to?'

'Search me. I tried her parents, her sister, her friends. No one has heard from her.'

'Did you have an argument?'

Grønfeldt looked at his hands and shook his head. Unconvincingly, in Henrik's professional opinion.

'Grønfeldt, is your wife frightened of you?'

'What?' said Grønfeldt, looking Henrik in the eye and half rising out of his seat.

The lawyer held out a hand to stop him and addressed herself to Henrik. 'Excuse me, but what has this got to do with the death of Ditte Mørk? What exactly are you accusing my client of?'

Henrik smiled and closed the folder in front of him with

elaborate slowness. He could feel Lisbeth shift in her seat beside him, but she was smart enough to keep her mouth shut.

'Christian Grønfeldt, you will be kept here for further questioning overnight. We will leave you a few moments with your lawyer and then Lisbeth here will take you down. We will speak more in the morning when you have had time to refresh your memory. Interview ends at twelve fifty-eight.'

He got up to leave, expecting noisy protests from Grønfeldt, but none came. When he turned to look, the man just sat there shaking his head and looking down at his shoes.

Not protesting his innocence.

Was that another sign that he was guilty?

Somehow it didn't fit.

Outside in the corridor, Henrik remembered the message from Jensen and dug out his phone.

It was Malene who provided Grønfeldt's alibi for the time of Sandra Mørk's murder!

She answered on the first ring.

'Well?' she said.

'Well what?'

'You're happy about Grønfeldt's future wife covering for him? He was probably already shagging her at the time, yet the police gladly accepted the alibi she gave him.'

Dammit. If he had had a krone for every time Jensen had ignored his advice to stop poking her nose into matters that didn't concern her. Where the hell had she laid her hands on that piece of information?

'So?' he said.

'So, isn't that supposed to be inadmissible?'

'There is no evidence to suggest that Malene was anything other than his assistant at the time. And Jensen, can I just remind you that there is no active investigation into the murder of Sandra Mørk? It's Thomas we're concerned about, and the other two, and now the aunt. As if that wasn't enough.'

'I bet Grønfeldt has an alibi for Ditte's murder as well. Let me guess, Malene says he was at home with her at the time?'

'No actually. Malene has gone missing. Grønfeldt claims he was at home by himself all night. We're keeping him for questioning.'

Jensen paused to think of the implications of what Henrik had just said. She thought of the steps she had heard upstairs in the Grønfeldts' bedroom when she last saw him, and his claim that Malene had retired early with a migraine. What if that hadn't been Malene at all, but some other woman?

'Wait, could he have harmed Malene?' she said. 'What if something has happened to her? You saw the text she sent to Gustav.'

'Jensen for the one hundredth time, will you just leave the investigation to me?'

'Because you are doing so well.'

'This is what police work is like. Slow. Ninety-nine per cent disappointment and frustration, one per cent achievement, if you're lucky. Anyway, I thought you were going back to London. Why are you still harping on about all of this?'

She hung up on him. He stared angrily at the phone, resisting the temptation to chuck it across the floor. No one was capable of infuriating him like Jensen.

Grønfeldt couldn't have had anything to do with Sandra's murder. Henrik had thought about it and dismissed the idea. It had been another DI's case, but he had been all over the paperwork, and everything had been done by the book. Had he been in charge at the time, he would have reached the same conclusion.

Thomas had killed his mother.

Whatever he had been playing at when he sat down in the street and pointed a sign with the word 'guilty' at Grønfeldt's clinic, Henrik felt fairly sure the boy had been deluded. He had seen it happening to people before. Inside, everyone was innocent, and Thomas had had plenty of time to convince himself.

But when it came to Thomas's own murder, and the three other bodies now stowed in the chiller cabinet at the morgue, Henrik hadn't a clue. Why would Grønfeldt have killed Thomas if he had nothing to fear from the boy? And what had happened to the other two homeless victims? With so many similarities between the three cases, how could there not be a link between them?

One thing was for certain: the dentist knew more than he was letting on. A night in the cells might jog the man's memory, and his detention would be something to tell Monsen. In the absence of any real progress, it would have to do.

74

Thursday 13:20

Jensen tapped her phone screen and declined the incoming call. 'No caller ID' never brought anything good, in her experience. Besides, she had just made Aziz pull up in front of her favourite sushi restaurant and was already salivating at the thought of their legendary miso soup.

The caller, however, was not minded to be ignored. She remembered that it might be Deep Throat chasing for her non-existent progress on the Carsten Vangede story, so she picked up, ready to defend herself.

And was surprised to hear a woman's voice.

'Malene?'

'I need to tell you something.'

'Where are you?'

'It doesn't matter. Listen.'

'I thought something might have happened to you. I thought Grønfeldt—'

'I wasn't feeling safe any more, not since Thomas was killed. Christian was acting so strangely, aggressive one minute, evasive the next. I tried to talk to him about it, but he just clammed up, so I left.'

'He has seemed very open the few times I have talked to him.'

Malene laughed cynically. 'He is great at putting people at ease; that's his speciality.'

Aziz eyed a traffic warden in the rear-view mirror and pulled away from the kerb to go round the block.

'What are you trying to say?'

'That Christian is not who he makes out to be. These past few weeks have really made me think. I should never have done what I did.'

'What did you do?'

'I lied for him.'

'About Thomas? Malene, if you have been hiding something for Grønfeldt, you need to talk to the police.'

'No, not the police, and it's not about Thomas. It's just ... I must tell someone. I tried to speak to that boy, your editor's nephew, but I can't seem to get hold of him now.'

'Gustav is ... indisposed at the moment.'

'So, I thought you might ... well, maybe you can use it in some way.'

'Tell me what it is, Malene, or I won't be able to do anything.'

'The day Thomas's mother was murdered, Christian wasn't at the clinic all day. I said he was, because I was in love with him, and because he persuaded me that he had nothing to do with what happened, but in fact I don't know where he was.'

'Are you saying that he could have done it after all?'

'No. I don't know. Maybe. I'm not sure what to think any more.'

'And Thomas? Christian said he slept through it all and didn't realise what had happened to him till the next morning, when he saw the emergency vehicles outside. Is that true?'

There was a brief pause. 'I don't know.'

'Will you at least meet me? Tell me where you're staying and we can talk, properly. I won't tell the police; you can trust me.'

293

'No. I've said enough. I've got to go. Don't tell anyone I called. Please!'

'Wait,' said Jensen, but Malene had already hung up.

The traffic warden had moved on, and Aziz was parked by the kerb once more. She looked at their reflection in the window of the restaurant. Sharp winter sunlight was bouncing off the black car, which had been polished to within an inch of its life.

The phone call from Malene had left Jensen with a funny feeling of something tugging away at her memory, but she resisted the urge to reach for her phone and call Henrik, knowing she was still too mad at him to be playing it cool. And if he wouldn't help her, why should she help him?

In any case, there was something more urgent she had to do. Resolutely, she pushed the best sushi takeaway in Copenhagen to the back of her mind, and told Aziz to drive.

75

Jensen spent the journey to Farum reading the coverage of Ditte Mørk's murder, but no new details had been released, and the newspapers, including *Dagbladet,* were treading water.

On one wall in Esben's summer house, she had built a time-line of Sandra's murder and on another a map with the locations of the three stabbings in Copenhagen, to which she had added Ditte's scene of crime, miles away out towards the Field's shopping mall and Kastrup airport.

The third victim had been identified as a Danish woman, a drug addict who had most likely been out for the count when she was killed. There was still no word on the first victim, though the newspapers reported that he was thought to have been Romanian, based on items found in his discarded rucksack.

She had found herself drawn back to Sandra's wall again and again. Why would Thomas have concocted the story about having been with a friend at the time of the murder when this could so easily be disproved? The address was in the files, a neighbouring street to Sandra's house in Farum.

Birkevej was not exactly prime property. The house was in the middle of a row of brown-brick terraced houses that had seen better days. The curtains of number forty-six were drawn. There was a carton of orange juice in one window, propped up against a white figurine of a boy in a hat. Were Lene Dollerup and her son Mickey still living there? That's what it said on the front door.

She waited for ages on the steps and was about to walk away when the door was jerked open. It was obvious that Lene had once been good-looking, but gravity had been unkind to her. Her loose clothing did little to hide the flab. Jensen recoiled at the smell of neglect escaping from the house.

'Is Mickey in?

'No,' said Lene.

Her folded arms told Jensen that Lene was as used to that question as she was to the answer she had given.

'Where can I find him?'

'No idea; he tells me nothing.'

Jensen nodded.

'You remember Thomas?' she said, 'The boy your son used to hang out with?'

'What's it to you?'

'It me was me who found Thomas dead, a couple of weeks ago. You must have seen it in the papers?'

'Don't read them.'

The woman's hostility was showing no sign of waning.

'I am shutting the door now,' she said. 'Not interested in whatever it is you've got to say.'

'Wait!' said Jensen. 'Thomas claimed he and Mickey were together at your house when his mother was killed. That they'd skived off school together and smoked weed all day. He said your son used to sell it to the kids from school.'

The door slammed in her face.

'Thomas was a lying little toad,' Lene shouted from inside. 'My son was at home with me all day. He was off sick. Now piss off, or I'll call the police.'

Jensen looked up and down the empty residential road. Perhaps Lene Dollerup had told the truth after all. In any case, it was too long in the past to challenge her statement effectively. According to Thomas's file, the school hadn't taken a register; apparently they wanted to treat the kids in the older classes 'like adults', which included refraining from checking on their coming and going, but none of those who had been interviewed could recall seeing Mickey at school that day. As to whether or not he had been with his mother, it was Mickey's word against Thomas's. And while, at the tender age of fifteen, Lene's son had already received a couple of slaps on the wrist for possessing recreational drugs, Thomas literally had blood on his hands. It was hardly a surprise that the police had chosen to believe his friend over him.

Jensen bent down and flicked open the letterbox, pushing through a scrap of paper with her mobile phone number and shouting into the empty hall.

'If you see Mickey, tell him to call me.'

She was within sight of Aziz when she heard running footsteps behind her on the snowy pavement. Aziz checked his wing mirror but didn't react, so he must have decided that whoever was approaching was harmless.

A man's voice: 'Wait, did you say you found Thomas?'

Mickey Dollerup was not what she expected, having read up on the teenage scumbag with a dealing habit who had testified to being at home with his mother on the day Sandra Mørk was murdered, and not with Thomas.

The man in front of Jensen wore his long, wavy hair tied up in a ponytail. His hands were buried deep in the pockets of his tracksuit bottoms. She had to remind herself that he was only in the start of his twenties. By the dark rings under his eyes and sallow cheeks, he could be at least ten years older. His facial expression was one of disappointment and regret more common in those of middle age.

297

'Mickey?'

'Actually, I don't call myself that any more. It's Mikael now. Sorry about mum.' He gestured with his thumb at the house behind him. 'She is not well.'

Nothing wrong with the woman that a course of Antabuse wouldn't sort out, thought Jensen, but she held her tongue.

'I read about Thomas. I am sorry. How was he, when you found him?' said Mikael.

'He looked peaceful. He had been stabbed multiple times, but there was no sign of a struggle,' she replied.

Mikael nodded, sniffing. 'That's good. Do they know who did it?'

She shook her head.

They stood for a moment in silence.

'Were you and Thomas close friends?' she asked.

He smiled, showing dirty teeth. 'Not really. A bit, maybe. I guess neither of us really got on with school.'

'Thomas said you were together the day his mother was killed. He said he left your house after two o'clock in the afternoon and came home to find his mother already dead, but according to your testimony, you didn't see him at all that day.'

Mikael looked down at his trainers. The laces were undone.

'It doesn't make sense. Why would Thomas say that he was with you that day if it wasn't true? There are so many other stories he could have come up with. Why this one?'

Mikael mumbled something inaudible. She moved closer to him. 'What?'

'I said, because it was the truth.'

Mikael buried his face in his hands.

'So, he wasn't lying?'

Mikael shook his head miserably. 'He wrote to me many times, tried to make me change my statement, but I never replied. I feel bad about it now, but I thought that, seeing as he had already been inside for the murder, it wouldn't do any good to rip it all up again. And now he is dead, and it's too late.'

He began to sob, trembling in his oversized hoodie. She let him get on with it. Thomas's alibi had been good after all, but he had been let down by a boy he thought was his friend. If Mikael thought he could get her sympathy, he could think again.

'I was fifteen and already in trouble with the police. Mum told me not to get involved, to say that I had been with her that day. She told me it wouldn't make a difference to Thomas anyway. That he would get done for the murder, because he was found on the scene holding the murder weapon.'

'So, you went along with it, knowing for certain that he couldn't have done it?'

'I guess I managed to persuade myself that he had somehow. I am not proud of myself.'

Jensen frowned at him, slowly shaking her head.

'What happens now,' he said, wiping away his tears. 'Will you interview me? I'll tell you everything for ten thousand kroner.'

'What?'

'You're a journalist, aren't you? I know you pay for stories. I know it happens, don't pretend it doesn't.'

Mikael appeared to have made a rapid recovery from the grief that had struck him a few moments ago.

'You're something else, do you know that?' she said.

'Eight thousand, then.'

'No, I am not going to pay you eight thousand to write your shitty little story, but I tell you what I *am* going to do.'

'What?'

'I am going to report you for perjury.'

'But I thought . . . What difference is that going to make now Thomas is dead?'

'If Thomas didn't do it, then the real killer is still out there, and thanks to you perverting the course of justice, they may never be found.'

'You can't report me. I'll deny everything. You and I never met.'

'Oh yes we did.'

She held up her mobile phone and pressed the red square to stop recording, thinking that Gustav would have been proud of her. Then she turned on her heel, closed her ears to Mickey's loud protests and got in the car, telling Aziz to drive.

76

Driving to the Forensic Institute, Henrik wondered how many times he had made this same journey. How many dead bodies he had seen since he became a police officer, many of them mutilated, robbed of every humanity. No matter how intimidating they had been when alive, or how much they had suffered, once naked and ensconced in the metal drawers of the morgue, they were all the same. If anyone ever got too big for their boots, all Henrik had to do was to imagine them under a white sheet with a tag attached to their toe. He reckoned that one day he might end up down there himself. God knew he had come within a whisker many times.

Jensen had called and texted him dozens of times, but he didn't have the energy, or frankly the patience, to discuss the Sandra Mørk case with her any more. She had a bee in her bonnet about Grønfeldt, but as far as Henrik was concerned, the dentist's only crime, aside from unbearable smarminess, was an inability to resist the weaker sex (which, frankly, would make a lot of men guilty, let alone Henrik himself).

In any case, it was wrong of Henrik to be sharing information with Jensen. Unprofessional and improper. From now on, she would have to manage on her own. Besides, all she had were questions to which he had no answers.

Hornbæk had been amazing, better than he had hoped it would be – he was still enjoying flashbacks of Jensen's lithe body arching under his – but her constant nagging for information was doing his head in. Like most of the women in his life, including his wife, she was considerably smarter than him, which was, admittedly, a worry. But what did she know about solving murders? Nothing.

His job was the boring and plodding real detective work they didn't show on TV. Most of the leads he followed led nowhere, but there was a certain reassurance in going through the steps methodically. And with a possible serial killer on the loose, he couldn't afford any more distractions.

He knew that he could simply have read the pathologist's post-mortem report on the latest victims, but he liked talking to David Goldschmidt. The man's deep tolerance of other human beings was something Henrik himself had lost through his years of policing.

He found David in his office in the cosy light from the anglepoise lamp, the blue screen reflecting in his reading glasses, and some sort of highbrow talk radio on the go in the background.

'Henrik, good to see you,' said David, smiling warmly.

That was another thing Henrik liked about David. He always seemed genuinely happy to see him. One of very few people who did these days. Despite being overworked and overexposed to the worst people were capable of doing to one another, David had never made an unfair or unsubstantiated judgment.

'Talk to me!' said Henrik.

'You know, Jungersen, you really should try and brush up on your social skills.'

This was their regular banter. David played the part of the charming, socially effortless urbanite, and Henrik the inarticulate caveman. He had often thought that he ought to be the one spending his days alone with the cadavers, with David moving among the living, but he also knew that policing wasn't about being nice. David was an excellent pathologist, but as an investigator of violent crime, he wouldn't last one minute.

Nevertheless, over the years, the two of them had developed a friendship of sorts. Henrik had lost count of the number of times he had consulted with David over some medical issue to do with himself or his family, trivial stuff. David had dealt with it all patiently, and these days he was the only member of staff at the Forensic Institute that Henrik had any time for. The circle of people fitting that description was growing ever smaller.

David made a show of looking behind Henrik. 'You didn't bring your friend with you this time?'

'Sorry about that,' said Henrik. 'I can't take her anywhere.'

'Not at all. I thought she was charming.'

'My wife would disagree with you violently.'

Laughing, David held up his hands in a leave-me-out-of-it gesture and headed for the door. 'Shall we?'

Henrik felt his feet grow heavy. He wished they could stay in David's warm office with the radio on, leaving the dead to their dreamless sleep in the refrigerated metal drawers where no further harm could befall them.

He followed David through the succession of security-protected doors that always reminded him of the airlocks in the spacecraft movies he had loved in his childhood, if a lot less fun.

In the autopsy room, David turned the light on, and it cut into Henrik's eyes, so he had to close them for a moment. The smell of decaying flesh hit him instantly, like a garbage bag of meat left out in the sun.

Two of the stainless-steel tables in the vast room were occupied.

On the first there was a slight, almost childlike, body covered in a green sheet.

'You ready?' said David.

'As I ever will be.'

David peeled back the sheet. If you wanted to see the damage heroin could do to someone, this was it.

'Tina Dyrby, twenty-six.'

You wouldn't have put her at a day under forty. Nothing aged a person as rapidly as drug addiction, and the lifestyle that came with it.

David nodded sadly, reading his thoughts. 'The state of her veins shows that she had been injecting for a long time,' he said.

'She had not eaten for at least twenty-four hours by the time she was killed. The amount of heroin in her system would suggest that she was unconscious at the time, which also explains why there are no signs of her putting up a fight.'

He pointed to her arms and abdomen, again reading Henrik's thoughts. 'Those bruises and cuts are of an older date. Looks like she was beaten up a while before she died, maybe several times. I would have expected to see recent scratches, skin and perhaps blood under her fingernails, but there was nothing.'

'Talk me through the stabbing,' said Henrik, fighting visions of his own daughter lying there, barely more than skin and bones.

Where was Tina Dyrby's parents now? And her siblings? Friends she had had when she was young with nothing but innocent thoughts in her head? That was another thing about heroin. In time, it left most people orphaned and friendless.

His eyes fell on the wide silver wedding band on David's left hand. He had heard that the pathologist was married to a man, another doctor at Riget. The two of them had had a baby the year before, through a surrogate mother. Henrik wondered if it was a girl, or whether David had nieces, or perhaps a sister. He was gentle with the corpse, respectful.

'She was stabbed five times, but this is the wound that would have killed her; it hit a major artery,' he said, pointing to Tina Dyrby's throat.

'And the amount of force used?'

'Considerable, but . . . not as much as the first victim.'

'Andrei Ciobanu, the Romanian?'

'Yes.'

'And compared to Thomas Mørk?'

'Again less. Thomas was stabbed twenty-two times and Andrei twelve.'

'If Thomas was unconscious like the others, there was hardly a need to stab him so many times.'

'Unless whoever did it was extremely angry or pumped up on something,' said David.

'Perhaps, with Tina being the third victim, the novelty was beginning to wear off? The killer no longer had his heart in it?'

'Or killers,' said David.

'Say that again?'

'We can't be sure these murders were committed by the same person. In all three cases, the stab wounds are consistent with a four-centimetre wide knife.'

'In other words, about as bog standard a kitchen knife as you can get.'

'Right.'

'So, it tells us nothing.'

The pathologist looked pained. 'You know I don't like speculating, Henrik. I deal only in facts; you and I have had that conversation many times.'

'I sense a but coming,' said Henrik

'But there is just something about Andrei Ciobanu's injuries, and the state he was in, that tells me that his was a different killer.'

'What?'

'More violence, more resistance. I could be wrong, of course. It's pure conjecture.'

'So the three murders might not be connected. Or they *are* connected, but there is more than one killer. Or the last two murders were committed by a person or persons who got the idea from the first. Or they are simply three random, unconnected murders.'

David laughed. 'That about sums it up. Oh, and by the way, the skin fragments we found under Andrei Ciobanu's fingernails?'

'Yes?'

'The DNA results are back. No match. Sorry.'

The pathologist gently replaced the sheet over Tina's abused body.

At least she is at peace now. The trite line reeled off to the bereaved ran through Henrik's head. In this instance, it seemed wholly appropriate.

David moved to the second autopsy table and its bulkier cargo. 'Now this one was a more frenzied attack than the other three. Stabbed thirty-nine times,' he said, lifting the sheet.

Henrik tried to ignore the mound of naked human flesh in front of him. Ditte Mørk was no more attractive in death than she had been alive.

'More anger? Stronger perpetrator? Like our first victim?'

'Not for me to say. Are you looking for a connection to the others?'

'There already is one. Ditte Mørk was sister to Thomas Mørk's mother. Though not exactly your stereotypical loving auntie.'

'Well, this one wouldn't have been able to put up much of a fight either.'

'Why?'

'She had vast quantities of alcohol in her blood.'

'So stabbing her would have been a relatively easy job for someone.'

'You could say that, yes.'

'Yet the person who did this stabbed her thirty-nine times, which again seems unnecessary.'

306

'Again, yes.'

Henrik thought about it. 'Only the first of these four victims seems to have done any damage to their killer.'

'Though we don't know if the tissue and blood found under Andrei Ciobanu's nails was from the murderer.'

Henrik was willing to bet on it. However, the fact that the DNA did not match anyone known to the police meant they could eliminate the drug dealer from their enquiries. At least as far as Andrei Ciobanu was concerned.

'What about Gustav Skov? Are the forensics back yet?'

David opened his laptop and searched.

'Yep,' he said. 'And no matches. Whoever attacked Gustav is also unknown to the police, and there is nothing connecting him to any of the four bodies.'

Henrik rubbed the top of his head.

'Tough case. I don't envy you, and I am not exactly helping. If only I had more to give you,' said David, removing his gloves and washing his hands.

'I'll get to the bottom of it,' said Henrik.

'I dare say you will. I have every faith in you,' said David as he switched off the lights and led them out of the room with one hand on Henrik's shoulder.

'By this time, I think it's safe to say that you are the only one who does,' said Henrik.

He wished he did not have to go back to the office. All hell had broken loose since the third body had been found. Anyone in the police who wasn't off sick or drawing a pension was now working on the case (getting in the way, more like). The government was breathing down Monsen's neck, and Monsen, adept at delegating if nothing else, was breathing down Henrik's. Armies of volunteers had taken to the streets to lead rough sleepers to safety, and hundreds of people had offered to open their homes.

'How can four people, FOUR PEOPLE, get stabbed in the

307

street, out in the open, without any CCTV or witnesses what-soever, and without any murder weapons having been found? How is it even possible?' Monsen had cried.

Henrik did not have the answer. The four victims could hardly be more different. It was now clear that there was probably more than one killer. And no crazy individual or organisation had claimed the murders publicly. But four in swift succession? Three of them sleeping on the street, four if you counted Ditte in her van? It seemed impossible that they weren't in some way linked.

There was only one thing for it: to trust in the method. It had always worked before. Henrik might take his time about it, but his detection record was the best on the force. He needed to remind Monsen of this again. That was another thing that usually worked with the chief super. To buy him time, at least.

There was just one problem. Method or no method, Henrik had no idea where to begin.

He felt his phone vibrate. Monsen.

Get your sorry arse back here. Now!

77

'Jensen who?'

Henning's gruff, deadpan voice came down the line. She could hear soft music in the background, imagined a cigar gently smouldering in the ashtray. In her absence, Henning could live without fear of impromptu visits to his office. None of her colleagues bothered with him, except Margrethe, and she merely humoured him as one does a dotty old relative.

'Come on, Henning, you can't have forgotten me *that* fast,' Jensen said.

She was waiting for Aziz in a coffee shop in Nørrebro while he collected one of his children from a friend's house. The café was the sort of place she would find it hard to leave Copenhagen for. Cosy and warm and smelling of home-made cakes, it was more like a living room than a place of business. She was having tea, the British way – strong, with milk. Liron had ruined coffee for her; these days, if it didn't come from his van, she wasn't buying it.

Outside in the street, in the cosy light from the café windows, was a line of prams the size of barges. A circle of young women, each with a baby in their lap, was sitting at the next table. They would all be on their year's maternity leave. Jensen couldn't help being drawn to their happy, animated faces.

It would have been easier to head down to *Dagbladet* to speak to Henning in person, but she was still an undesirable at the newspaper and would be for the foreseeable, unless she redeemed herself with Margrethe in some way, which seemed increasingly unlikely. She had texted her boss several times, saying sorry in a variety of ways, but there had been no reply.

Henning coughed, a deep wet cough, before speaking.

'So, Margrethe finally got rid of you. I thought she probably would.'

'Yep.'

'What do you want?'

'When we spoke about Christian Grønfeldt, you mentioned that he was fond of the ladies.'

'Did I? I don't recall.'

She left him to think a bit, a tried and tested method as far as getting anything out of Henning was concerned.

'Grønfeldt. I knew his father, Anton. We were at school together at Ordrup Gymnasium.'

'You never said.'

'You never asked.'

Long pause.

'Good-looking family – Spanish blood down the line. Anton was always chased by some skirt or another. Surgeon, good with his hands, so to speak.'

Henning chuckled softly to himself. Then his tone turned more sombre. 'He operated on my wife when she got sick, you know.'

'Did he?' said Jensen, astonished not so much that Anton Grønfeldt had wielded the scalpel, but that Henning had a wife.

'She passed away.'

'Oh, sorry.'

310

'Not Anton's fault. Patient died, operation was a success. Complicated heart thing.'

'I see.'

'Years ago now.'

There was another long pause. Jensen wondered if Henning had fallen asleep. The radio announcer came on in the background. She was about to hang up when Henning spoke again, as if he had merely paused for breath mid-sentence.

'Now, Christian. Understand that he was a chip off the old block as far as women were concerned.'

'What makes you say that?'

'His father mentioned it once or twice. Something along those lines. The boy was a dreadful disappointment to him. Only child, scraped into medical school at the University of Copenhagen, but got expelled for laziness.'

Henning drew deep on his cigar. He never blew the smoke, just sort of breathed it out so it stood about him in a cloud. Which is what she imagined he was doing now. She waited. Henning could not be hurried. Too much pressure and he would clam shut.

'His father tried to intervene, personally went and got him out of whatever mess he was in, then worked some sort of connection to get him into dental college. God only knows how ... how he ... how ... he ...'

Jensen waited until the sound of steady breathing came down the line, accompanied by a soft piano on the radio. This time Henning definitely had fallen asleep. She hung up. Sometimes she was unsure whether he was in fact just a figment of her imagination.

It came as no surprise to her that Christian was a womaniser. She could have worked that one out for herself. Malene had seemed jealous on seeing the two of them together at the clinic, and he had clearly made a big impression on Charlotte Friis.

Something was niggling at the back of Jensen's mind when

311

she thought of Charlotte, while absentmindedly looking at the women on maternity leave, a few of whom were feeding their babies from heavy breasts.

Charlotte was good-looking and must have been even more so seven years ago. Had Christian been able to keep his hands to himself? Had Charlotte?

Jensen got out her phone as one of the babies launched into an ear-splitting wail. She pressed a finger to her other ear and turned away, conscious of how intolerant she must look.

'Not you again,' said Charlotte. 'Didn't I tell you to get lost?'

She sounded drunk, or as if Jensen had woken her from a nap. A slow day in the boutique, Jensen guessed.

'Wait,' she said. 'Just wanted to ask you about Christian. He finds it very hard to resist women, doesn't he?'

'Here you go again, trying to make out as if he is some sort of dodgy character. He loved Sandra and was devastated to lose her. Trust me.'

Time to play her best card.

'Look, Charlotte, the reason I am calling is that Malene admitted to me that she provided a false alibi for Christian on the day Sandra was murdered. In fact, he didn't turn up at the clinic that day at all, so technically at least, he *could* have killed her.'

'And you think he did?'

'I only know he wasn't where he said he was.'

'Well, he didn't do it.'

Down the line came the sound of Charlotte lighting a cigarette and exhaling aggressively.

'How can you be so sure?'

'Because it it's the truth.'

'But how do you know?'

'BECAUSE HE WAS WITH ME!' she screamed.

Jensen waited patiently for more, listening while Charlotte took a deep drag on her cigarette.

'I was married then. I had no intention of leaving my husband. He and Christian knew each other from the golf club. It was only a few times. A bit of a fumble. Christian can be very persistent when he wants something, until he doesn't, and then you never hear from him again. But that's Christian for you.'

Jensen guessed that, in her time, Charlotte would have been the sort to call the shots in relationships. Being used and then dumped by Grønfeldt wouldn't have suited her.

'So, there's no way he could have killed Sandra, all right?'

Grønfeldt had asked for an alibi from Malene, his dental assistant. Had he confessed his embarrassment about two-timing Sandra, or persuaded her in some other way to lie for him? What sort of hold was it that Christian had over women?

Grønfeldt and Malene had married eighteen months after Sandra was killed. Had he gone on to cheat on Malene during their marriage, or had they agreed on an open relationship? Tricky to ask her, seeing as she had disappeared, but Jensen found it impossible to believe that Christian had kept on the straight and narrow.

'So you say he was with you all that day?'

'Until the time he would usually have left the clinic. Then he went home and found Sandra in a pool of blood. Just like he said. It was horrible for him. Can't you get that into your stupid little head? Don't call me again.'

She hung up.

Skyldig.

Of what?

Neglect?

Adultery?

Low integrity?

That was just about the sum of the accusations that could be levelled at Grønfeldt over his relationship with Sandra. None of them was murder. If Charlotte was to be believed, and Jensen's instincts told her she was telling the truth.

But Malene had told Gustav that she was feeling unsafe, and now she appeared to have vanished off the face of the earth. Jensen reminded herself that Grønfeldt might still be violent, that perhaps he had had something to do with Ditte's death, if not Sandra's.

The group of young mothers got up to leave, bundling their babies into padded bodysuits and knitted bonnets. Jensen felt a deep sense of despondency rising within her. Not for her, sitting around in cafés during the day chatting with a baby bouncing on her lap.

It wasn't too late. She could still find someone, move into a flat in the neighbourhood, have kids and ferry them around in a front carriage attached to her bicycle, like a proper Copenhagen parent.

And pigs could fly.

Maybe Frank and the rest of the media were right. Thomas had been a troubled soul who had chosen the wrong place and the wrong time to make his point, and whoever had killed him had two other murders on their conscience, or three, if you counted Ditte. As far as Jensen was concerned, with the mouth she had on her, Thomas's aunt could have got herself killed in any one of a hundred ways. Grønfeldt might have had nothing whatsoever to do with it.

'Ready to go?'

Aziz towered over her. It never ceased to amaze her how a man so big was capable of entering a room so inconspicuously. She made a face at him.

'What happened?' he said, immediately on high alert. 'What's the problem?'

'Nothing happened, Aziz. Nothing at all, and that's the problem.'

78

Henrik only partially succeeded in suppressing a grin when he entered Monsen's office and saw the man himself standing by the window like an extra from a period drama. He was wearing his gala uniform, black with the royal crown and three medium-sized stars that signalled his rank. The jacket was held together by an uncomfortably tight-looking gold belt. Monsen spun round, saw the upturned corners of Henrik's mouth and told him in no uncertain terms to shut his face.

'I am accompanying the commissioner to a reception at the palace. What would you like me to say if she asks me how the investigation is going?'

Henrik, no royalist himself, knew that Monsen harboured a deep veneration for Queen Margrethe. Any occasion to don his finest in the proximity of the monarch was the highlight of his working life, always had been, no matter that these days the uniform jacket was tighter than ever over his midriff and the peaked cap seemed to have transformed itself into a prop from a children's fancy-dress party. The mere thought of being hauled over hot coals by the commissioner at such an auspicious occasion would trouble him deeply, not to mention the failure of his team to capture the lunatic street killer everyone in Denmark was talking about.

'We're working on a few leads,' Henrik said. 'There's this person we're looking for, a Romanian who has been living on the streets until recently and was seen arguing with our first victim on at least one occasion.'

'So you're close to making an arrest, is that it?'

'We have to track the guy down first. It's not like you can look him up in the National Register.'

'Well, use your sources. You used to tell me you could get any information you wanted off the streets of Copenhagen.'

True, thought Henrik, but that was years ago, and though he didn't like to admit it, he did not have the easy passage through the city's criminal underworld that he once did.

'We'll get him. I've got several officers on it, don't worry.'

'Hmph,' said Monsen. 'And we think this chap could be our serial killer?'

'Whoa, I didn't say that.'

'But you've got three very similar stabbings, all of people on the streets, and then that woman in the van. If our man committed the first murder, who's to say he isn't behind all of them?'

'We'll do some tests when we find him.'

'Mind you do that and let me know the minute you have any news. You've been at this for three weeks. I'll take you off the case if you haven't made any significant progress by the end of tomorrow.'

'Now hang on a minute . . .'

Monsen raised a white-gloved hand.

'I don't want to hear it.'

'You can't do that.'

'Watch me,' said Monsen, checking his watch. 'Now get out of my office. Mrs Hansen has spent all day having her hair done, and I am late enough as it is.'

Henrik doubted very much that this was true. Monsen's wife Rigmor was a highly respected and level-headed history lecturer at the University of Copenhagen whom Henrik had a lot of time for, not least because he suspected that she cut her husband little slack at home. He somehow couldn't imagine her with her hair in curlers, nor that she would be impressed with the promise of a glass of champagne in a draughty ban-queting hall.

Monsen's threat, on the other hand, he was willing to take more seriously. It wasn't unheard of for stale cases to be passed to other teams; Henrik had often been the recipient of such cases, but never the one they were taken from, and no way was that going to start now.

As he left Monsen and walked across the dingy office floor, where most people had left for the day, Henrik got out his phone to warn his wife that he wouldn't be home any time soon. Not that she would care, or even acknowledge the message, but he hadn't yet sunk so low that he didn't tell her when work held him late. Whether she believed him or not was another matter.

Now, where the hell was Mark when you needed him?

79

Thursday 21:07

The Nørrebro apartment block was covered in graffiti to the maximum reach of a human with a spray can. The graffiti was everywhere in Copenhagen, something else Henrik deeply resented about his city. That and the tattoos covering virtually every bit of exposed human flesh. Even Mark, the perpetually energetic if somewhat boring family man from Hvidovre, had several. One, a hideous Viking motif on his wrist, was visible now that he was driving.

They were in an unmarked car, but Henrik knew they might as well have shouted from a megaphone that they were police. People around this neighbourhood were born with the kind of nose that could smell police a mile off. He looked up at the building to the fourth floor where Daniel Cuțov was staying, according to the tip-off they had received. Their informant, a petty criminal detained for an unrelated offence, had told Mark that Daniel had been boasting about killing Andrei Ciobanu. There was every possibility that this was a false statement, but at this point, with four unsolved murders to contend with, he wasn't going to argue.

The curtains were drawn on the fourth floor, but the lights were on. Henrik thought about it. He and Mark were unlike to be welcomed with open arms.

'Let me go up,' he said to Mark. 'Wait by the back entrance. These flats all have kitchen stairs.'

'Let's call for back-up, and I can go up with you.'

'No time. Someone will have seen us coming. The guy will be long gone by the time the others get here.'

'But—'

'Do it, Mark, it's an order!'

Mark wasn't happy, but he did what he was told. That and his methodical, hard-working nature were the only reasons he was still on Henrik's team. He and Lisbeth were the two colleagues who had managed for the longest time not to get kicked out by him.

The stairwell stank of fifty kinds of fried food with undernotes of urine. Most of the doors were reinforced with steel, including the fourth-floor flat. Henrik could hear music and voices inside. He rang the doorbell. A man in a leather jacket with a gold necklace opened the door and immediately slammed it shut again.

Or almost slammed it shut. Henrik had managed to stick his foot in the door and rammed the door back hard into the man's face with delicious force.

'Police,' he shouted to the dozen men watching him.

'Now which of you is Daniel Cuțov?'

'What do you want with him?' said one of the men in perfect Danish.

'A word,' said Henrik.

'Why?'

It was just a very small movement in the man's face, so small it could have been an involuntary contraction of the muscles round one eye, but Henrik instinctively turned. Just in time to see a man slip out behind him and take the stairs.

319

The main stairs.

Shit.

Fifty per cent chance, and the odds had gone against him. He took off after the man, thundering down the steps behind him. Fast but not fast enough.

'Stop,' he shouted, but Daniel Cuțov was already out the door and halfway down the street.

Henrik emerged just in time to see Mark set off in sharp pursuit. Leaning over his knees and panting hard (Jesus, when had he become so unfit?), he watched in amazement as his younger colleague caught up with the man and knocked him to the ground. Before Henrik could catch up, he had Daniel in handcuffs.

The man was completely silent as they bundled him into the back of the car. As Mark slammed the blue blink on the roof and swung out into evening traffic, Henrik permitted himself a little smile. Finally, things were starting to go his way.

80

Thursday 22:16

On impulse, he parked a couple of streets away from his house, out of the street light, and rang Jensen on the hands-free. This was how he had spent most of their phone conversations over the years, in the car looking idly at other people's back gardens or the front of shops where he had gone on the pretext of picking up milk (often arriving home without the milk and having to go back out again). Together those places had formed a blank canvas against which he had been able to imagine Jensen's face and the feel of her body in his hands.

He hadn't meant to call her, but he couldn't stop thinking about what had happened in Hornbæk. It was an illness, an obsession. When she picked up, she was breathless, tearing him brutally from his reveries.

'Finally he answers my call! What took you so long?'

'I thought you said you were leaving the country?'

'I told you, Sunday. Did you bring Grønfeldt in? Have you asked him about the things I told you?'

'I did and I have.'

'Well?'

'Not that it is any of your business, but we have just released him.'

'What?'

'There is no evidence whatsoever to connect him with either Thomas Mørk's or Ditte Mørk's murders.'

'So it's pure coincidence that the boy who served time for killing Grønfeldt's former girlfriend is murdered outside his very own dental clinic holding a sign with the word "guilty" on it?'

'It was a coincidence that he happened to be murdered while sitting there, yes. Probably by whoever is going around killing rough sleepers. The rest was not a coincidence. We can all have our theories about why he did it.'

'What about the third victim?' said Jensen. 'What have you found out?'

'Nothing I am going to share with you.'

He knew he was breaking every rule in the book even by talking to Jensen; it was his guilty conscience that was making him do it. Despite many declarations to the contrary over the years, he had never managed to leave his wife for her. He had wanted to, of course he had, but every time there had been the inevitable conclusion that he would lose Oliver. His other children had long since sided against him, but with Oliver he hadn't managed to ruin things. Not yet. His youngest son represented his only hope of redemption.

'OK,' said Jensen, in that infuriatingly obstinate manner of hers. 'Have it your way.'

'Stop,' he said. 'You said it yourself – you no longer have a newspaper to write for, so what's the point of all this? Is it to get at me, is that it?'

Jensen laughed. 'Don't flatter yourself, Henrik. You may believe in coincidences, but I don't. It was me who found Thomas and to me that means something. I can't just walk away, I can't.'

'Well, like you said, come Sunday night you will be on a

322

plane to London. Not much you will be able to do about it then, is there?'

She fell silent. Love flushed through him, love and regret and a wish that everything could have been different. The thought came to him that Jensen was the female version of himself, that the two of them were too alike for it ever to work between them. Was there such a thing as being too well matched? Man and woman in one piece, no visible join?

When she spoke, her voice was small and cut into him.

'See you around, Henrik.'

81

Friday 11:22

It had taken all night and most of the morning to track down a Romanian translator but, in the end, they may as well have saved themselves the trouble. Daniel Cuțov, younger and slighter of stature than Henrik would have expected, was staring at his handcuffed hands and saying nothing. His legs were bobbing up and down furiously under the table, creating ripples across the surface of the untouched glass of water in front of him.

Nothing whatsoever was going to come from the interview, but they had to go through the motions.

As ever.

'Daniel, why were you resisting arrest?'

The translator, a man dressed in multiple shades of brown, who reminded Henrik unhappily of his primary-school geography teacher, did his bit. The answer came back immediately in English.

'No comment.'

'We have a signed statement from a witness who has identified you as the man he saw arguing with Andrei Ciobanu on the night he died. What did you argue with Andrei about?'

'No comment.'

'Was it about money? Or someone back home? We know that Andrei came from the same town in Romania as you.'

'No comment.'

'Daniel, isn't it true that you lost your temper with Andrei that night, and that you stabbed him twelve times, leaving him for dead?'

'No comment.'

'What did you do with the knife, Daniel?'

'No comment.'

'Daniel, did you kill Thomas Mørk and Tina Dyrby?'

For a brief second, the man stopped bobbing his knees and looked straight at Henrik. Then he looked down again and carried on.

'No comment.'

One by one, Henrik set out the photos from the first three crime scenes. The man didn't look at them once.

'Did you kill Ditte Mørk?'

He set down his pièce de resistance, the photos from the inside of the orange camper van. The crimson streaks of blood all over the images swam before his eyes, but still Daniel didn't look up.

'Let me guess, no comment?' said Henrik.

'No comment.'

'Fine,' said Henrik. 'You don't want to chat. I get that. To tell you the truth, I am not bothered either way. Your DNA will do all the talking we need. The results should be back any time soon.'

He looked at his watch.

'Interview ends at eleven forty-four a.m.,' he said, stopping the recording.

The translator shuffled his unused notepad and pen into his worn, brown-leather satchel. Mark gathered his papers, moving his chair back to get up, as the door opened and a uniformed officer came to take Daniel back to the cells.

325

And then.

Maybe it was because of the blood, all that blood spilled on the table in front of him.

Maybe it was lack of sleep after Jensen had made her goodbye sound so devastatingly final.

Or maybe it was Daniel Cuțov, bobbing his legs up and down, like his oldest child did when he was impatient to flee from one of his father's lectures, or their team was losing at football, which had happened far too often lately.

In his mind it wasn't clear to Henrik why he suddenly leapt out of his chair and shoved the table hard at Daniel, roaring into the man's horror-stricken face, so the uniformed officer jumped, and the translator dropped his spectacles onto the floor.

But it felt great.

Thankfully, before he could get his punch in, Mark's tattooed arms closed round his, and led him quickly from the room.

82

Aside from a lone dog walker, who paid Jensen no attention, the suburban streets of Farum were deserted. These were the dead hours between children returning from school and their parents heading home from work. It was almost dark. Jensen was grateful for the fading light as she turned into Langelandsvej, having left Aziz parked round the corner.

She had spent most of the day going over everything again, checking her timeline and notes. Fruitlessly, as it turned out. Nothing fitted. If Grønfeldt had been with Charlotte all day, and Thomas had been off his head with his friend, then who had killed Sandra? Could it have been a complete stranger?

She looked across the street to the Mørks' house for clues. It looked different from the pictures printed in the newspapers at the time. Someone had changed the façade with wooden cladding. The estate agent must have had a job selling it after Sandra's murder. No amount of ripping up the flooring and replacing the kitchen units could make up for the common knowledge of how the previous owner had died.

There was no sign of life. The windows stared back at her darkly, making her shudder.

The door to the opposite neighbour's house was answered almost as soon as she rang the bell. Mette Isager was tall and carried a significant amount of weight. Her hands and face had a swollen look about them, but her body was well proportioned and graceful. She reminded Jensen of the ice-white marble statues of the gods on display at the Ny Carlsberg Glyptotek museum in Copenhagen.

'Come in,' Mette said, pressing Jensen's hand hard. 'I baked a cake. It hasn't turned out very well, I'm afraid.'

The smell of burnt sponge clung to the air, though the rooms had been aired, judging by the chill.

'You should see *my* baking. Last time, I had to get the kitchen repainted,' said Jensen, eliciting a laugh from the woman.

She had never baked in her life. Baking, like marriage or babies, wasn't her thing, but Mette need not know that. Jensen looked more closely at her. Whatever psychiatric issue had caused her evidence to be disallowed in Thomas Mørk case was not immediately obvious.

Mette led her to two armchairs facing the living-room window. One of the two chairs was worn threadbare, obviously where she spent most of the time. When Jensen sat down in the other, her eyes quickly found the Mørks' front door across the street.

She nodded at the window: 'Did you know the Mørks well?'

'No,' Mette said.

'I understand you had children around the same age?'

'Yes, two daughters. They went to school with Thomas. They weren't friends, though.'

'And you? Did you ever speak to Sandra? You must have bumped into her from time to time?'

'No,' said Mette. 'I used to be severely agoraphobic. Never left the house, if I could help it.'

'But you seem so . . .'

'Normal? I am much better these days. Different drugs, I no longer feel like a zombie the whole time, though the anxiety is still with me. Now,' she said, 'wait here, and I will bring us some tea, and whatever I can salvage of the cake.'

Jensen could hear the kettle being filled, cupboard doors opening and closing. She took a tour of the lounge. It was full of pictures, mostly of the family's two daughters in various stages of growing up. It seemed one of them had got married and had a baby recently. The room was cosy and gratifyingly untidy. There was a Bible on the coffee table and an embroidered Bible quote in a wooden frame over the settee: *Not a Sparrow Falls Without God Knowing*.

Mette returned with a thermos of tea, finger-painted mugs (her daughters' work, Jensen assumed) and a plate of sponge cake with the burnt bits surgically removed.

They both looked at it and laughed.

'You don't have to,' Mette said, when Jensen helped herself to a slice.

'I want to,' said Jensen.

The sponge tasted bittersweet and not at all unpleasant. She found that she was hungry.

'Do you work?' she asked, mouth full of crumbs.

'Sometimes,' said Mette. 'My husband is a GP. I cover for his secretary whenever she is off sick. I think he prefers her to me, to be honest, but he is very good about it. And it gets me out of the house.'

'But back then you didn't?'

'No. I . . . was very unwell back then.'

There was a moment's silence.

'I can feel there is something you are burning to ask me. Come on, spit it out,' said Mette.

'Well, when I rang, I told you it was I who found Thomas. In Magstræde.'

329

'Yes, I remember. It was such dreadful news. That poor lad, he went through so much. Tell me ...' She looked up at the Bible quote, as if for guidance.

'Yes?'

'Are you here because of what he'd been doing?'

Jensen swallowed hard, the cake suddenly dry and mealy in her mouth.

'What do you mean?'

'Well, going around investigating? He came here, you know, just before Christmas. Sat where you are sitting now and asked me loads of questions.'

'You let him in?'

'Jesus taught us to forgive. He had done his time. Besides, he was such a scrap of a thing, I could hardly feel threatened by him.'

'What did he ask you?' said Jensen.

'What I saw that day. He said it wasn't him who did it. That he had come home from school and found his mother already dead in a pool of blood. But there is no getting away from it, is there? I mean, he was found holding the knife, covered in blood himself. I'd imagine that sort of evidence is pretty difficult to dismiss.' Mette shook her head slowly. 'I am not sure I can work it all out.'

'You saw something,' said Jensen. 'You told the police about it, but for whatever reason your testimony wasn't admitted as evidence. What was it? What did you tell them?'

'I was so ill back then, I no longer know what I saw. Something happened. A couple of months before the murder. My husband told me afterwards, I don't remember anything about it myself. It was a psychotic episode, I believe. I hadn't been taking my drugs. That is, I thought I was cured. Yes, I know now that sounds ridiculous, but back then I really thought I had some sort of control. I was OK at first, but one day apparently, I stood in our doorway and just screamed into the street. All I remember

330

is waking up in hospital and feeling this huge fear for my life, this utter terror. I struck one of the nurses apparently. I must have thought she had it in for me. I went back on the drugs and recovered. By the time the murder happened, I was back home, a zombie again. That's why, when my husband took me down to the police station, insisting on me telling them what I had seen, no one believed me. I am not sure I really saw anything after all, to be honest. It was all so confusing.'

'Do you remember much about that day?'

'I remember it was winter, because it had been snowing and it was completely white outside. The children had been talking about tobogganing after school.'

Jensen kept quiet. Mette was thinking, calling up deeply stored memories. She brushed cake crumbs off her dress. She had finished three large pieces already.

'When you sit here, day in day out, staring out the window, you notice stuff. You see people coming and going, get used to their habits.'

'And that day?'

'There was nothing really out of the ordinary.'

'Did you see Thomas leaving for school?'

'No, though I would have been giving my own two breakfast at the time and getting them out of the door, so that doesn't necessarily mean anything. But I saw him come home later on in the day.'

'You did?'

'Yes, that's what I thought,' said Mette.

'We know he hadn't been at school. He said he was at a friend's house. The friend denied this at the time but has since told me that it was in fact true, and that he *was* with Thomas that day. Only he can't remember exactly what time Thomas left his house. Do you recall what time it was that you saw him?'

'Not any more, sorry.'

'I see.'

'But it wasn't long before *he* came home.'

'Sandra's partner Christian, you mean?'

'Yes.'

'Was he often around in the daytime?'

'Oh yes. He had his own clinic, see. My husband always used to joke about dentists having an easy life.'

'And then what happened?'

'Well, I think everyone knows that. He, Christian, came rushing out of the house, covered in blood and sank to his knees in the snow, screaming.'

'Did you go to him?'

'No, but I did call the police. When they got here, all hell broke loose. I still can't believe that Thomas did it. He was always so tiny and frail-looking. They said the stabbing was a "frenzied attack". But they also said that he had been taking drugs. He really was a poor, neglected soul.'

'And all this, you told the police?'

'Yes. My husband brought me down to the station. And they took my statement. It was only later that I was sent to see a psychiatrist and my testimony got disregarded. We were told that, because of what happened to me when I went to hospital that time, and because now and again I still suffered from hallucinations, I was an unreliable witness.'

'And were you? Could you have been mistaken?'

'I didn't think so, but after they began to question me, I suddenly felt unsure. It was really important they said, and if I was in the least bit uncertain then it would be better not to say anything. It felt like a dreadful responsibility. And then when we got the psychiatrist's report it didn't matter because they didn't believe me anyway.'

'And how did that make you feel?'

'Not very good, I suppose. But my husband made me see that it was better that way. That we wouldn't want anyone convicted on the basis of my evidence, if I had got it wrong.'

Instead, someone had got convicted in the absence of her evidence, Jensen thought. Surely, that made things a hell of a lot worse, not better? She felt her patience drain out of her.

'And Thomas, when he came to see you, what did you tell him?'

'The same as I just told you.'

Jensen thought about it. Thomas's insistence that he had been with his friend all day and only returned home after his mother had been murdered had not been corroborated by the woman's evidence. Nor had it exactly been disproved.

'I'll see myself out,' she said, reaching out for her coat. 'Thanks for the tea.'

'Was I helpful to you in some way? I do hope I can help you find out what happened to him.'

'You have been extremely helpful. For what it's worth, I think the police ought to have believed you.'

'I did tell them exactly what I thought to be true. It was also me who told them about the woman.'

Jensen went cold all over.

'What woman?'

'The one who came to the house earlier that day, before Thomas and Christian. Sandra let her in herself; I assumed she was a friend. 'I thought you knew?'

'No.'

There had been no mention of a woman in any of the notes.

Jensen sat down again. 'Tell me exactly what you saw.'

83

Friday 17:08

Henrik stared at the sheet of paper on his desk, flanked by Lisbeth and Mark. Who sent letters these days? Was this someone born before the internet? Or just wary of having their email traced? No prints (of course!) and given the unreliable nature of the Danish postal service, the butt of jokes across the land, it was impossible to tell with any accuracy when it had been sent. He supposed the technicians would be able to confirm that it had come from a particular printer, but that wouldn't help them till they had a suspect. The contents were the usual drivel, portraying immigrants, beggars and addicts as vermin that needed eradicating. The increasingly racist rhetoric of the election campaign had a lot to answer for there. Though Henrik couldn't help noticing that the letter was properly spelled and put together, with sentences that actually made sense, if only on their own warped terms. The lunatic right-wing fringe seldom covered themselves in glory when it came to correct usage of Danish; ironic, considering their complaints about foreigners not being Danish enough. Henrik knew they were lucky the letter had reached them at all. A racist, xenophobic letter addressed to the 'Copenhagen Police' on a printed letter was pretty much guaranteed to be binned straight away, but some bright spark had read it properly and thought it might warrant a closer look.

Scourges of our streets: who will be number four?

Number four? Interesting that Ditte Mørk was unaccounted for in the tally. Below the message there was a picture of a knife dripping with blood. Not much of a lead.

'So, Andrei Ciobanu was the immigrant, Thomas Mørk was the beggar, or at least the killer thought they were, and Tina Dyrby was the drug addict. And number four ... what?' said Lisbeth.

'Street vendor?' said Mark.

They both fell silent and waited for Henrik to speak. He felt weary. They were desperate for a clue, anything at all, but this wasn't it, and he suspected they were heading into a third weekend during which the case would remain unsolved.

Monsen was bound to relieve him of his duties now. There would be plenty of takers. All the work Henrik had put in, and now someone else was going to take the credit.

'Something doesn't feel right,' he said.

'What do you mean?' said Lisbeth.

Good question. Something about the whole thing was too neat, a serial killing spree all tied up in a bow. And Daniel Cuțov didn't strike him as a cold-blooded criminal mastermind.

'Wait,' said Mark, opening his laptop.

Good old dependable Mark. After his little outburst in the interview room, Henrik had duffed him affectionately on the head, and though Mark had ducked and wriggled away, Henrik could tell that he had been pleased. There had been no need to actually apologise; no harm done, just a letting off of steam after a tough few weeks in the office. Mark knew that, and things used to be a hell of a lot worse as far as Henrik controlling his temper was concerned. There would be an official complaint,

335

of course, but he could deal with that. Especially if he solved the case promptly.

'We've got a match,' said Mark, pointing triumphantly at his laptop screen. 'Daniel Cuţov's blood was found under Andrei's fingernails, and on his torn shirt.'

'Thank God for that.'

Henrik reached for his phone to tell Monsen the good news. There was bad weather coming; the big man would have left the office hours ago for his house in Lyngby. Henrik imagined that he would be seeing in the weekend with the first of many single malts by now.

'Get Daniel whatshisname back to the interview room and confront him with the results. I want a confession. And check his alibi for the other three murders,' he said to Mark.

'Sure thing, boss.'

'So, what do we do with this?' said Lisbeth, waving the anonymous letter with the picture of the knife.

'Fake news.'

'You mean it's just someone who wants us to think *they* are the serial killer?' said Lisbeth.

Henrik pondered her question. Serial killers were extremely rare. In Denmark they were virtually non-existent. Most murders were solved long before they could turn into serials. Which meant that, right now, Henrik was doing extraordinarily badly.

'Or someone who wants us to think there is a serial killer on the loose in the first place,' he said, tapping Monsen's number on the screen and sighing deeply.

84

'There's loads here. You will have to read it for yourself,' said Fie and handed Jensen the USB memory stick with the contents of Thomas's computer, holding on to it for a bit longer than strictly necessary.

She wiped her nose with the back of her hand and glanced back up the road at Skovhøj's low-lying brick buildings as though she longed to be back in her warm cave, as though she wished she had never become involved. Her eyes were weary.

Jensen put the USB in her pocket and thought of how she could get Fie to talk. There was no time to read through dozens of emails to learn the truth for herself.

The air had a wet taste to it and the cloud cover felt ominously close. The Met Office had warned of another blizzard. Apparently it had already begun to snow heavily in Jutland and was sweeping fast across the country towards Zealand. The Storebælt Bridge had just been closed.

'Tell me what you found' she said.

'All sorts of stuff.'

'About the case?'

'That too. He had worked on it for months. I had no idea. He never told me any of it. I could have helped, I could have . . .'

Fie looked close to tears.

'No,' said Jensen, placing her hand firmly on her arm. 'He didn't want you to know.'

'But why?'

'He was used to no one believing a word he said.'

'But I would have done, I would . . .'

'Don't torture yourself, Fie.'

'There are emails, loads and loads of them. Most of them to someone called Christian, who had been his mother's boyfriend.'

Jensen nodded. 'He's the one who found her, with Thomas still holding the knife.'

'But Thomas didn't do it. That's what he wrote to Christian. He said that he had come home to find his mother lying there with a knife sticking out of her stomach. He said that he slipped in the blood and got it all over him, then removed the knife. Which is when Christian walked in and found him.'

'And what was Christian's reply?'

'He didn't believe him. He just kept saying that all the evidence pointed to Thomas, and that there was no one else who could have done it. And that Thomas should go away and get on with his life and stop writing to him. Which eventually Thomas did, for a while just after Christmas. But then he started emailing again.'

'Right, and he accused Grønfeldt of having done it.'

'No, that's just it. Well, he did in the beginning, and he was angry. He said Christian could just as easily have come home earlier in the day and killed Sandra. Then wandered back in the afternoon to discover the body, and conveniently Thomas had been there to take the blame.'

'But Thomas changed his mind about that. Why?'

'When he started emailing again after the pause, he was asking Christian to have a think about what his dental assistant had been doing that day.'

'Malene? The woman he later married?'

'Yes. She is supposed to have given Christian an alibi for the time of the murder. She said he was at the clinic with her, but he wasn't. Thomas had found out that on the day of the murder Christian had been with a friend of Sandra's, so he couldn't have done it.'

'Charlotte.'

'Yes! How did you know?'

'Spoke to her myself.'

'Then you know that Charlotte was married and didn't want it all to come out in court. Anyway, Malene covered for him, and it was meant to be just the two of them at the clinic that day, which raises a big question.'

'If Christian was with Charlotte, what was Malene doing?' said Jensen.

'Exactly. Thomas reckoned that Malene had developed a crush on Christian by then, and that she was jealous of Sandra. He thought Christian must have confided in Malene that Sandra was pregnant, and that Malene would have wanted Sandra out of her way.'

Jensen thought of Mette Isager's statement that a woman had come to Sandra's house on the day she had died. Malene would have told Sandra that she and Grønfeldt worked together and come up with some sort of story that would have gained her access to the house.

'And what did Christian say to all that?'

'He called Thomas crazy, and threatened to call the police. He told him again to stop contacting him, and then, in the end, he stopped responding altogether.'

'And when did Thomas last email Christian?'

'Two days before he went down to Copenhagen.'

Guilty.

The sign had not been intended for Grønfeldt.

It had been pointed at Malene.

Fie looked relieved to be dismissed from the conversation. Jensen sensed that as far as she was concerned, the relationship she thought she had had with Thomas was valueless because he had failed to be honest with her.

'You were a good friend to Thomas, Fie, and he had never had any before you. Always remember that.'

'I have to go now,' said Fie.

Jensen took a deep breath. 'Fie, you know you don't have to stay here – at Skovhøj, I mean. You could find a job. I could help you, get you somewhere to live?'

Fie pulled back from her, shutting down. Too soon to make that kind of suggestion. Jensen noticed that Tobias had appeared at the top of the drive. Fie glanced back at him and Jensen felt happier leaving her, knowing that he was there.

'No,' said Fie. 'Thank you, but I don't want that.'

Then as if she had only just remembered it: 'Karina is leaving. They sacked her.'

'Glad to hear it.'

'I keep telling Tobias to go for her job. Then maybe we will get the money from the council so we can all stay here and not all have to find new homes.'

They shook hands like they had done the first time they met, and Jensen watched Fie walk back up the drive to Tobias. As they went inside the building, Tobias put his arm round her.

'I have to get Esben from the airport and take him back to Klampenborg now,' said Aziz when he and Jensen were back in the car. 'Can I drop you somewhere on the way?'

'Yes, take me to the police out at Teglholmen. I need to see someone urgently.'

'The policeman?'

Aziz's black eyes in the rear-view mirror revealed nothing, but it was obvious he must have been speaking to his employer about her. Esben had always detested Henrik. Not because of who he was; Esben had no idea whatsoever of Henrik. But because he hadn't done the 'honourable thing' and left his wife for Jensen.

'How am I different from all the women *you* have shagged and not left your wife for, Esben?' was her regular refrain.

'Oh Jensen, where do you want me to start?' was his.

'Yes, the policeman,' she said, a little more angrily than she had intended.

Was it possible that Aziz did not appreciate how annoying it was to take lectures in morality originating from a man like Esben? Obviously, it was. To Aziz, Esben could do no wrong.

She got out her phone.

No reply from Henrik. She couldn't exactly blame him after the way they had parted the last time. She left another message.

'Pick up, Henrik, for God's sake. Thomas had changed his mind at the end. He was no longer accusing Grønfeldt. It was all about Malene. His sign was for her. I think Grønfeldt may be in danger. Call me back as soon as you get this.'

She rang three more times as they approached Copenhagen. Then she rang the switchboard at the police station and was told that Henrik Jungersen was out of the office.

When she got off the phone, she saw that she had four missed calls from Gustav.

Oh Gustav, not now!

Then she recalled his text message. He had remembered something. What was it? And what if he had got himself in some kind of trouble again? This time Margrethe most definitely *would* kill her.

'Aziz? Change of plan. Drop me at Margrethe's instead. I need to speak to Gustav.'

'And afterwards?'

'I'll head back to the newspaper and, if need be, stay there overnight till the blizzard has cleared.'

'I can be back for you in an hour.'

'That won't be necessary. Besides, you don't know what the

driving conditions are going to be like by then. The streets might not be passable.'

'They will be for me,' said Aziz.

She reckoned they would be. In the sleek black car, Aziz looked as unstoppable as a bullet.

'No, Aziz. I am grateful for everything you've done, but you look after Esben now. I will be absolutely fine.'

85

Gustav stood by the gate to the courtyard, just out of the street light, trembling with cold. His white neck brace shone like a polished bone in the darkness. He had told Margrethe that he was grabbing some fresh air, but he was vaping furiously. The steam stood about him in a cloud of vanilla. You could tell from his stiff movements that he was still in a lot of pain.

'I can't stay long. She is cooking,' he said.

Margrethe cooking? Again, Jensen marvelled at the ability of Gustav to transform the boss she thought she knew into a total stranger.

'How are you doing?'

'All right, as long as I don't turn my neck. Why haven't you answered my calls?'

'I've been busy. The case has moved on. But you had something to tell me?'

They fell silent as a woman walked past the gate. Her eyes flicked nervously between the two of them. Jensen smiled and lifted a hand in greeting, which sent the woman skittering away.

'You know last Friday when I had been to see Fie and got off

343

the train at the Central Station?' said Gustav when they were alone.

'Yes. You remember seeing the drug dealer now?'

'No,' said Gustav. 'But I remember that I'd got a message from someone, and I was on my way to meet them. I had been given directions and was using Google Maps.'

'What?'

'I always assumed, because of what the police told me, that it was the drug dealer who beat me up, but I don't actually think I even went to see him.'

'Do you remember getting to the meeting place?'

Gustav sniffed loudly and buried his hands deep in the pockets of his hoodie. 'No, and before you ask, I didn't see who did this to me. I just remember jumbled-up stuff. Like holding onto this rusty bicycle rail while I got hit. Watching blood splash onto my trainers.'

'Do you remember the person talking?'

'No. I don't think there was any talking.'

'Who was it you were on your way to meet?'

'That's just it, which is why I don't understand the text message she sent me later, the one I shared with you, saying that we had kept missing each other. Because I think we really did meet up on that occasion.'

He pointed to his neck brace. 'I think she is the one who did this.'

'Gustav, who?'

'She said she had something to tell me but that it wasn't safe over the phone.'

'WHO?'

'Malene Grønfeldt.'

86

'Come on, pick up!'

No one was answering the phone at the dental clinic. She didn't have Grønfeldt's mobile number, but she had to get to him before it was too late. She had to warn him.

The snow had begun to fall, little white pinpricks heralding the approaching storm. The roads were emptying fast and the few pedestrians still out and about were rushing along the pavements, anxious to get to their destinations.

Having left the relative shelter of Margrethe's courtyard, Jensen felt the full force of the cold on her face. The snow was falling horizontally in the phosphorous light from the street lamps, obscuring the buildings around her so they might be mountains or trees. There were no buses or taxis to be seen.

She ran down Østerbrogade, past the Lakes, to Østerport, but they had closed both the S-train and the metro, and there were no city bikes in sight. Cursing her poor form, she continued on foot, running through the dark King's Garden, past the fairy-tale Rosenborg Castle and onwards towards the canals.

In Magstræde the snow had already begun to settle thickly

on the cobbles. She stopped and leaned over with her hands on her knees to catch her breath, her throat burning. Grønfeldt's house was in darkness. With the forecast as it was, and being on his own, perhaps he hadn't bothered opening the clinic.

Perhaps he was out.

Perhaps he had decided to lock up shop for a while and go away somewhere.

Perhaps she was already too late.

Malene must have known that she would be found out eventually. Perhaps she had allowed herself to relax when Thomas had been put away for Sandra's murder. Jensen shook her head at the thought that Malene had let an innocent, grieving fifteen-year-old boy take the blame. She would have gone to Sandra's house in a red mist after finding out from Grønfeldt that Sandra was pregnant with his child. But she would have cleaned up after herself, making it look as though Sandra had been stabbed by a stranger.

Then, serendipitously, Thomas had turned up at the house, slipped in the blood and grabbed the handle of the knife to pull it from his mother's belly just where it had begun to swell. Grønfeldt, wandering in after spending all morning in the bed of Sandra's married friend, could have reached but one conclusion. All Malene had to do was to stay quiet.

But when Thomas began to email Grønfeldt, having discovered the truth about Malene, what then? Had he dismissed it as yet more rambling nonsense by a damaged child desperate to offload the guilt of having murdered his mother?

Or had he known the truth, deep down?

Jensen felt the sweat running down her back as she leaned one shoulder against the door, surprised when it yielded to her pressure.

'Hello? Anyone there?'

No answer. Quickly, the snow began to blow into the dark stairwell and collect on the floor.

346

Jensen went inside and closed the door, peering up the stairs, just as she had done on the day when she first met Grønfeldt. How little she had understood then. She turned on the torch on her mobile phone and peered through the open door to the clinic.

The cone of light caught the lilies on the reception desk. They had bent over the edge of the vase and filled the room with a stench of decay. The waiting room was empty, and so was Christian's office and the treatment room with the black leather dental chair and the lavatory in the hallway. The pyramid of black boxes with the 'CG' white lettering was fuzzy with dust.

A floorboard above her creaked.

'Christian?'

She went upstairs to the flat cautiously.

'Grønfeldt?'

She pushed the door open.

There was something on the floor.

It was wet and sticky, like syrup.

She felt her legs slide out from under her as she landed in it.

There was someone else there.

A body.

Still warm.

She felt a presence above her, breathing in the dark, then a bright light flashed before her eyes as she felt a sharp pain in her shoulder.

She looked up. 'You?'

87

Friday 20:17

'*Hej.*'

Nothing.

It had got so he entered and left his own house unacknowl-
edged. ('And whose fault is that?' his wife would say.) He stared
at himself in the hallway mirror. Monsen frequently chided him
for looking rougher than many of the criminals they hauled in,
and his boss was right. Henrik reckoned it wasn't his looks per
se (though he was no beauty) but something in his eyes, a cynical slant that hadn't been there when he was young. The skin
on his face had thickened over the years, burying his features
deeper. His hands had got calloused all over, the nails tough,
as if he was growing himself a suit of armour, and that was just
on the outside.

He could hear his wife and two older children chatting in the
kitchen over the noise of the TV. Sometimes he would stand in
the hall for ages, not wanting to spoil it, not wanting to bring
his grim world into the house.

His children scuttled off as soon as he entered the kitchen.
He suppressed an urge to join them. His wife was standing in

348

her usual place at the kitchen island, queen of all she surveyed. She didn't look up from the cream she was whipping, but he could tell by the way she wielded the whisk that she wasn't in the best of moods. She too had acquired a hard look over the years, drawing her thin black eyebrows with an ever-more-unforgiving pencil.

Henrik pitied the poor souls who found themselves on the receiving end of his wife's inquisition at the high school where she was head teacher. She had always been smarter than him, even when they were teenagers, but somehow, magically, she had chosen him. ('I could have had anyone I wanted.') Back then it had been his jack-the-lad demeanour that had won her over, his rough sexual appeal (ha!). None of that attraction left now; they only had sex once in a blue moon, if one of them was willing to humiliate themselves enough to initiate it.

'Where is Oliver?' he said.

His wife looked up sharply. Henrik realised that he might have said anything in that moment, anything at all, and his wife would have seized on it as an extreme provocation.

'Where is Oliver? Where is Oliver? Change the bloody record, will you? You have three children – three.'

She was right, he was obsessed with Oliver, the third child he hadn't wanted. Not out of a guilty conscience, though he had enough of that to fill a book, but because Oliver was straightforward, and the two of them got on. ('Of course he's straightforward; he's only bloody seven years old.') The only thing he wanted to do these days when he was at home was to watch football with Oliver or sit next to him on the sofa in the den playing some inane game on the PlayStation. He knew it was because Oliver was still young enough to engross himself in simple pleasures, too young to talk back. And in contrast to the others, Oliver seemed to tolerate his company, even sometimes enjoy it. The older two children were on his wife's side, but Oliver was still on Team Henrik.

349

He wondered for how much longer it would last.

His phone dinged in his pocket: Jensen.

Of all the moments she could have chosen.

He blushed immediately and could not bring himself to look at his wife. She went straight for the jugular.

'Who is it?' she said.

He didn't get a chance to reply.

'Come on, Henrik, you've been weird for weeks. Is there someone else?'

The *someone* hung between them.

She didn't have to be specific.

'Why do you say that?'

'Come on, who?'

It was the only slight hold he had on her these days. She rarely showed any affection towards him, but at the smallest sign of him being interested in someone else, he could feel her breathing down his neck.

He looked at her defiantly, summoning the streetwise, silver-tongued lad she had fallen for a hundred years ago.

'No, but if there were, or if you had someone, neither of us could blame the other. This is no way for two people to live together.'

That stumped her. She was biting her lip in the way she did when she was pondering something.

His wife pondering was never a good thing.

He knew that she would be thinking of 'him', her colleague, Bo Petersen, who had come on to her once at a work Christmas do. ('He fancied the pants off me, and I wanted to go home with him, but I didn't, because unlike some, I don't capitulate to every single sexual urge that strikes me.')

Henrik wasn't proud of what happened next, and if his wife ever found out, he would deny it strenuously, but he had followed the man for a week, all around his tawdry little life, before confronting him. He hadn't needed to say anything. He had just stood in a doorway opposite the high school, in the pouring rain, staring at Bo Petersen, as he emerged from the building at the end of the day.

He had a good stare, perfected over many years. The man had clocked him instantly and scuttled off, like his children had done a moment ago.

For a few months afterwards, he and his wife had had amazing sex, but their desire had soon cooled. Nothing ever lasted. Henrik blamed himself, of course he did. He would take the entire blame in a heartbeat. His wife and Jensen: he had let both of them down. Together they had him by the balls.

There was another ping, this time a text message.

'Well,' said his wife. 'Aren't you going to answer her?'

They stood with their eyes locked for a while before he could no longer resist the temptation to look at the screen and conceded victory to his wife.

There were several missed calls and a voicemail from Jensen. The second message was from Mark.

Back to the drawing board, boss. Daniel Cuțov had an alibi for both Thomas Mørk's and Tina Dyrby's murders. We have a signed statement from a witness.

'Fuck,' said Henrik.

Then he played back Jensen's message.

'Fuck,' he said. 'Fuck.'

He grabbed his keys.

'What is it?' said his wife.

'I have to go.'

'But my parents are coming for over for coffee and cake tonight. I told you ages ago. They'll be here in twenty minutes.'

'Sorry,' he said halfway down the hall. 'It's work.'

The excuse of police officers everywhere. Work. Over the years it had come in handy more than once when the atmosphere in his home had become unbearable.

He reckoned that if all the words he had ever spoken to his

351

wife were counted, sorry would be the one he had used most often.

It would be an understatement to say that his in-laws hadn't exactly been overjoyed when their eldest daughter had come home with the naughtiest boy at school. But they had mellowed over the years and, if affection had failed to evolve, at the least there had been a state of truce, dependent on his presence at key family events and general acquiescence.

His father-in-law, a self-made man who had thought himself too good for the working-class neighbourhood where he was born and bred, mostly ignored him and, whenever Henrik piped up at the dinner table, would turn on him a sort of absent-minded look as if noticing him for the first time.

As he started the car and slapped the blue light on the roof, Henrik reckoned that this particular evening, much like any other, they would all be better off without him.

88

Jensen tried and failed to get to her feet. She was conscious that by now she would be covered in blood, her own mixed with the blood on the floor, and tried to ignore the iodine smell of it. Below her, Malene's body was soft and wet. She tried to press one hand into the wound in her shoulder but found the strength had left her. Strangely, there was no pain.

'Don't move!'

Grønfeldt was holding the knife out in front of him with both hands, like a sabre. Jensen felt in the dark for Malene's pulse. There wasn't one.

'She was waiting for me, hiding up here behind the door.'

'I believe you,' said Jensen, holding up her hands. 'Now can you put the knife down?'

Grønfeldt ignored her. It was as though he was speaking to himself. 'She wanted to do a deal. She said that if I covered for her, she would come home and turn the police's suspicion the other way. If not, then she'd land me in it.'

'She killed Sandra. Thomas was telling the truth the whole time,' said Jensen.

353

'I swear to you I had no idea.'

'You were with Charlotte that day, Sandra's friend.'

'I thought it would make things unnecessarily complicated if the police were to find out about that, what with Sandra being pregnant, so Malene covered for me.'

'Were the two of you an item then?'

'No. Except maybe in Malene's head. I knew she liked me. When Sandra died, she was really understanding and sympathetic. She offered to sort everything, to speak to the police and say that she had been with me at the clinic that day. It all happened so quickly, and my head was in a mess. I didn't think a little white lie could hurt anyone.'

'So, you began to sleep together.'

'Not straight away. It just sort of evolved. Malene is a good-looking woman, I was grieving, and she was there for me. Before long we were talking about getting married.'

'And you had no inkling whatsoever what she had done to Sandra? Do you expect anyone to believe that?'

'Believe what you like, it's the truth. She pulled me aside on our wedding day and said that if I were ever unfaithful to her, she would tell the police that I had forced her to give me a false alibi. But I thought that was just her being jealous. It didn't occur to me that it was herself she was covering for.'

'Thomas wrote to you many times to say that he didn't do it, that he had nothing to do with his mother's murder. Why didn't you believe him?'

'Because it was me who found him sitting there on the kitchen floor, high as a kite with the knife in his hand, covered in his mother's blood. How could I have believed that he was innocent? Impossible. Besides, he was horrible to Sandra, a liar and a thief who stole money out of her purse. He would have been horrified that she was having my baby.'

'There is no evidence to suggest that he knew anything about his mother's pregnancy. He was telling the truth: he had nothing to do with her murder. But Malene knew about the baby, didn't she?'

'I told her I didn't want the kid.'

'When was that?'

'A few days before Sandra was killed. Yes, I know how it looks! Malene threatened to tell the police that too.'

'And it really never crossed your mind that she may have had her own reasons for threatening you?'

'No. Never. I told you I had no reason to believe anything other than that Thomas killed Sandra.'

'Except he told you. After he was released from the young offenders' institution, he put it all together. He found out what really happened that day, and he contacted you, again and again, but you did nothing. You didn't even reply.'

'I thought he was just mad, that he'd lost it in prison,' Grønfeldt roared, gesturing wildly with the knife.

'So, when *did* you discover the truth?'

Jensen was starting to feel cold, her teeth clattering. It was like she was running out of breath.

'She told me herself. I found her in the kitchen in the middle of the night. I watched her washing blood off the knife, drying it carefully and replacing it in the kitchen drawer. She burned the cardboard sign in the sink and flushed the ashes down the plughole.'

'And Thomas's rucksack?'

'She made me fill it with hand weights and push it through a hole in the ice. It's at the bottom of the canal. No one will find it.'

'You could have gone to the police. So what, if she had told them about your false alibi for Sandra's murder? You were with Charlotte Friis that day; you couldn't have killed Sandra.'

'You don't understand. She threatened to tell the police that I killed Thomas. She said she had taken a picture of me and him and would be handing it over.'

'What? When?'

'I am not blind. I saw him sitting there that day, with his little sign. I felt sorry for him. It was Malene who encouraged me to go out and talk to him, persuade him to leave. I looked up this shelter nearby, wrote the address on a scrap of paper and gave it to him. Malene must have taken the photo of us then.'

'The Bird's Nest.'

'That's the one.'

'And Malene?'

'Like I said, she pushed me to do it. She even made a flask of hot chocolate for me to give to him.'

The benzos. Malene had been thinking ahead.

'And did you?'

'Yes. He wouldn't drink it at first, but I talked him into it. I tried to tell him that he was wrong about Malene, but he got angry with me and pushed me away. I yanked his arm, tried to drag him up to standing, but he just flopped, making me pull him along the street. So I lost my patience, left him where he was, went back indoors and went to bed. I guess Malene must have gone out there after me.'

'And Ditte?'

'Wasn't me but can't say I was sorry. Ditte took money off me for years. She had found out somehow that I wasn't at the clinic the day her sister was murdered. I stopped paying her when Thomas was killed, and that sent her ballistic. She came here demanding money, or else she would go to the police. Made a complete nuisance of herself.'

Jensen lay down on the floor, ignoring the blood, ignoring Malene's body. She was overcome by sleepiness. When she spoke, her voice was faint and distant. 'Malene stabbed Tina Dyrby to make it look like Thomas had got caught up in a serial killing. And when Ditte got too loud, she killed her too.'

'I didn't know.'

'I don't believe you,' said Jensen.

356

She thought of the dog. Malene must have found the address of Esben's summer house in Gustav's phone after she beat him up.

'I never stabbed anyone; this was self-defence,' Grønfeldt went on, his voice climbing up the register. 'I told her to turn herself in, but she said the police had no evidence on her. That we could still make it, both of us.'

Jensen closed her eyes, feeling her strength ebb away. Grønfeldt might be innocent of the other crimes, but he could have prevented them, had he been prepared for once is his life to take responsibility for something.

'She wouldn't listen to reason, kept threatening to report me to the police. Then she got the knife out, we wrestled for it, and somehow in the tussle she must have got stabbed.'

Jensen reckoned the amount of blood on the floor would have taken a good deal more than an accidental stab wound, but who was she to argue? David at Riget would be able to tell for sure.

She saw Malene and herself lying side by side on the autopsy tables, as David and Henrik pored dispassionately over their corpses. Would Henrik shed a tear for her? She couldn't see it, somehow.

'I've met someone else,' said Grønfeldt. 'Maja. She's beautiful, not a bad bone in her body. I want to start again.'

'They won't let you get away with it,' whispered Jensen.

'You're the only one who knows what happened.'

'I passed what I know on to the police. It's only a question of time before they turn up.'

'Bullshit,' said Grønfeldt. 'No one even knows you're here. No one is going to come.'

She felt her phone buzz in her back pocket, but plucking up the energy to reach for it was beyond her. It was probably Aziz, checking up on her. But he would remember the time when he had slept overnight in the lane at Esben's summer house and everything had turned out fine, even though she hadn't texted him as promised. It would be a while before he got truly concerned and, even then, he would look for her at *Dagbladet* first.

'There is no evidence that I knew anything.'

'And me,' said Jensen weakly. 'How are you going to explain me?'

'You came to see me and found Malene. You killed her in self-defence but died of the wounds she inflicted on you. Tragically, you couldn't be saved.'

'What?' said Jensen.

Grønfeldt made his move.

89

Sometimes things were simple. You had one moment, knew what you had to do and did it without stopping to ask yourself why. Most of the time, things were not like that. There were nuances of right and wrong, and self-doubt to contend with, and you inevitably walked away from the one opportunity you had been given with a sense of dissatisfaction.

Henrik almost hadn't made it. He had got into the car fast enough, but the tarmac had filled quickly with snow and the wind had whipped it up and made it almost impossible to see where he was going. On the news, they had advised people not to go out unless strictly necessary.

Soon he had found himself completely alone on the road and been forced to keep his speed to ten miles an hour with his nose pressed up against the windscreen and his hands running with sweat. Meanwhile, he had must have called Jensen a dozen times, but kept getting her voicemail. ('Come on, answer me for once, woman!' he had yelled at the phone display.)

He thought of the grainy CCTV images from Magstræde. He had been right after all: it had been a woman running away in the snow that night. Had Malene Grønfeldt been surprised by someone, perhaps, or just anxious to get away? They might never know.

Jensen never had been able to leave anything alone. If she wasn't dead already, he would strangle her himself. Though he knew he had only himself to blame for what had happened. He had gone off on a tangent looking for a serial killer, precisely as Malene Grønfeldt had intended, even though his every instinct had told him it was wrong. He had allowed himself to succumb to Monsen's pressure when he should have listened to Jensen. Thomas hadn't got himself killed by coincidence. Everything was linked, and now Malene Grønfeldt had not two, but four murders on her conscience, and God knew what else besides.

Copenhagen was like a ghost town, a tundra with a howling wind, emptied of cars, with only a scattering of foolhardy pedestrians leaning into the gale. In places it was difficult to see where the pavement ended and the road began. He had to abandon his car by Christiansborg and run the rest of the way to Magstræde, pulling his service pistol out of its hoister as he went. The power had gone, taking out the street lights and leaving the buildings in darkness; it was no longer his city, but a strange topsy-turvy world lit bluishly from below.

Grønfeldt's house was in total darkness, no sign of life. Perhaps Henrik had got the wrong end of the stick? Perhaps Jensen was back in Hornbæk by now, safe and sound? ('Yeah right, you believe that, Jungersen.')

He pushed against the door with his shoulder and stumbled into the stairwell. The floor was wet. He thought he heard voices above him. That's when his police training kicked in, and the many years of getting it wrong, time and time again.

He didn't shout or run but moved fast up the stairs without making a sound, flicking on his police torch as he went and pointing it with his gun.

Grønfeldt never heard him. Henrik opened the door and

he had his one moment, and the sight of Jensen, slumped on the floor covered in blood, removed any trace of self-doubt he might have felt when pulling the trigger at the man with the knife.

The shot rang out, deafening him momentarily.

'Please,' he said, praying to the God he didn't believe in. 'Let her be alive.'

90

Saturday 14:42

'You have a badly injured shoulder. Apart from anything else, you'll be in immense pain if I remove that cannula from your hand,' said the nurse.

'I'll be fine with some morphine tablets,' said Jensen. 'Take it out, please.'

'May as well give in now. She doesn't take no for an answer, that one,' said a familiar voice from the door.

'Aziz!'

'You should have called me. Why didn't you call me?' he said.

The nurse looked from Aziz to Jensen and back to Aziz. 'Oh, so *you* must be her partner,' she said.

'No,' said Jensen. 'Whatever gave you that idea?'

'Well, I just assumed ... There was another man here this morning when I started my shift. He had slept all night on a row of chairs in the corridor. He asked me if you were going to be all right, and refused to leave until he had spoken to one of the doctors. From the way he talked about you, I assumed he was your partner or husband, but he said he was just a friend.'

'Big man? Bald? Leather jacket? Kind of a rough face?'

The nurse nodded. 'Do you know him?'

'Yeah, I know him.' Jensen smiled.

She turned to Aziz, wincing at the pain in her shoulder as she swung her legs out of the bed and set her feet on the floor. The room wobbled around her.

'Where are my trousers?' she said.

'You should be getting out of bed,' said Aziz.

'The police took your clothes away. Evidence, apparently. Besides, you are nowhere near ready to be getting out of bed,' said the nurse.

Aziz held up a Netto plastic bag. 'I went to Hornbæk and got some clothes for you. Hope these are OK?'

'That's it. I'm getting the doctor,' said the nurse and left the room.

Aziz had packed tracksuit bottoms and a jumper and a pair of socks and trainers. There was even a toothbrush and fresh underwear.

'Why are you here, Aziz?' she said, inexplicably blushing when she removed her knickers from the bag.

'Esben sent me. He thought you might want to leave, so he asked me to collect you. There's a room ready for you at d'Angleterre. He also wanted me to give you this.'

Aziz produced an enormous bouquet of flowers from behind his back. Jensen pictured Esben walking into a posh flower shop and asking for the most expensive bunch they were capable of putting together.

She smiled. 'Very Esben.'

'There's a card, too.'

The message was scribbled in blue fountain pen, in Esben's dreadful, childish scrawl. The sight of it moved her.

Now go do your thing.

'Flowers are not allowed,' said the nurse, re-entering the room, followed by a tall woman with a long silver-grey plait hanging down the back of her white coat.

'So, I understand you want to leave us,' said the doctor, smiling tiredly.

'If that's all right with you?' said Jensen.

'Actually, your injury is not as bad as we feared when we first got you in and saw you covered in blood.'

'Most of it wasn't mine.'

'Still, you'll be very weak for a while.'

'I will look after her,' said Aziz, holding up the giant bouquet of flowers, like an anxious suitor.

'I can't force you,' said the doctor.

'No, you can't, but thanks all the same,' said Jensen.

'I will take her to her hotel room and make sure she stays there till she is better,' said Aziz.

He virtually carried Jensen out of the room, down in the lift and into the black car. He had left a fleece blanket for her on the back seat and she swaddled herself in it woozily.

They left Riget, heading towards the Lakes and the centre of town. Copenhagen was a sunlit white blanket. She saw a man skiing by the side of the road, towing a little girl on a sleigh.

She rested her forehead on the cool windowpane and found Aziz's eyes in the rear-view mirror. 'We are not going to d'Angleterre, are we?' she said.

'No,' he said, his eyes smiling. 'Not yet. Esben gave me strict instructions.'

'Thank you, Aziz. Thank you for everything.'

'Don't mention it,' he said, and she saw a flicker of embarrassment pass across his features.

Despite all the time they had spent together, she didn't really know him. Not his wife's name, nor the names of his children. But even before City Hall Square glided into view, she knew exactly where he was taking her.

91

Saturday 12:01

Margrethe and Yasmine were waiting for her in the lobby with Gustav.

'Some line-up,' said Jensen.

'Your friend the MP gave us a tip-off,' said Margrethe. 'Odious man. Never understood what you saw in that idiot.'

Gustav stepped up to Jensen, hugging her awkwardly.

'Ouch,' she said.

'You won't be able to type properly with one hand.'

'No, but I reckon you could type for me.'

He looked from her to Margrethe and back again, pointing to his chest. 'Me?'

'There you go,' said Margrethe. 'We finally found a use for you.'

'Two uses,' said Jensen. 'Run down to Liron first and fetch me a coffee, would you?'

Margrethe accompanied Jensen upstairs to her office under the eaves. She made a move to support Jensen's good arm, but changed her mind and skipped ahead awkwardly, leaving Jensen to support herself on the wall. For all that she was probably the best editor in the world, Margrethe would make a terrible nurse.

Jensen walked over to the dormer window and looked out at the snow-topped rooftops of Copenhagen. In the winter sunlight they looked innocent and melancholy, like a Danish Golden Age painting.

'Margrethe, I—' she began, but Margrethe interrupted, clasping her hands over her ears.

'Whatever it is, I don't want to hear it. Now, I trust you have everything you need. If not, call me.' She pointed to the desk phone, which was covered in a thick layer of dust. 'You do know how to use one of those?''

While she waited for Gustav, Jensen got out the pictures she had taken of Thomas as he sat dead in Magstræde and sent them to Margrethe.

I lied. I did take some photos that morning. Sorry.

The sound of two-fingered typing came from Henning's room. She guessed he might be working on Christian Grønfeldt's obituary. Or perhaps the dentist wasn't important enough, just a weak man who had disappointed his father and every single woman he had ever been involved with. There was some kind of poetic justice in Malene dying at Grønfeldt's hand, and himself now lying critically injured in a heavily guarded intensive-care bed. No justice whatsoever for Tina Dyrby, though, murdered by Malene to make the stabbing of Thomas look like the work of a single lunatic picking off rough sleepers at random.

Hardly anything was random. She would need to have another word with Henrik about that. She checked her phone. Still no message from him. Perhaps he didn't trust himself around her. ('I need to knock you out of my head for good,' he had once said to her.)

Though Henrik wouldn't hesitate to shoot an adversary dead – particularly not for her – she knew he would want Grønfeldt to survive and not evade justice by copping it. He was

366

probably at the hospital now, waiting to question Grønfeldt the second he woke up.

Jensen looked round the office. It had never really had a chance to become her own since she returned to Denmark, yet, inexplicably, it felt like home. She would miss the view.

'Liron says hi and this one is on the house.'

Gustav stood in the doorway with a tall paper cup smelling sweetly of cardamom.

'He said he is glad we are both alive, so we can start paying our way again. No more freebies.'

Jensen smiled.

'Will you be staying now?' Gustav asked.

'No,' she said. 'There is nothing for me here.'

'There's me.'

'You'll be a lot better off on your own. I'll talk to Frank, put in a good word for you.'

'Nah,' said Gustav. 'I'll be looking for something else to do. Liron says he needs an assistant. Perhaps I can branch out, get my own van.'

Jensen smiled. 'In your dreams,' she said. 'Take a seat and start typing.'

'I am very slow.'

'Not as slow as me,' she said holding up her bandaged arm. 'You ready ...? Here goes. *Innocent*. By Gustav Skov and Jensen.'

'What?'

'We worked on the story together. This is how it goes, partner.'

It took them more than two hours. By five in the afternoon, the piece was the 'most read' on *Dagbladet*'s website and had been picked up by every news outlet in Denmark. Jensen had declined twelve offers of interviews, including three to appear on TV later that evening.

'Just so you know, if you're expecting me to beg you to stay,

I am not going to,' said Margrethe, escorting her back down in the lift with Yasmine and Gustav.

Jensen laughed. 'I think I had better start looking for another profession. Won't be long before all of you are gone.'

'You are writing us off too soon,' said Margrethe. 'Can you seriously see yourself in some corporate press office fielding calls from substandard journos the rest of your life?'

'Maybe I won't. Maybe I'll open a hotel or drive a bus.'

'Ha,' said Margrethe. 'You'd be useless at anything else, and that's the truth of it. We'll be doing this till they carry us out, feet first.'

92

What had she imagined? That Henrik would honour a pledge he had made several days ago before Grønfeldt had tried to kill her? Henrik, who had never kept a promise as long as he had lived? She was doing it again: expecting him to behave like a normal person, waiting for him to call her.

She had messaged him several times to say thank you, and to let him know that she was staying at d'Angleterre and what time her flight was, all of which had been met with total silence. She and Esben had stood around in the lobby until Esben had forced the issue and marched her out to Aziz, who was waiting in the car in front of the hotel.

'That bastard cop.'

'He *did* save my life, Esben.'

'Doing his job, hardly some romantic gesture, and he hasn't even bothered to turn up and see you off.'

But in the car, as they drove to the airport, Jensen felt no resentment. It never ended well anyway when she and Henrik met up. It was better when they were in different countries, dreaming of what might have been and could still be.

If pigs could fly.

In Kastrup Airport, she waved to Esben and Aziz from the escalator.

'Don't do anything stupid with that rich Englishman of yours. I'll be coming over as soon as this damn election is behind us, and then you and I are going to Claridge's to celebrate,' Esben had said, hugging her too close and hurting her shoulder.

'How can you be so certain you'll win?'

'Ha! You've obviously not seen the polls this morning. That story of yours, turning out to have nothing whatsoever to do with provision for society's weakest, has caused the opposition to implode. Margrethe Skov will be furious.'

'You mean I have inadvertently helped keep you lot in power?'

'I can't thank you enough, darling, but I would like to try, if you'll let me,' Esben had said, beaming with his sauciest smile.

She had buried her face in one hand. 'God, what have I done?'

'Too late.'

Far below, standing out from the bustling crowd with his massive static form, Aziz raised a hand to farewell. She blew him a kiss, turned away and headed for the gates to security. She was fumbling with her boarding pass when her phone buzzed in her back pocket.

Bloody Henrik never got his timing right.

The phone buzzed again.

And again.

Finally, she answered. Unknown number.

'Hello Miss Jensen.'

Deep Throat.

'How did you get my number?'

'Never reveal your source. Isn't that what you journalists always say?'

'There's a lot of noise on the line ... Wait, is that a helicopter?' she said.

'Yes, and it's about to take off with me on it, so listen. Carsten Vangede was found hanged this morning.'

'Where?'

'At his flat in Gentofte.'

And she hadn't even bothered to call the man back, too busy on the story she wasn't supposed to be working on to bother with the one Margrethe had actually asked her to look into.

She felt for the accountant's spectacle case in her bag. It was still there. 'So, he killed himself,' she said. 'That's tragic. I must say he seemed very depressed about his business going down.'

'That's precisely what the police will conclude, but they'll be wrong.'

'What do you mean?'

'Ask yourself. Why does a man about to hang himself book a flight to Thailand?'

'He did?'

The engine sound in the background grew to a deafening roar. 'Must go,' shouted Deep Throat at the top of his voice.

'Wait . . . What do you mean?'

The call was disconnected. Perhaps Deep Throat would speak to Frank once he found out that she had left the country. Or maybe he already knew that she was about to? She looked into the blank faces of the other travellers to check if she was being followed, scanned the ceiling for cameras.

Carsten Vangede had been down, but had he, a bloke who seemed more than capable of handling himself, really been suicidal? She felt a familiar tingling all over.

Come to think of it, Deep Throat's tip-off wasn't the only unfinished business she had in Copenhagen: Gustav still hadn't told her why he had been expelled from school. He seemed like a decent boy. Annoying as hell, with a temper on him, but his heart was in the right place. What could he have done that was so bad that his school had thrown him out?

He could tell her all about it on the way to Gentofte. She dialled his number.

93

After a hairy ride from the centre of town, with his blue blink plonked on the roof of his car, Henrik had thrown the 'Police' sign on the dashboard and parked up right outside the terminal.

He was a hero to Monsen now. And with the case solved, his boss was off limits to the trigger-happy prime minister, whose star was rising in the polls again. Monsen had insisted on having him back to his house in Lyngby to thank him in person, an awkward few hours that had made him late for picking up Jensen from the hotel. All afternoon he had felt her calls buzzing in his pocket.

It wasn't too late. With a bit of luck she would still be there, dropping her suitcase off, fumbling with her boarding pass.

Pissed off, but there.

Very pissed off.

When it came to it, he couldn't bring himself to leave his car and go inside the airport terminal.

He hadn't cried since he was a boy, but now the tears were coming thick and fast. Tears of regret, mostly for things that might have been. ('Self-pity more like,' his wife would have said.)

372

It had always been Jensen, since he had first set eyes on her. His wife also, years ago when she had been fifteen and as beautiful as a goddess, but the two of them had worn each other down, and now there was nothing left but the promise they had once made to one another. Still, was he ready to turn his back on that? Lose the house, have the kids turned against him (even, God forbid, Oliver) and end up in some shitty bedsit by himself, with fifty per cent of the so-called fantastic life he and his wife had built together?

He doubted Jensen would give him the time of day, considering how he had treated her over the years. Yet, somehow, she still had a dominant place in his heart, and here he was, sobbing like a lovesick teenager at the airport because she was flying away and leaving him. Well, it was too late for loving farewells now.

Too late for most things but to try and salvage what was left of his marriage and get back to reality. The football would be on later. He had promised Oliver to be home in time for the match. They were going to get takeaway pizza.

He removed the blue blink from the roof and tossed it in the back along with the 'Police' sign. Then he wiped his nose on the back of his hand, leaned over to the glove compartment and took out the souvenir he had collected from that clown Esben's summer house. A juvenile thing to do, but Jensen's black knickers felt strangely comforting in his hand. He would be OK. It wasn't like anyone had died; things were just going back to how they had been before.

And who knew what might happen one day?

Or in another lifetime

'What the fuck?'

He dropped the knickers in his lap and stared through the windscreen in disbelief. It was Jensen, hobbling out of the terminal building with her arm in a sling and a phone clamped to her ear. A security guard towing her luggage was following closely behind. She was heading for the taxis like a woman on a mission.

'Fuck, fuck, fuck.'

What was she up to now? Since the first day he had met her, at the ambassador's fusty do in London all those years ago, the woman had been trouble.

Nothing but.

Before that morning in Magstræde when he had seen her again, he had forgotten what it felt like to be in love. He had been afraid that he would never experience it in his life again. Now he was afraid that he would.

Jensen got into the black Mercedes at the front of the taxi rank, leaving the driver and security guard to dump her luggage in the boot. Cursing loudly to himself, Henrik followed the cab as it darted out into the Sunday-evening traffic, heading for the motorway back to Copenhagen and the fifty kinds of fresh hell awaiting him.

Acknowledgements

I was born in Copenhagen and still live there in my imagination, if not in the flesh, which may explain certain idiosyncrasies in my portrayal of this greatest small city on Earth. While some locations are real, all characters and events in this book are fictional. I would like to thank Lars Jung, special consultant in the Danish police, and Hanne Nørgaard Heje, GP, for their wisdom and generosity in putting up with my endless questions. Any mistakes are entirely my own. Thank you to Kate and Sarah Beal of Muswell Press for being the best publishers a writer could wish for, and to Kate Quarry for her eagle-eyed copy editing. Thanks also to my first readers, Jules Walkden, Helen Pike, Suzanne Hellier, Philippa Curtis and Lone Theils, whose encouragement meant the world; to Frederik Walkden for creating the map of Copenhagen that accompanies this book; and to Jeremy Osborne – who started it all by putting my dark tales from home on BBC Radio 4 – for his enduring friendship.

COPENHAGEN

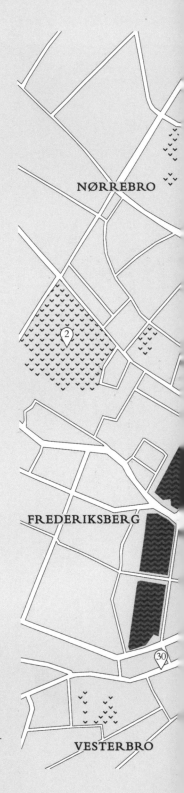

1. Amalienborg
2. Assistens Cemetery
3. Badstuestræde
4. Central Station
5. Christiansborg (Borgen)
6. City Hall Square
7. Hotel D'Angleterre
8. Farvergade
9. Forensic Institute
10. Frederiksholms Kanal
11. Grønnegade
12. King's Garden
13. Magstræde
14. Marble Bridge
15. Marmorkirken
16. National Art Gallery
17. National Museum
18. Nyhavn
19. Østerport
20. Riget (Rigshospitalet)
21. Rosenborg
22. Royal Library
23. Royal Theatre
24. Rysensteensgade
25. Sankt Peders Stræde
26. Strøget
27. The Lakes
28. The Little Mermaid
29. Tivoli
30. Vesterbrogade

NØRREBRO

FREDERIKSBERG

VESTERBRO